Mr. PANtS

IT'S GO TIME!

WORDS BY
SCOTT MCCORMICK

PICTURES BY
R. H. LAZZELL

Dial Books for Young Readers
an imprint of Penguin Group (USA) LLC

TO SOEN AND SADIE, THE COOLEST CATS I KNOW
"ALL . . ." —S.M.

FOR MY PARENTS, CAROLE AND BOB
—R.H.L.

Dial Books for Young Readers
Published by the Penguin Group | Penguin Group (USA) LLC
375 Hudson Street | New York, New York 10014

USA / Canada / UK / Ireland / Australia / New Zealand / India / South Africa / China
PENGUIN.COM
A Penguin Random House Company

Text copyright © 2014 by Scott McCormick | Pictures copyright © 2014 by R. H. Lazzell

Library of Congress Cataloging-in-Publication Data   McCormick, Scott, date.
Mr. Pants: it's go time! / words by Scott McCormick ; pictures by R. H. Lazzell.   pages cm
Summary: On the last day of summer vacation, all Mr. Pants wants to do is play laser tag, but Mom and his sisters, Foot Foot and Grommy, have other ideas. ISBN 978-0-8037-4007-5 (hardcover)
[1. Brothers and sisters—Fiction. 2. Cats—Fiction. 3. Behavior—Fiction.]
I. Lazzell, R. H., illustrator. II. Title. PZ7.M47841437Mqi 2014   [E]—dc23   2013001969

Manufactured in China on acid-free paper

1 3 5 7 9 10 8 6 4 2

Designed by Jennifer Kelly | Text set in Archer

The publisher does not have any control over and does not assume any responsibility for author or third-party websites or their content.

CONTENTS

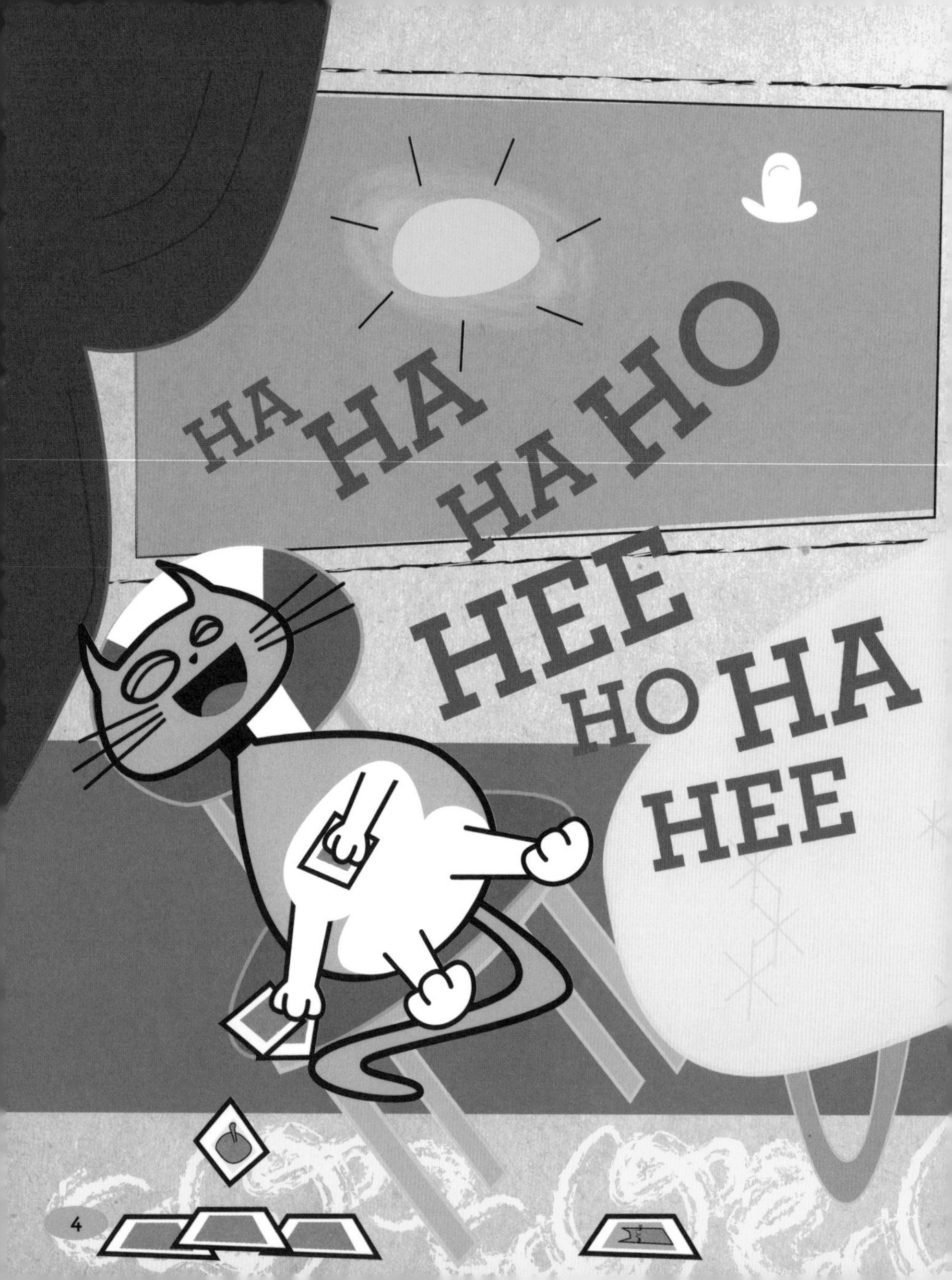
HA
HA
HA
HO
HEE
HO
HA
HEE

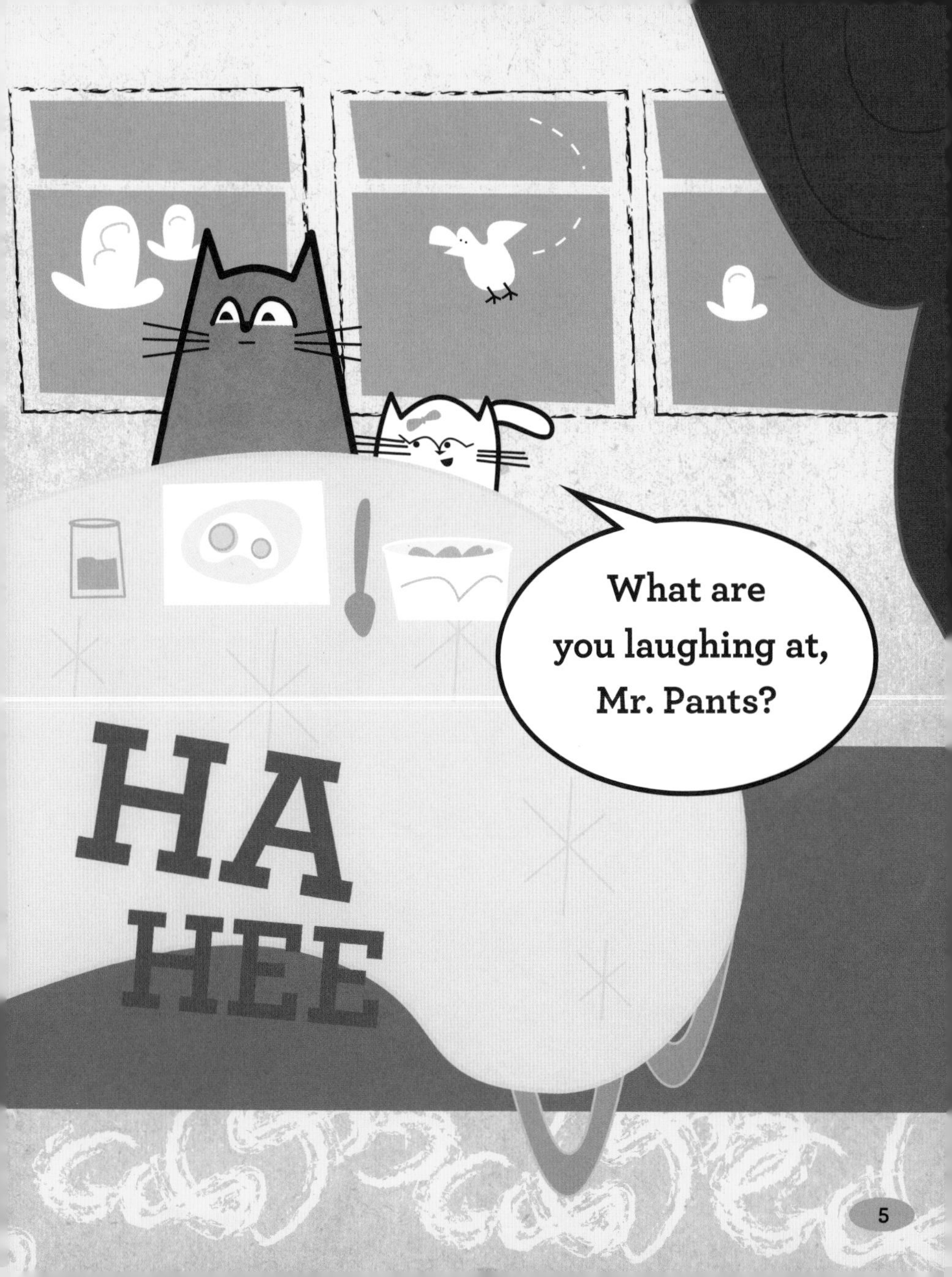
What are you laughing at, Mr. Pants?
HA
HEE

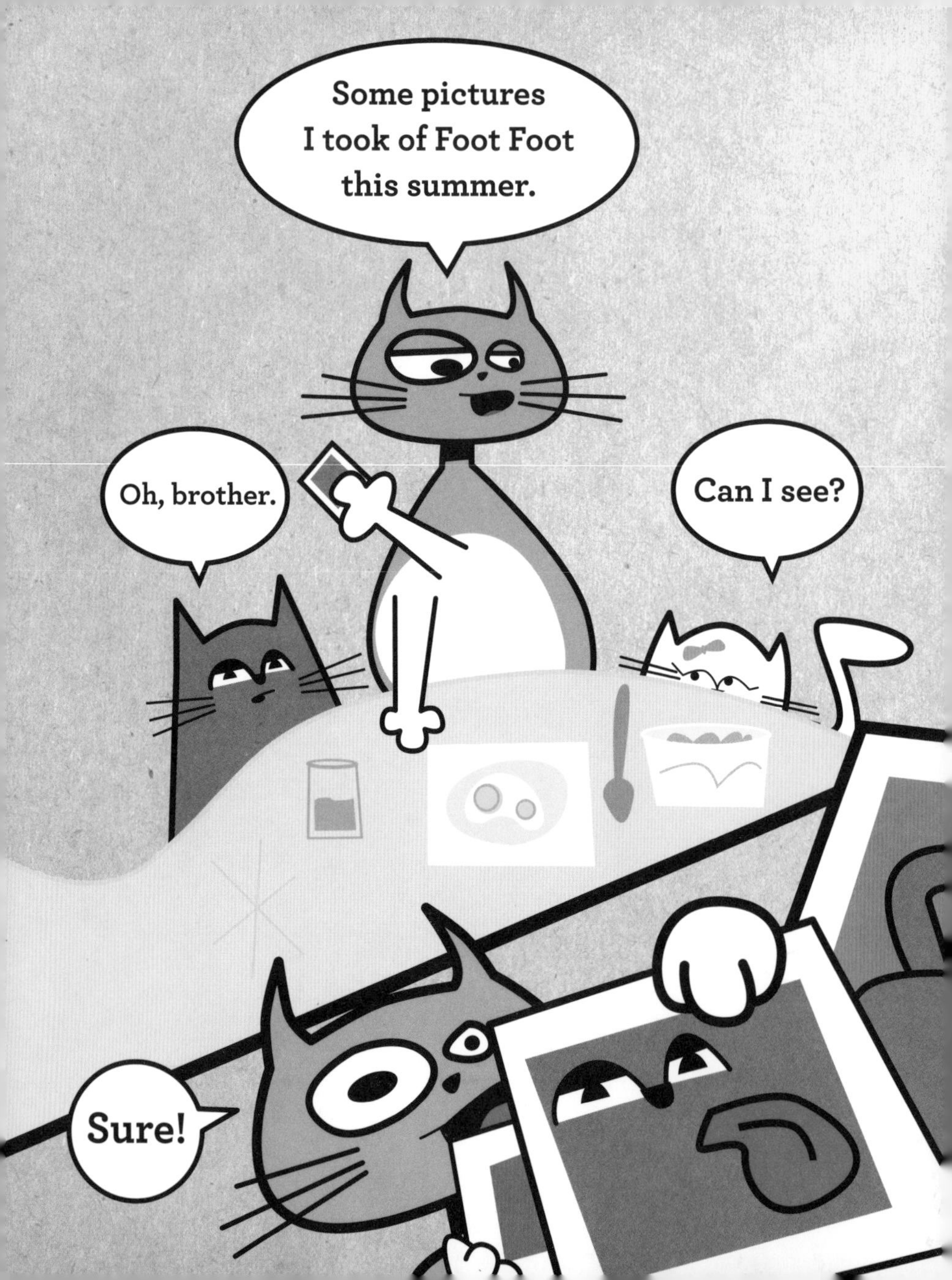
Some pictures I took of Foot Foot this summer.
Oh, brother.
Can I see?
Sure!

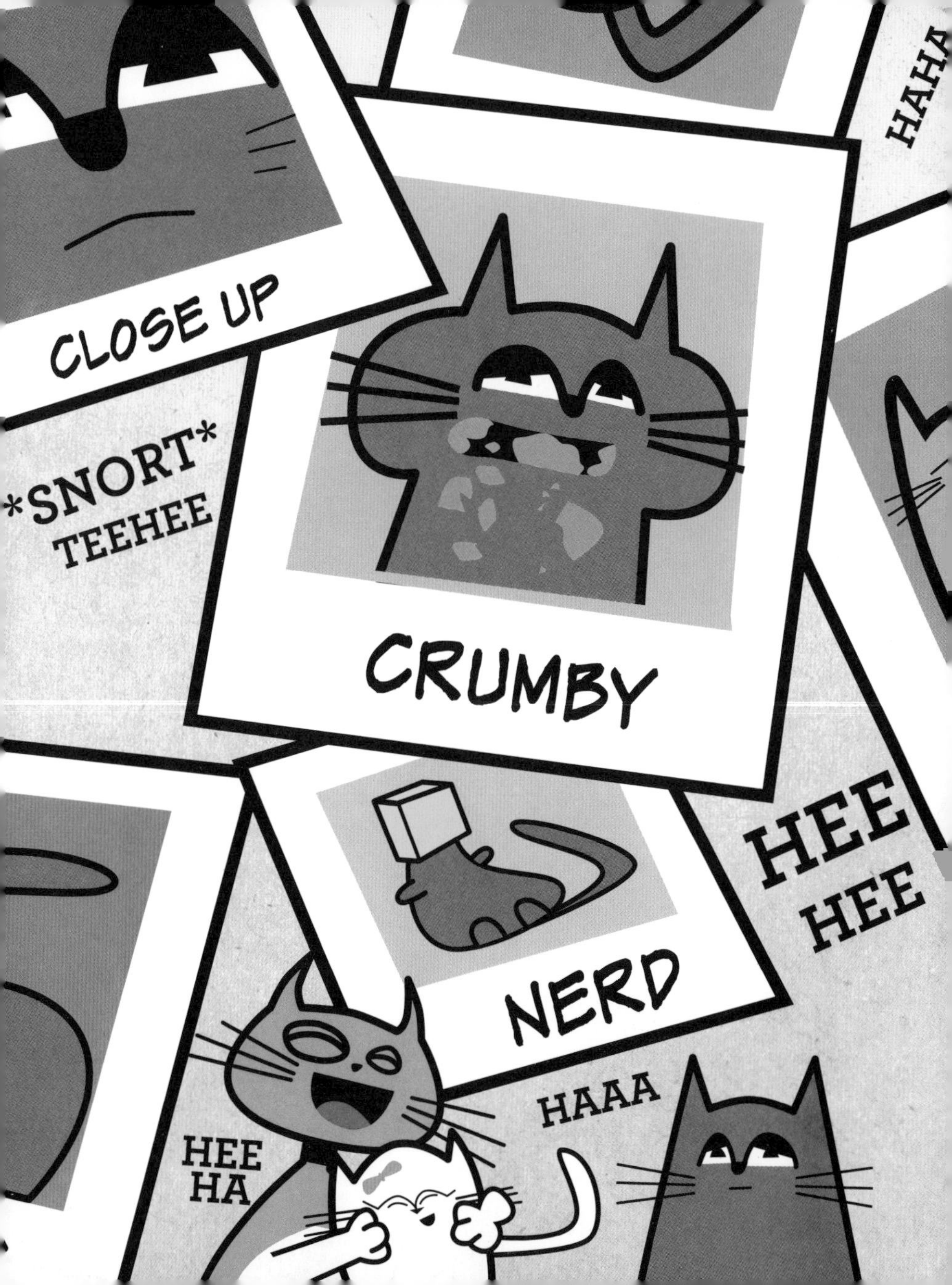
CLOSE UP
HAHA
SNORT
TEEHEE
CRUMBY
HEE
HEE
NERD
HAAA
HEE
HA

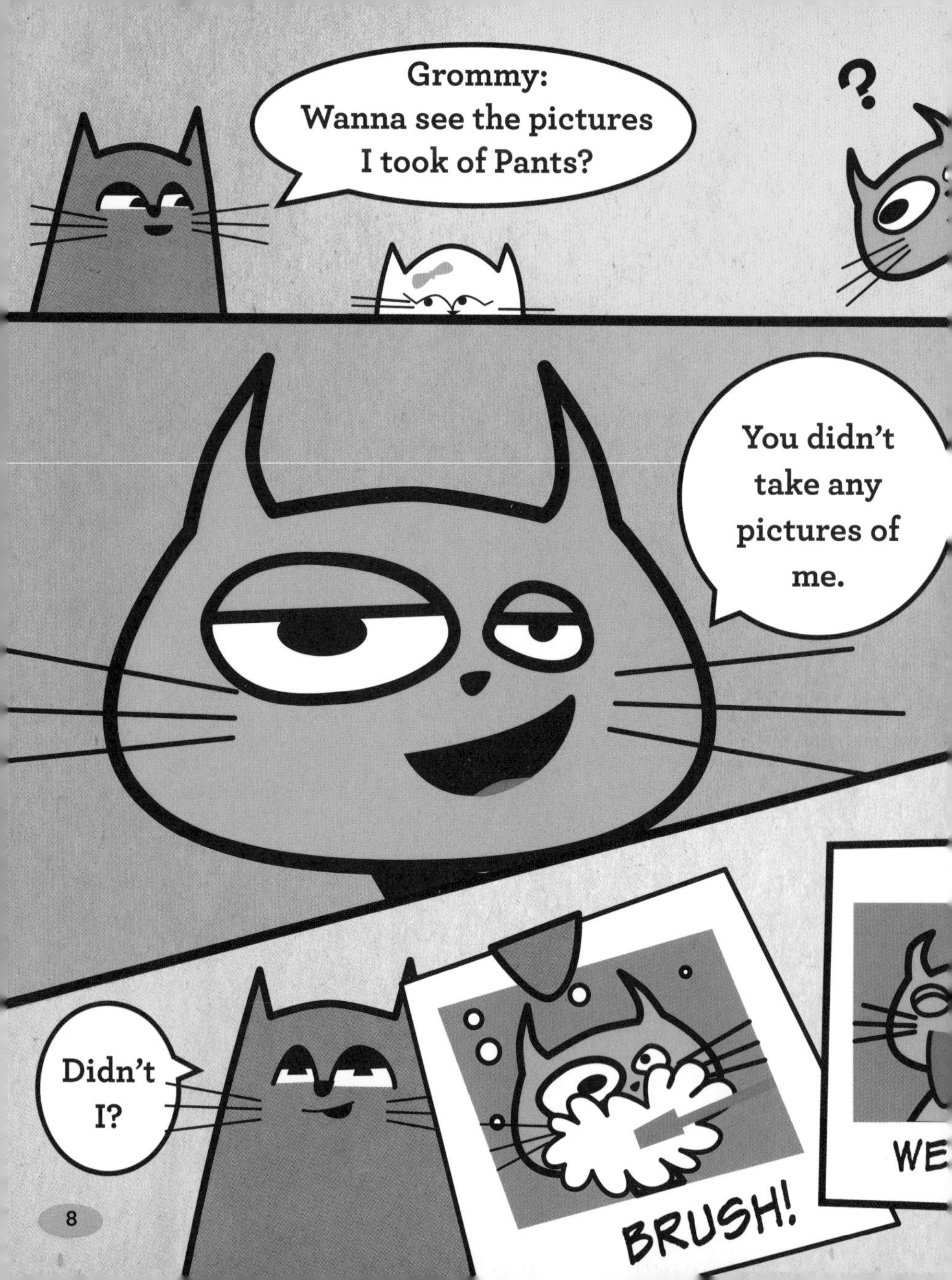
Grommy:
Wanna see the pictures I took of Pants?
?
You didn't take any pictures of me.
Didn't I?
BRUSH!
WE

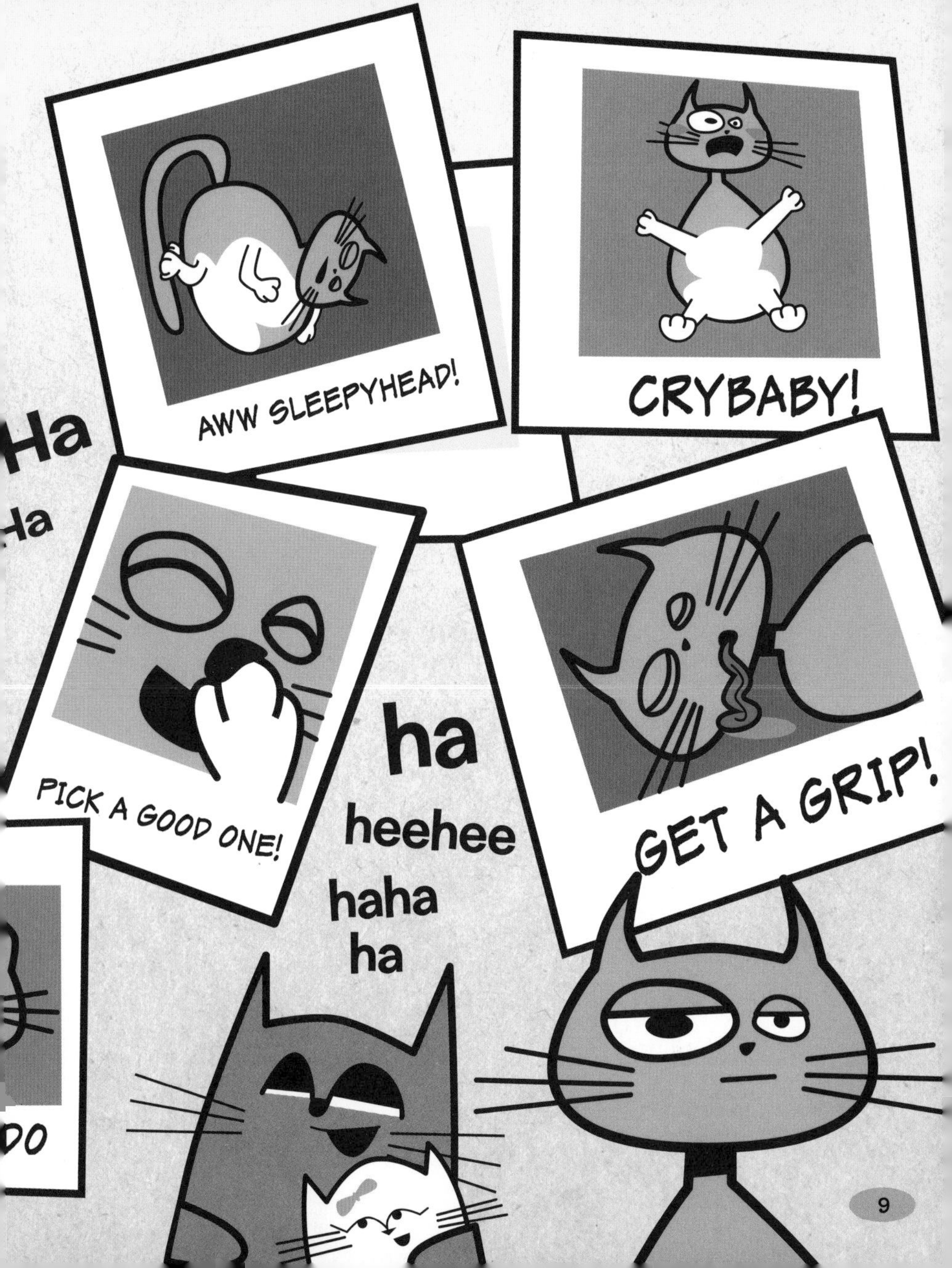
AWW SLEEPYHEAD!
CRYBABY!
Ha
Ha
PICK A GOOD ONE!
GET A GRIP!
ha
heehee
haha
ha
DO

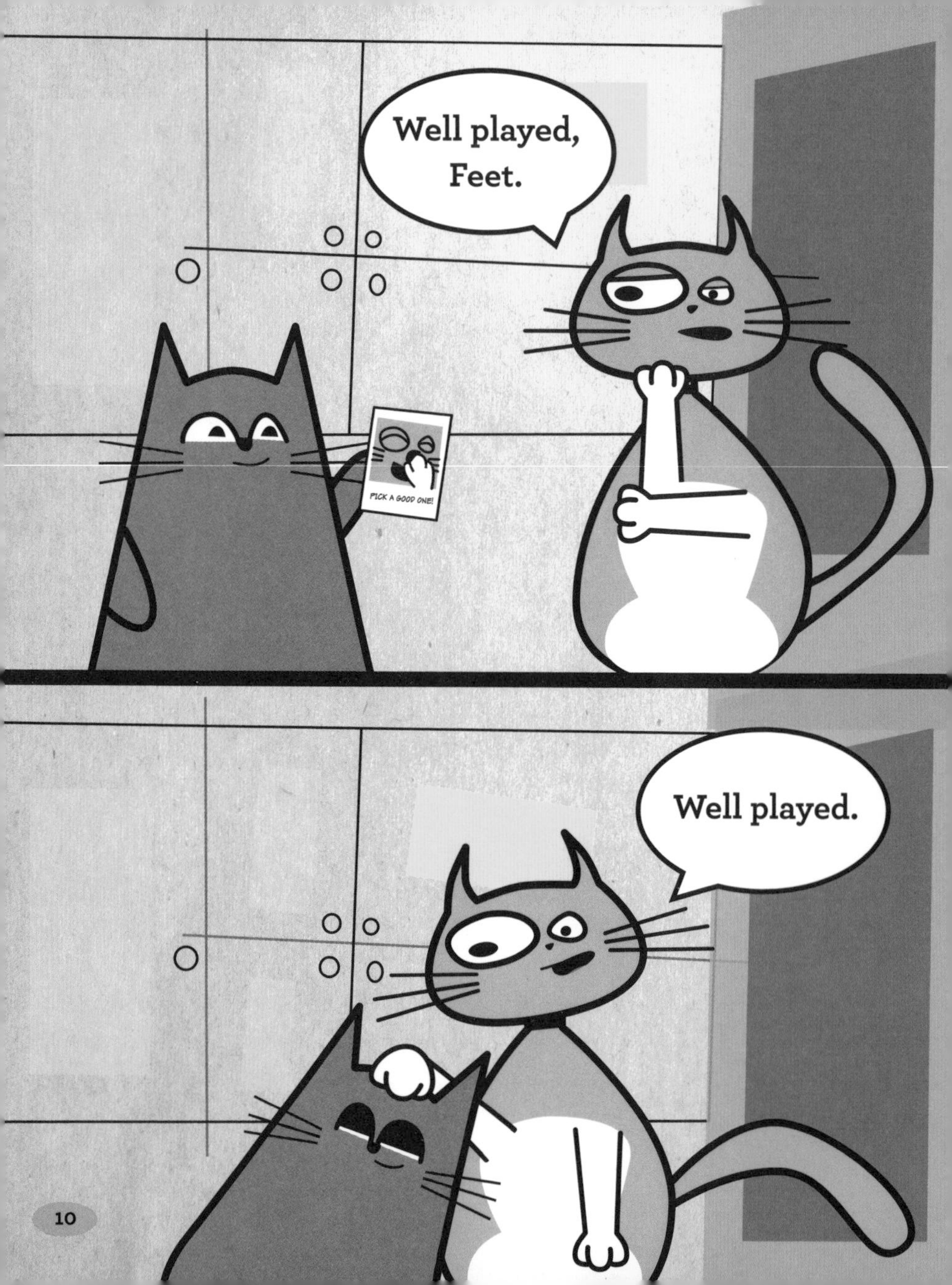
Well played, Feet.
PICK A GOOD ONE!
Well played.

Chapter One:
THE DEAL

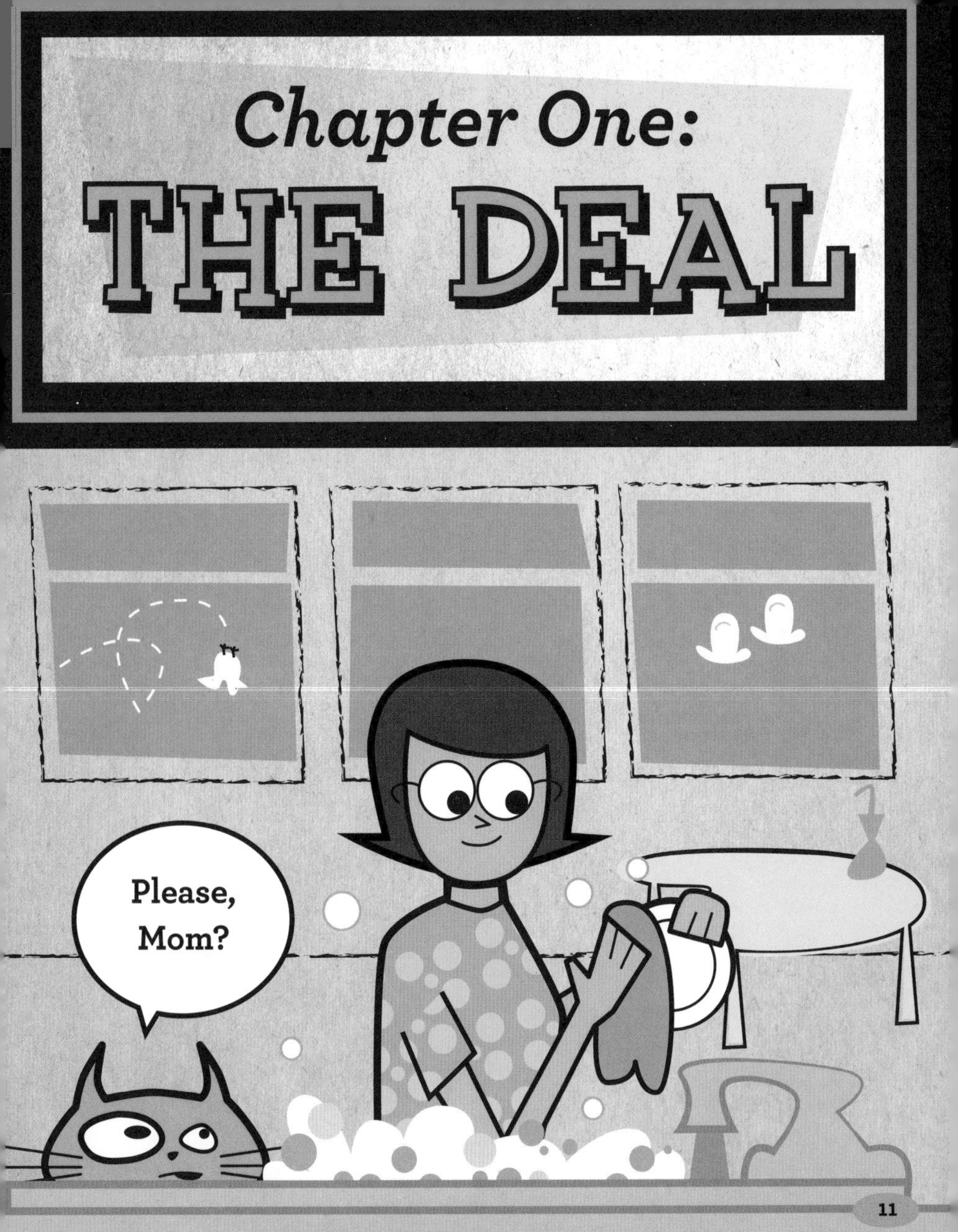
Please, Mom?

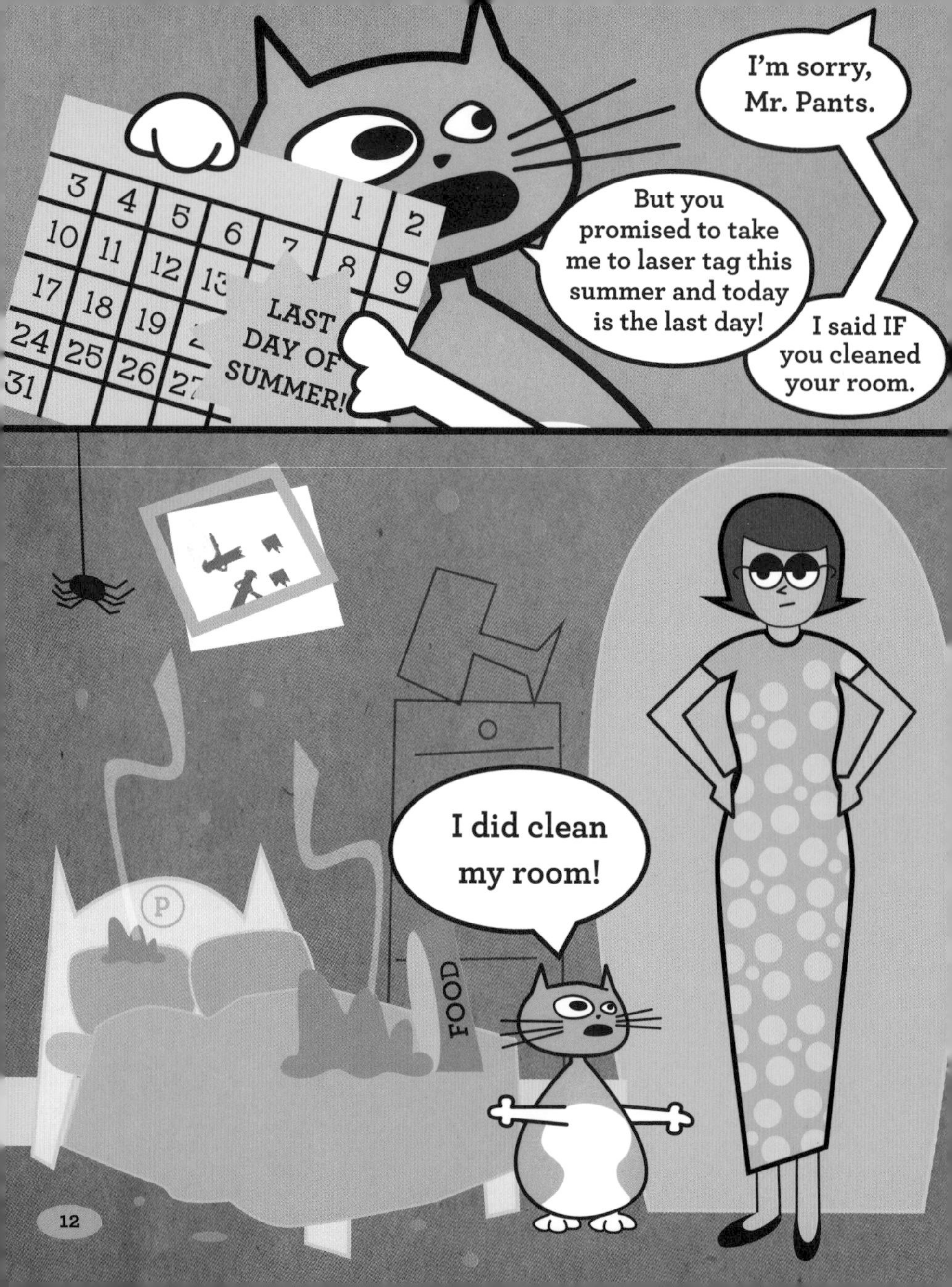
LAST DAY OF SUMMER!
But you promised to take me to laser tag this summer and today is the last day!
I'm sorry, Mr. Pants.
I said IF you cleaned your room.
FOOD
I did clean my room!

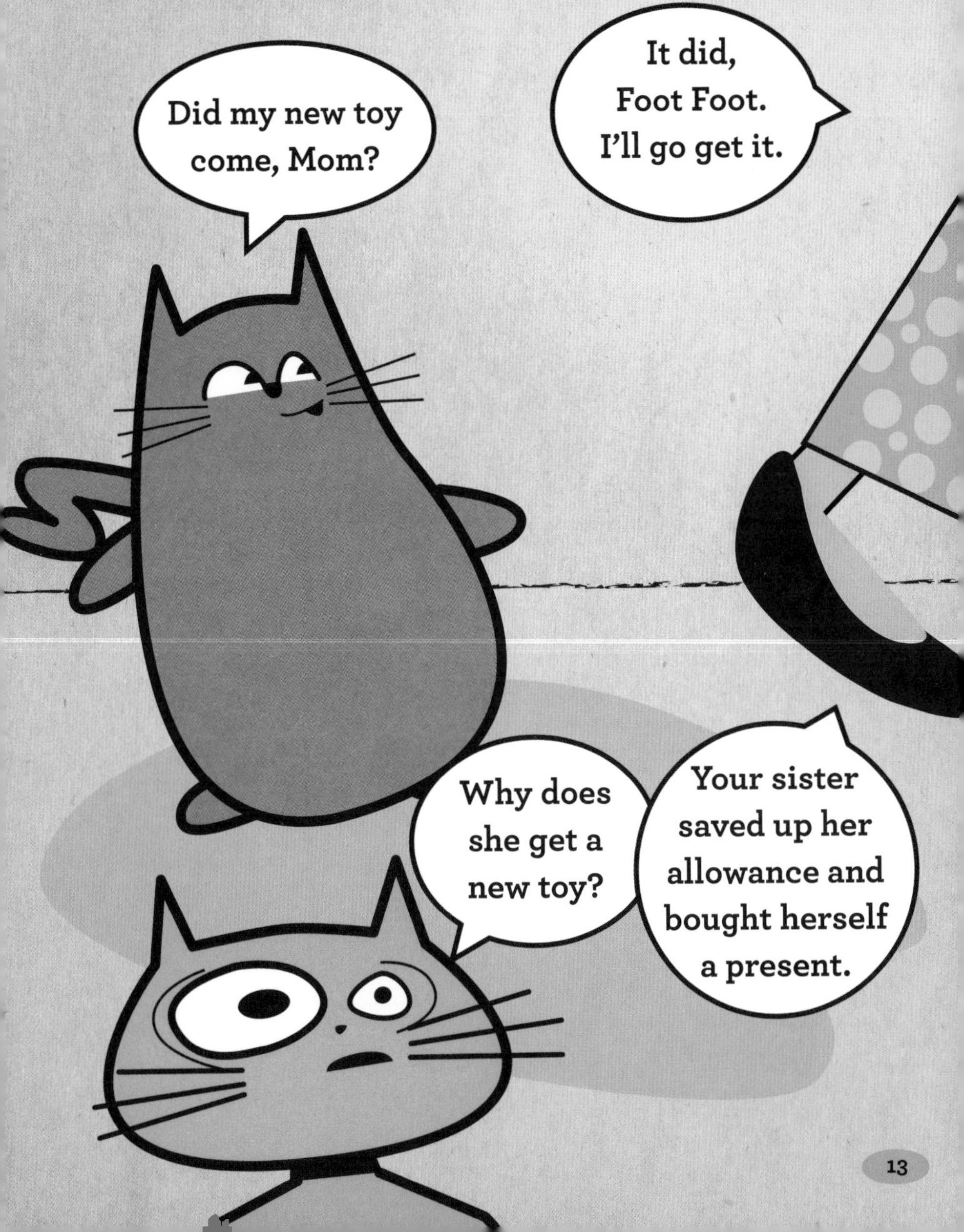
Did my new toy come, Mom?
It did, Foot Foot. I'll go get it.
Why does she get a new toy?
Your sister saved up her allowance and bought herself a present.

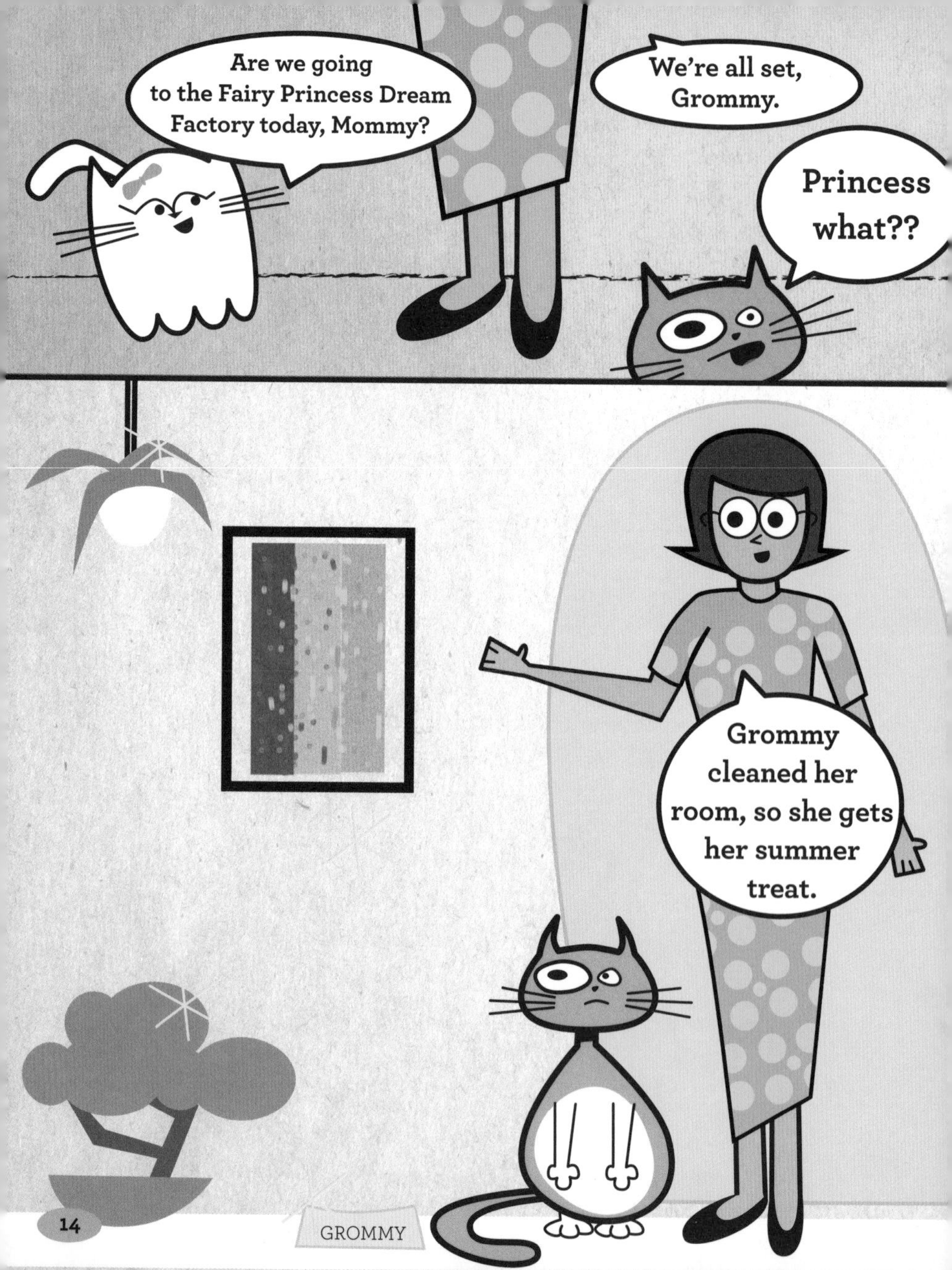
Are we going to the Fairy Princess Dream Factory today, Mommy?
We're all set, Grommy.
Princess what??
Grommy cleaned her room, so she gets her summer treat.

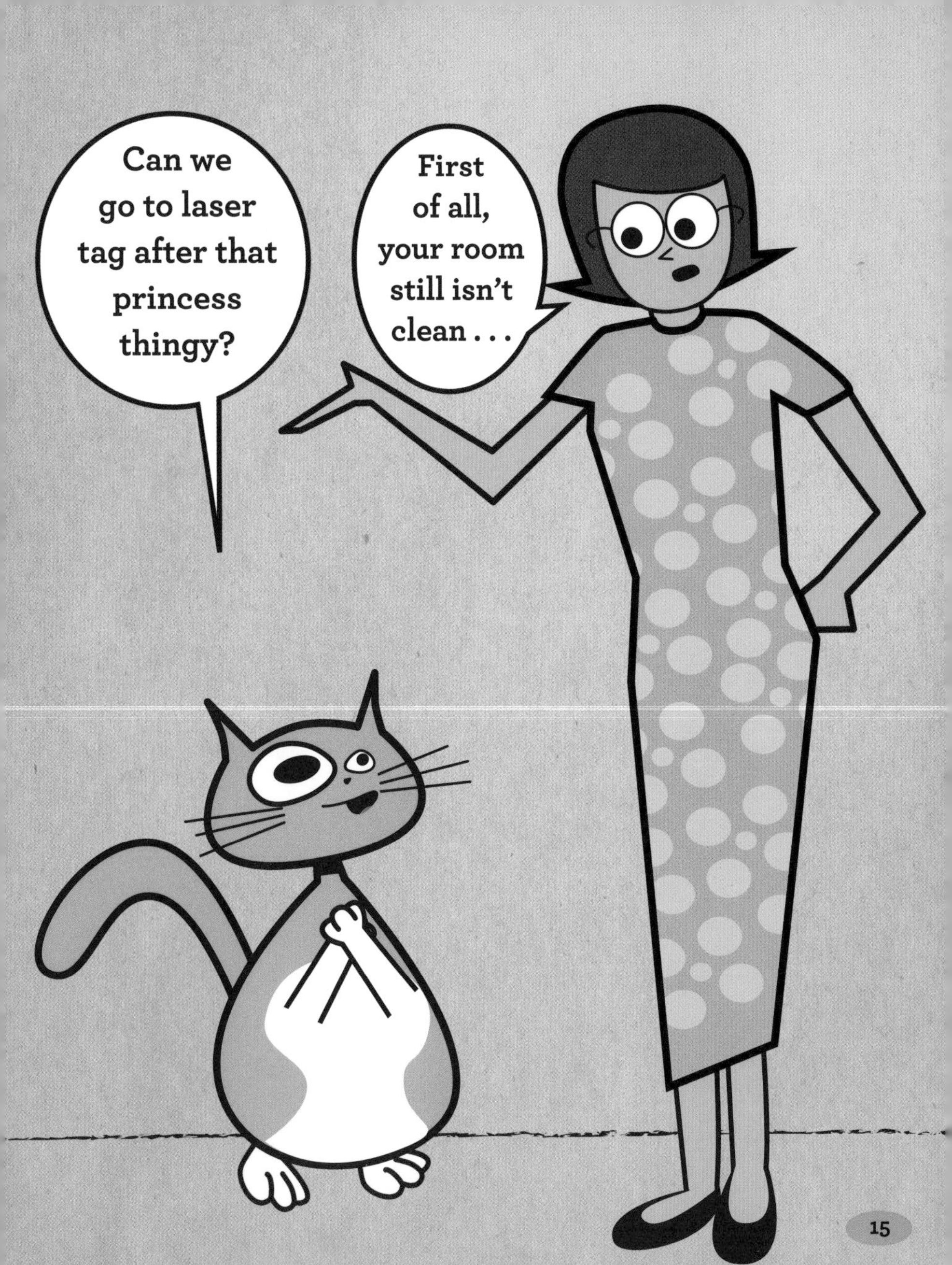
Can we go to laser tag after that princess thingy?
First of all, your room still isn't clean . . .

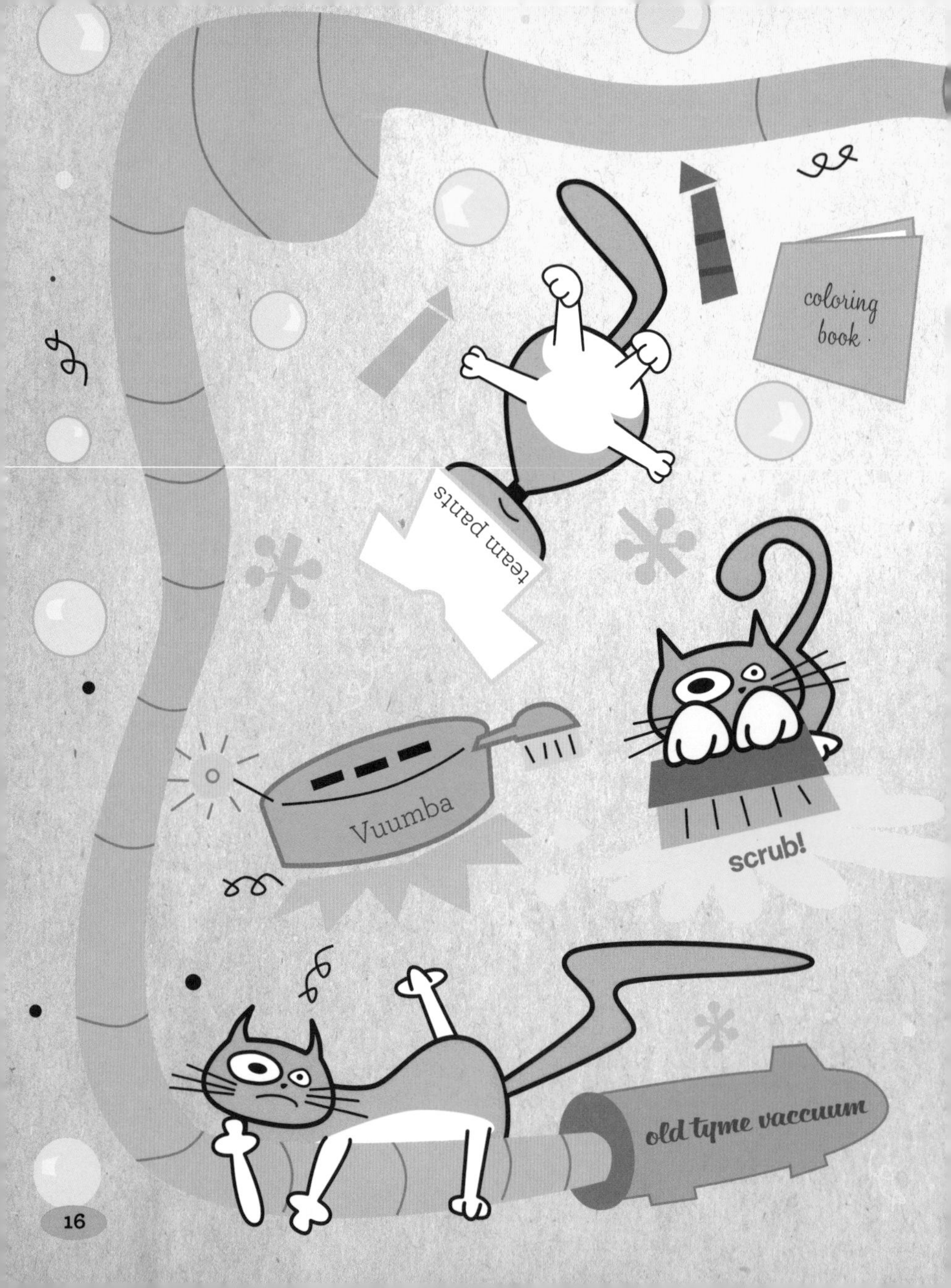
coloring book
team pants
Vuumba
scrub!
old tyme vaccuum

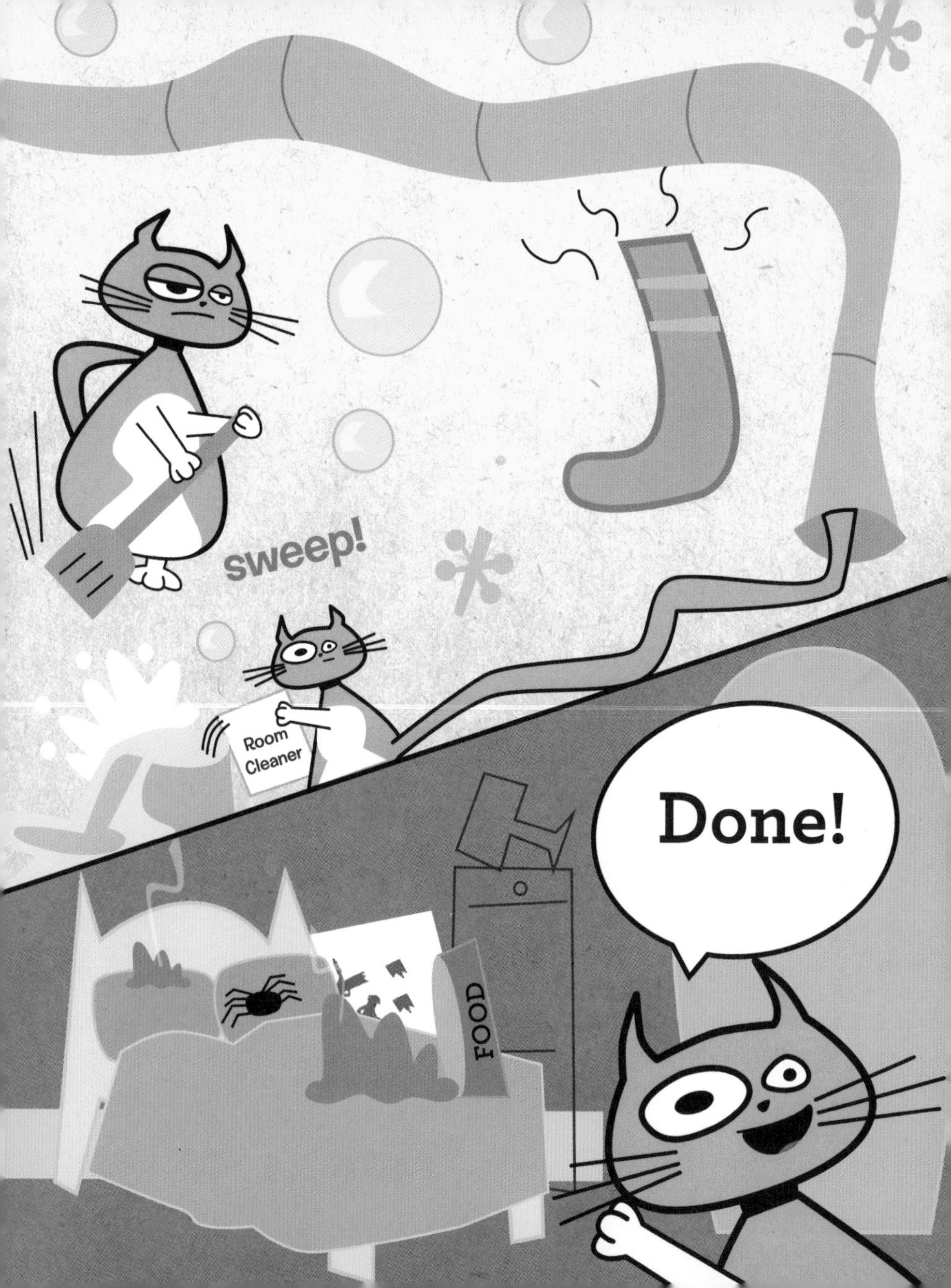
sweep!
Room Cleaner
FOOD
Done!

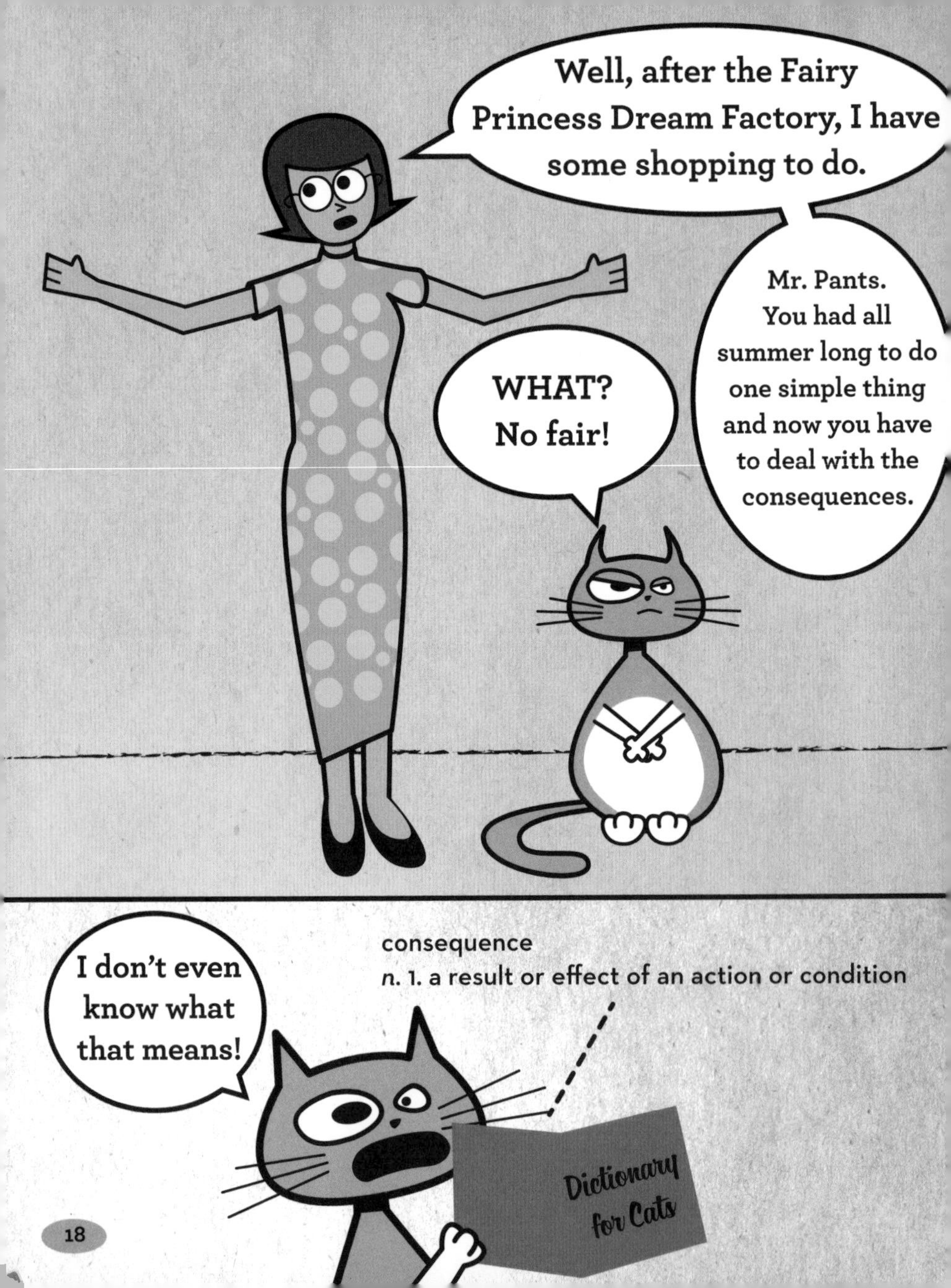
Well, after the Fairy Princess Dream Factory, I have some shopping to do.
Mr. Pants. You had all summer long to do one simple thing and now you have to deal with the consequences.
WHAT? No fair!
I don't even know what that means!
consequence
n. 1. a result or effect of an action or condition
Dictionary for Cats

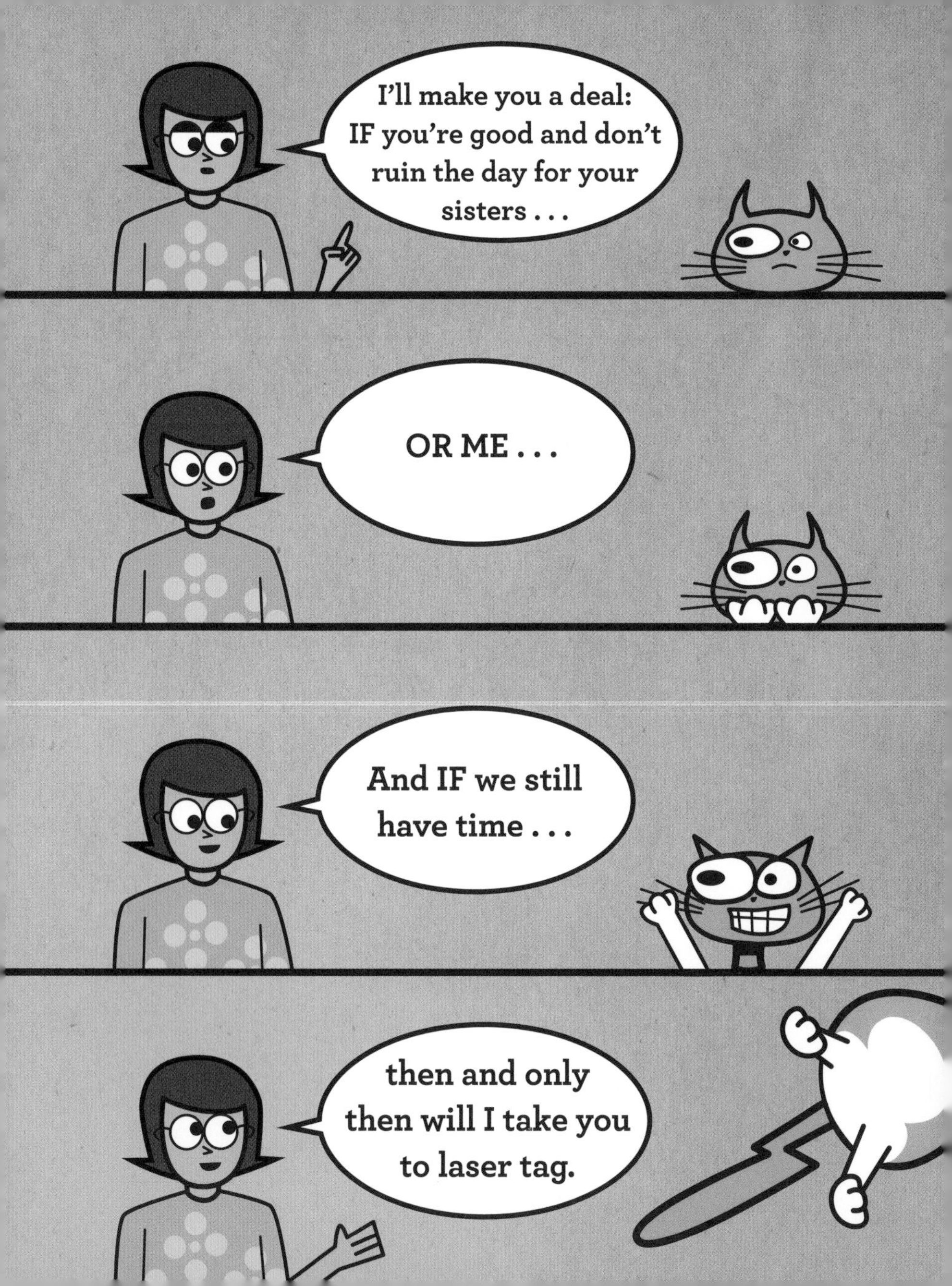
I'll make you a deal: IF you're good and don't ruin the day for your sisters . . .
OR ME . . .
And IF we still have time . . .
then and only then will I take you to laser tag.

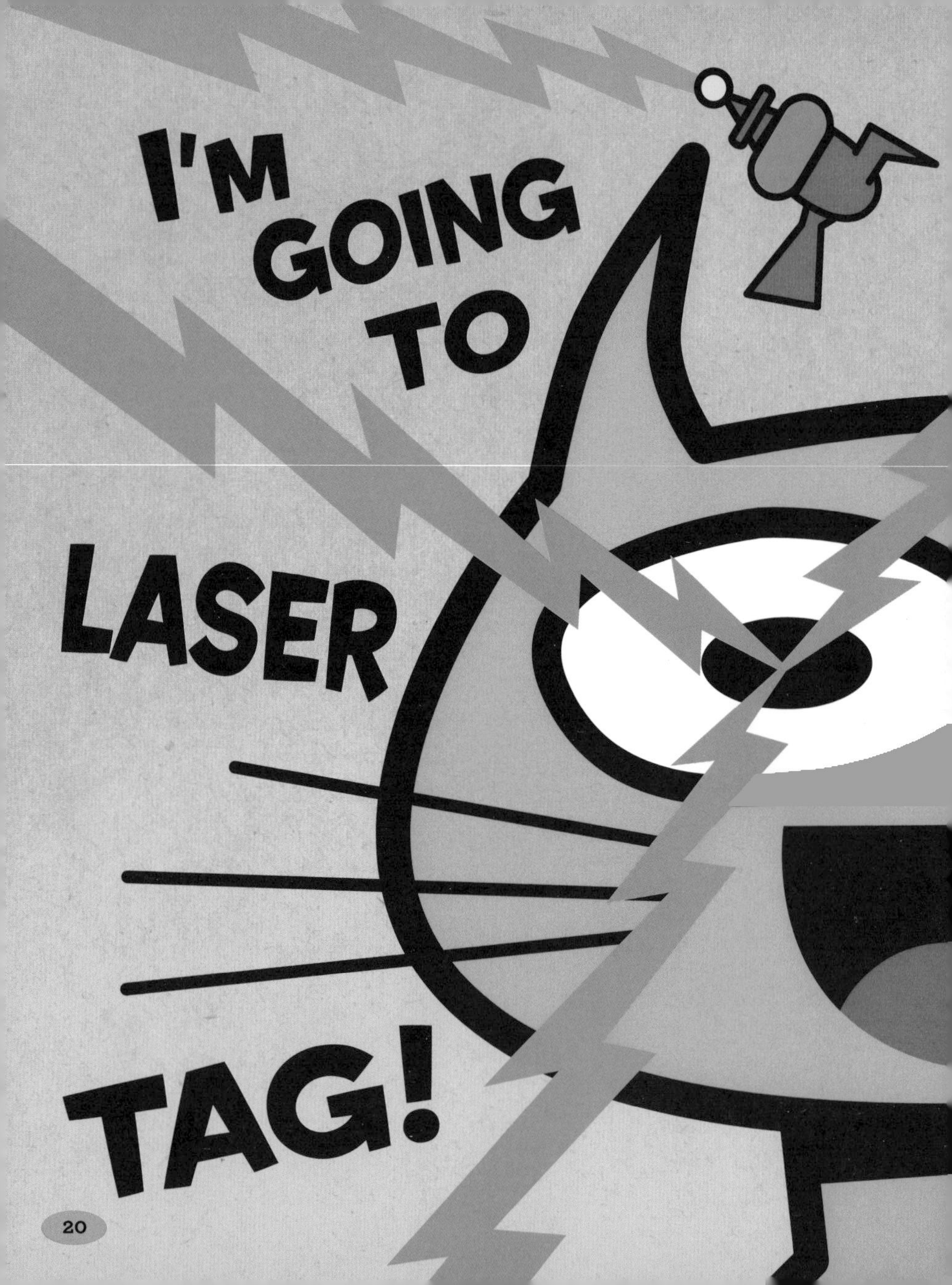
I'M
GOING
TO
LASER
TAG!

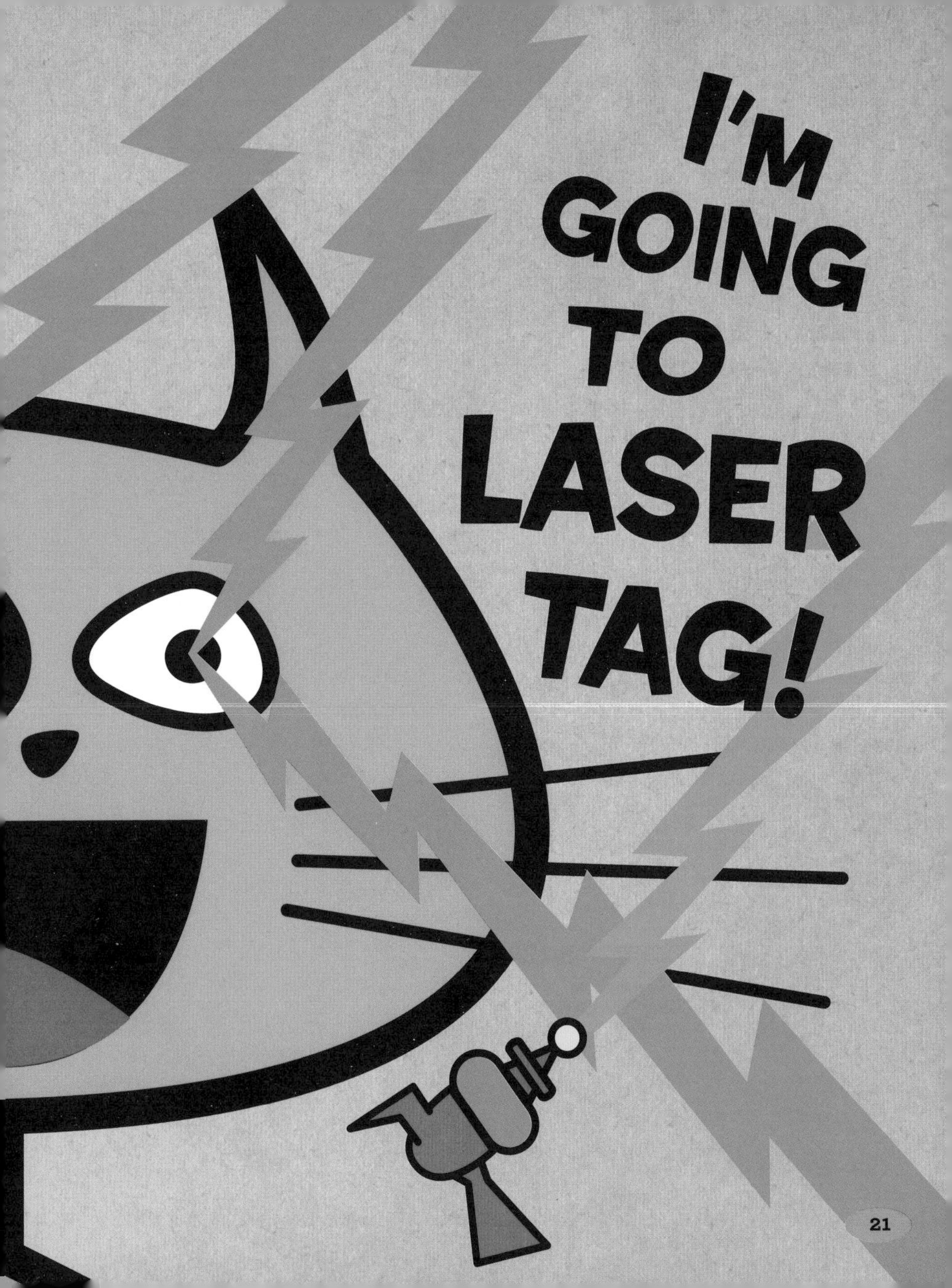
I'M GOING TO LASER TAG!

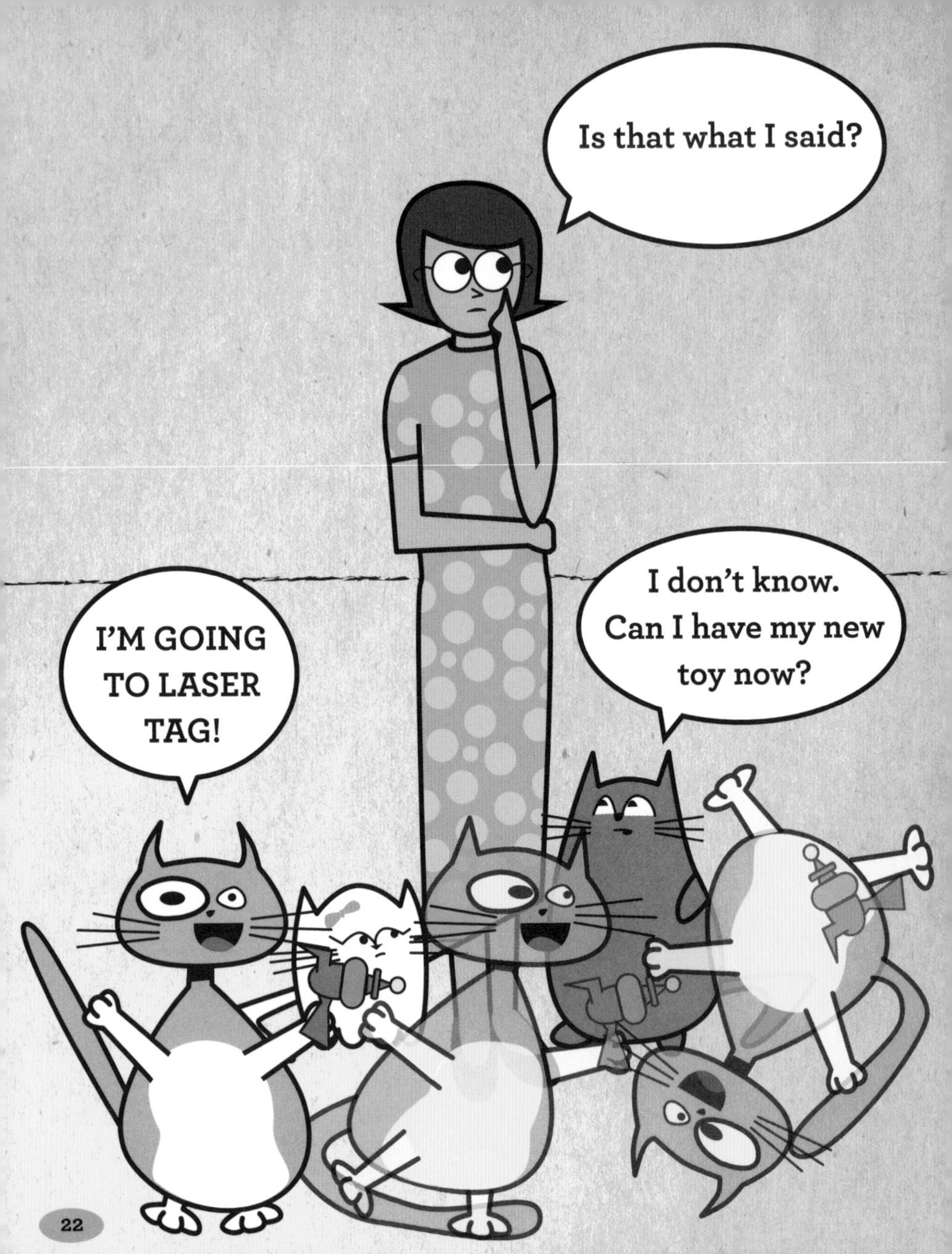
Is that what I said?
I'M GOING TO LASER TAG!
I don't know. Can I have my new toy now?

Chapter Two: BOXY

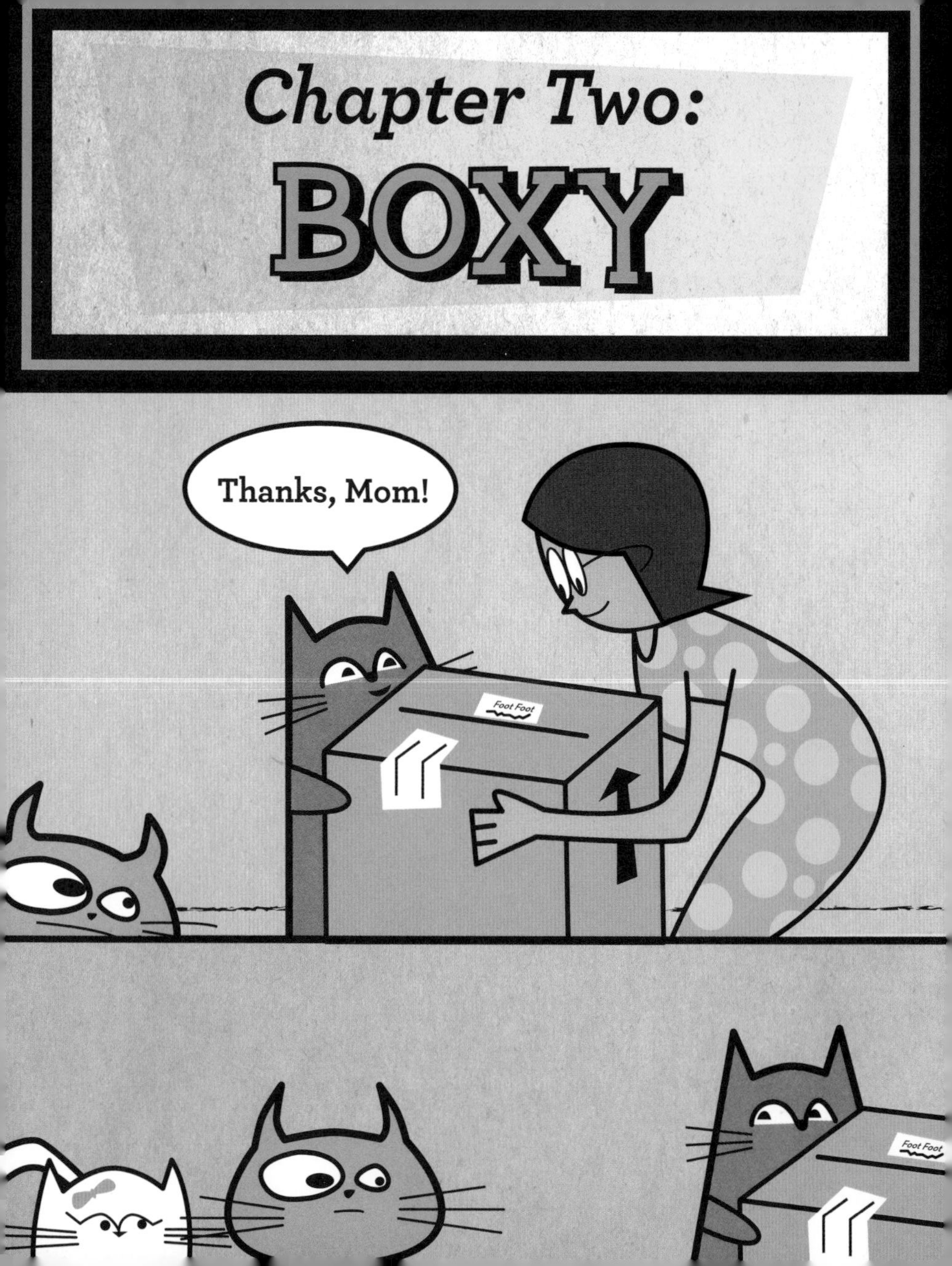
Thanks, Mom!
Foot Foot
Foot Foot

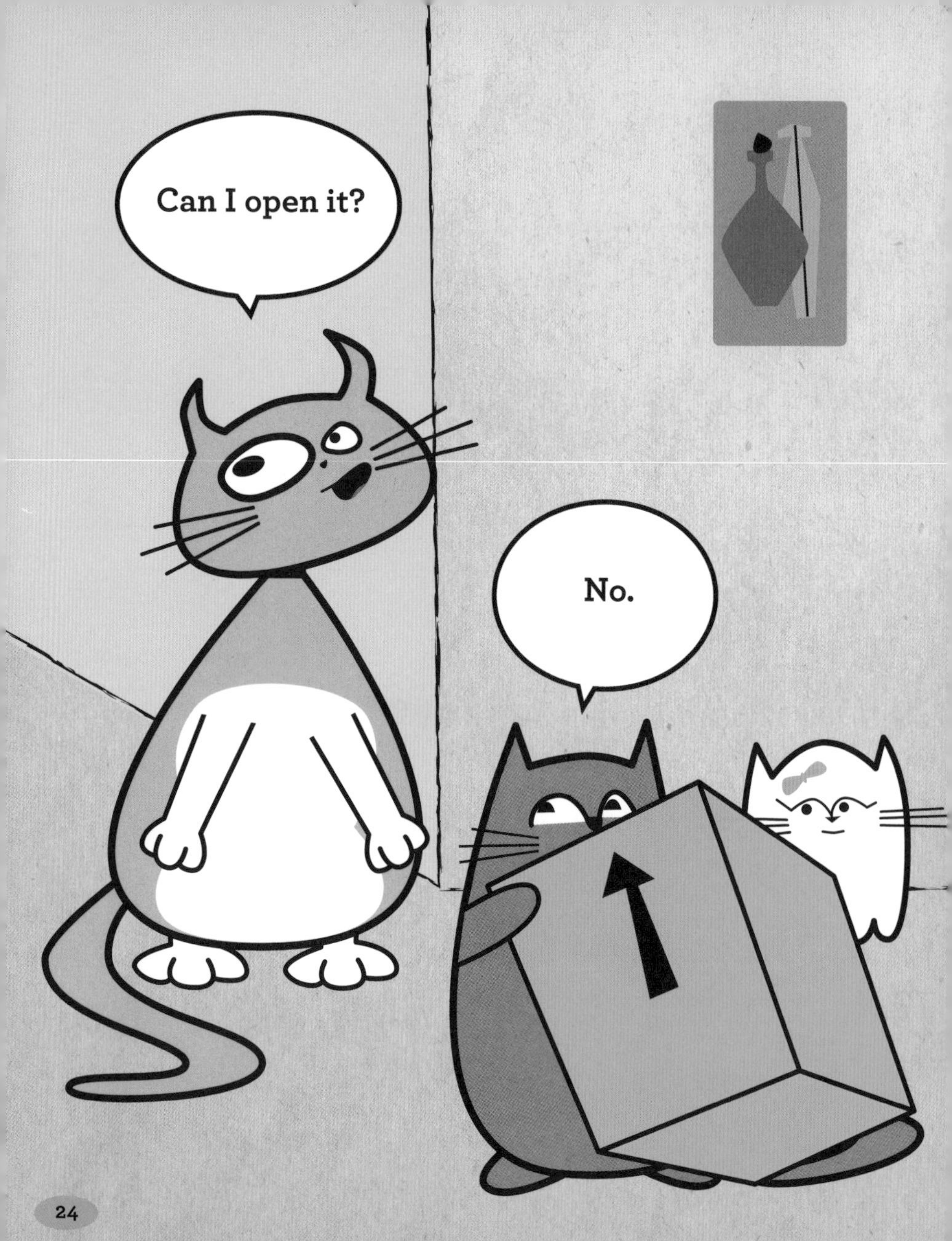
Can I open it?
No.

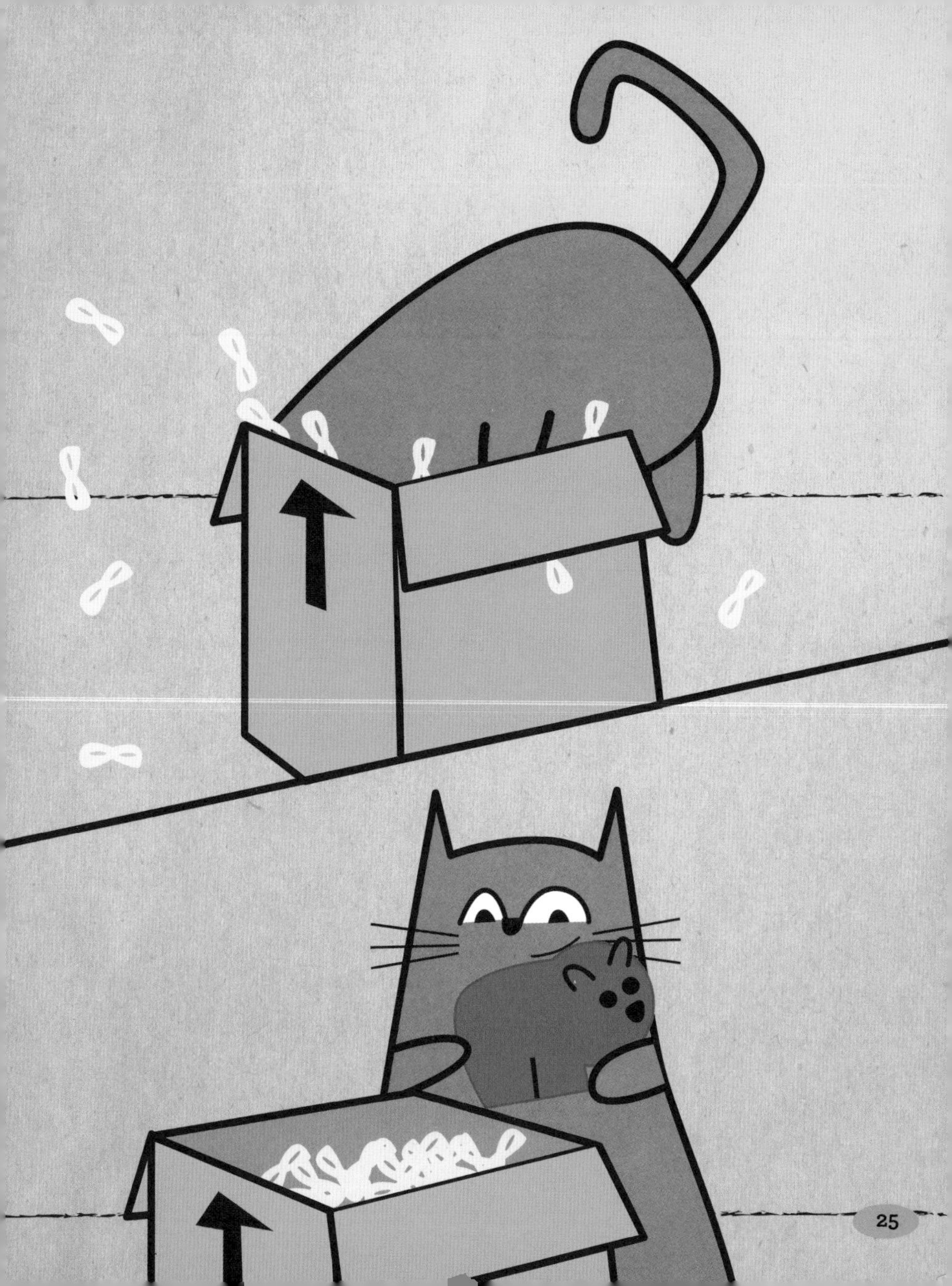

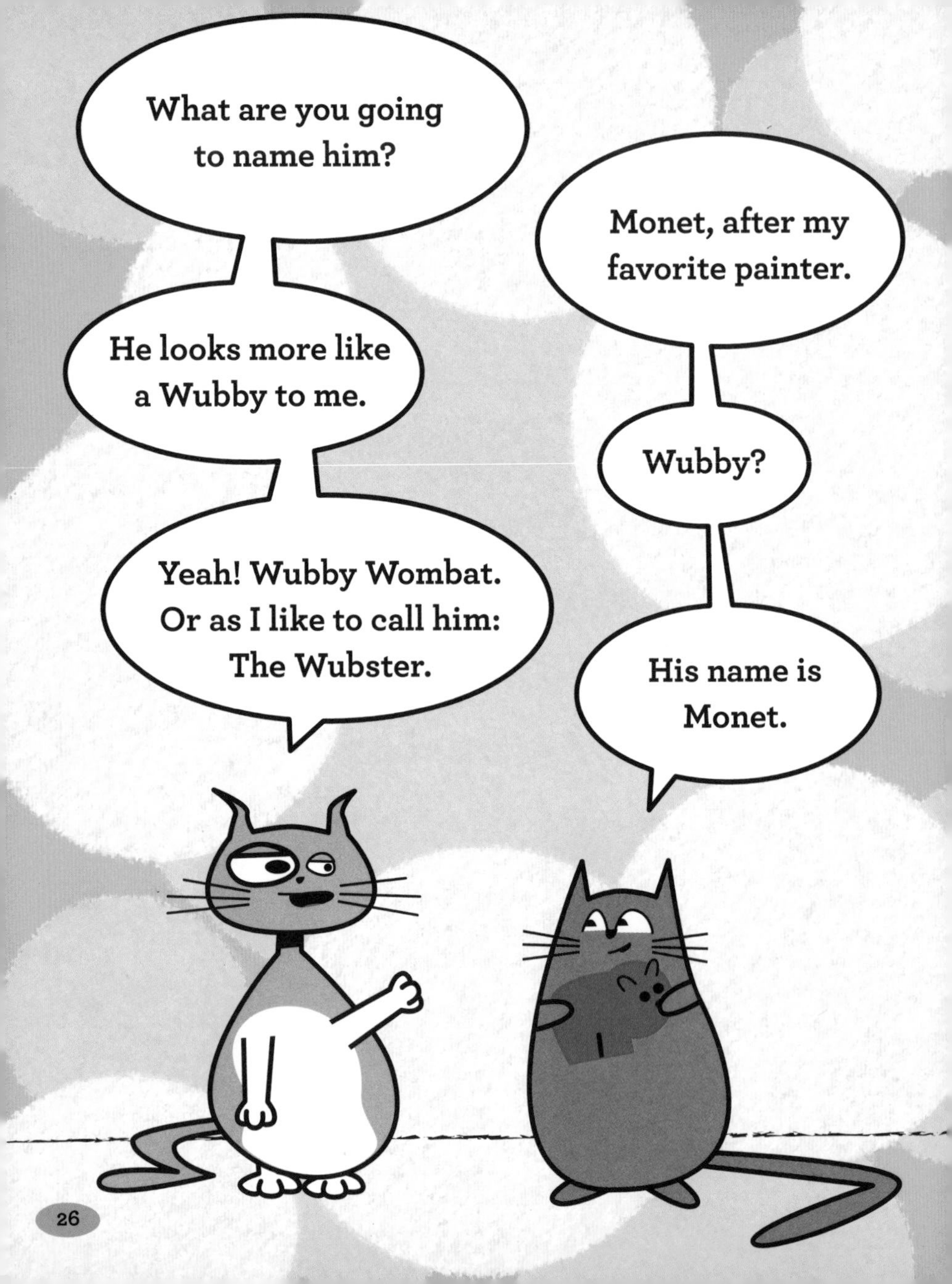
What are you going to name him?
Monet, after my favorite painter.
He looks more like a Wubby to me.
Wubby?
Yeah! Wubby Wombat. Or as I like to call him: The Wubster.
His name is Monet.

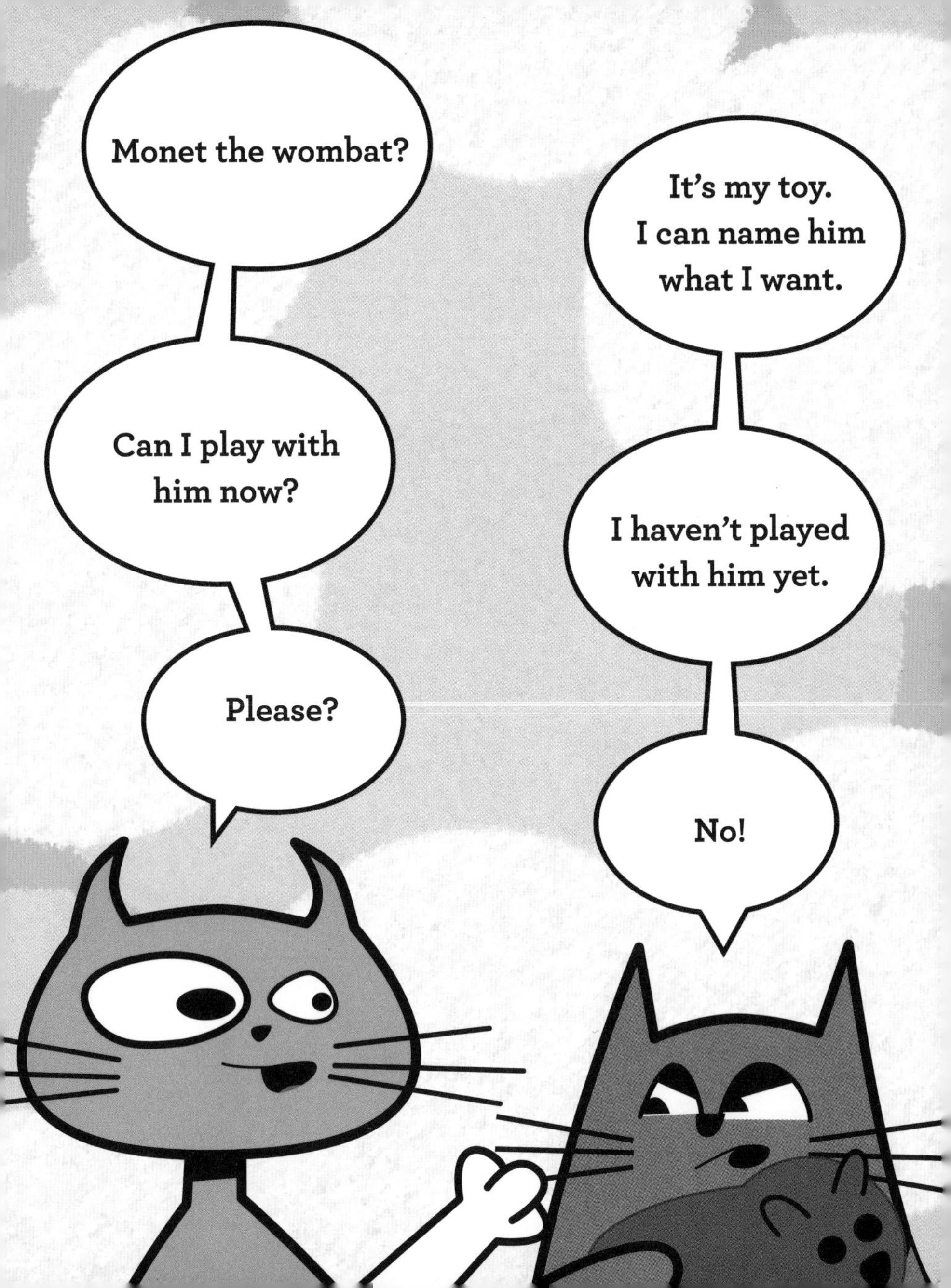
Monet the wombat?
Can I play with him now?
Please?
It's my toy. I can name him what I want.
I haven't played with him yet.
No!

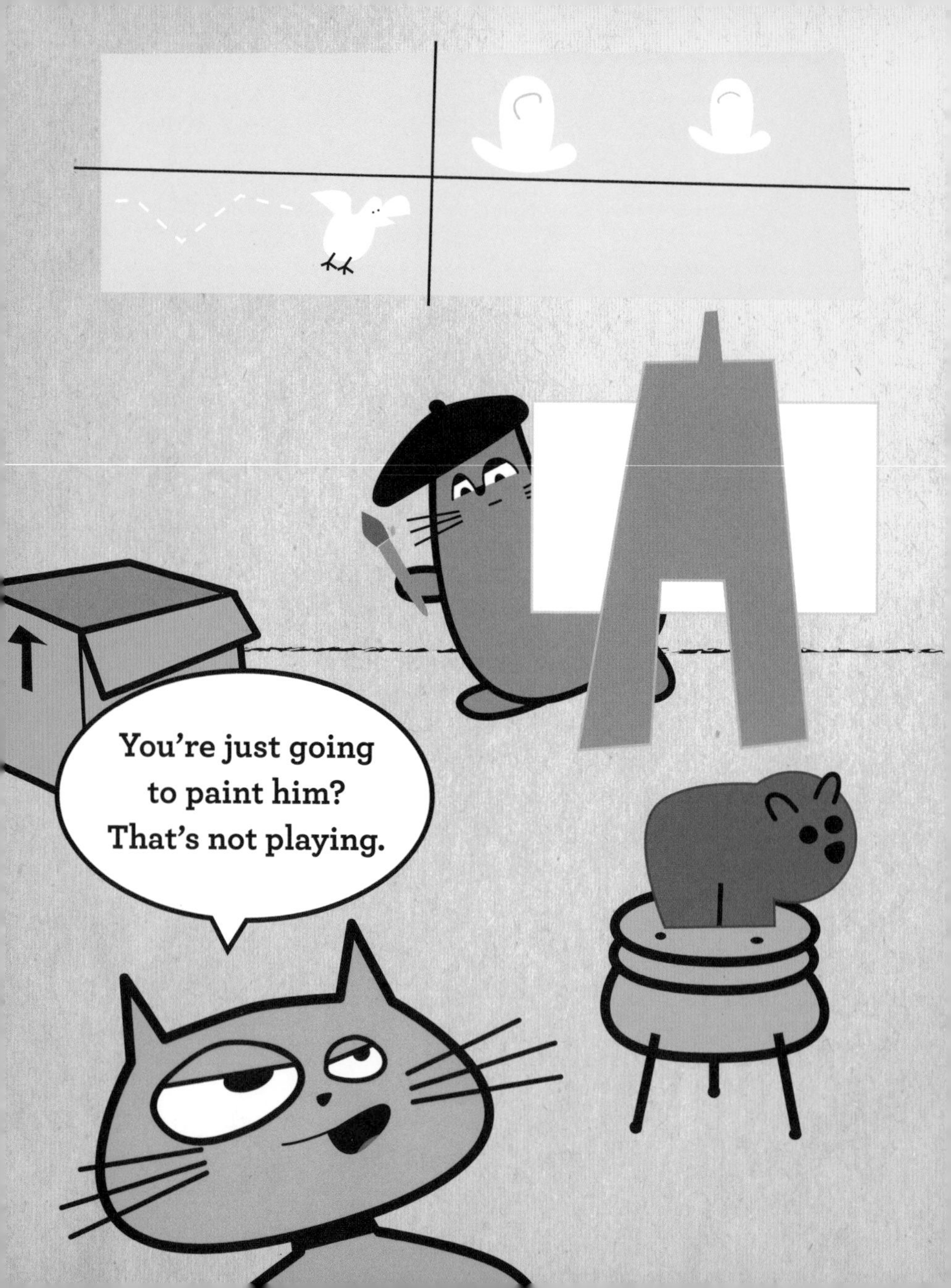
You're just going to paint him? That's not playing.

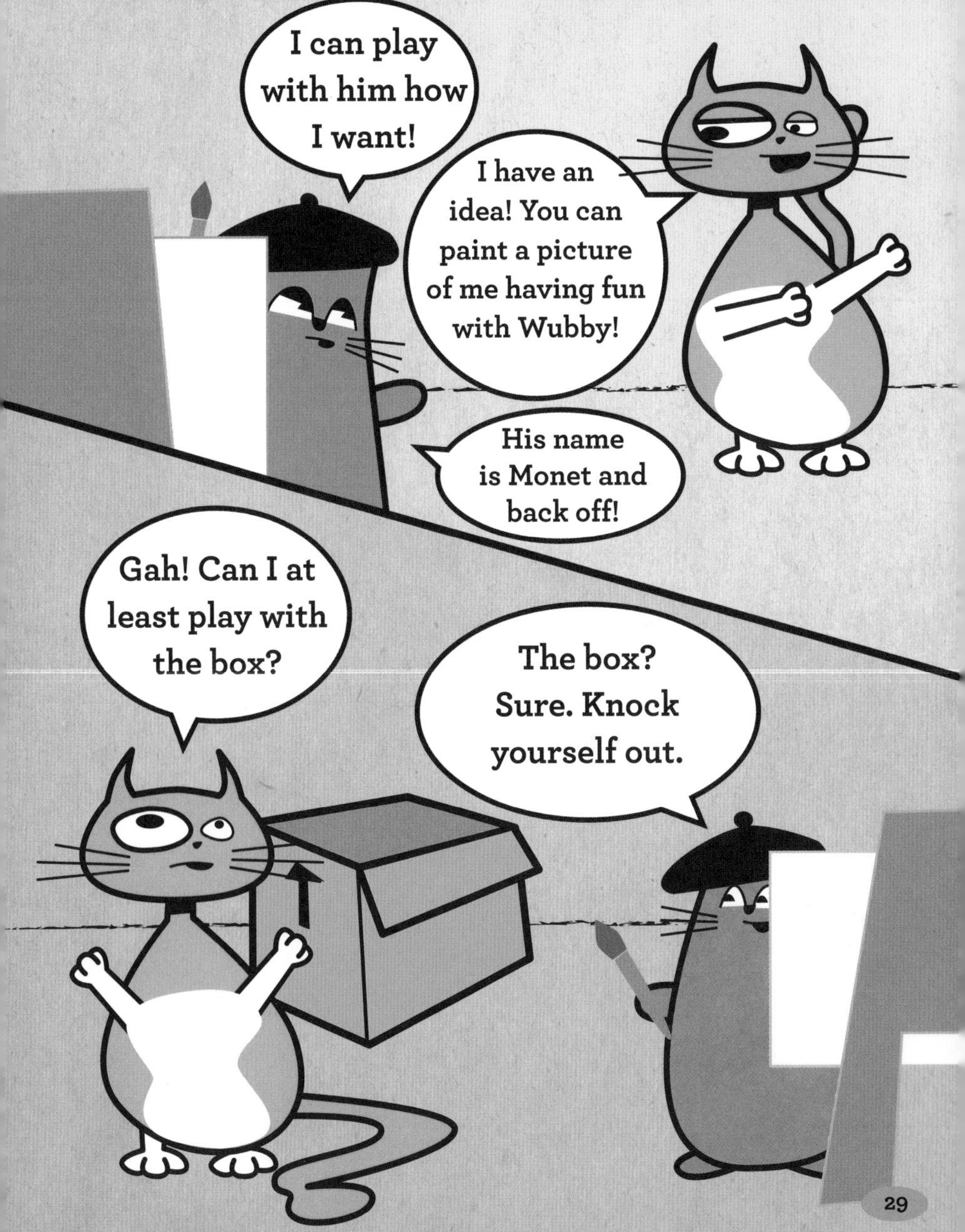
I can play with him how I want!
I have an idea! You can paint a picture of me having fun with Wubby!
His name is Monet and back off!
Gah! Can I at least play with the box?
The box? Sure. Knock yourself out.

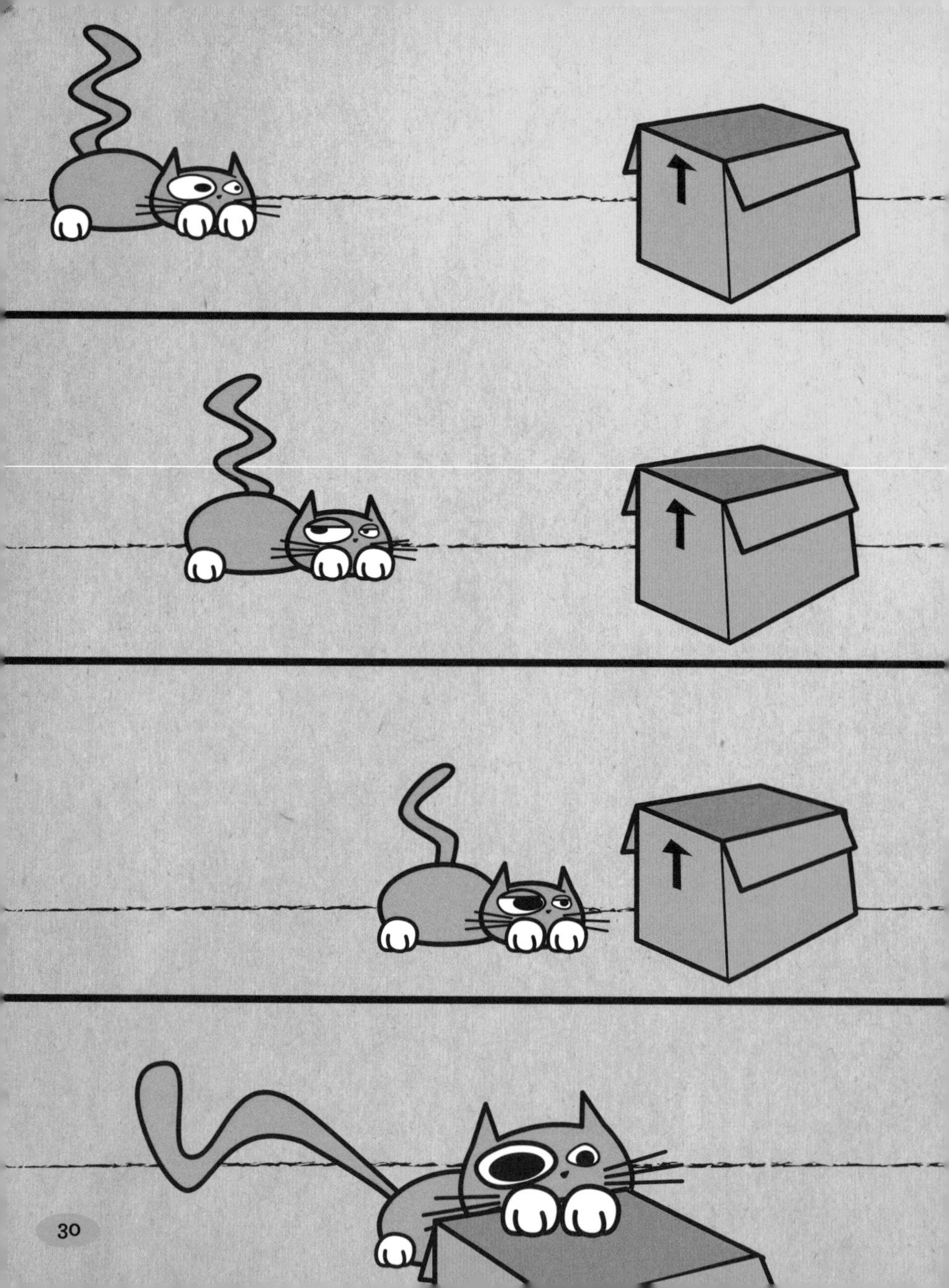

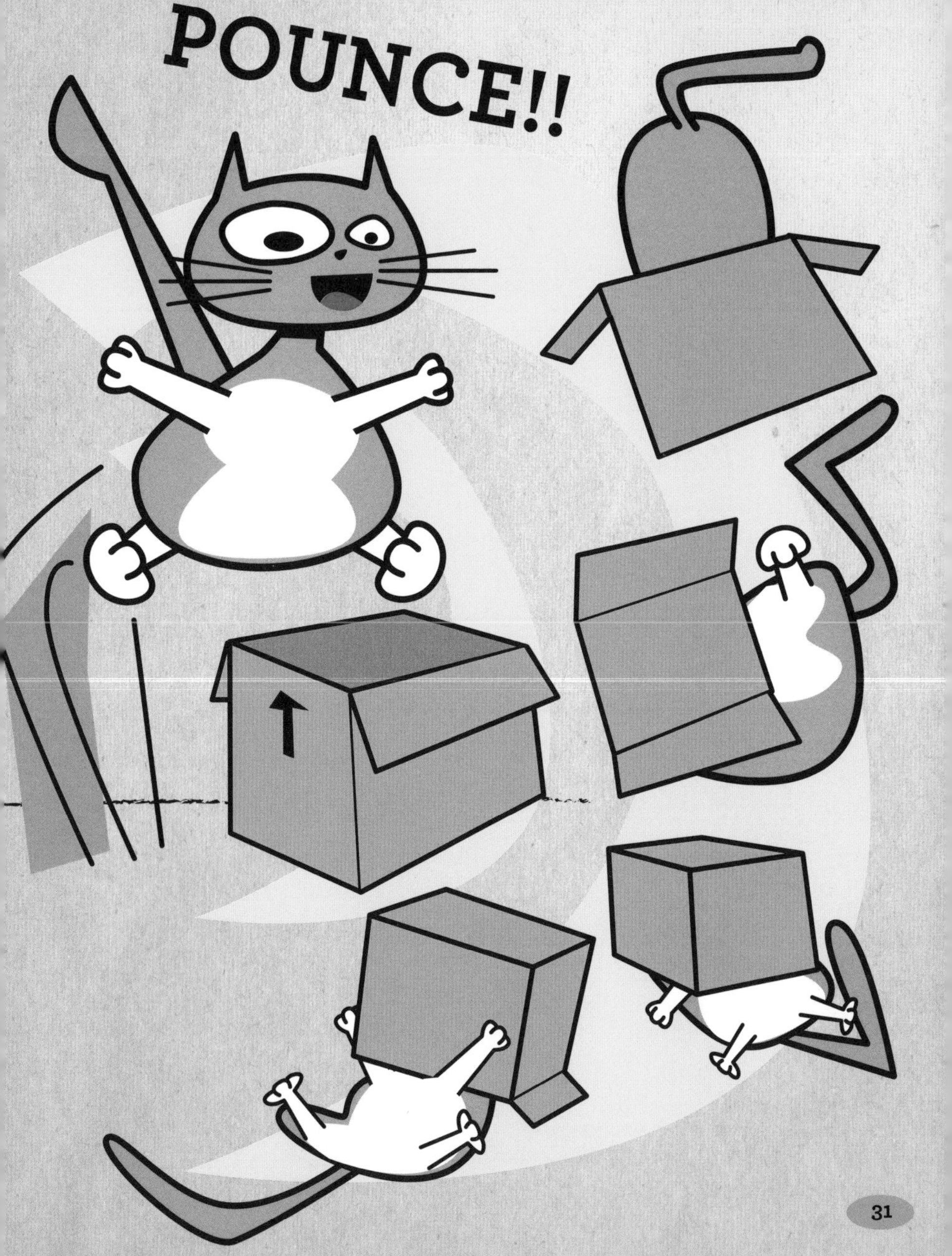
POUNCE!!

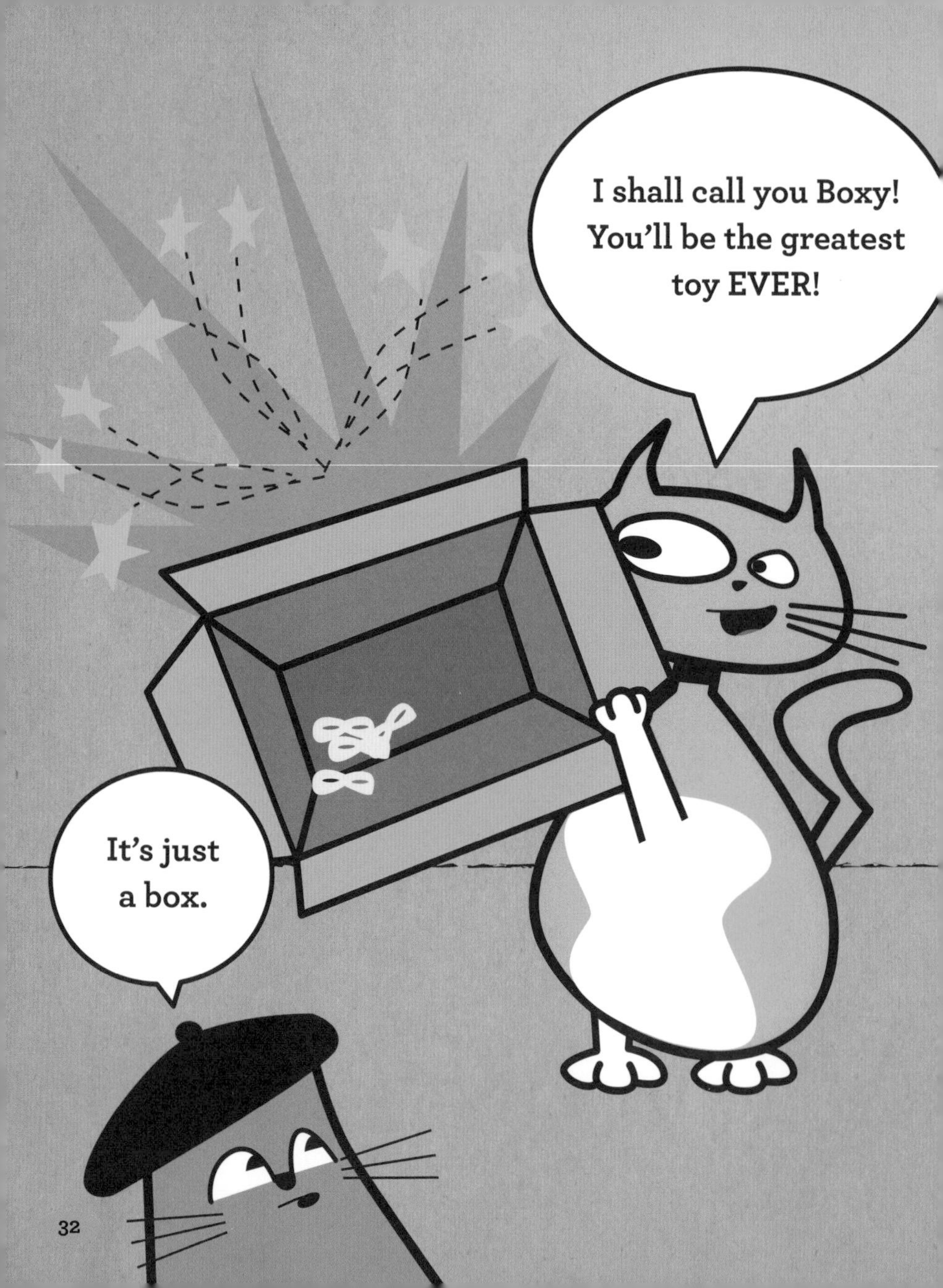
I shall call you Boxy! You'll be the greatest toy EVER!
It's just a box.

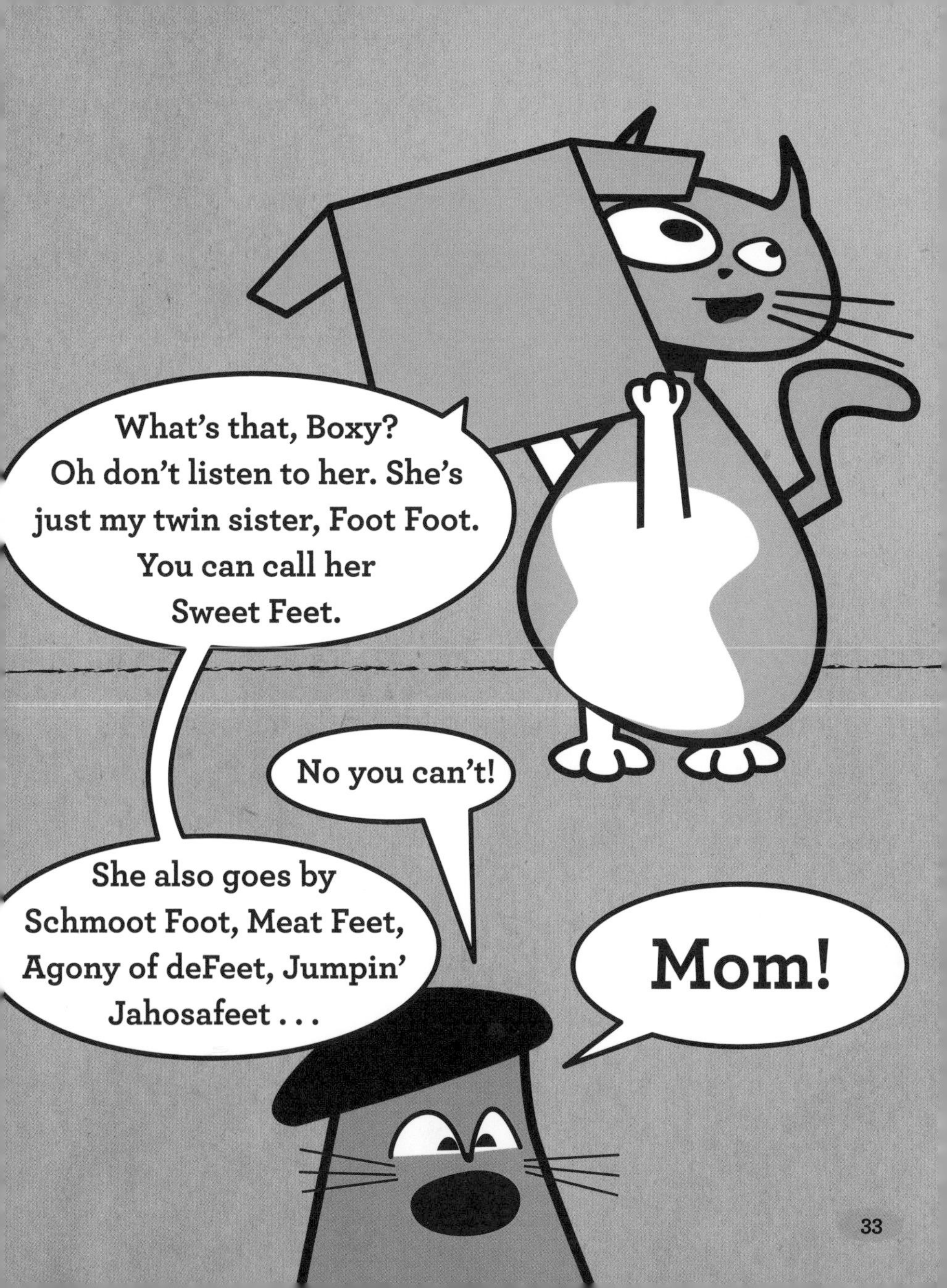
What's that, Boxy? Oh don't listen to her. She's just my twin sister, Foot Foot. You can call her Sweet Feet.
No you can't!
She also goes by Schmoot Foot, Meat Feet, Agony of deFeet, Jumpin' Jahosafeet . . .
Mom!

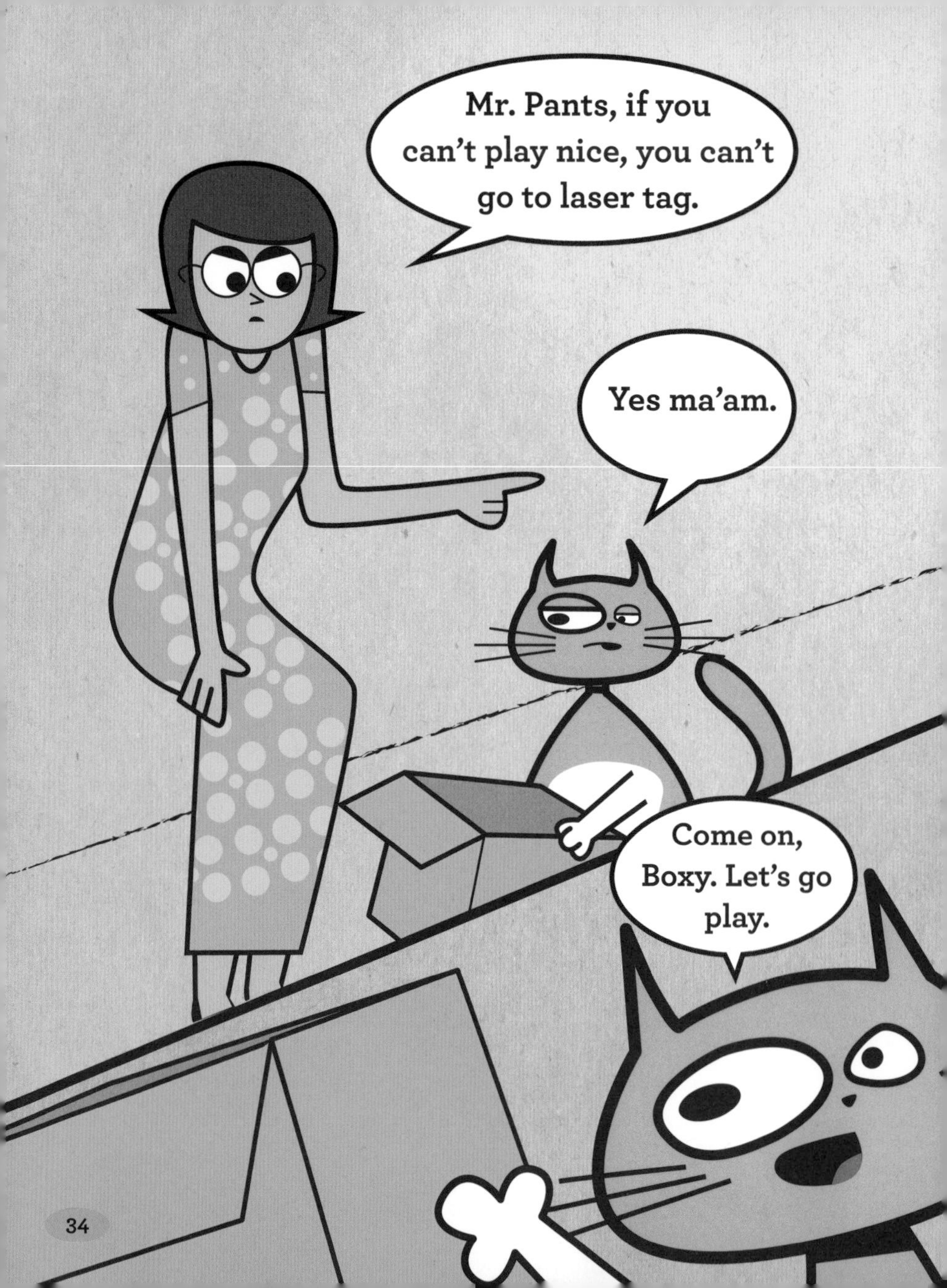
Mr. Pants, if you can't play nice, you can't go to laser tag.
Yes ma'am.
Come on, Boxy. Let's go play.

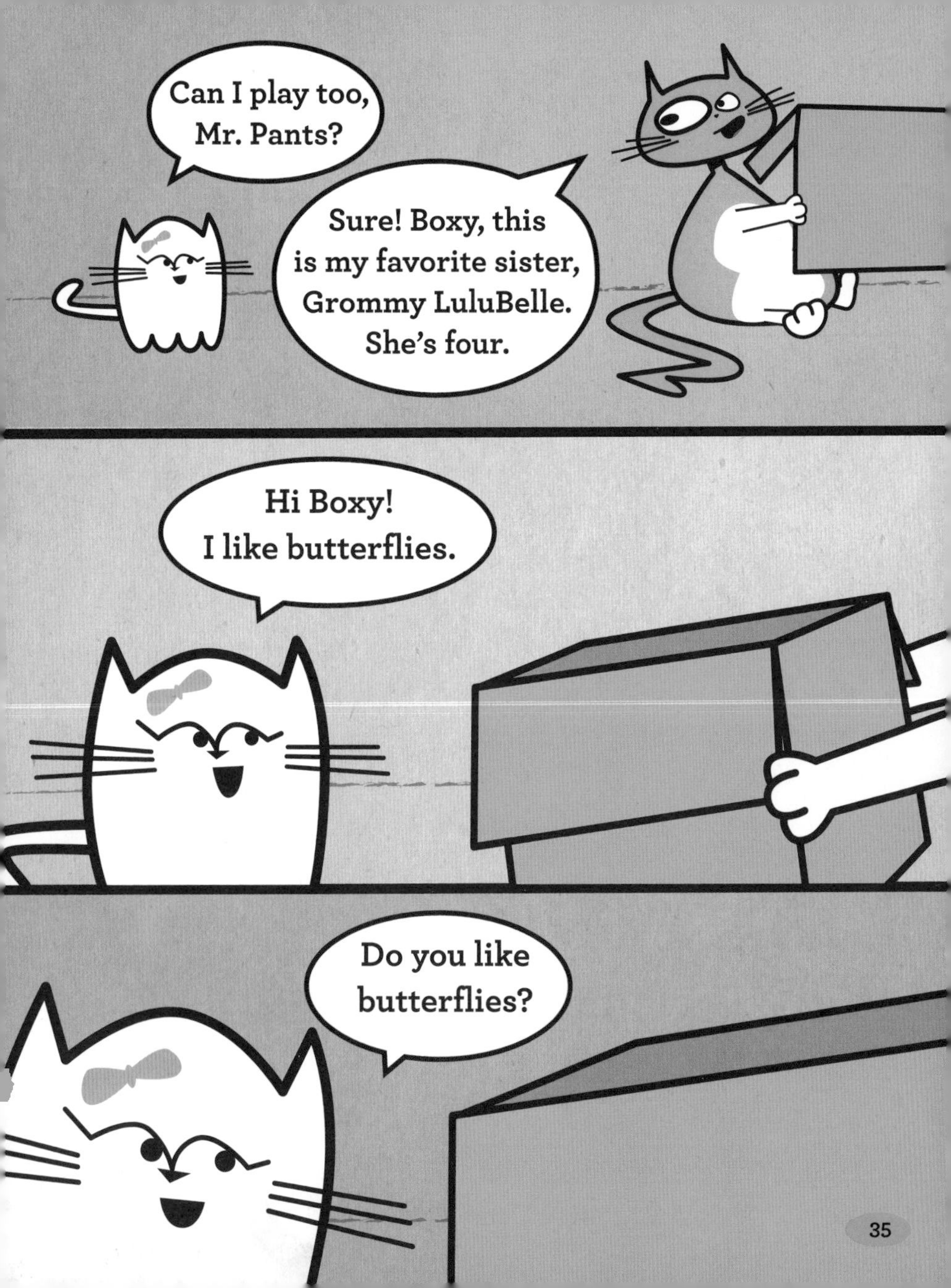
Can I play too, Mr. Pants?
Sure! Boxy, this is my favorite sister, Grommy LuluBelle. She's four.
Hi Boxy! I like butterflies.
Do you like butterflies?

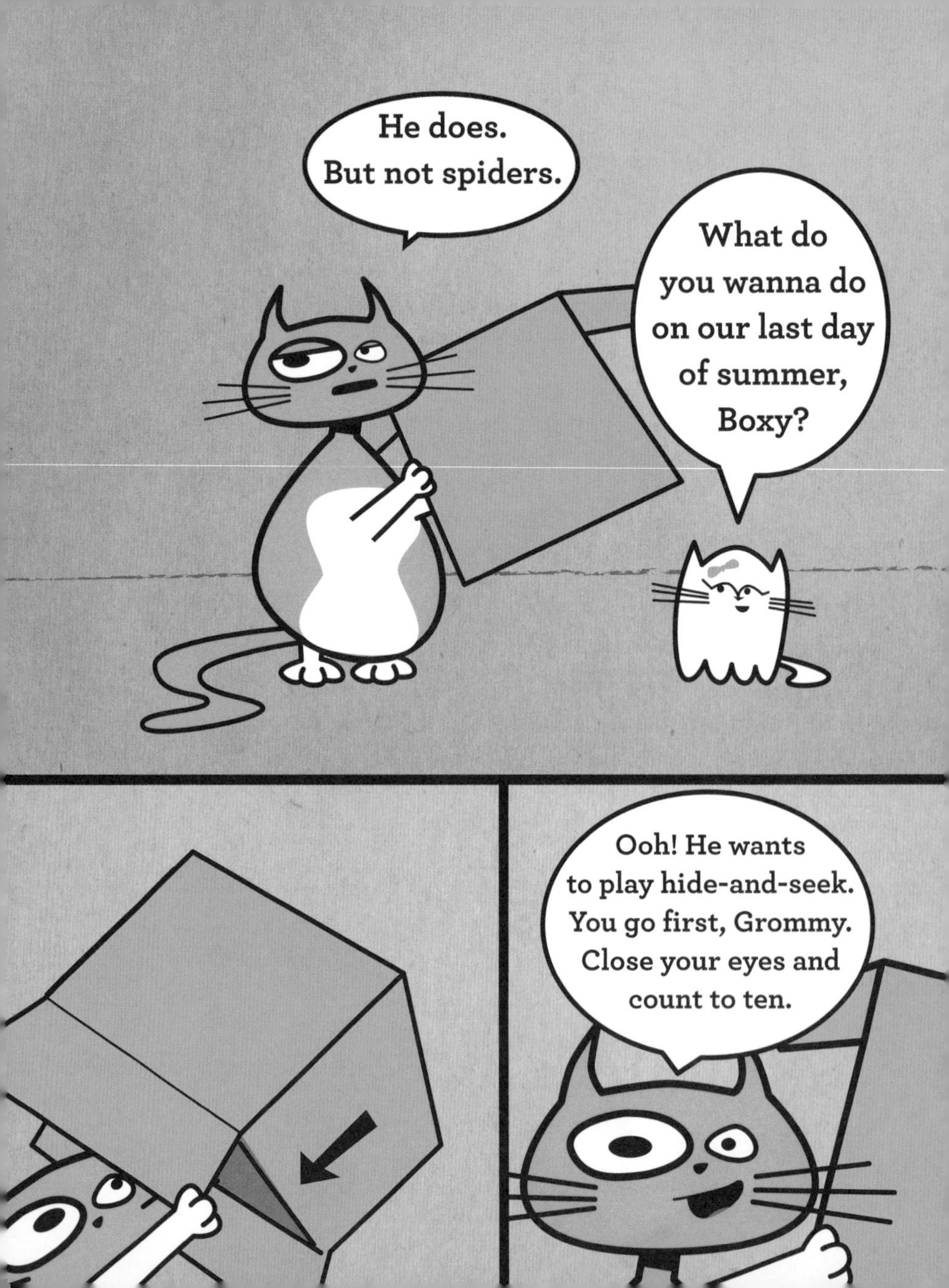
He does. But not spiders.
What do you wanna do on our last day of summer, Boxy?
Ooh! He wants to play hide-and-seek. You go first, Grommy. Close your eyes and count to ten.

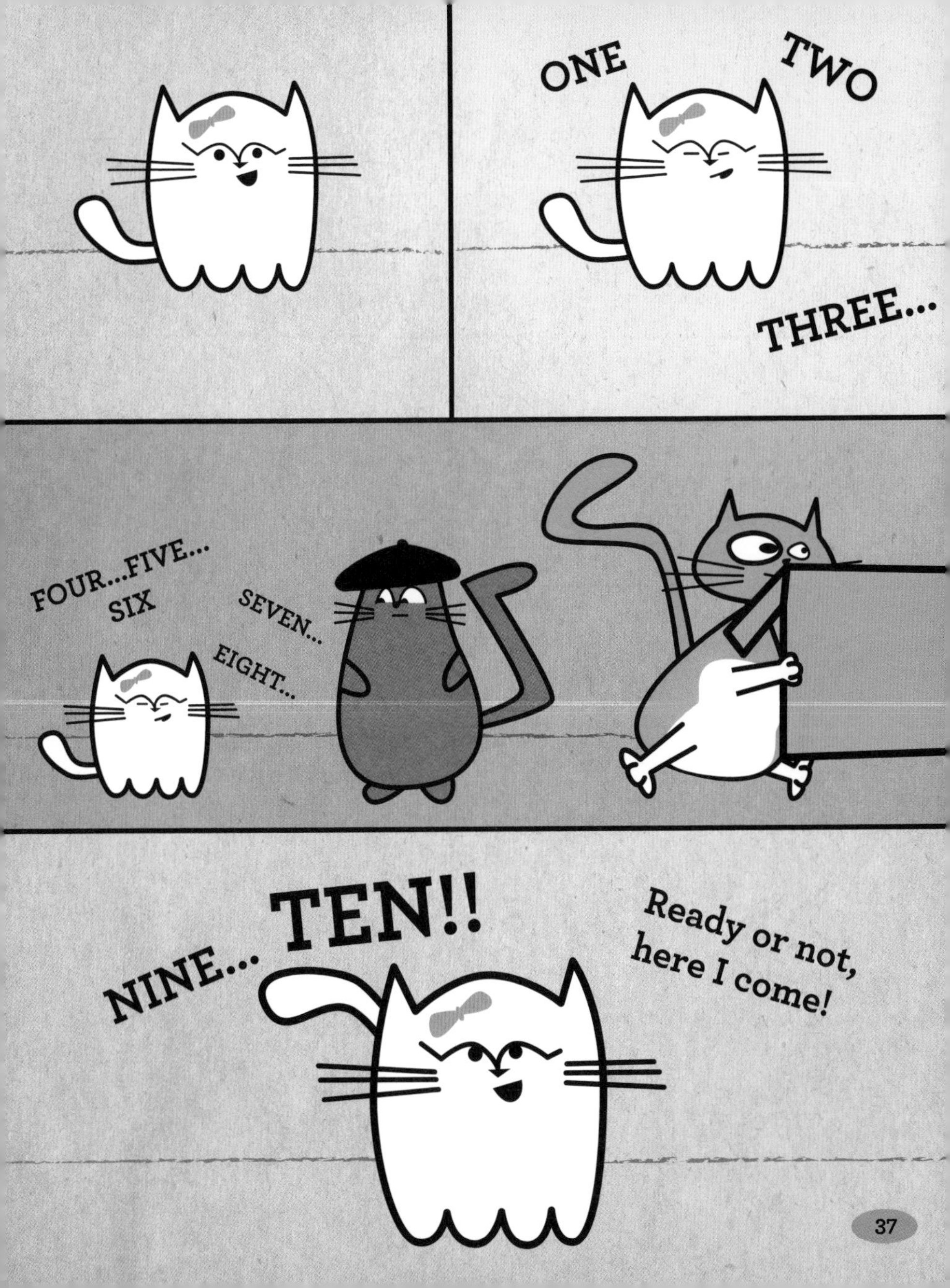
ONE
TWO
THREE...
FOUR...FIVE...
SIX
SEVEN...
EIGHT...
NINE...
TEN!!
Ready or not,
here I come!

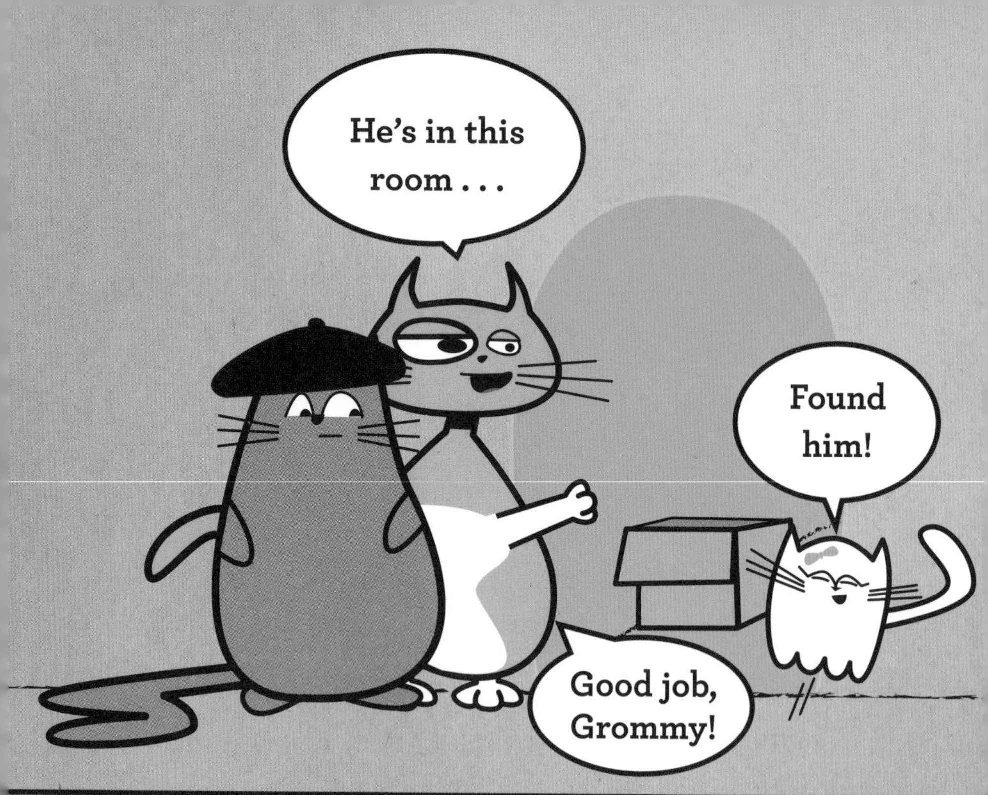
He's in this room . . .
Found him!
Good job, Grommy!

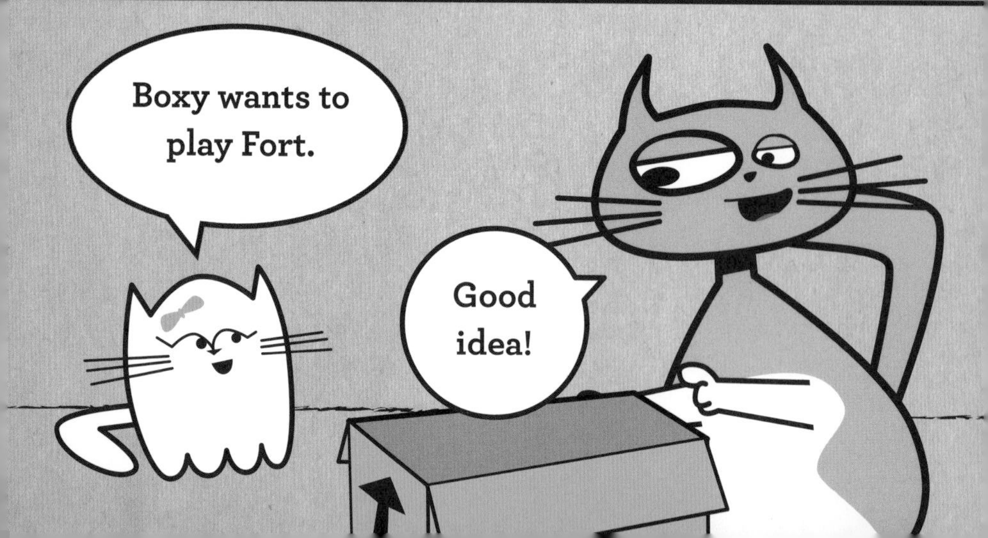
Boxy wants to play Fort.
Good idea!

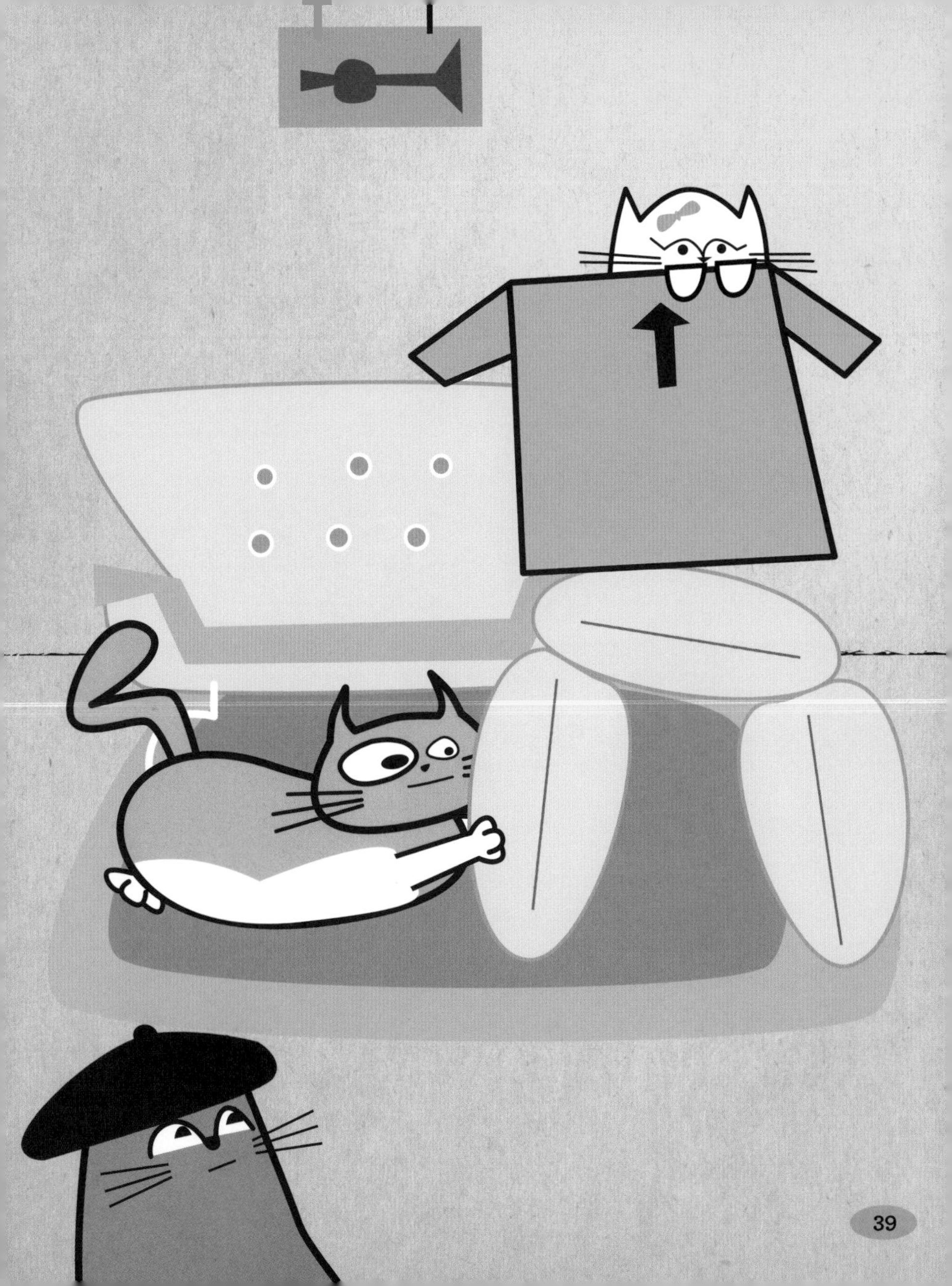

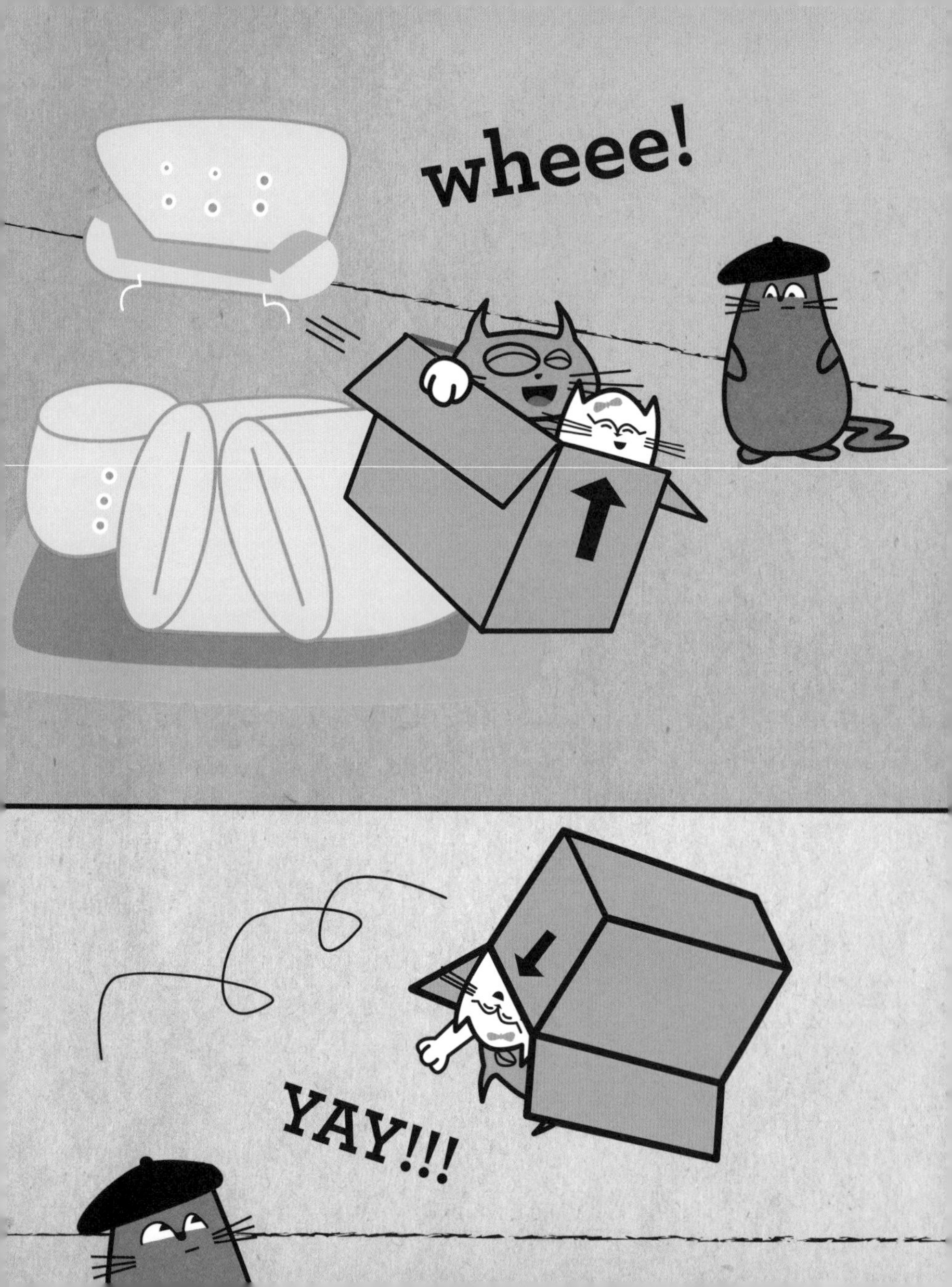

wheee!
YAY!!!

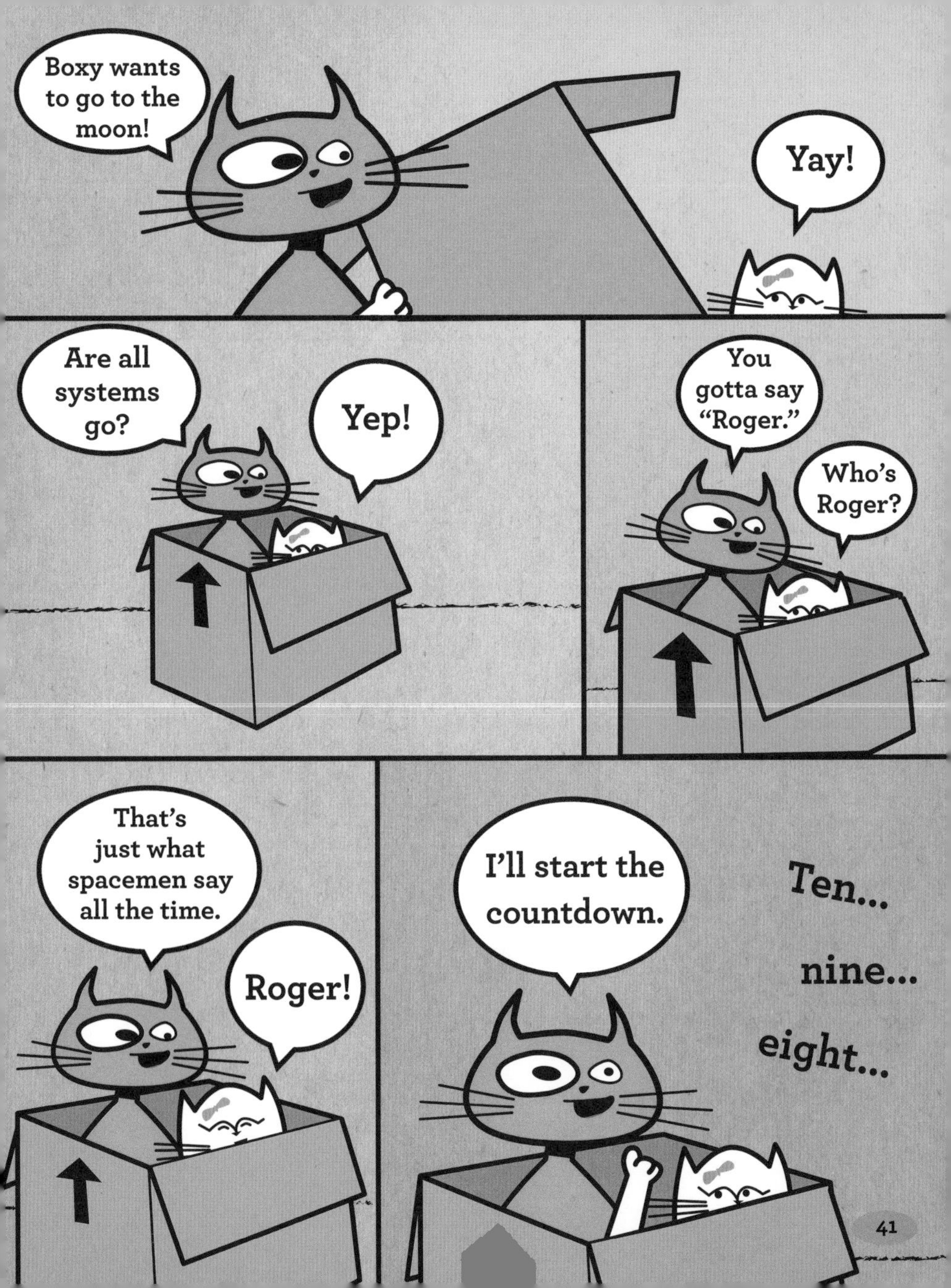
Boxy wants to go to the moon!
Yay!
Are all systems go?
Yep!
You gotta say "Roger."
Who's Roger?
That's just what spacemen say all the time.
Roger!
I'll start the countdown.
Ten...
nine...
eight...

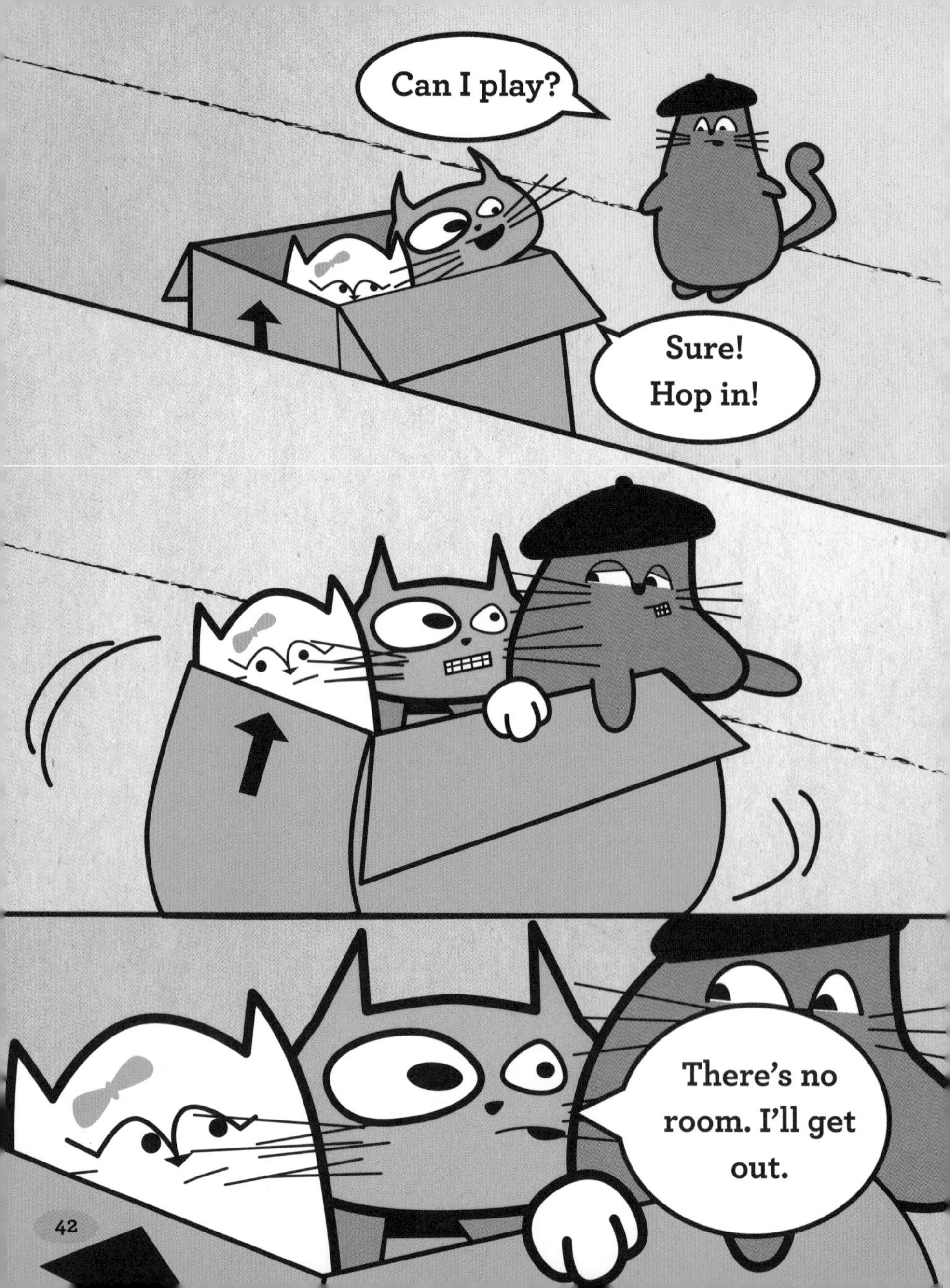
Can I play?
Sure! Hop in!
There's no room. I'll get out.

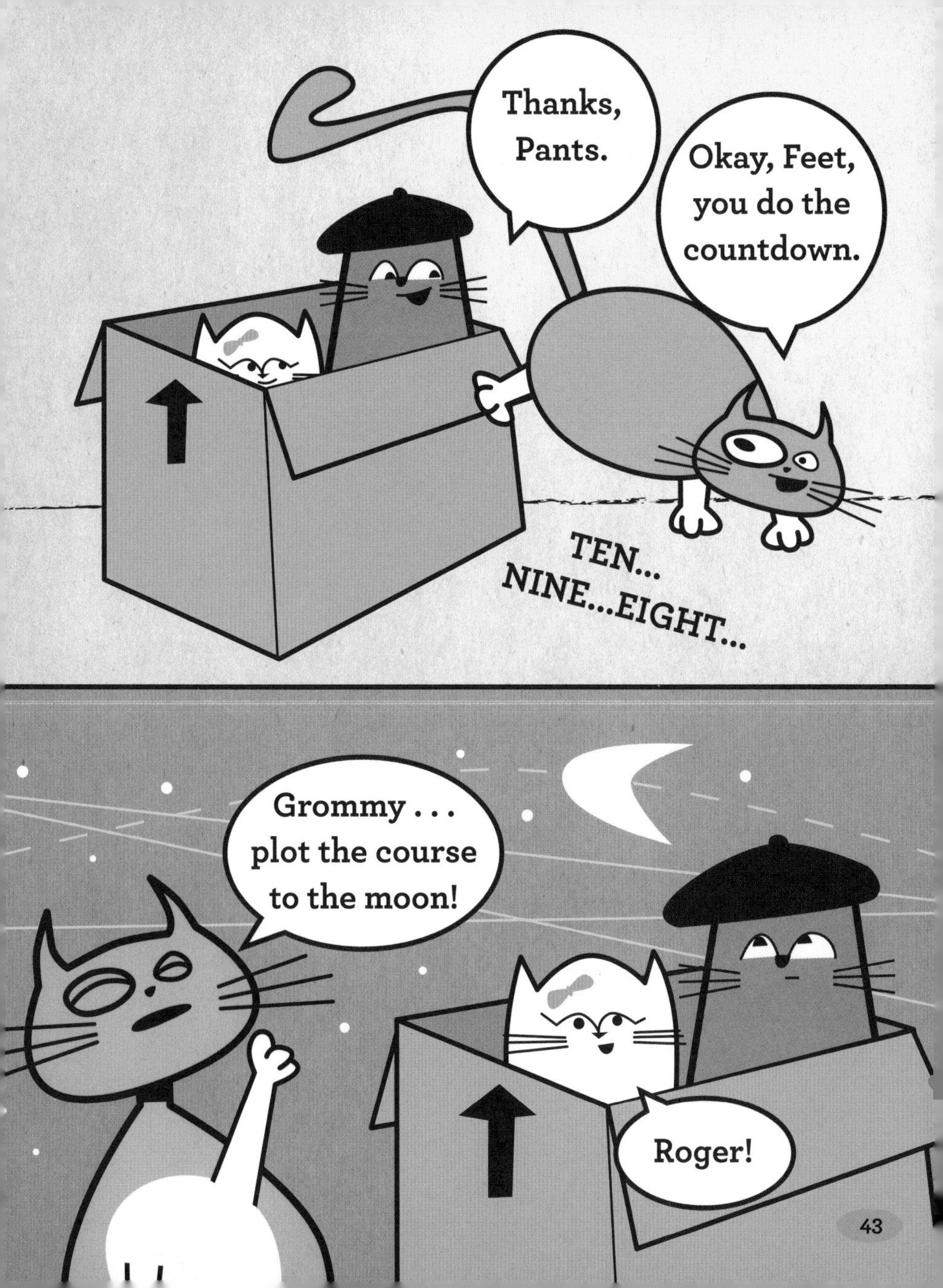
Thanks,
Pants.
Okay, Feet,
you do the
countdown.
TEN...
NINE...EIGHT...
Grommy . . .
plot the course
to the moon!
Roger!

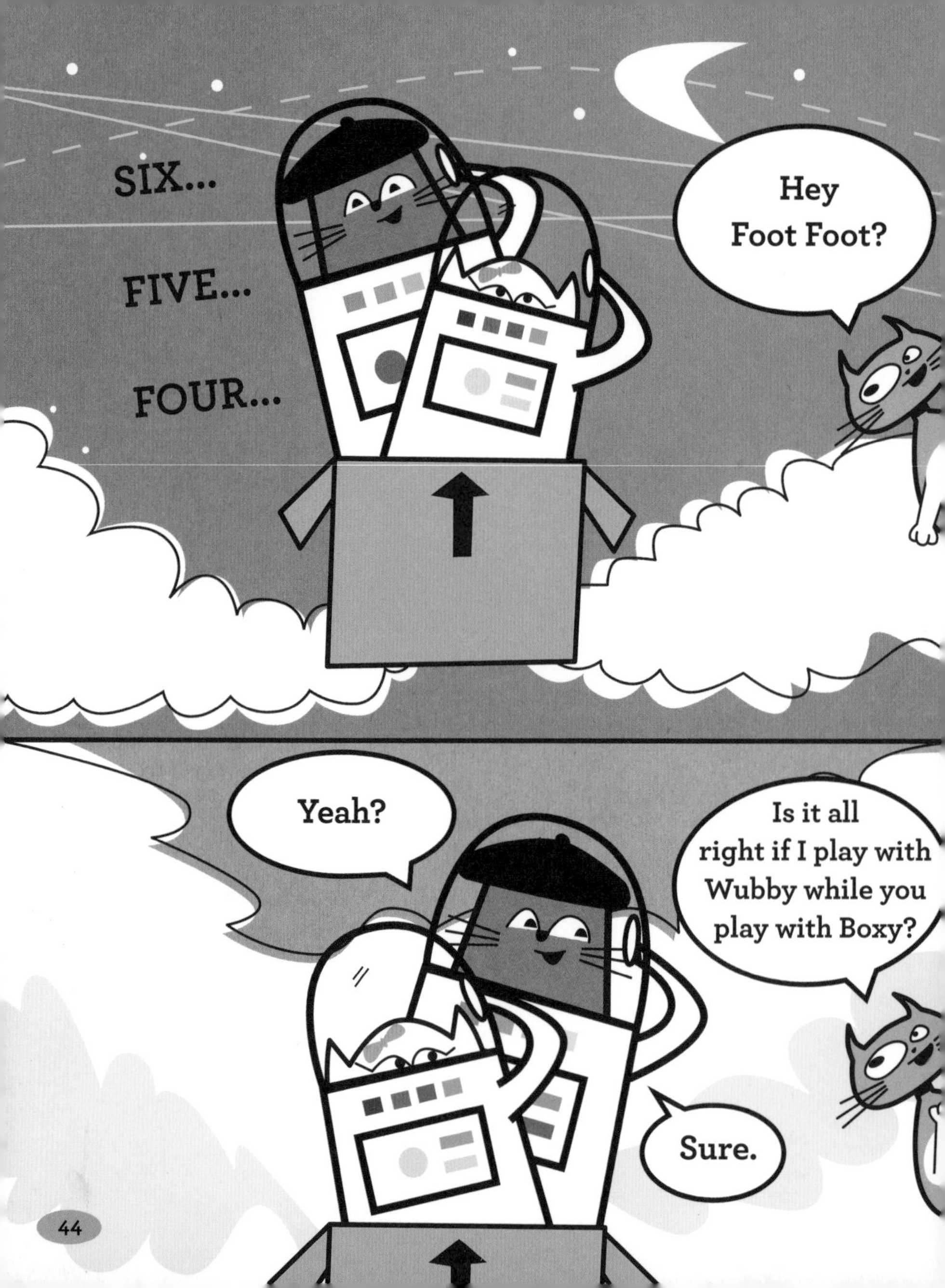

SIX...
FIVE...
FOUR...
Hey Foot Foot?
Yeah?
Is it all right if I play with Wubby while you play with Boxy?
Sure.

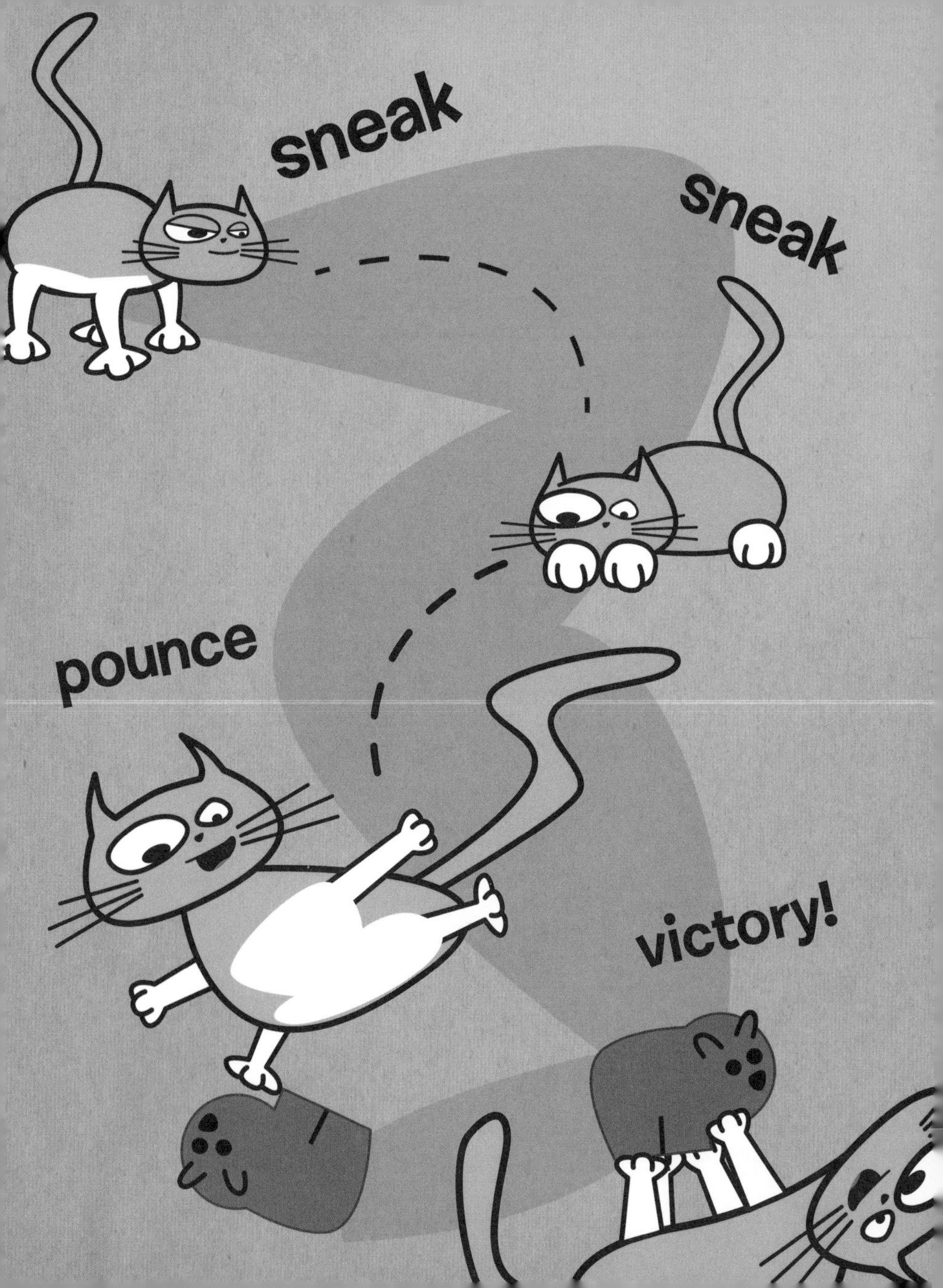
sneak
sneak
pounce
victory!

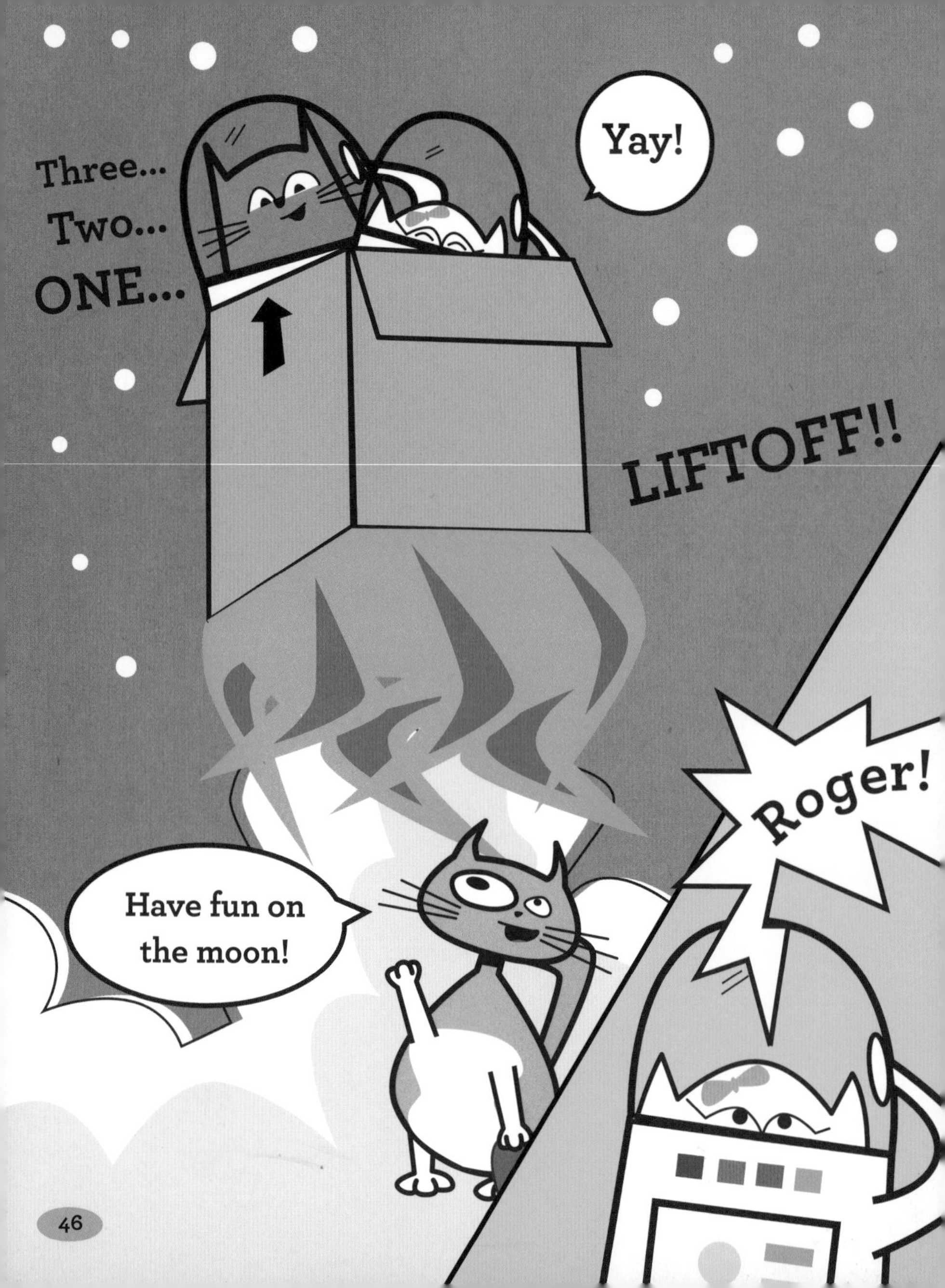
Three...
Two...
ONE...
Yay!
LIFTOFF!!
Roger!
Have fun on the moon!

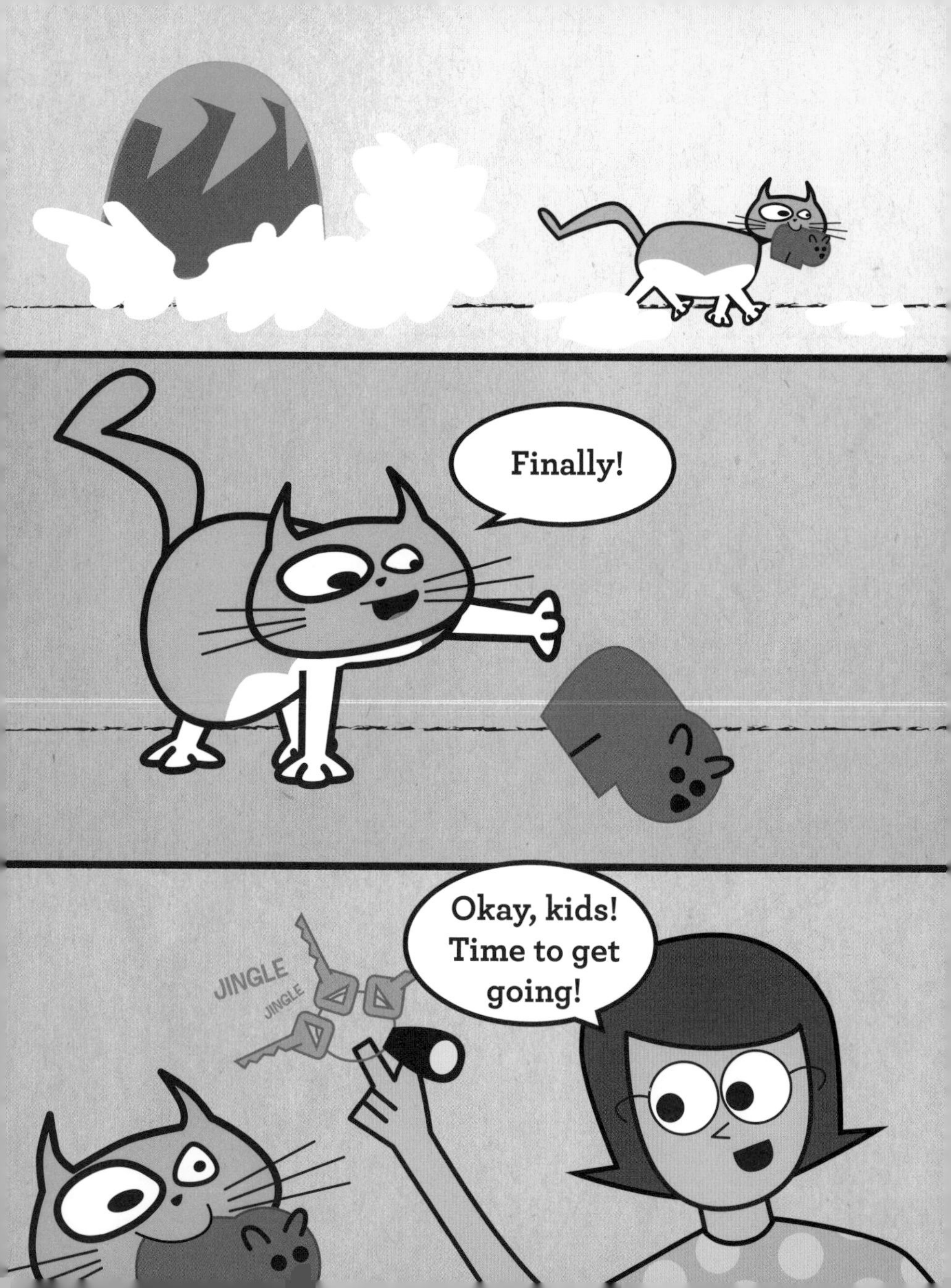
Finally!
Okay, kids! Time to get going!
JINGLE
JINGLE

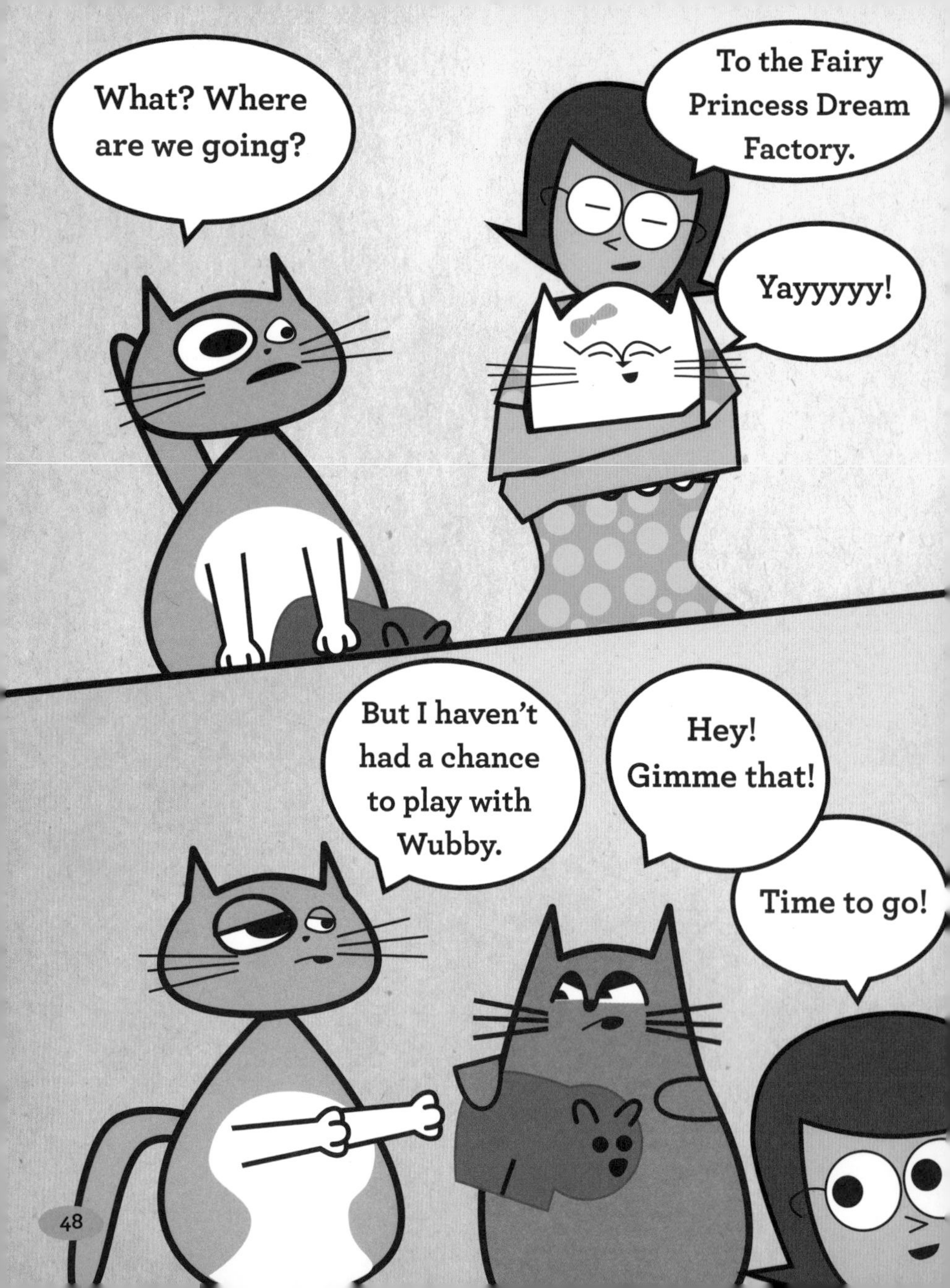
What? Where are we going?
To the Fairy Princess Dream Factory.
Yayyyyy!
But I haven't had a chance to play with Wubby.
Hey! Gimme that!
Time to go!

Chapter Three: PRINCESS PANTS

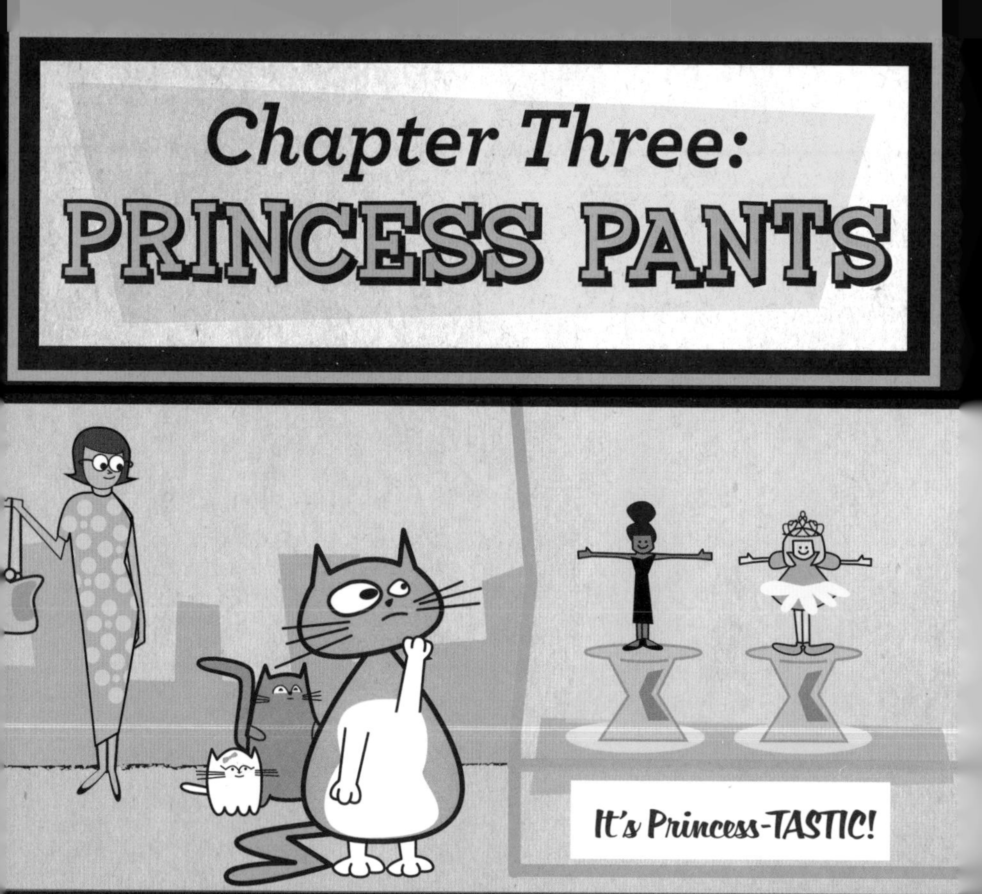
It's Princess-TASTIC!

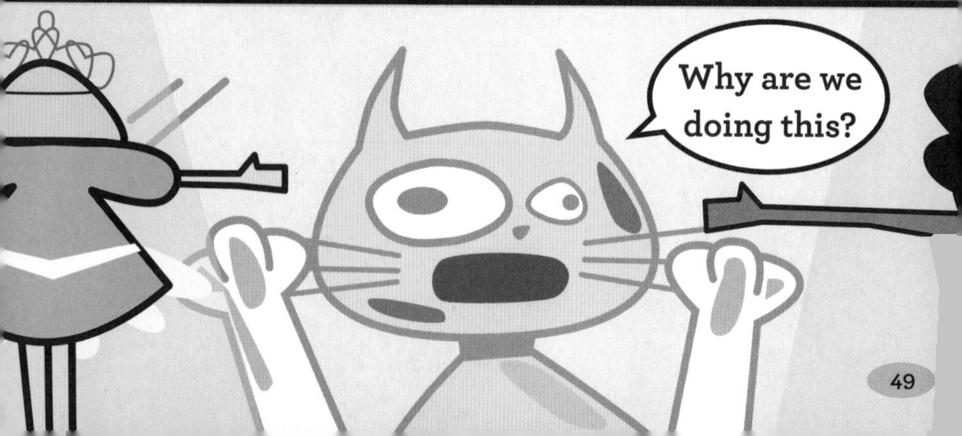
Why are we doing this?

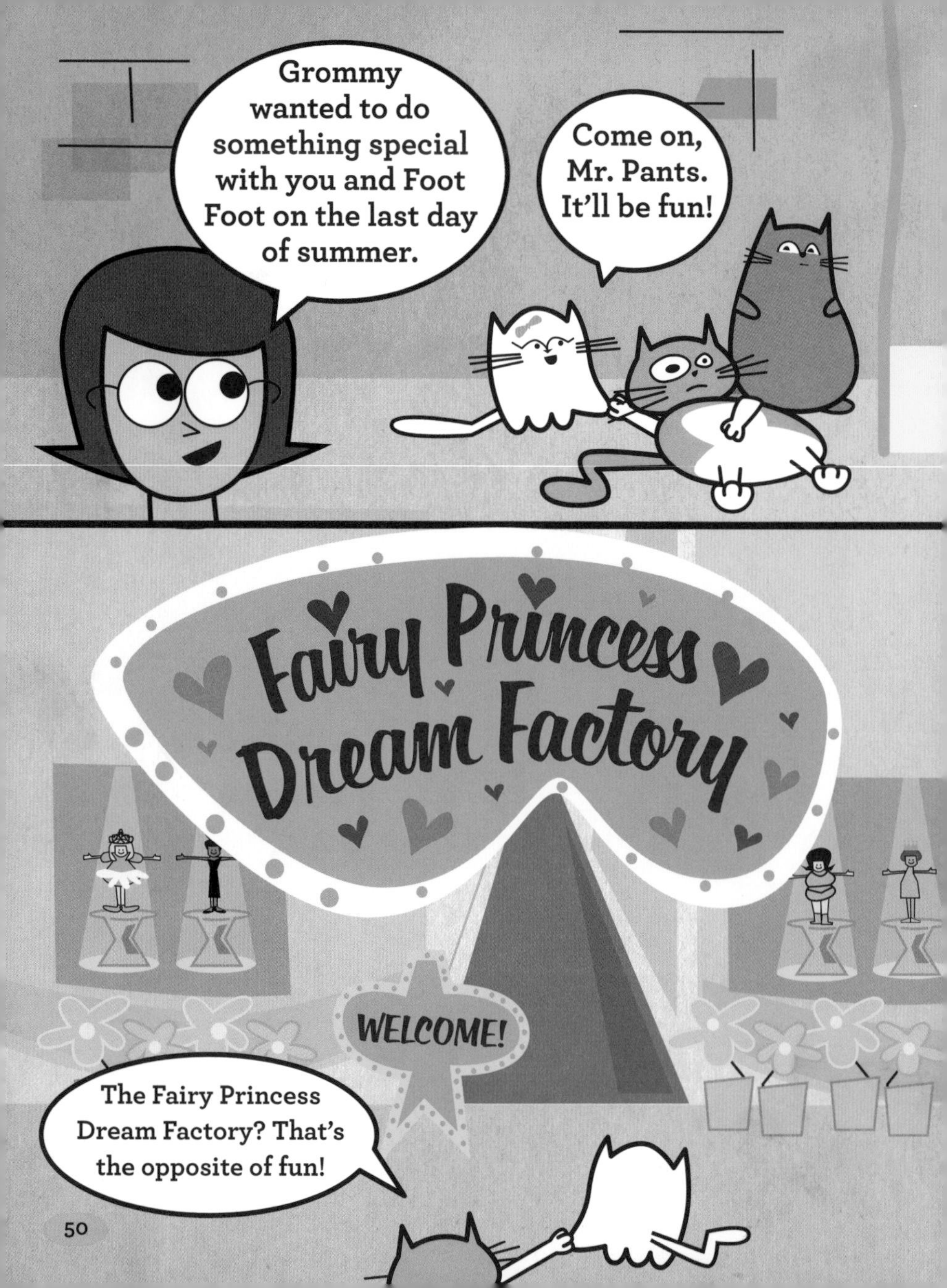
Grommy wanted to do something special with you and Foot Foot on the last day of summer.
Come on, Mr. Pants. It'll be fun!
Fairy Princess Dream Factory
WELCOME!
The Fairy Princess Dream Factory? That's the opposite of fun!

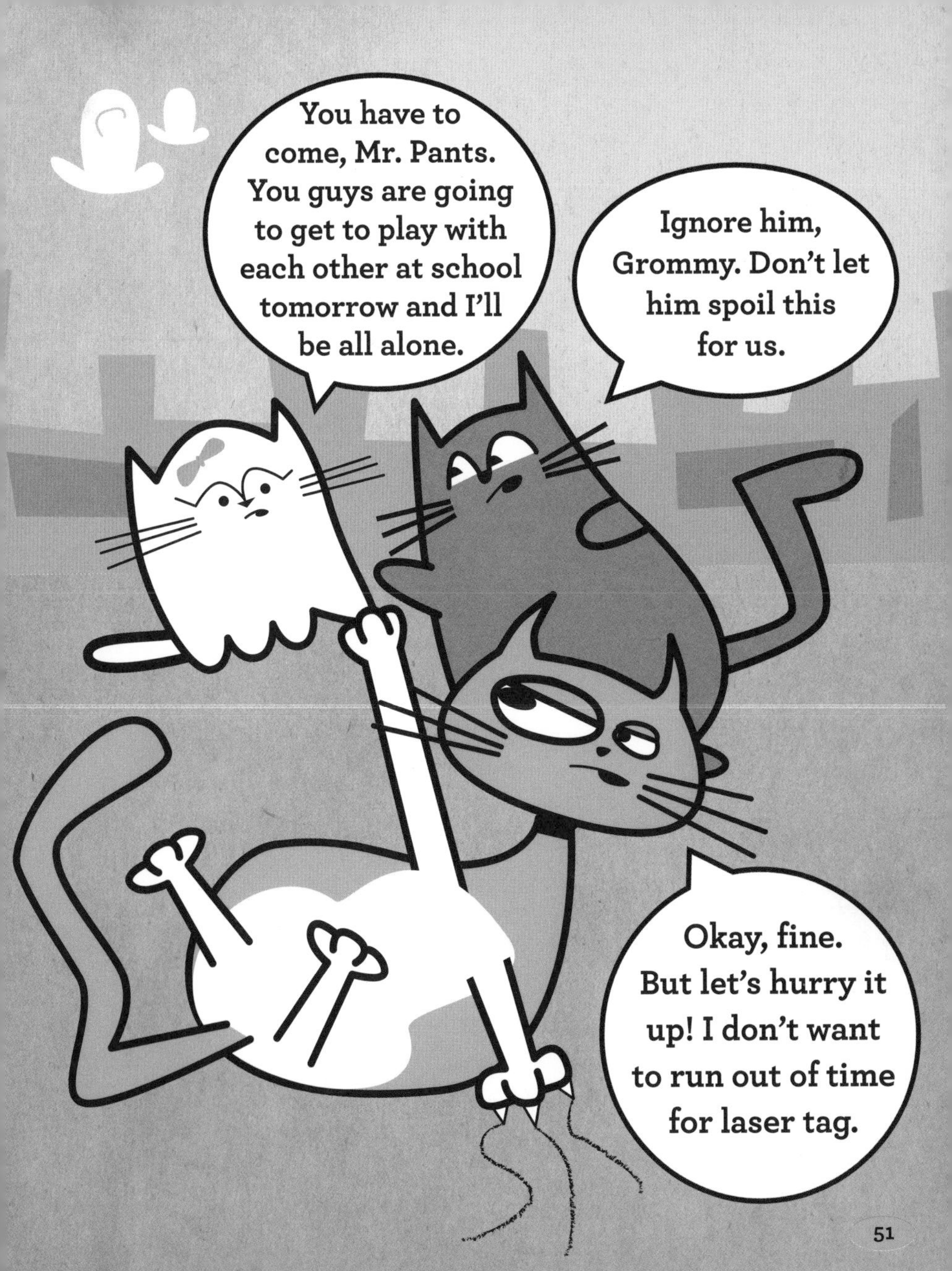
You have to come, Mr. Pants. You guys are going to get to play with each other at school tomorrow and I'll be all alone.
Ignore him, Grommy. Don't let him spoil this for us.
Okay, fine. But let's hurry it up! I don't want to run out of time for laser tag.

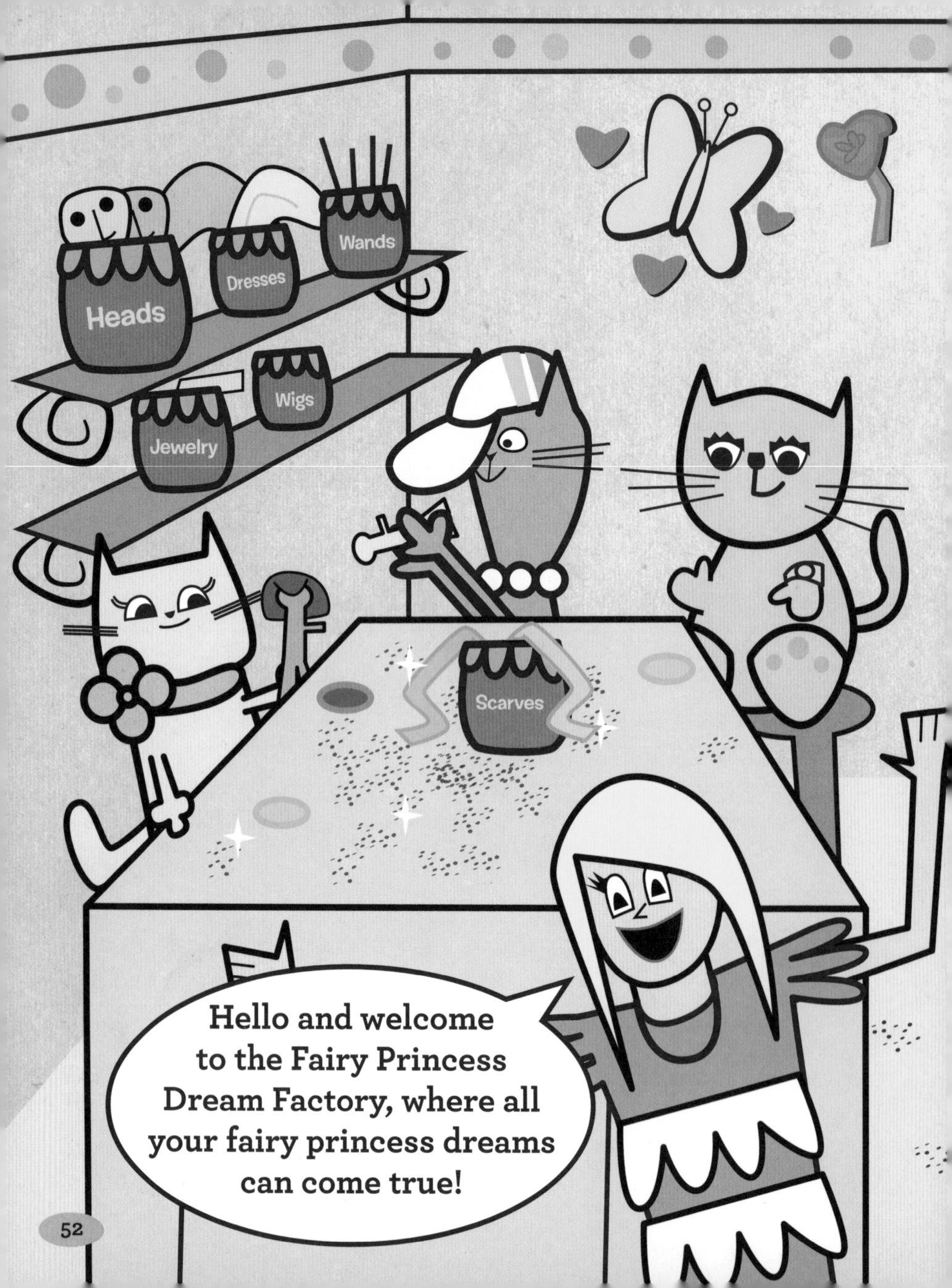
Heads
Dresses
Wands
Wigs
Jewelry
Scarves
Hello and welcome to the Fairy Princess Dream Factory, where all your fairy princess dreams can come true!

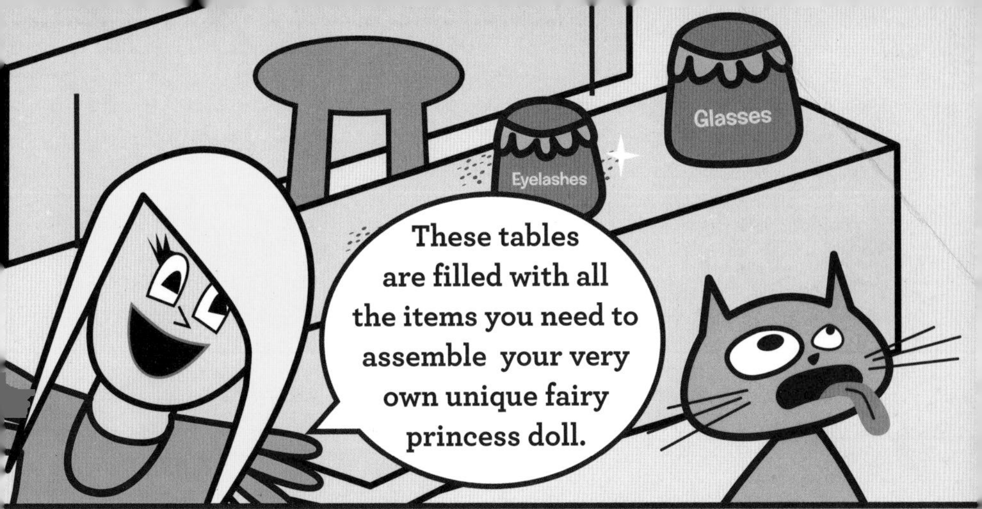
Glasses
Eyelashes
These tables are filled with all the items you need to assemble your very own unique fairy princess doll.

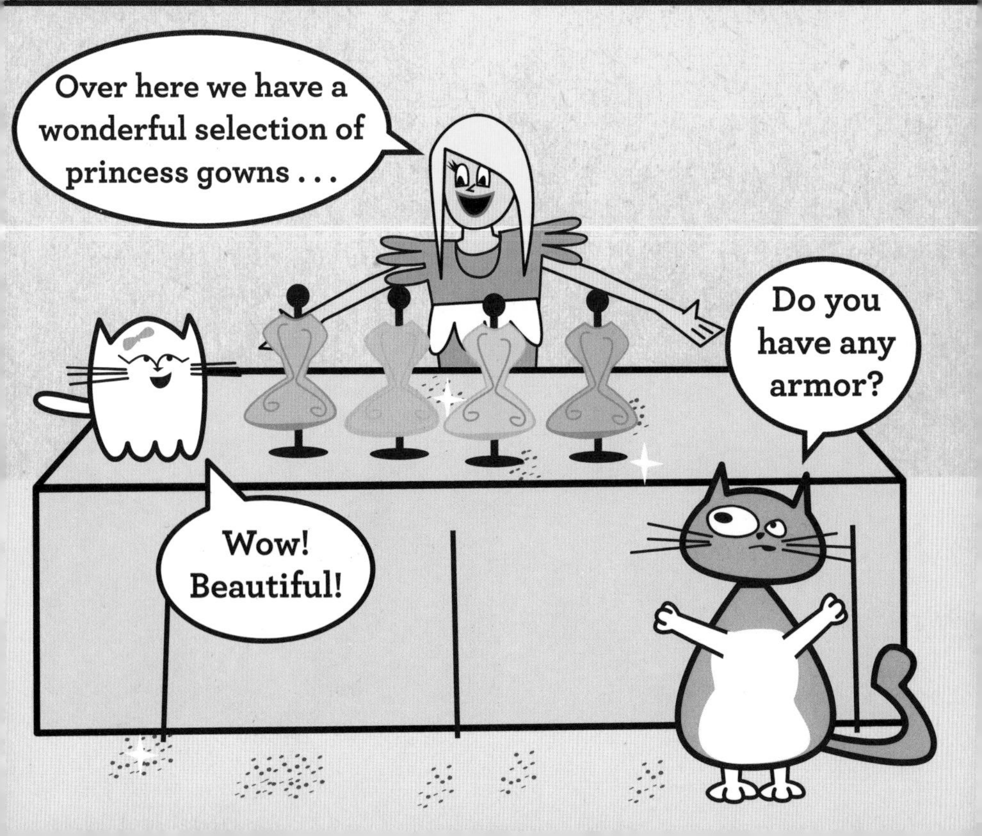
Over here we have a wonderful selection of princess gowns . . .
Do you have any armor?
Wow! Beautiful!

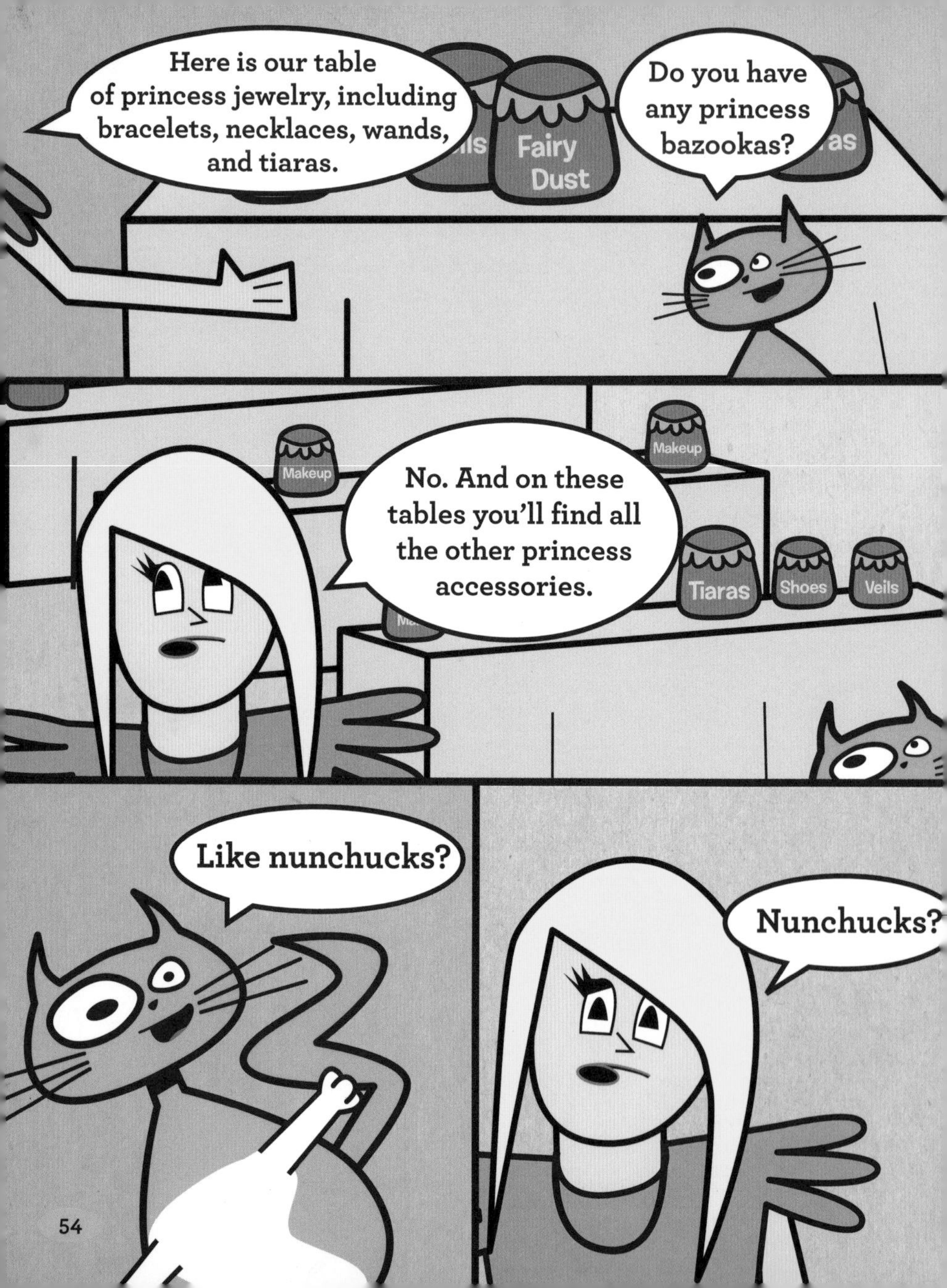
Here is our table of princess jewelry, including bracelets, necklaces, wands, and tiaras.
Fairy Dust
Do you have any princess bazookas?
Makeup
Makeup
No. And on these tables you'll find all the other princess accessories.
Tiaras
Shoes
Veils
Like nunchucks?
Nunchucks?

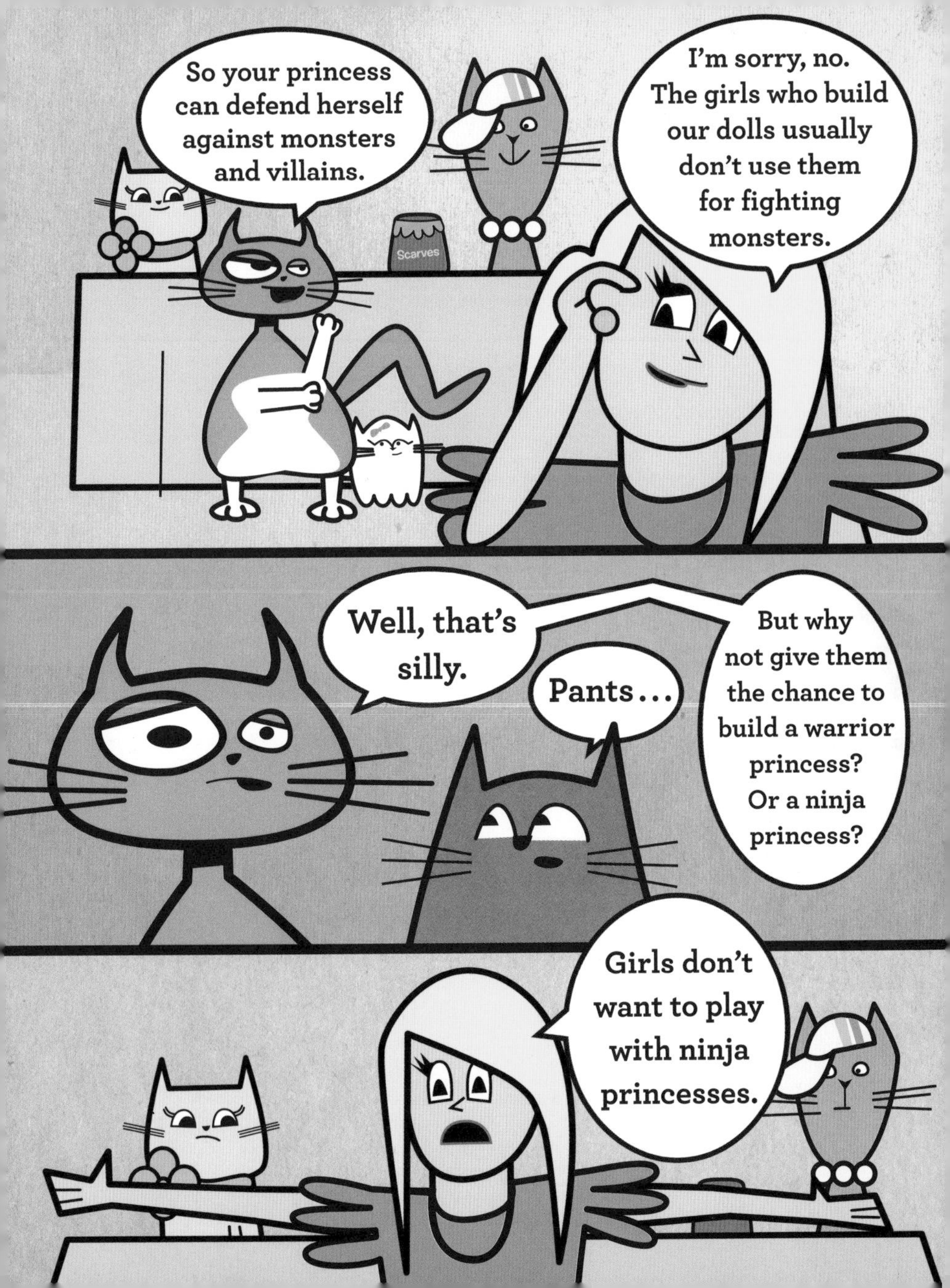
So your princess can defend herself against monsters and villains.
I'm sorry, no. The girls who build our dolls usually don't use them for fighting monsters.
Scarves
Well, that's silly.
But why not give them the chance to build a warrior princess? Or a ninja princess?
Pants . . .
Girls don't want to play with ninja princesses.

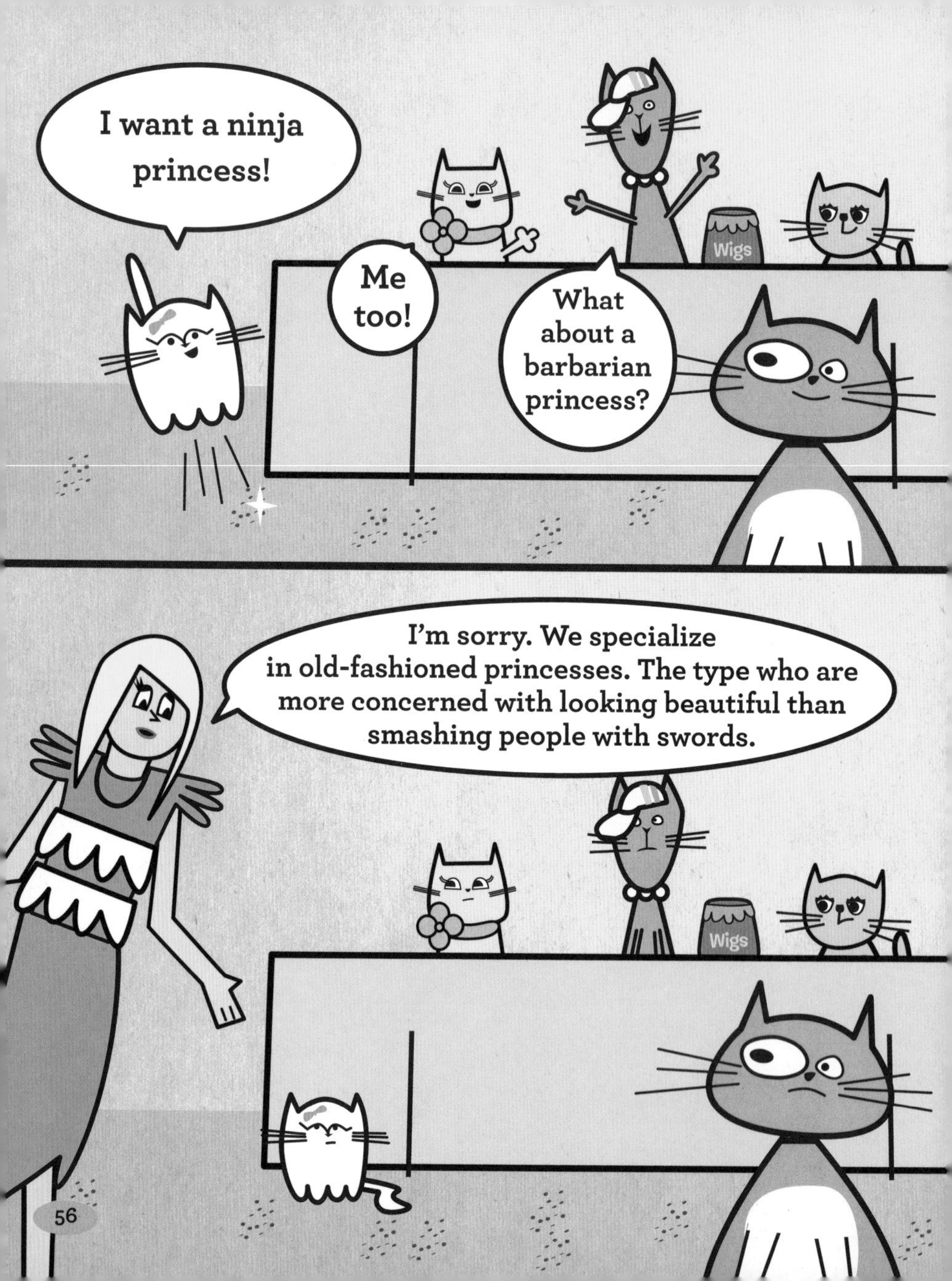
I want a ninja princess!
Me too!
What about a barbarian princess?
Wigs
I'm sorry. We specialize in old-fashioned princesses. The type who are more concerned with looking beautiful than smashing people with swords.
Wigs

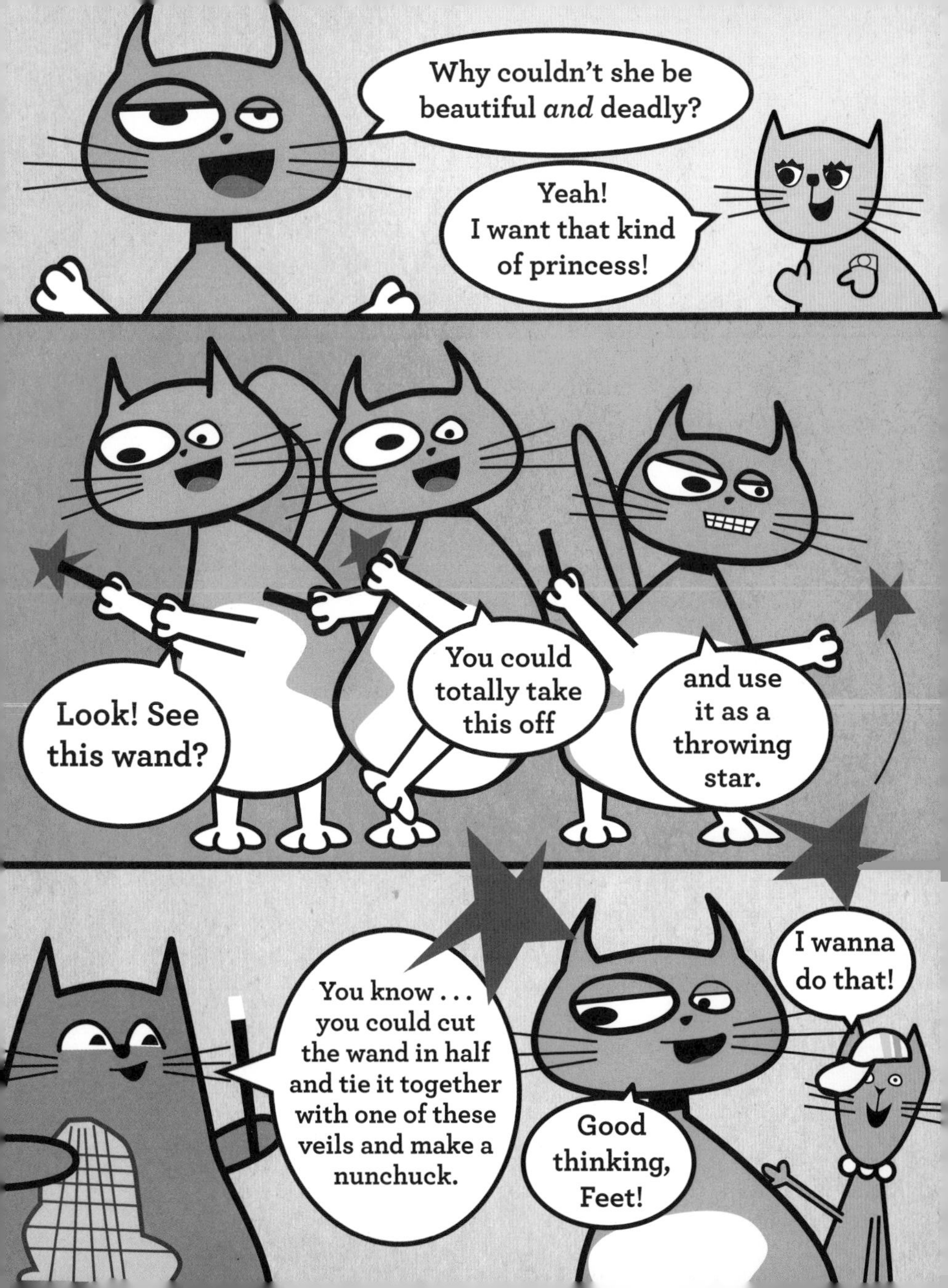
Why couldn't she be beautiful *and* deadly?
Yeah! I want that kind of princess!
Look! See this wand?
You could totally take this off
and use it as a throwing star.
You know . . . you could cut the wand in half and tie it together with one of these veils and make a nunchuck.
Good thinking, Feet!
I wanna do that!

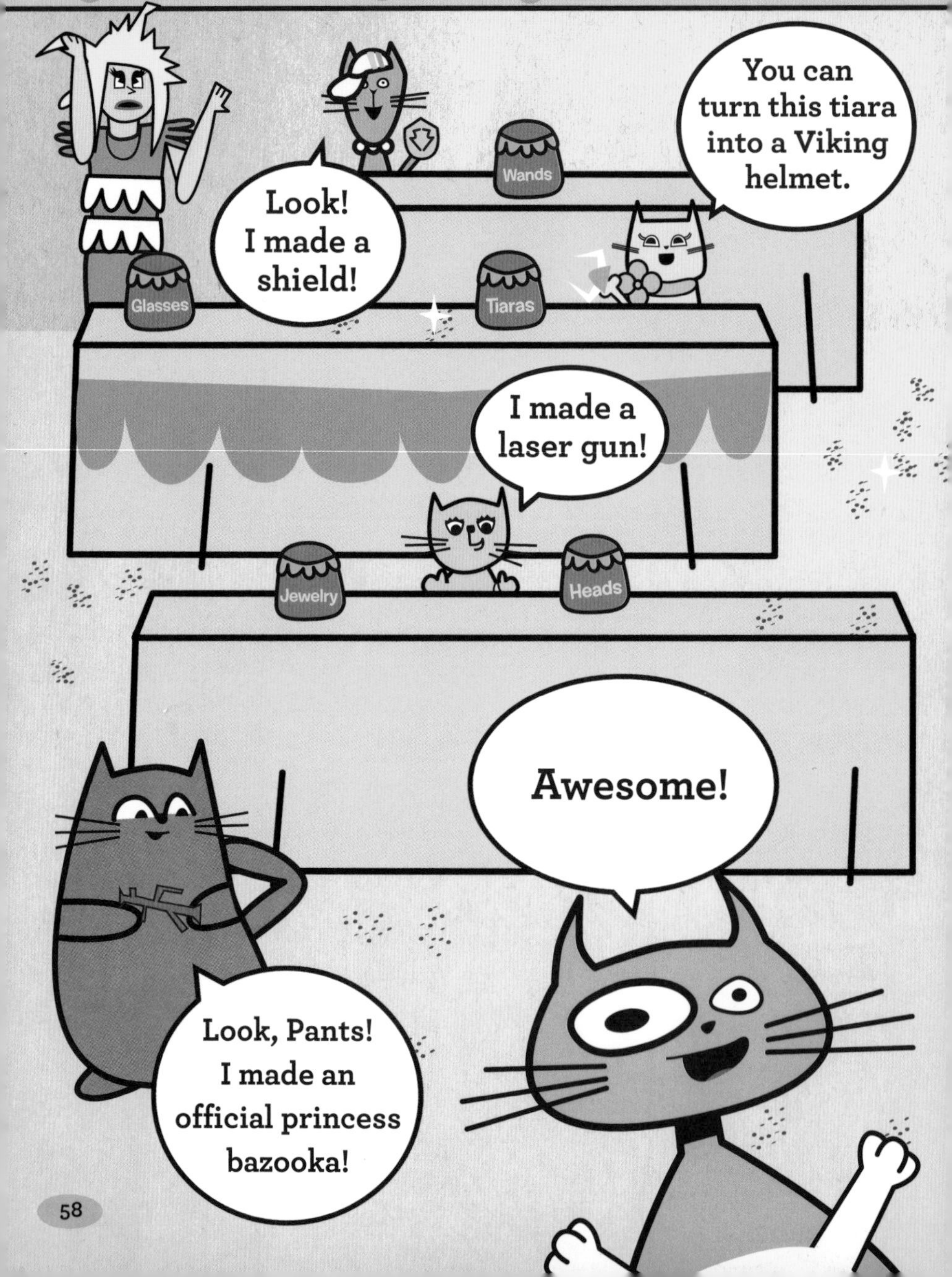
Wands
Look! I made a shield!
You can turn this tiara into a Viking helmet.
Glasses
Tiaras
I made a laser gun!
Jewelry
Heads
Awesome!
Look, Pants! I made an official princess bazooka!

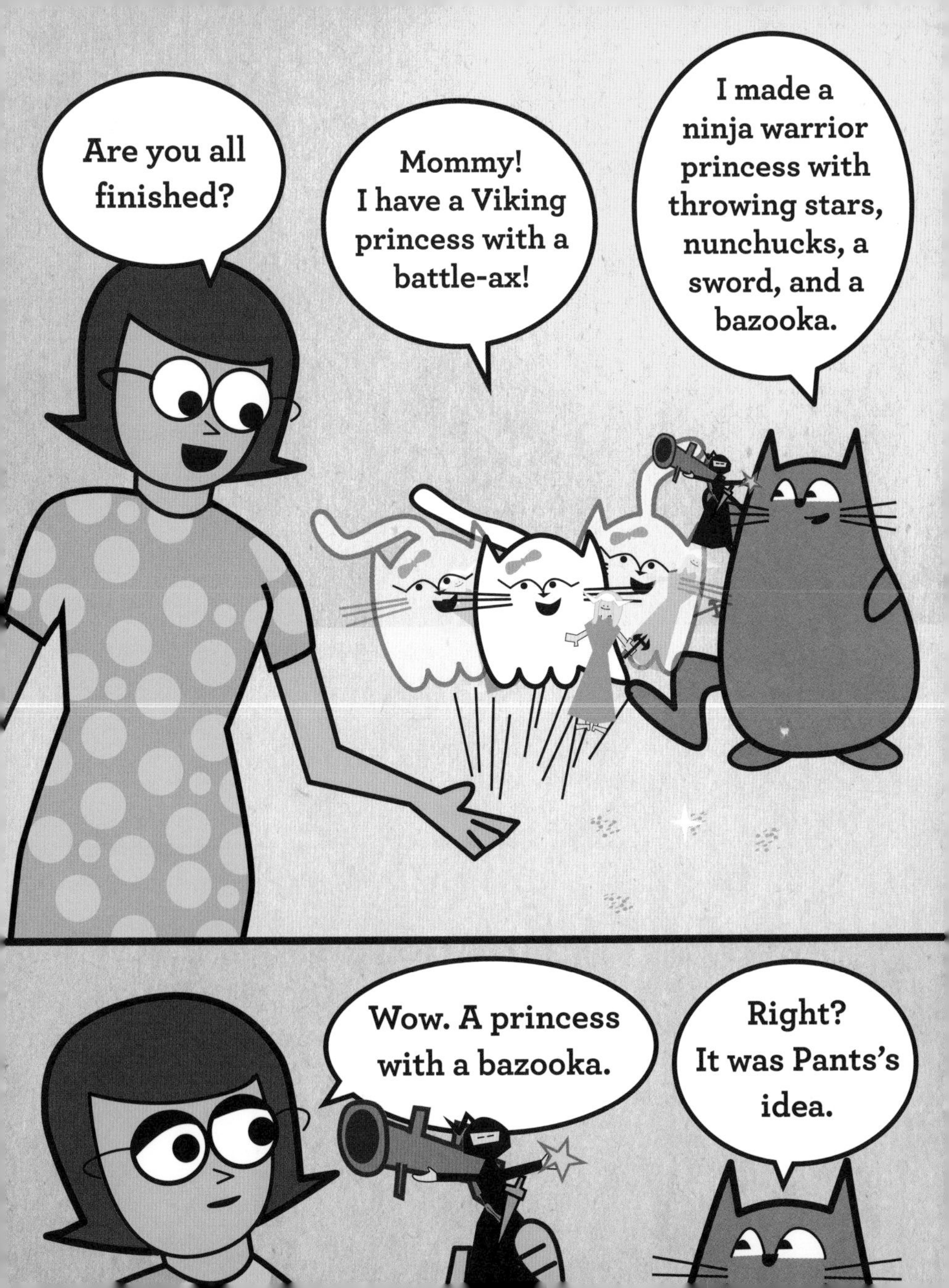

Are you all finished?
Mommy! I have a Viking princess with a battle-ax!
I made a ninja warrior princess with throwing stars, nunchucks, a sword, and a bazooka.
Wow. A princess with a bazooka.
Right? It was Pants's idea.

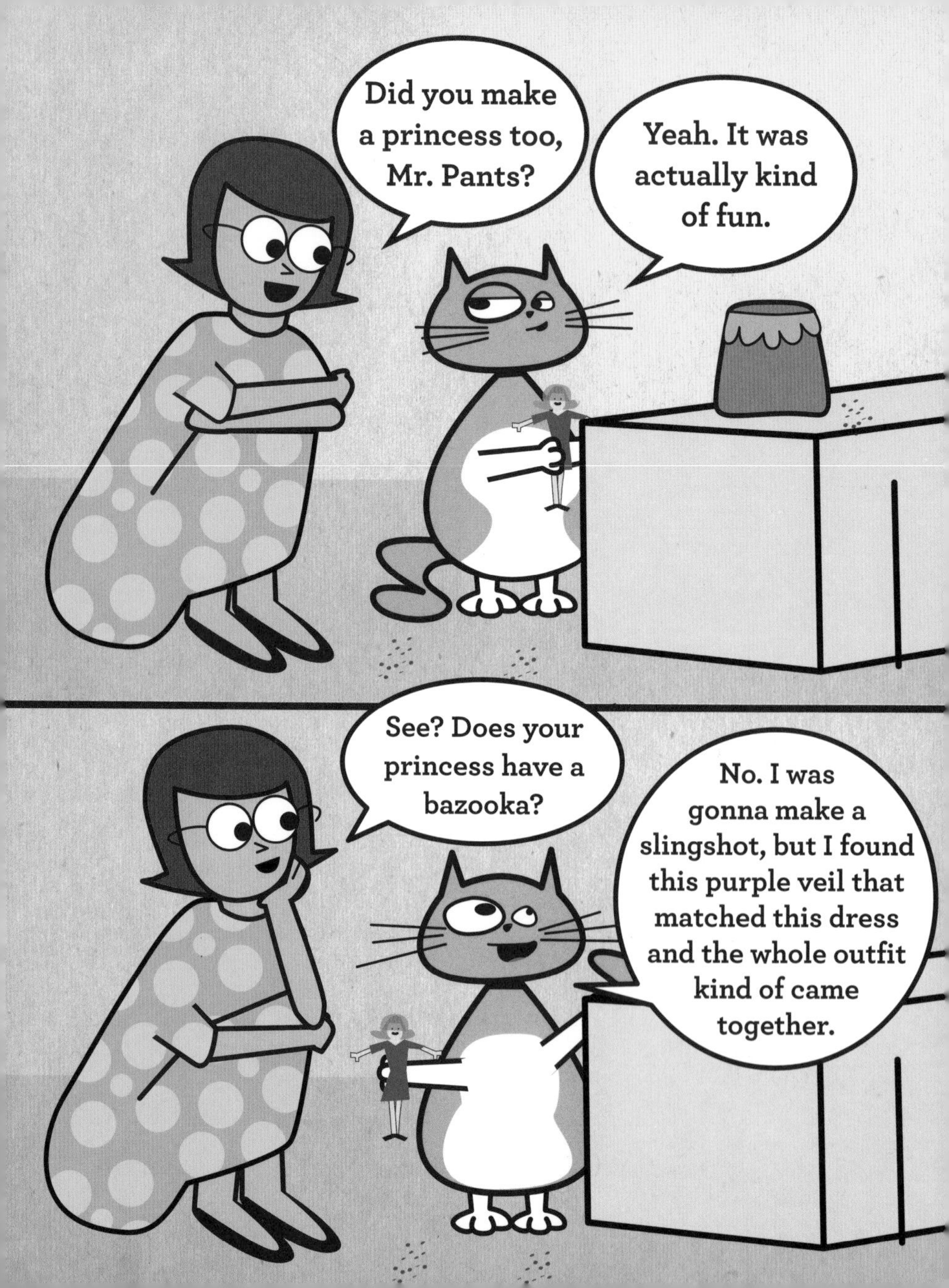
Did you make a princess too, Mr. Pants?
Yeah. It was actually kind of fun.
See? Does your princess have a bazooka?
No. I was gonna make a slingshot, but I found this purple veil that matched this dress and the whole outfit kind of came together.

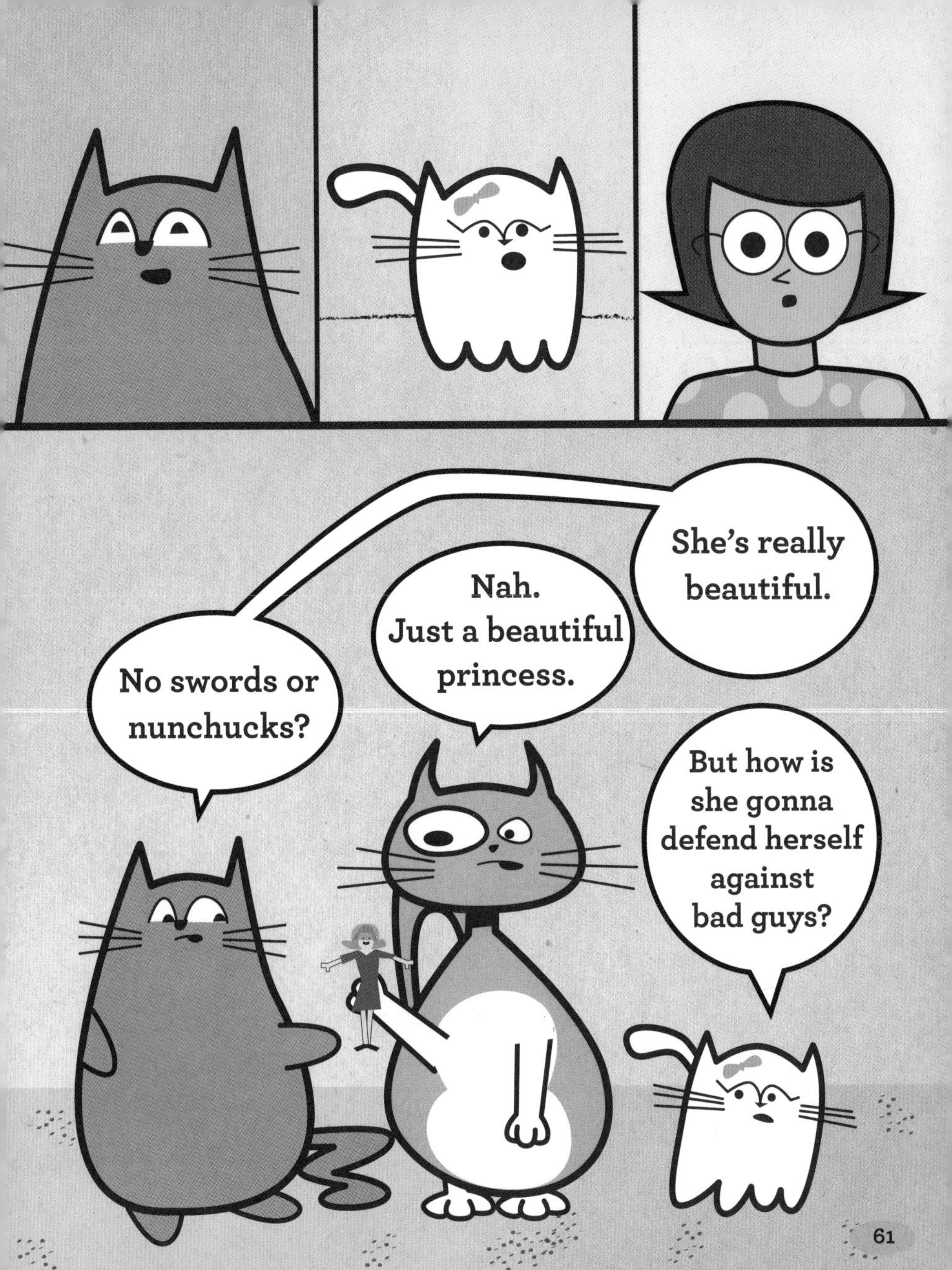
She's really beautiful.
No swords or nunchucks?
Nah. Just a beautiful princess.
But how is she gonna defend herself against bad guys?

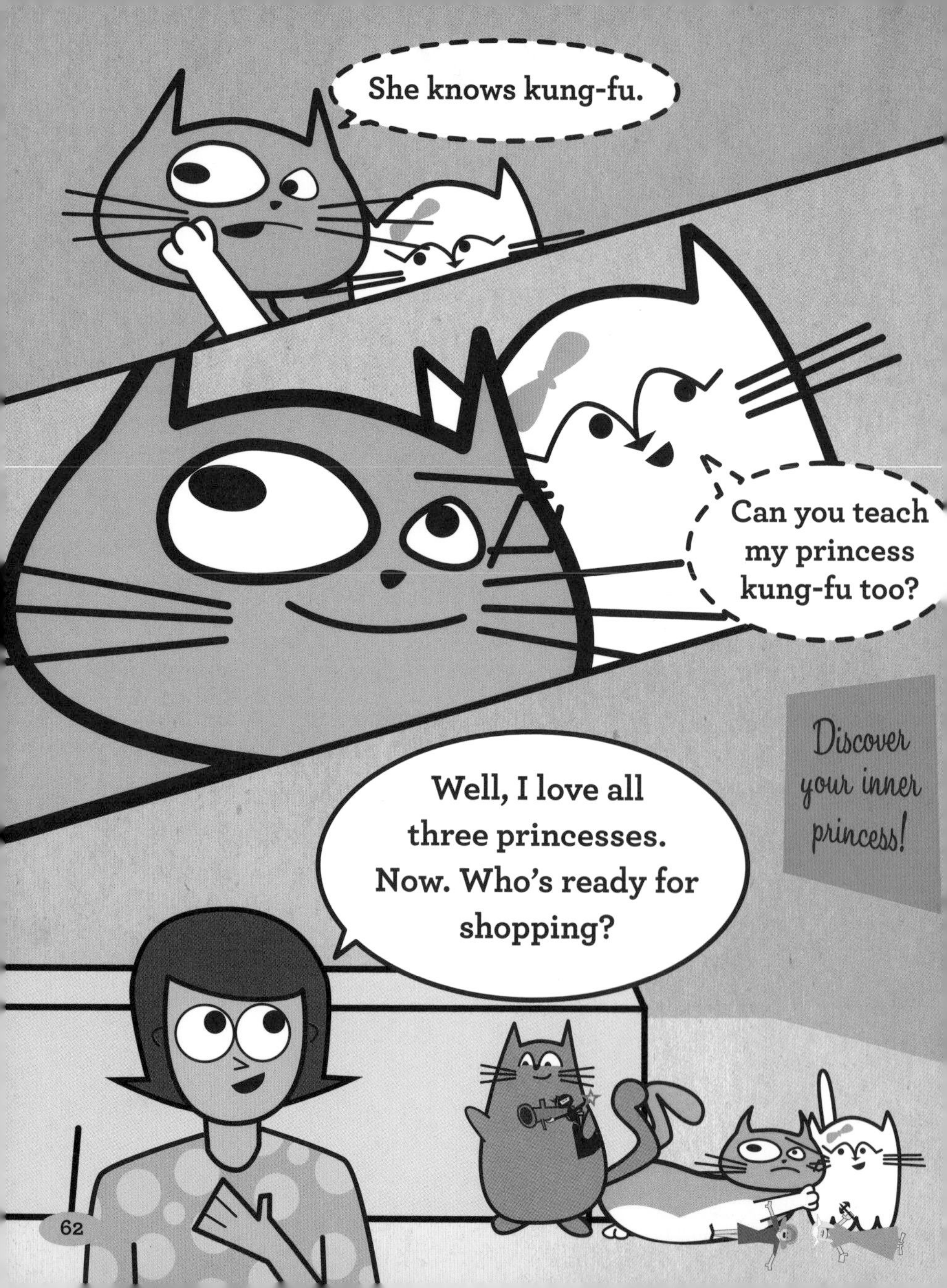
She knows kung-fu.
Can you teach my princess kung-fu too?
Discover your inner princess!
Well, I love all three princesses. Now. Who's ready for shopping?

Chapter Four:
IT'S GO TIME

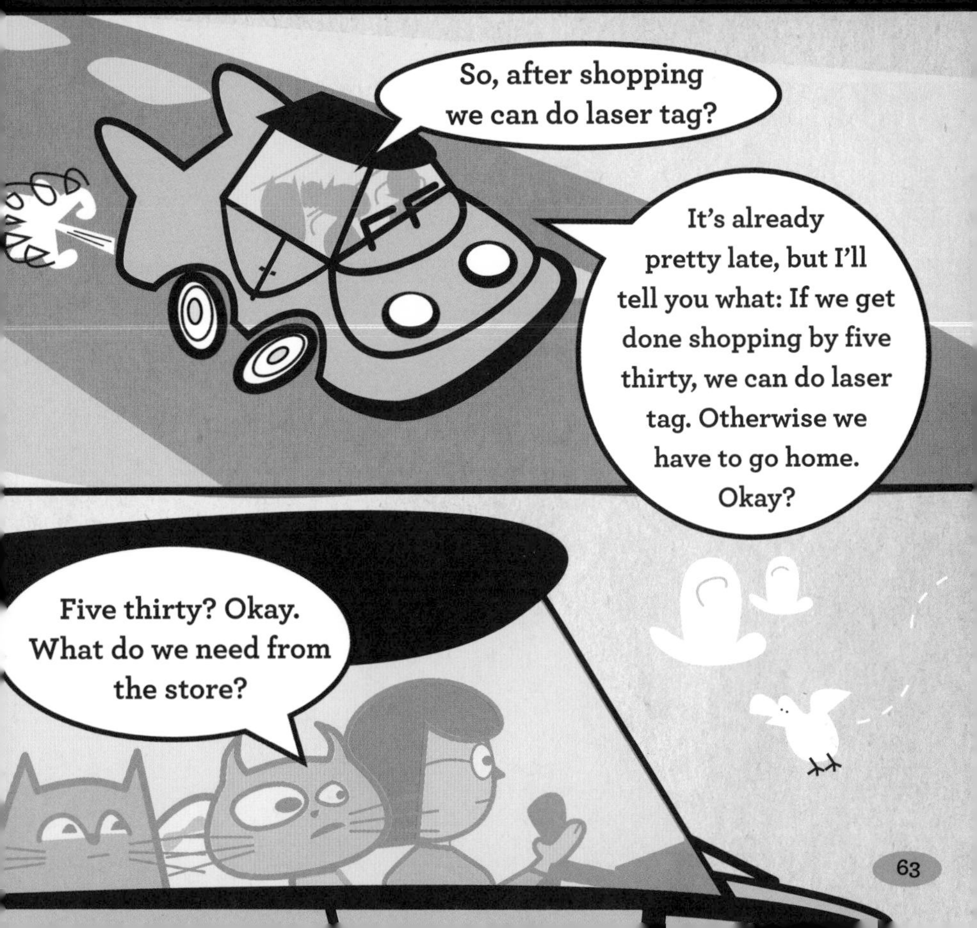

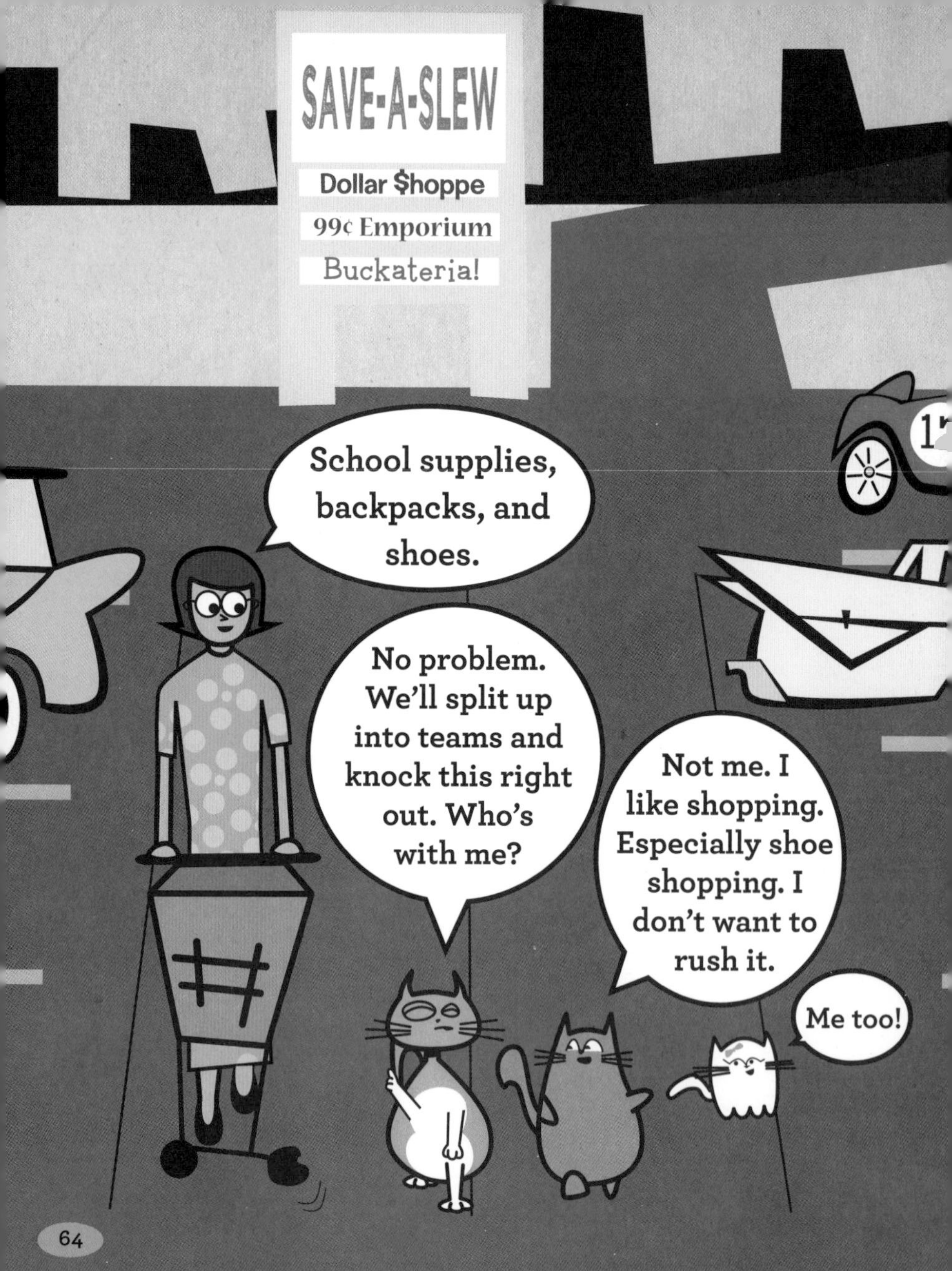
SAVE-A-SLEW
Dollar $hoppe
99¢ Emporium
Buckateria!
School supplies, backpacks, and shoes.
No problem. We'll split up into teams and knock this right out. Who's with me?
Not me. I like shopping. Especially shoe shopping. I don't want to rush it.
Me too!

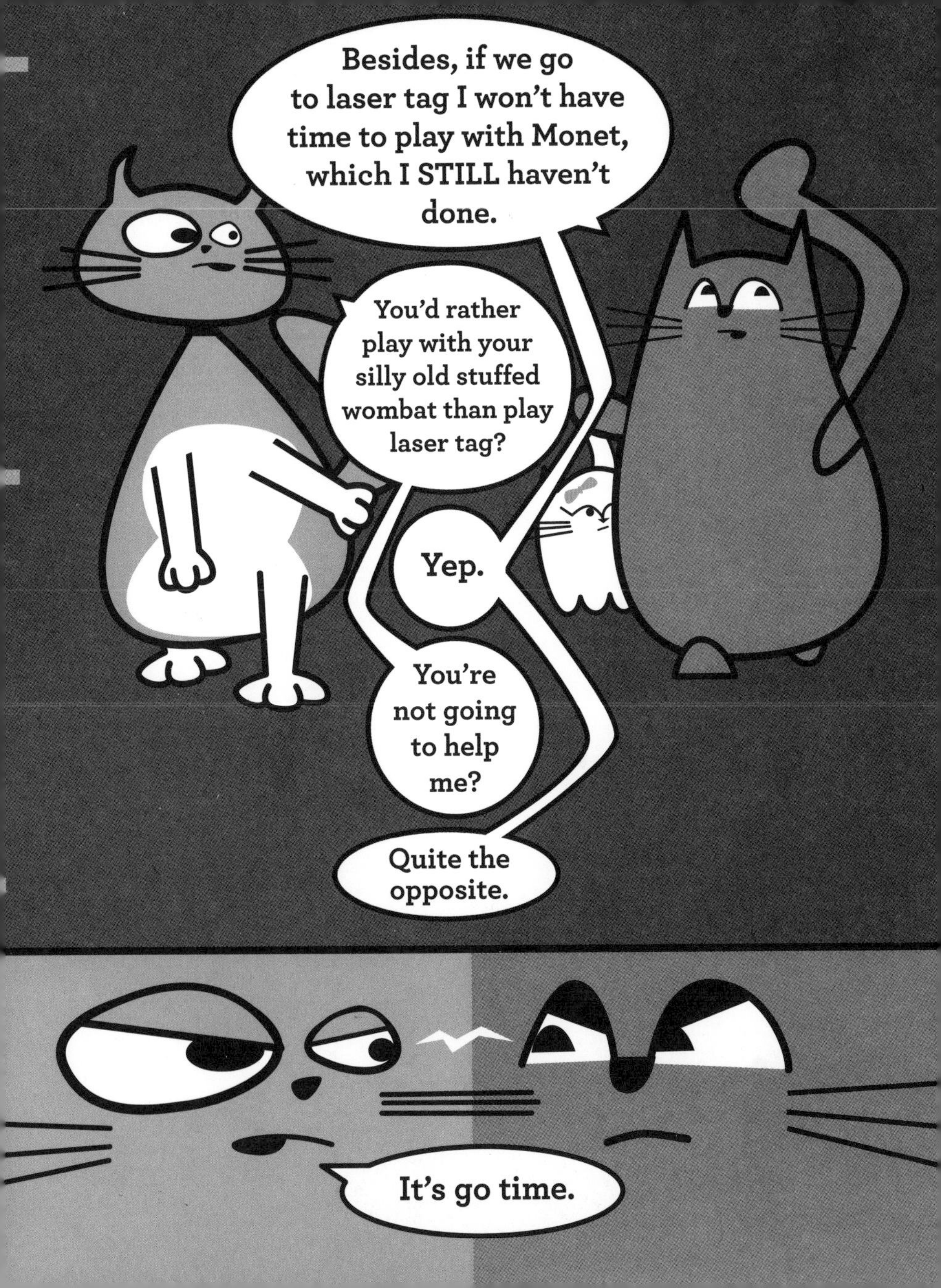
Besides, if we go to laser tag I won't have time to play with Monet, which I STILL haven't done.
You'd rather play with your silly old stuffed wombat than play laser tag?
Yep.
You're not going to help me?
Quite the opposite.
It's go time.

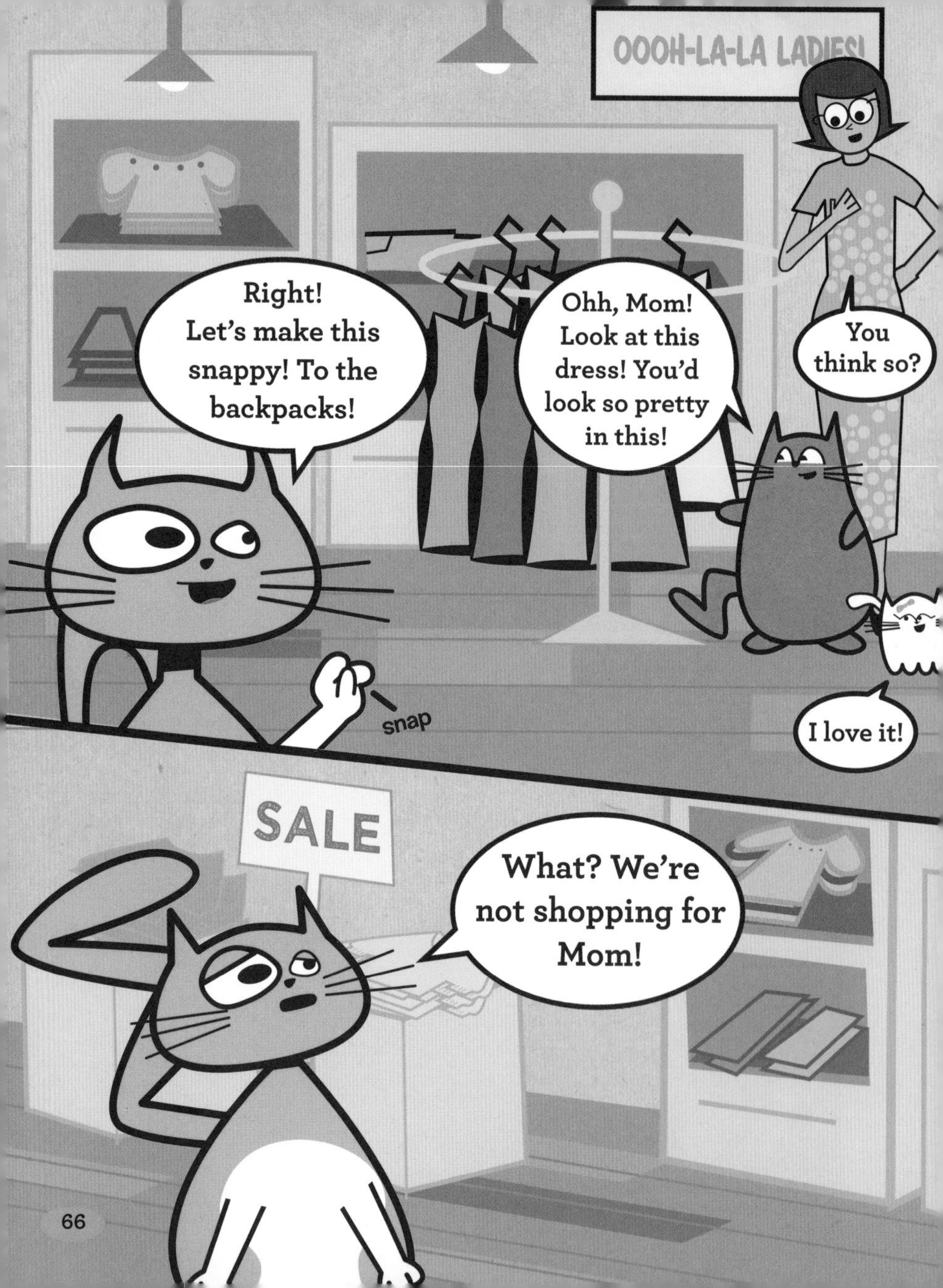
OOOH-LA-LA LADIES!
Right! Let's make this snappy! To the backpacks!
snap
Ohh, Mom! Look at this dress! You'd look so pretty in this!
You think so?
I love it!
SALE
What? We're not shopping for Mom!

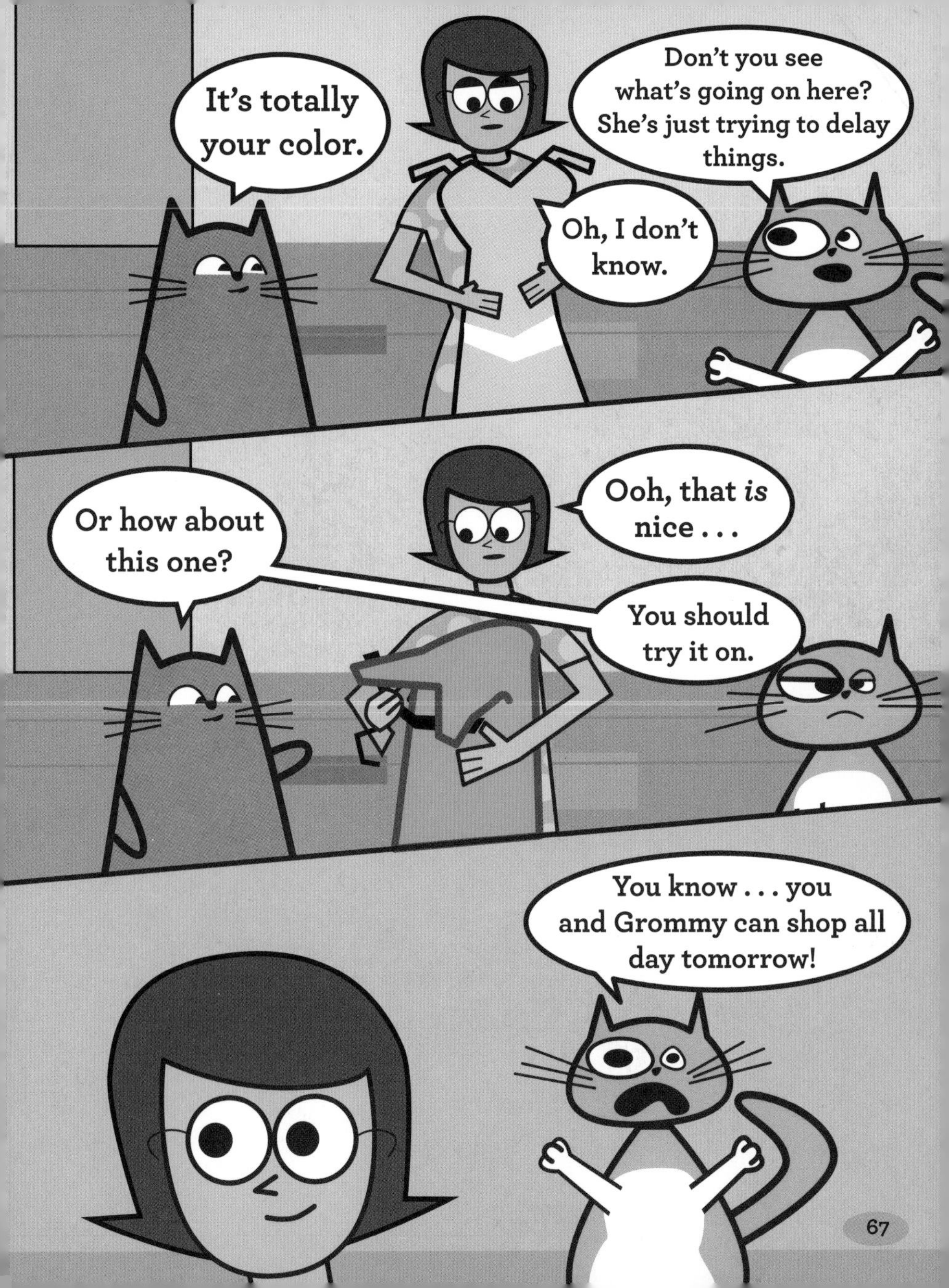
It's totally your color.
Oh, I don't know.
Don't you see what's going on here? She's just trying to delay things.
Or how about this one?
Ooh, that *is* nice . . .
You should try it on.
You know . . . you and Grommy can shop all day tomorrow!

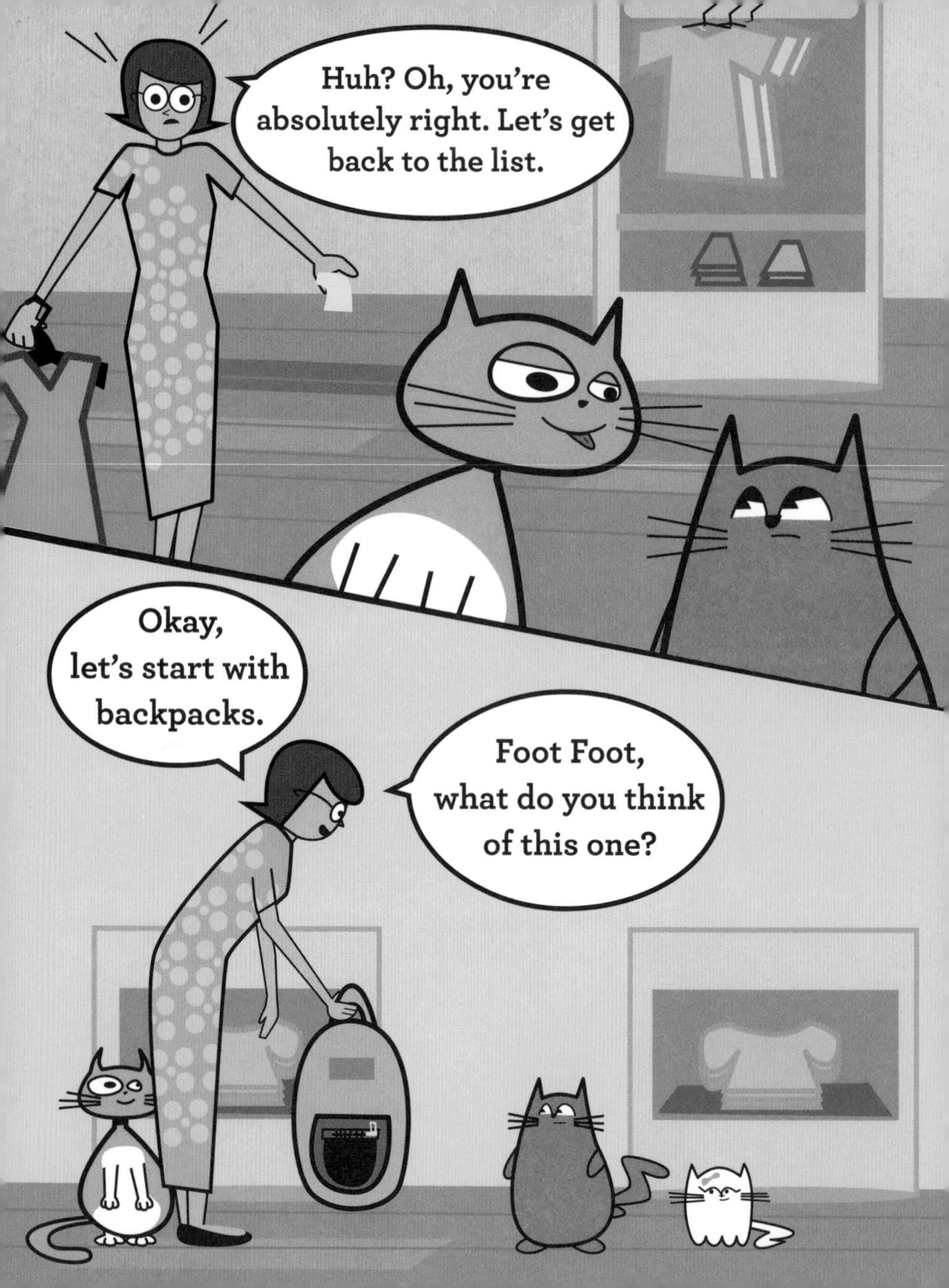
Huh? Oh, you're absolutely right. Let's get back to the list.
Okay, let's start with backpacks.
Foot Foot, what do you think of this one?

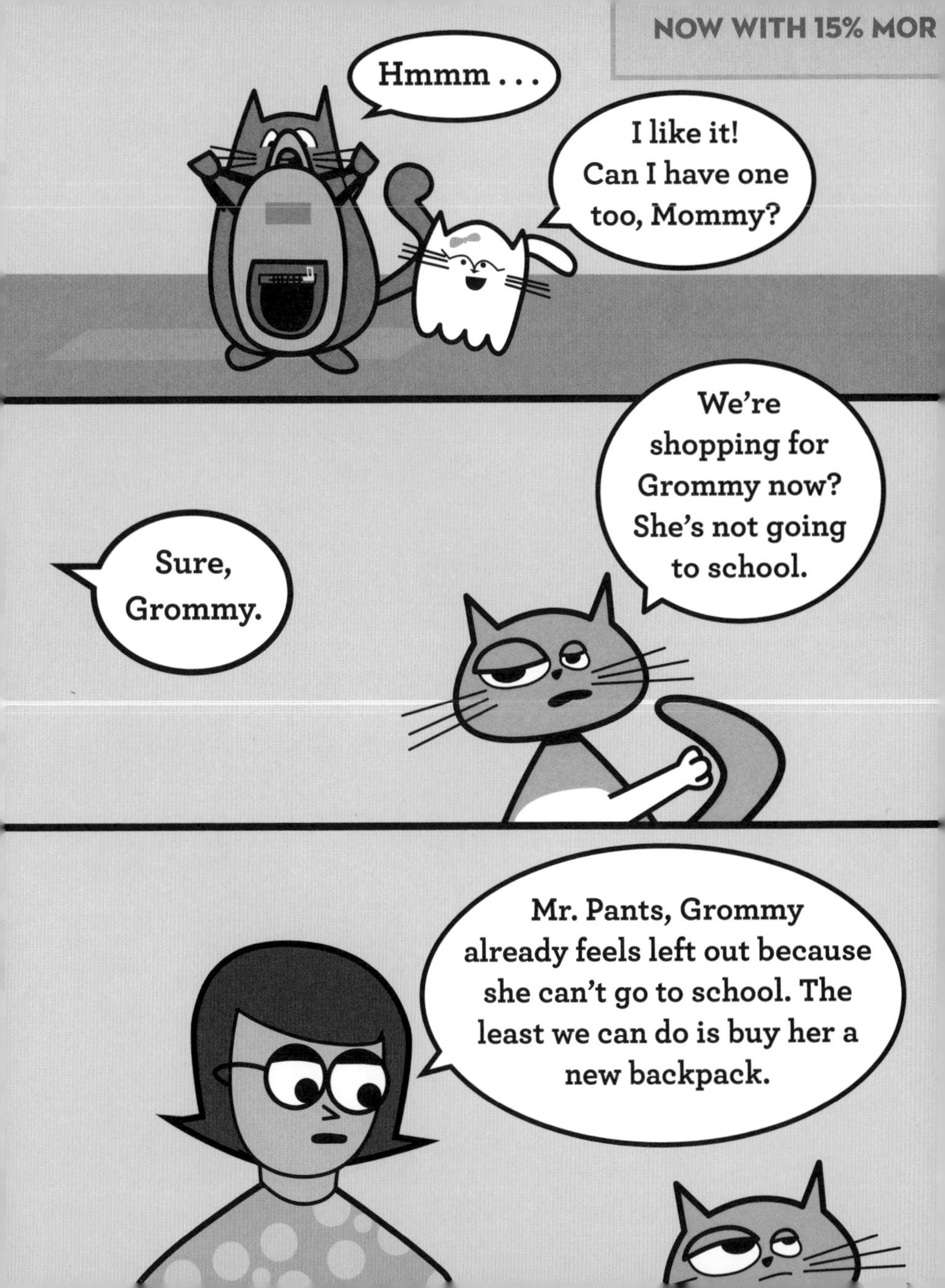
NOW WITH 15% MOR
Hmmm . . .
I like it! Can I have one too, Mommy?
We're shopping for Grommy now? She's not going to school.
Sure, Grommy.
Mr. Pants, Grommy already feels left out because she can't go to school. The least we can do is buy her a new backpack.

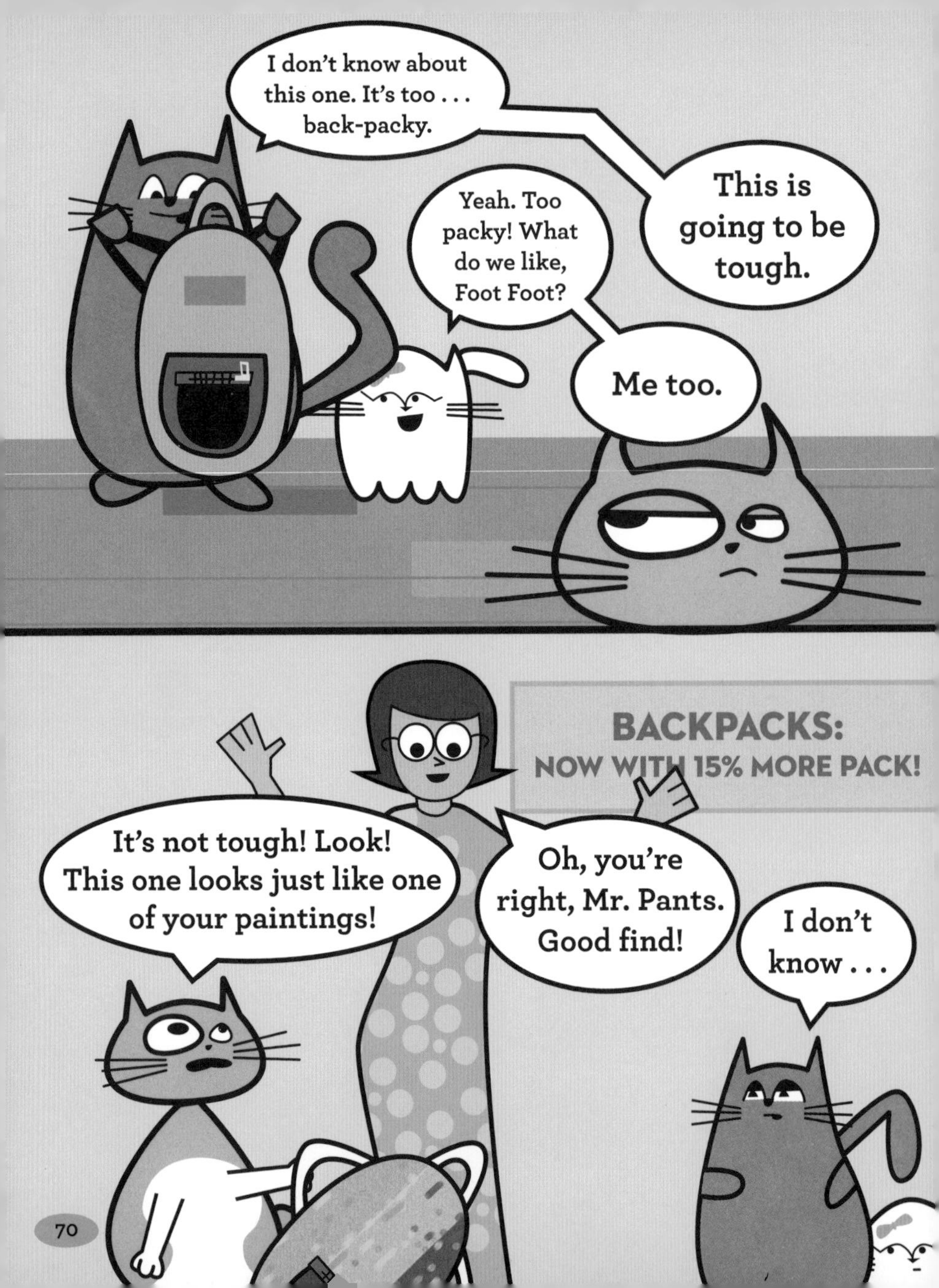
I don't know about this one. It's too . . . back-packy.
This is going to be tough.
Yeah. Too packy! What do we like, Foot Foot?
Me too.
BACKPACKS: NOW WITH 15% MORE PACK!
It's not tough! Look! This one looks just like one of your paintings!
Oh, you're right, Mr. Pants. Good find!
I don't know . . .

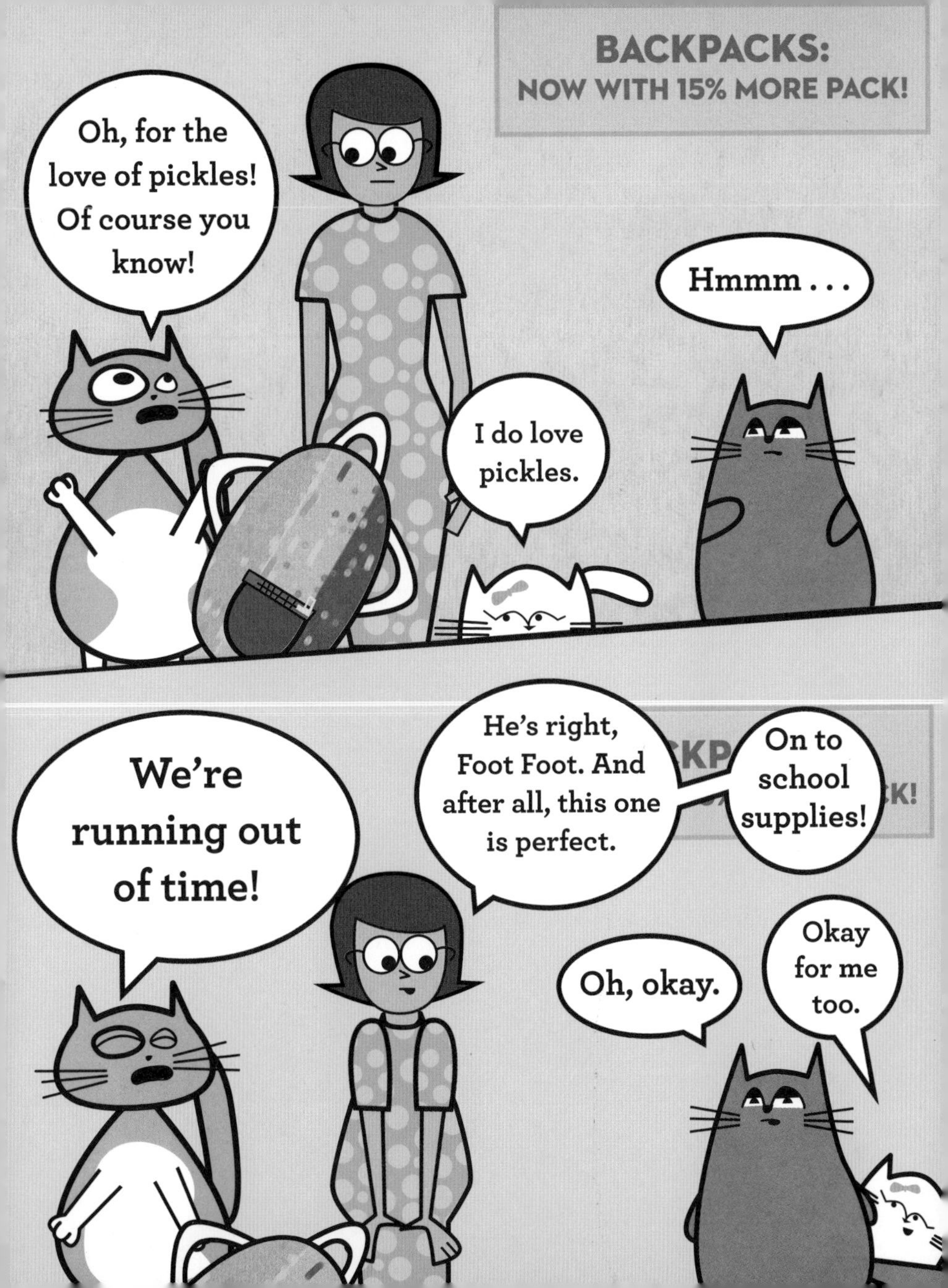
BACKPACKS:
NOW WITH 15% MORE PACK!
Oh, for the love of pickles! Of course you know!
I do love pickles.
Hmmm . . .
We're running out of time!
He's right, Foot Foot. And after all, this one is perfect.
On to school supplies!
Oh, okay.
Okay for me too.

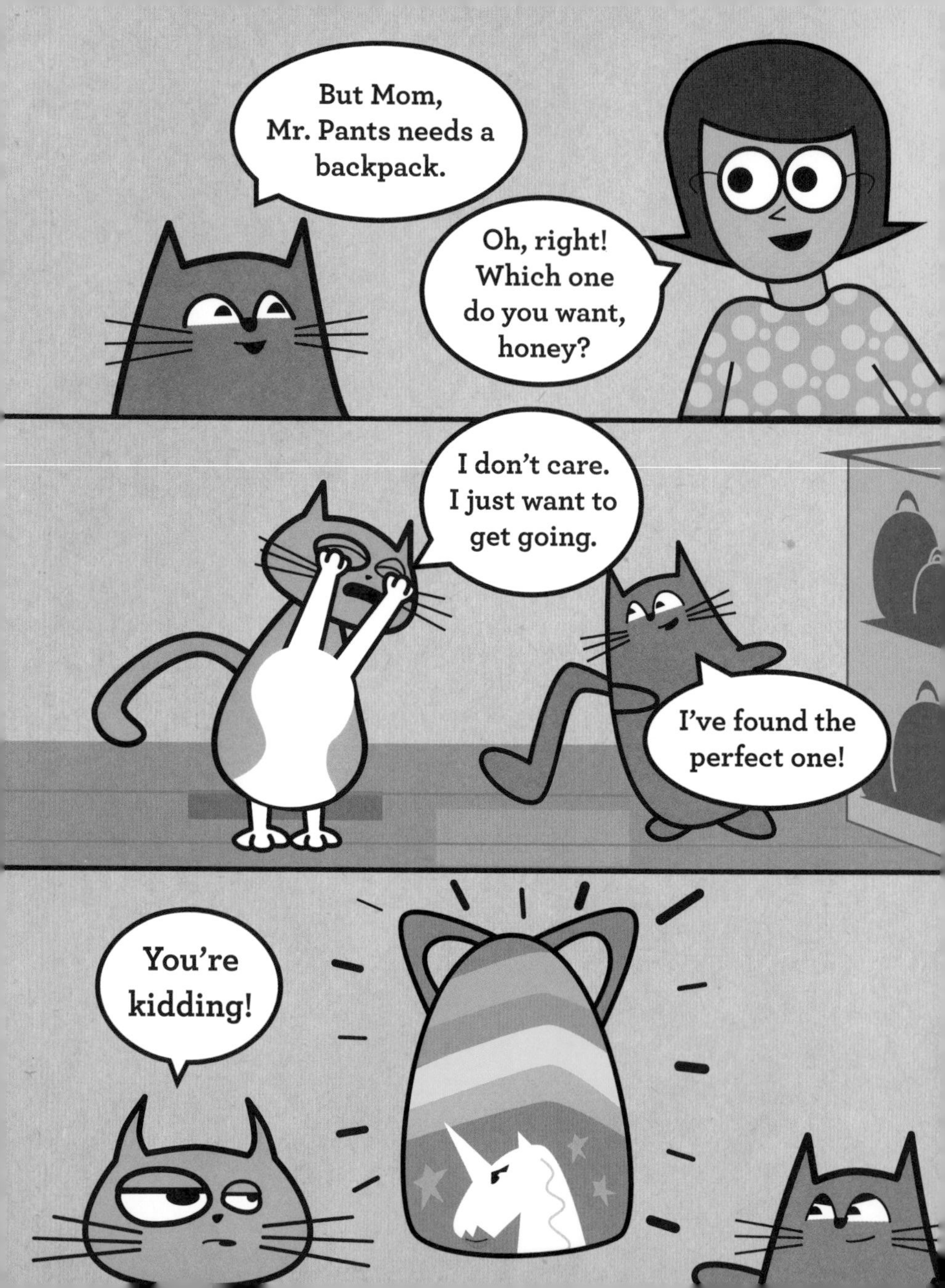
But Mom, Mr. Pants needs a backpack.
Oh, right! Which one do you want, honey?
I don't care. I just want to get going.
I've found the perfect one!
You're kidding!

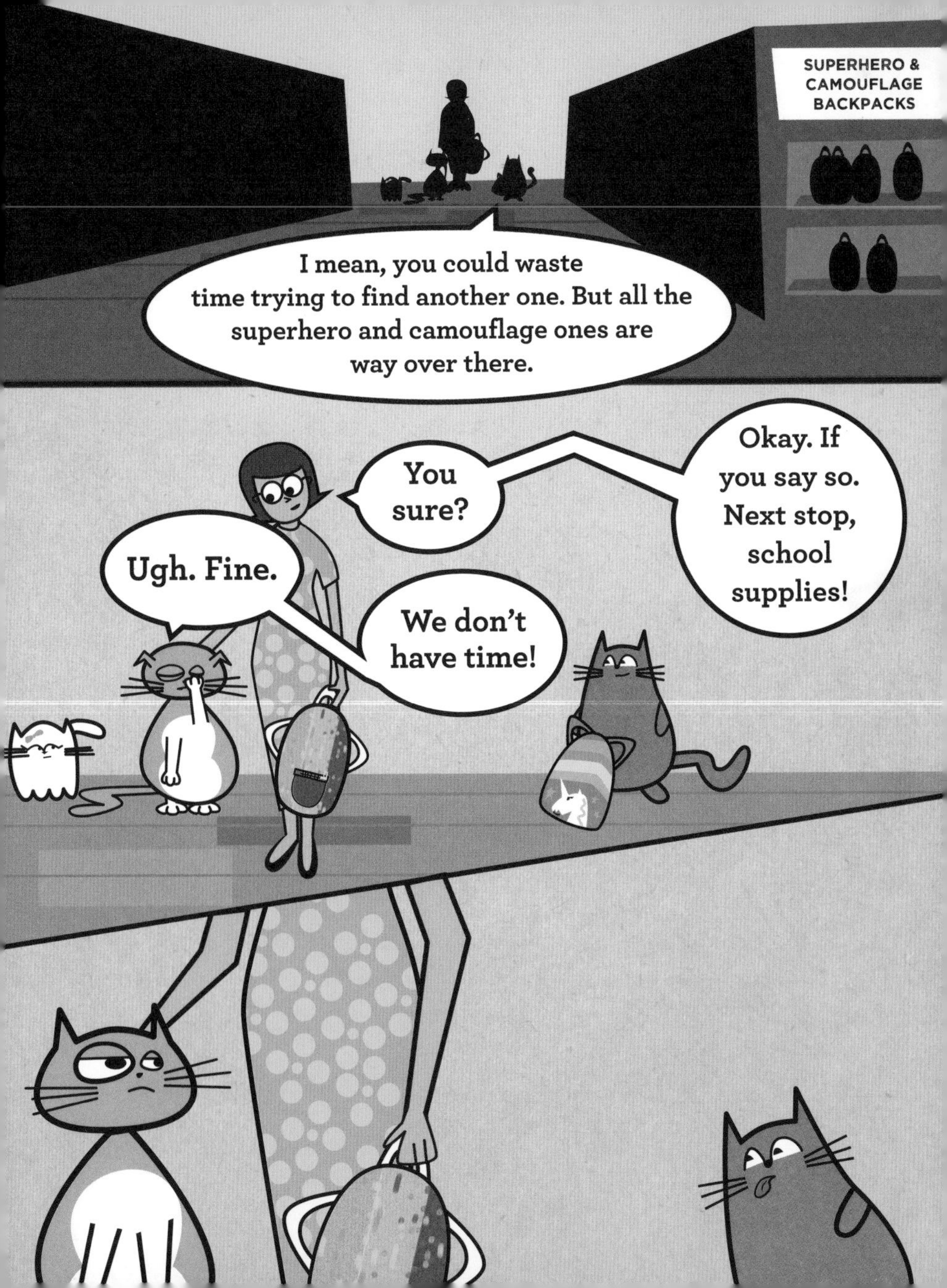
SUPERHERO & CAMOUFLAGE BACKPACKS
I mean, you could waste time trying to find another one. But all the superhero and camouflage ones are way over there.
You sure?
Okay. If you say so. Next stop, school supplies!
Ugh. Fine.
We don't have time!

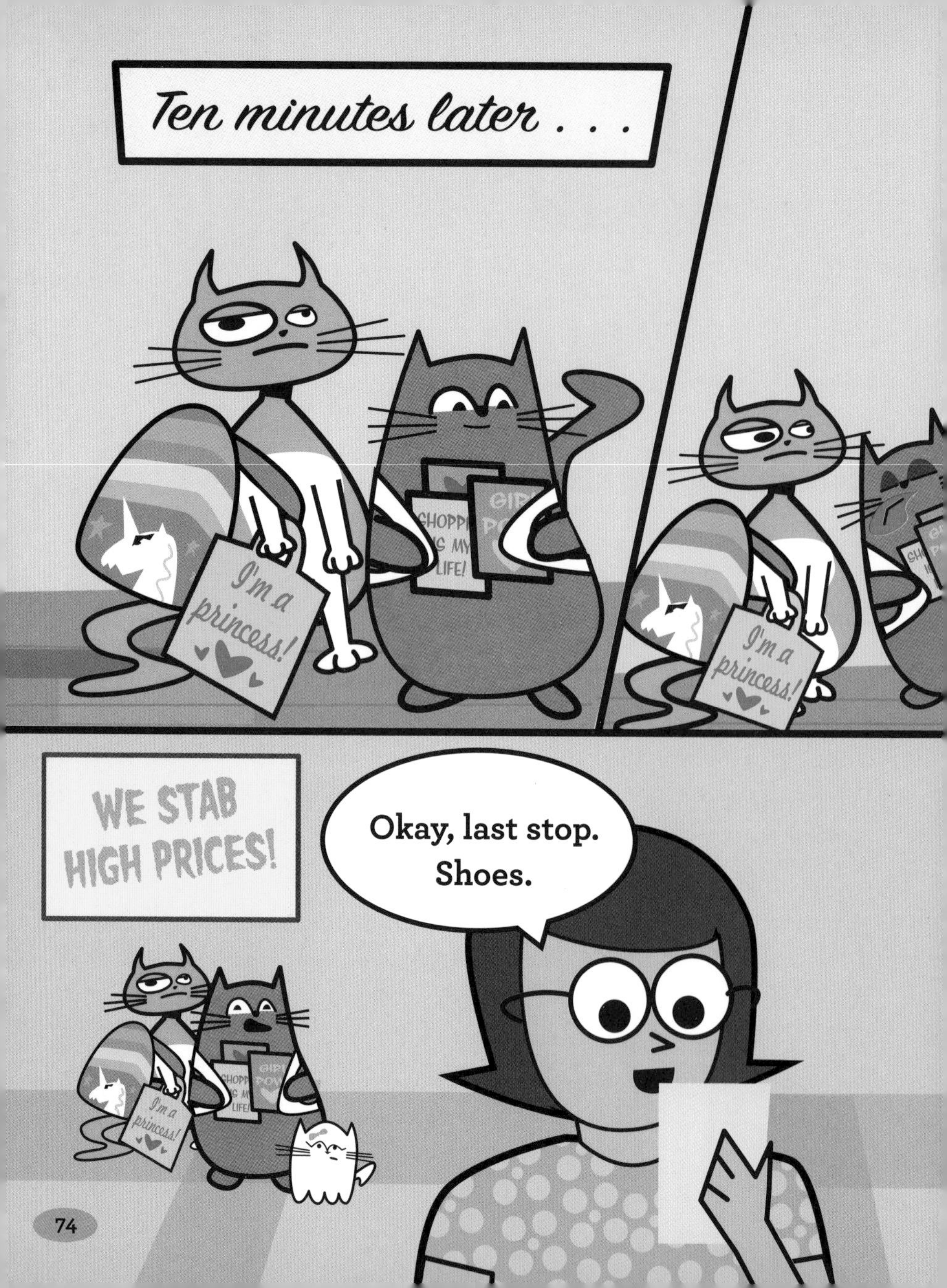
Ten minutes later . . .
SHOPPING IS MY LIFE!
GIRL POWER
I'm a princess!
WE STAB HIGH PRICES!
Okay, last stop. Shoes.

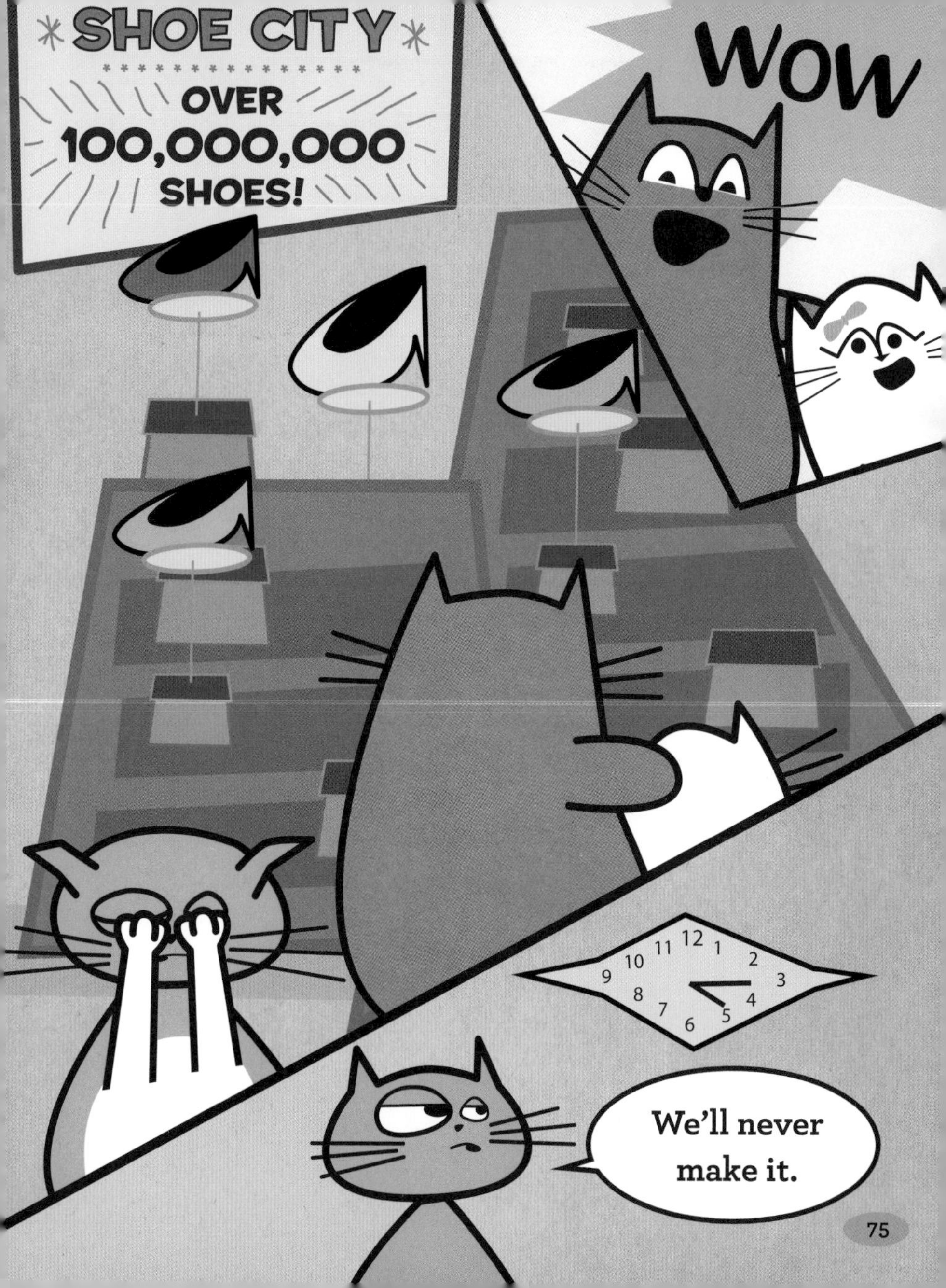
SHOE CITY
OVER 100,000,000 SHOES!
WOW
We'll never make it.

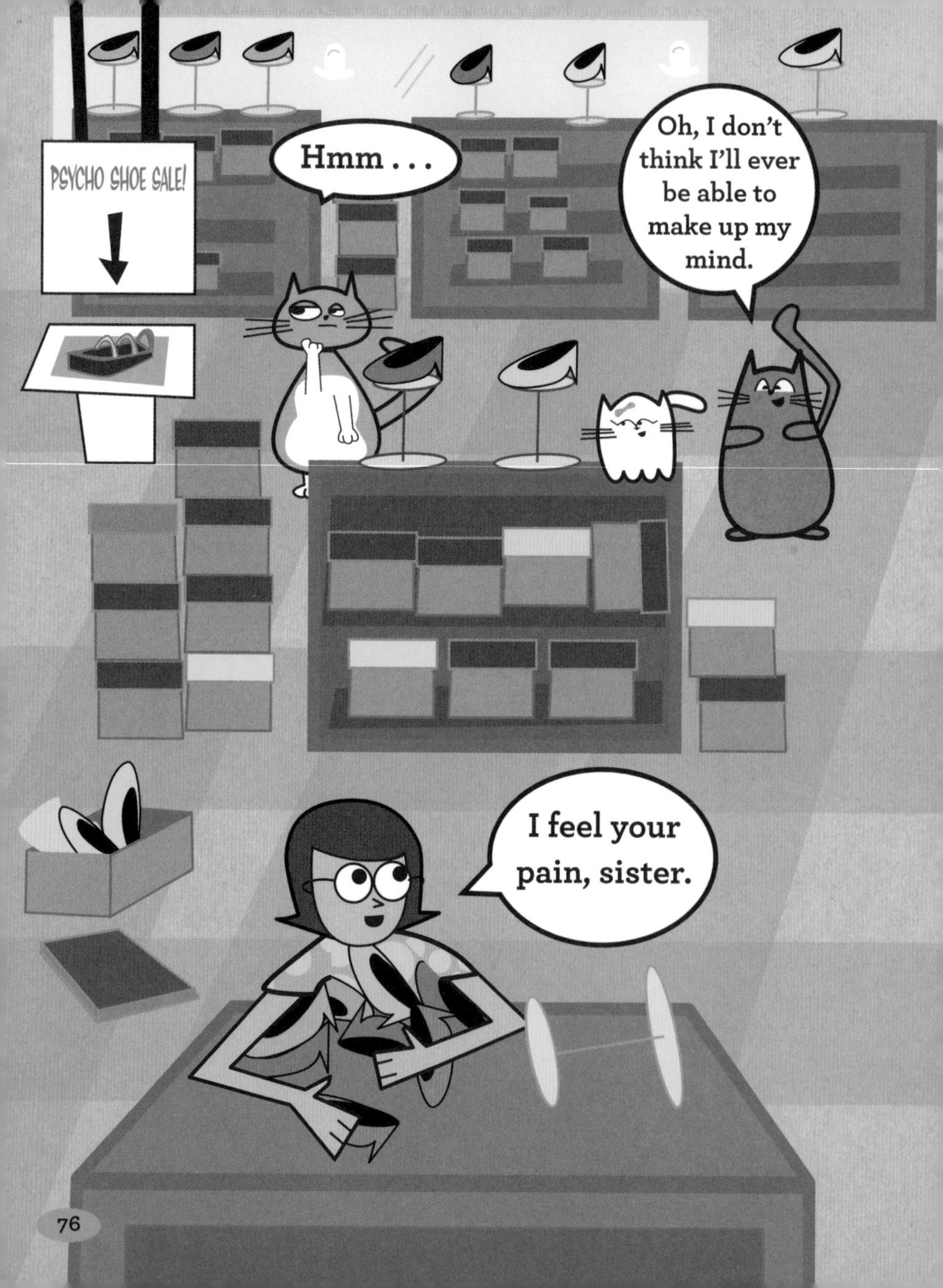
PSYCHO SHOE SALE!
Hmm . . .
Oh, I don't think I'll ever be able to make up my mind.
I feel your pain, sister.

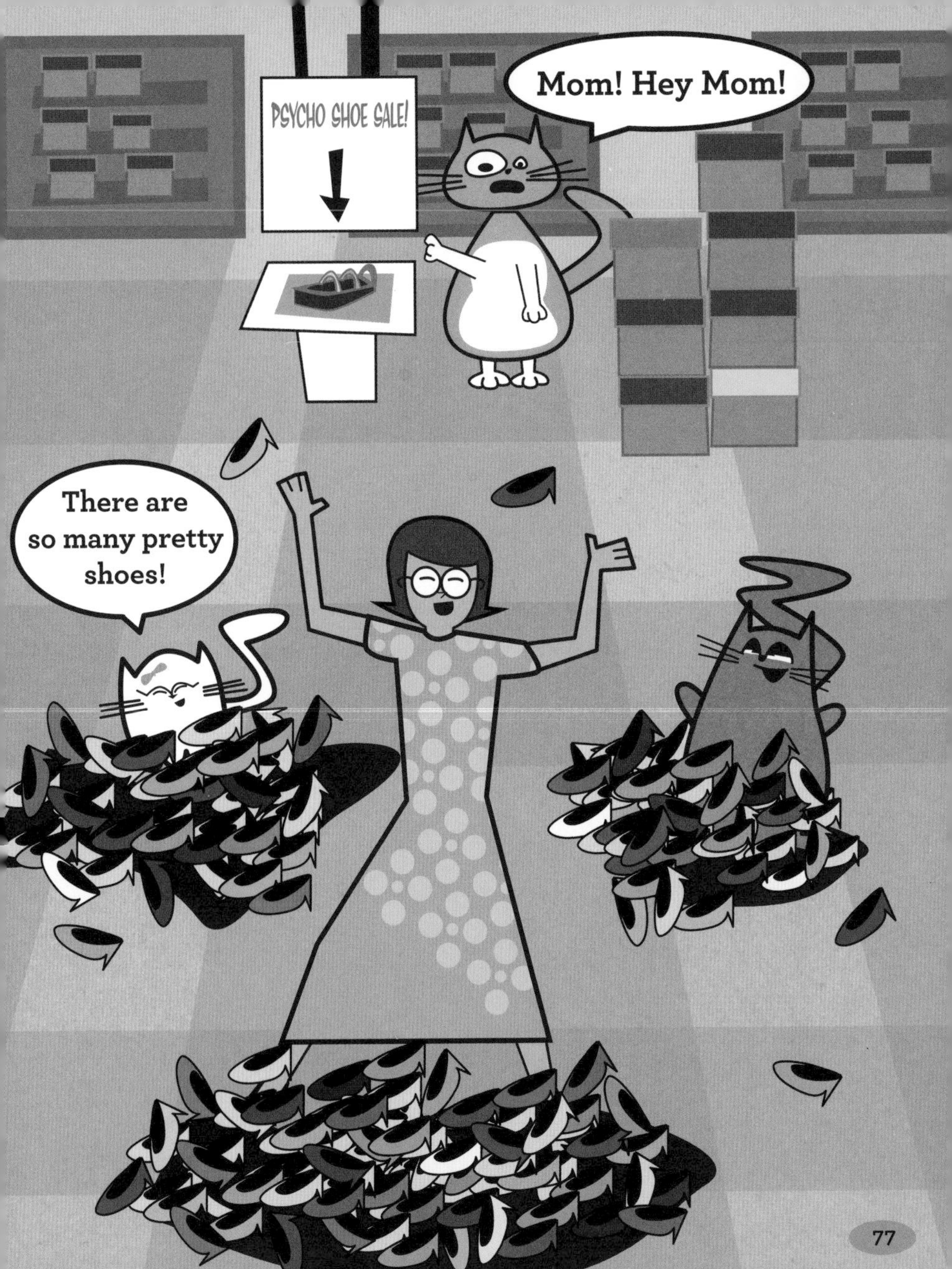
PSYCHO SHOE SALE!
Mom! Hey Mom!
There are so many pretty shoes!

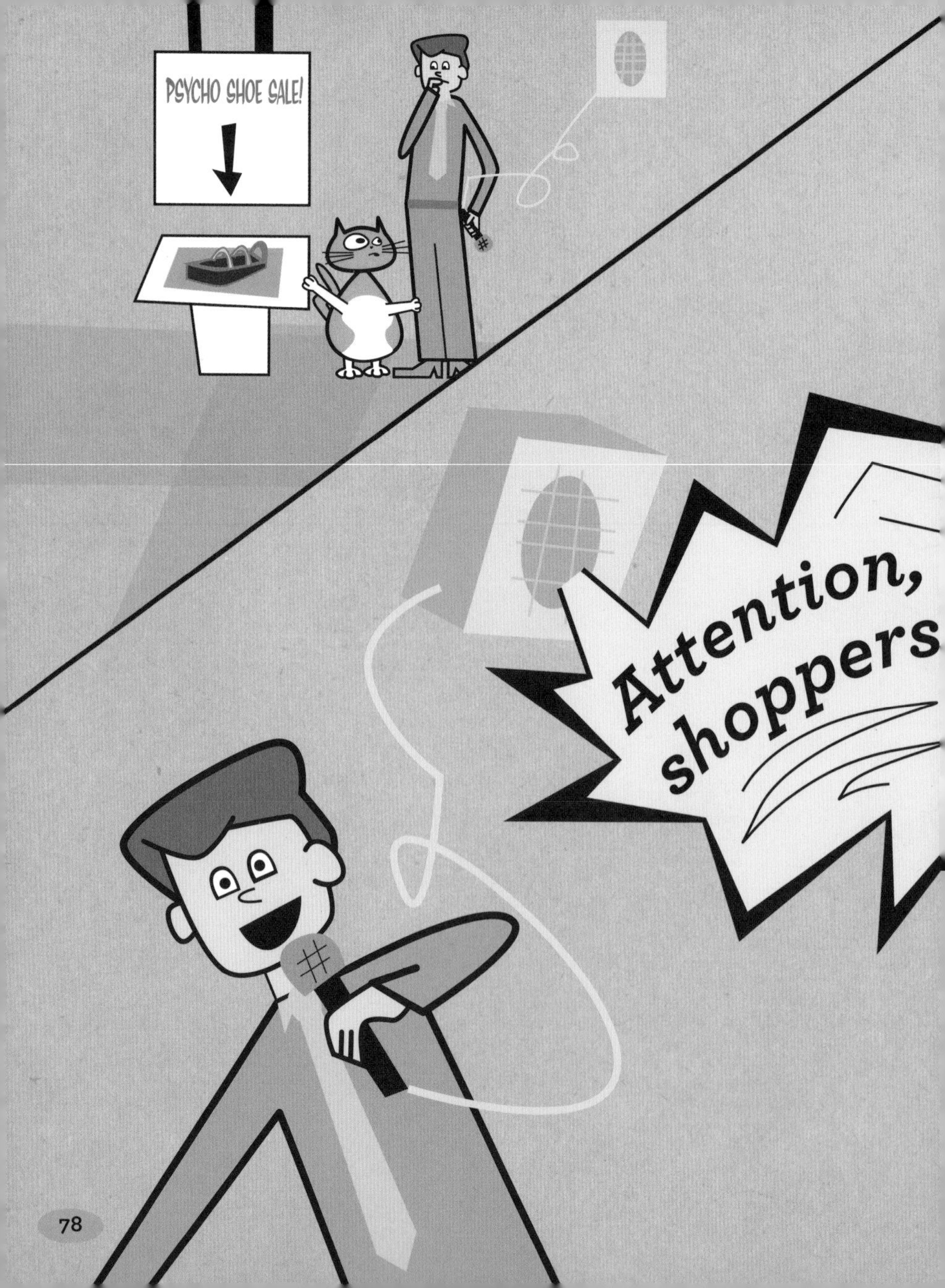
PSYCHO SHOE SALE!
Attention, shoppers

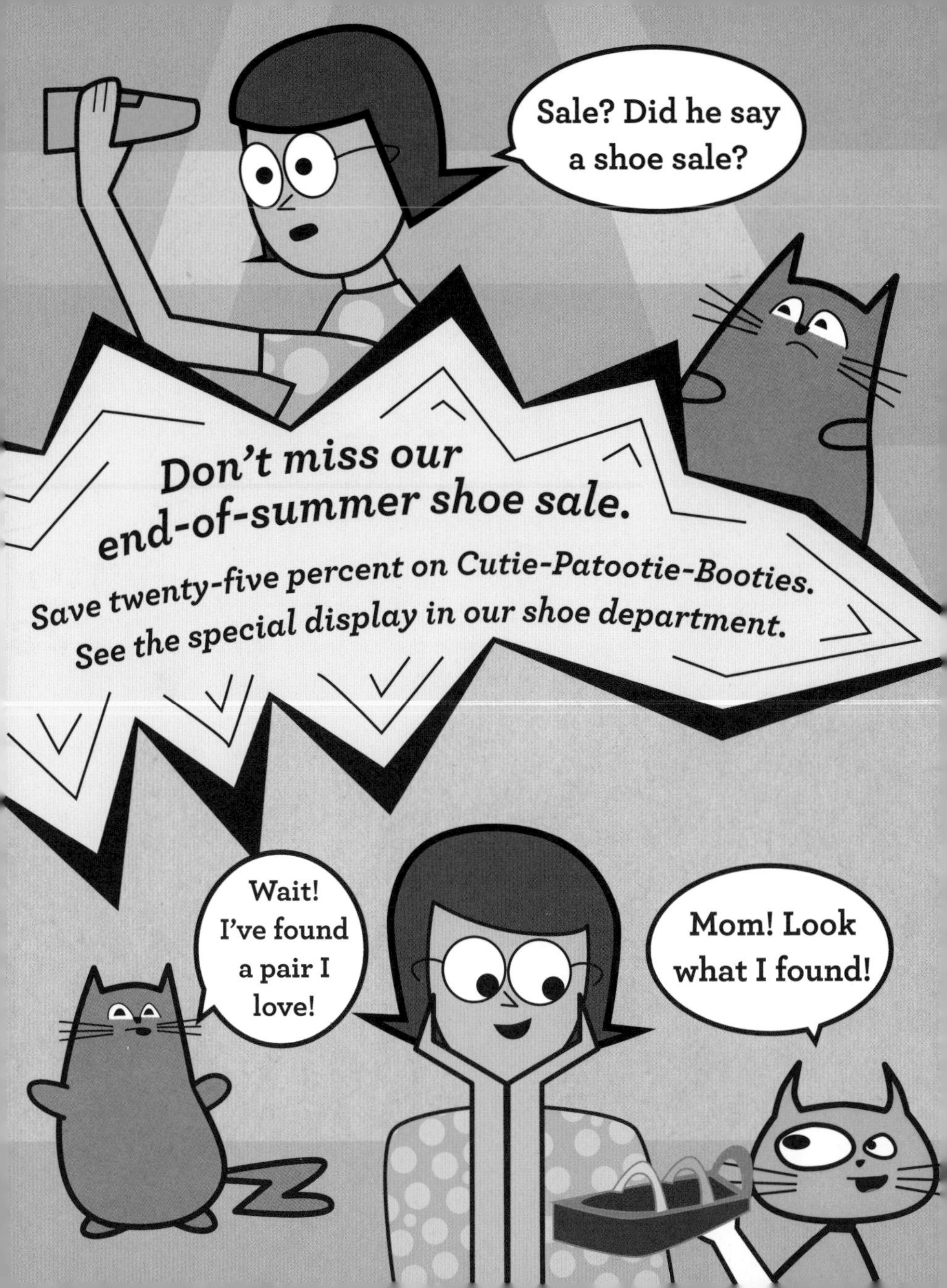
Sale? Did he say a shoe sale?
Don't miss our end-of-summer shoe sale.
Save twenty-five percent on Cutie-Patootie-Booties.
See the special display in our shoe department.
Wait! I've found a pair I love!
Mom! Look what I found!

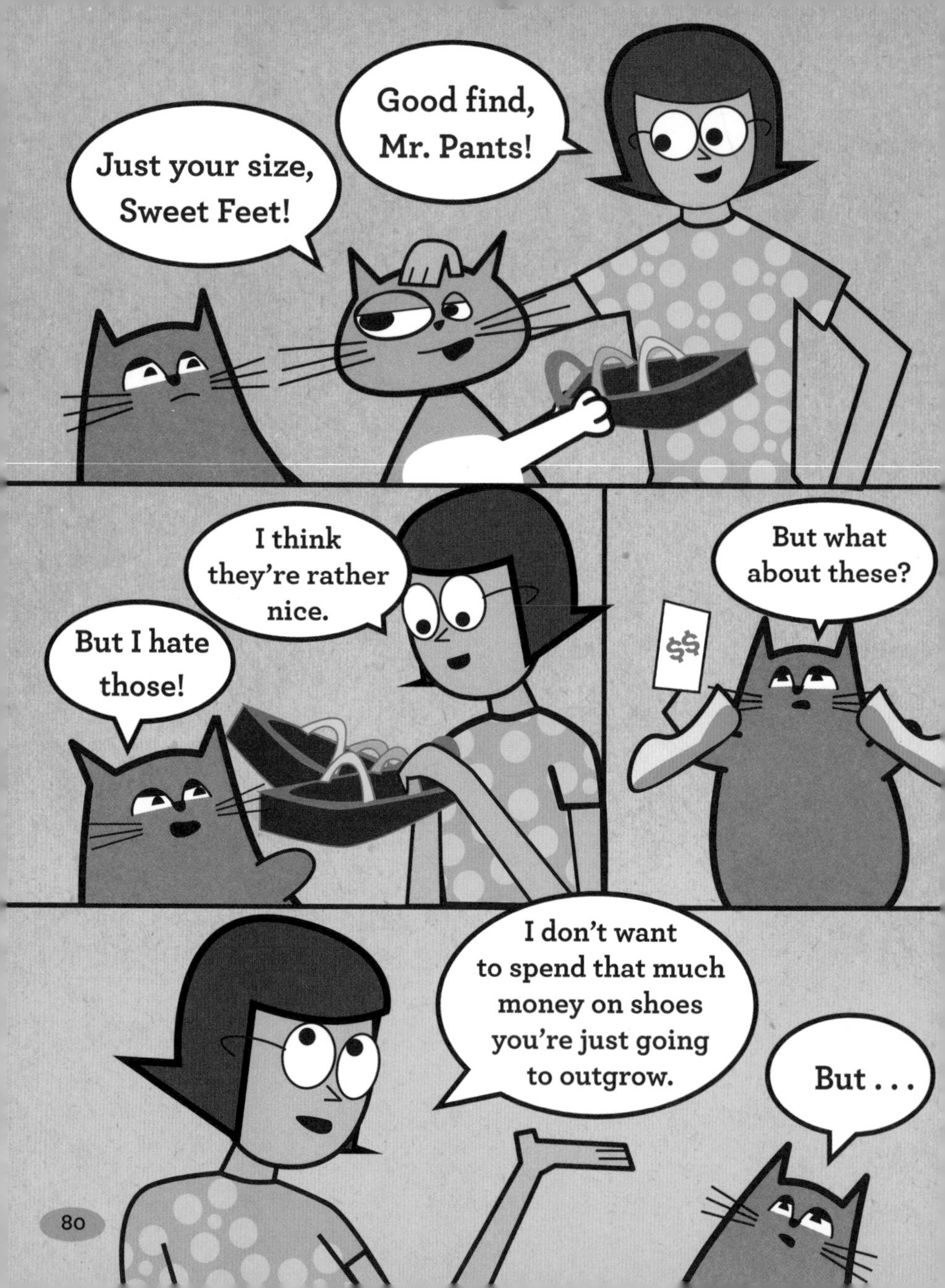
Just your size, Sweet Feet!
Good find, Mr. Pants!
I think they're rather nice.
But I hate those!
But what about these?
$$
I don't want to spend that much money on shoes you're just going to outgrow.
But . . .

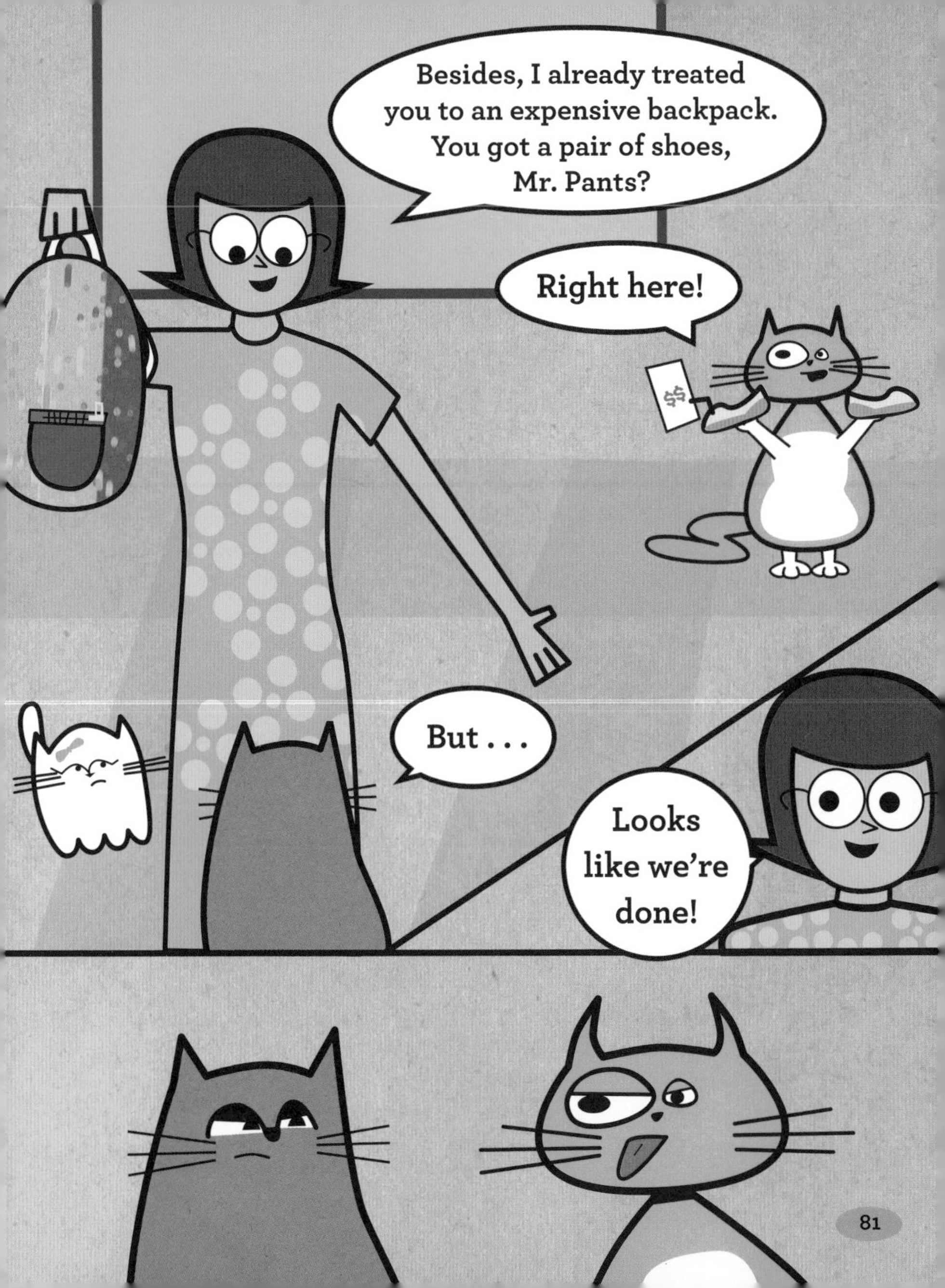
Besides, I already treated you to an expensive backpack. You got a pair of shoes, Mr. Pants?
Right here!
$$
But . . .
Looks like we're done!

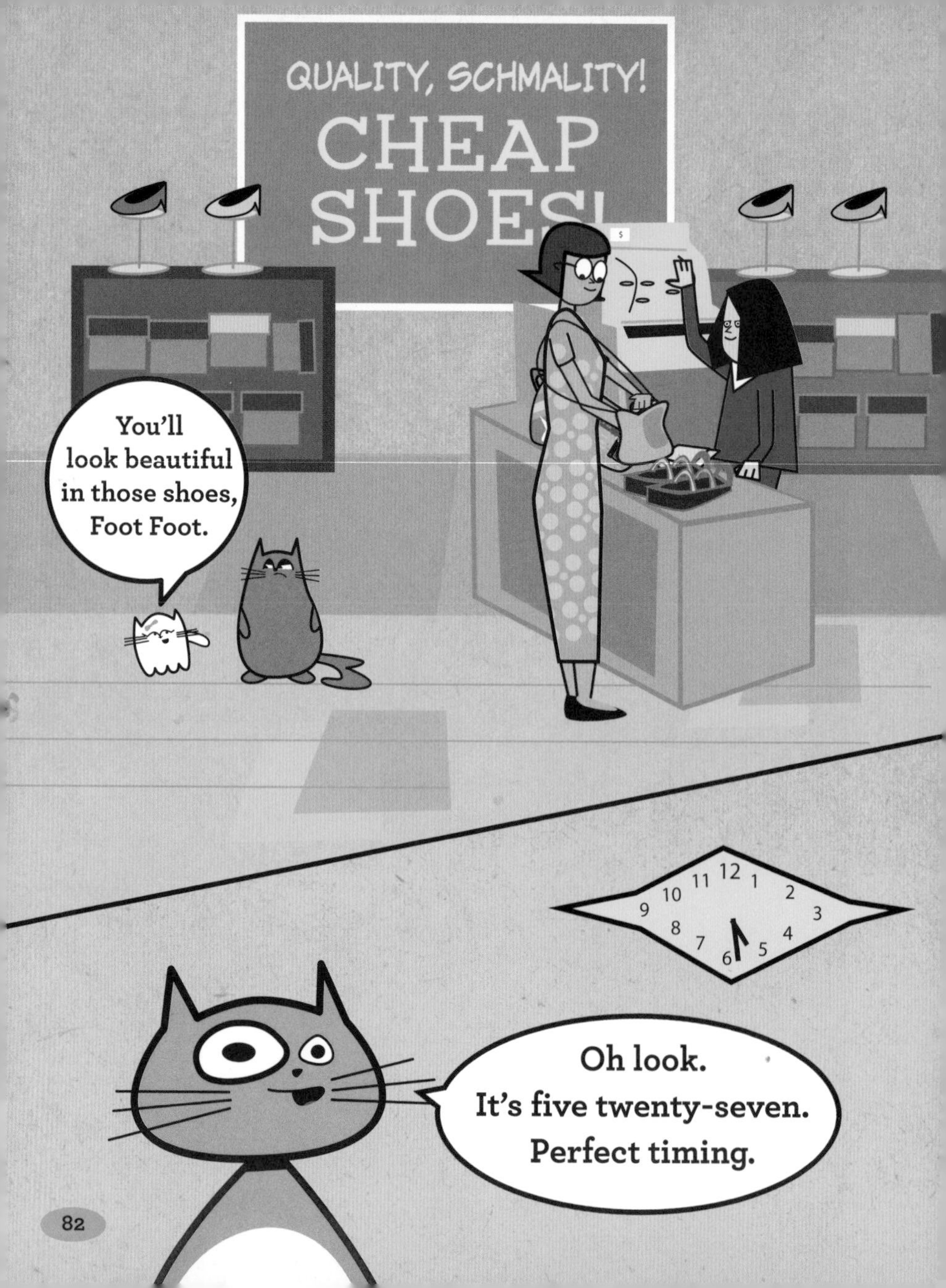
QUALITY, SCHMALITY!
CHEAP SHOES!
You'll look beautiful in those shoes, Foot Foot.
Oh look. It's five twenty-seven. Perfect timing.

Chapter Five: A TREAT FOR FEET

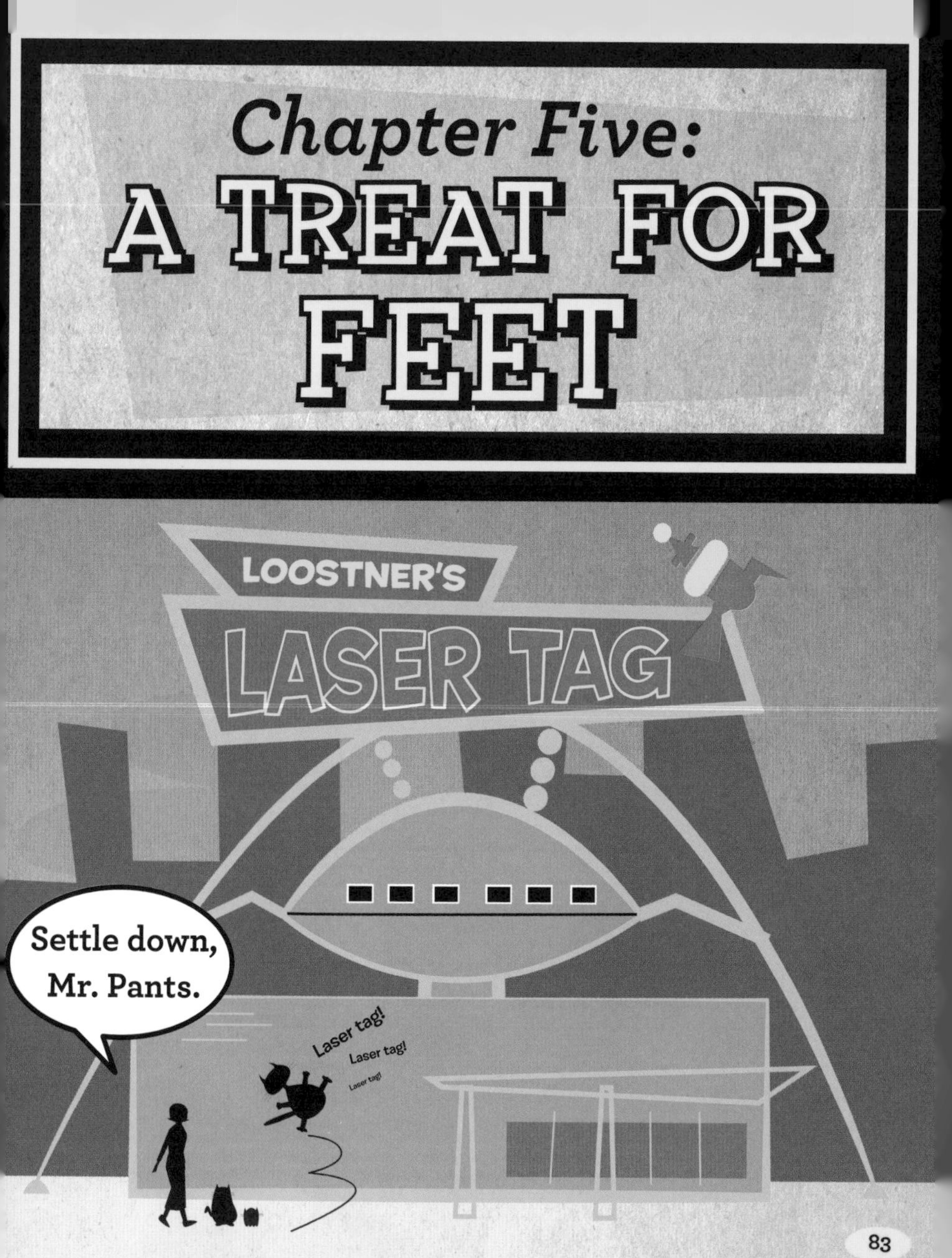
LOOSTNER'S
LASER TAG
Settle down, Mr. Pants.
Laser tag!
Laser tag!
Laser tag!

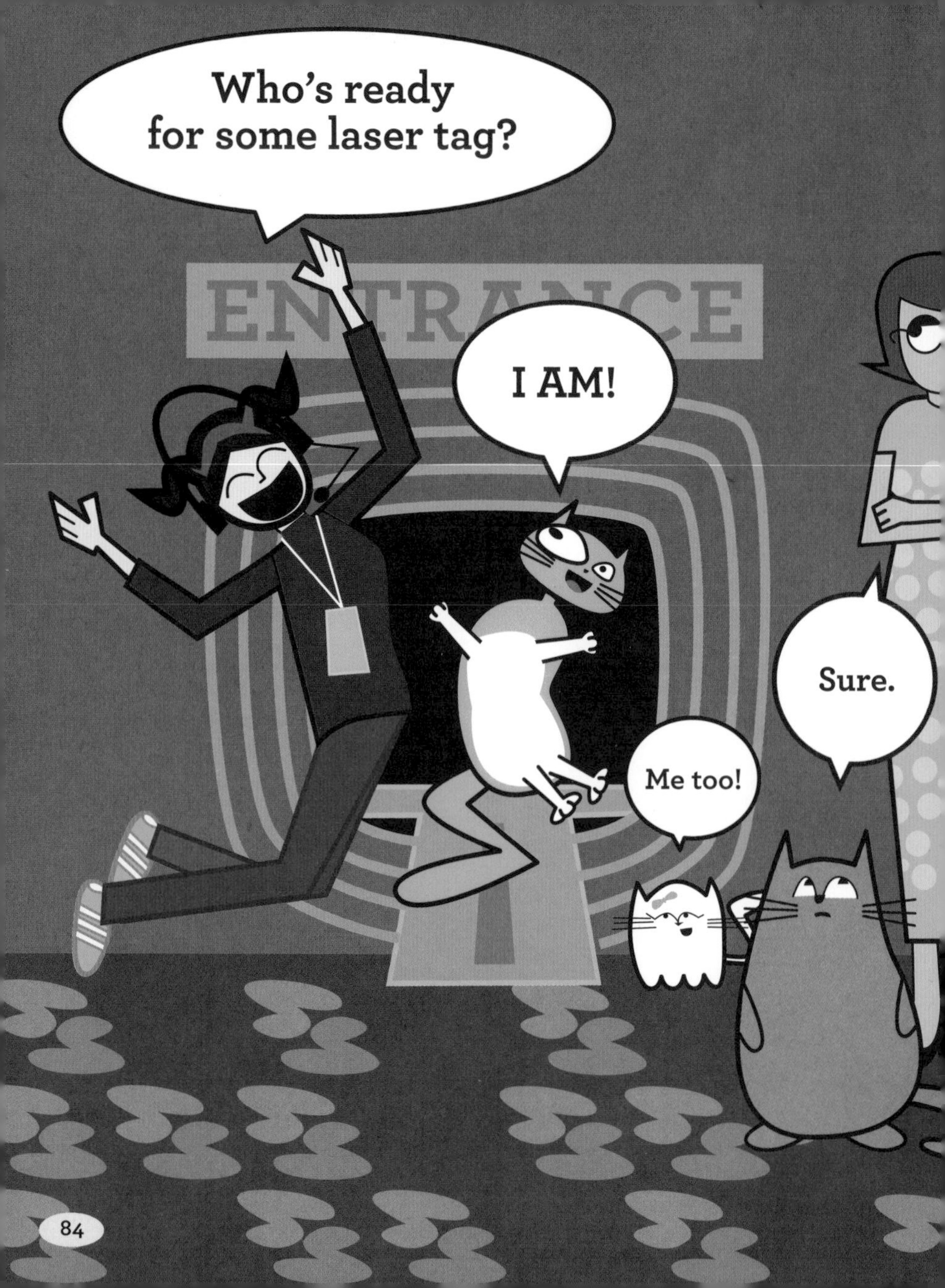
Who's ready
for some laser tag?
ENTRANCE
I AM!
Sure.
Me too!

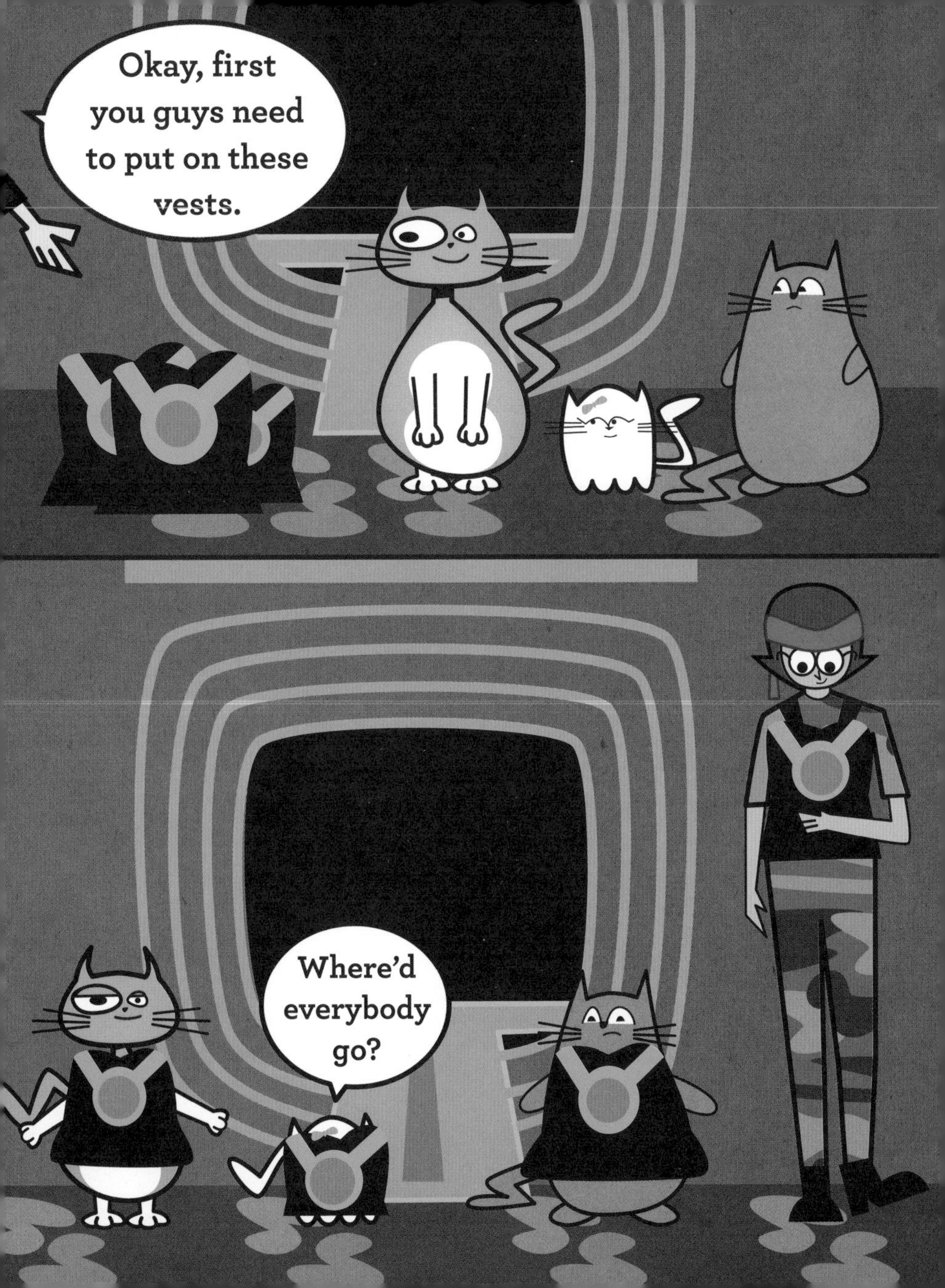
Okay, first you guys need to put on these vests.
Where'd everybody go?

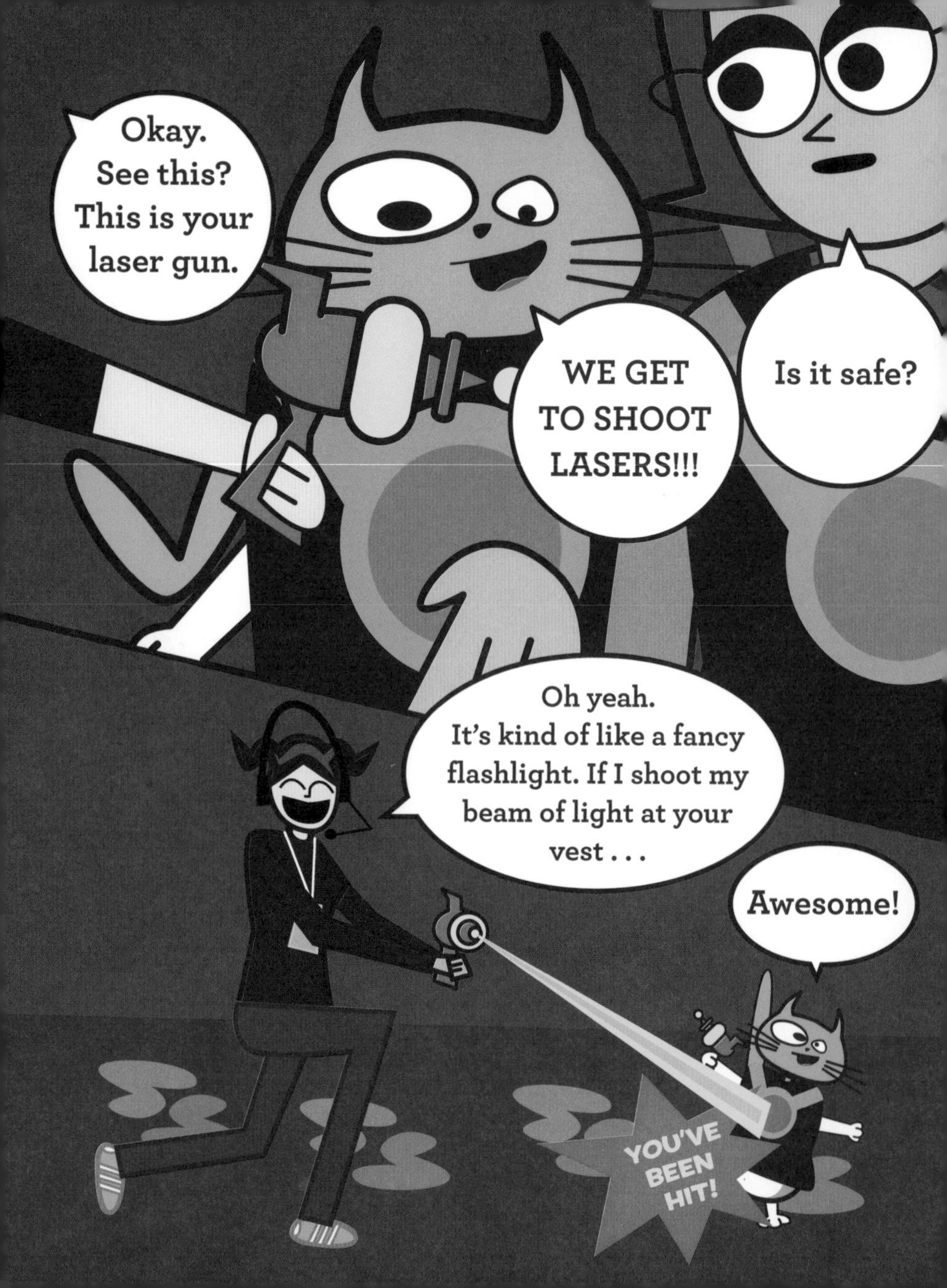

Okay. See this? This is your laser gun.
WE GET TO SHOOT LASERS!!!
Is it safe?
Oh yeah. It's kind of like a fancy flashlight. If I shoot my beam of light at your vest . . .
Awesome!
YOU'VE BEEN HIT!

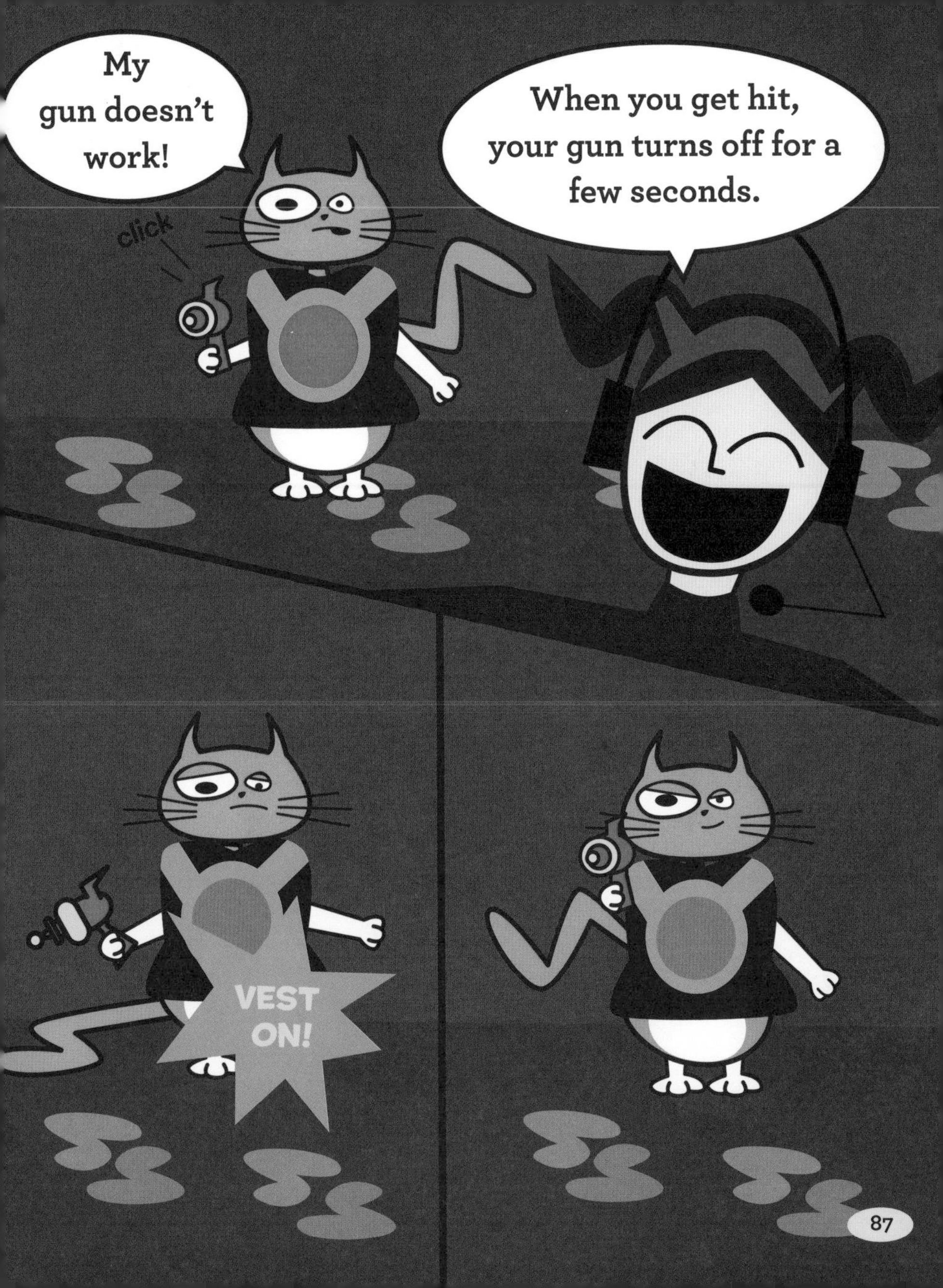
My gun doesn't work!
click
When you get hit, your gun turns off for a few seconds.
VEST ON!

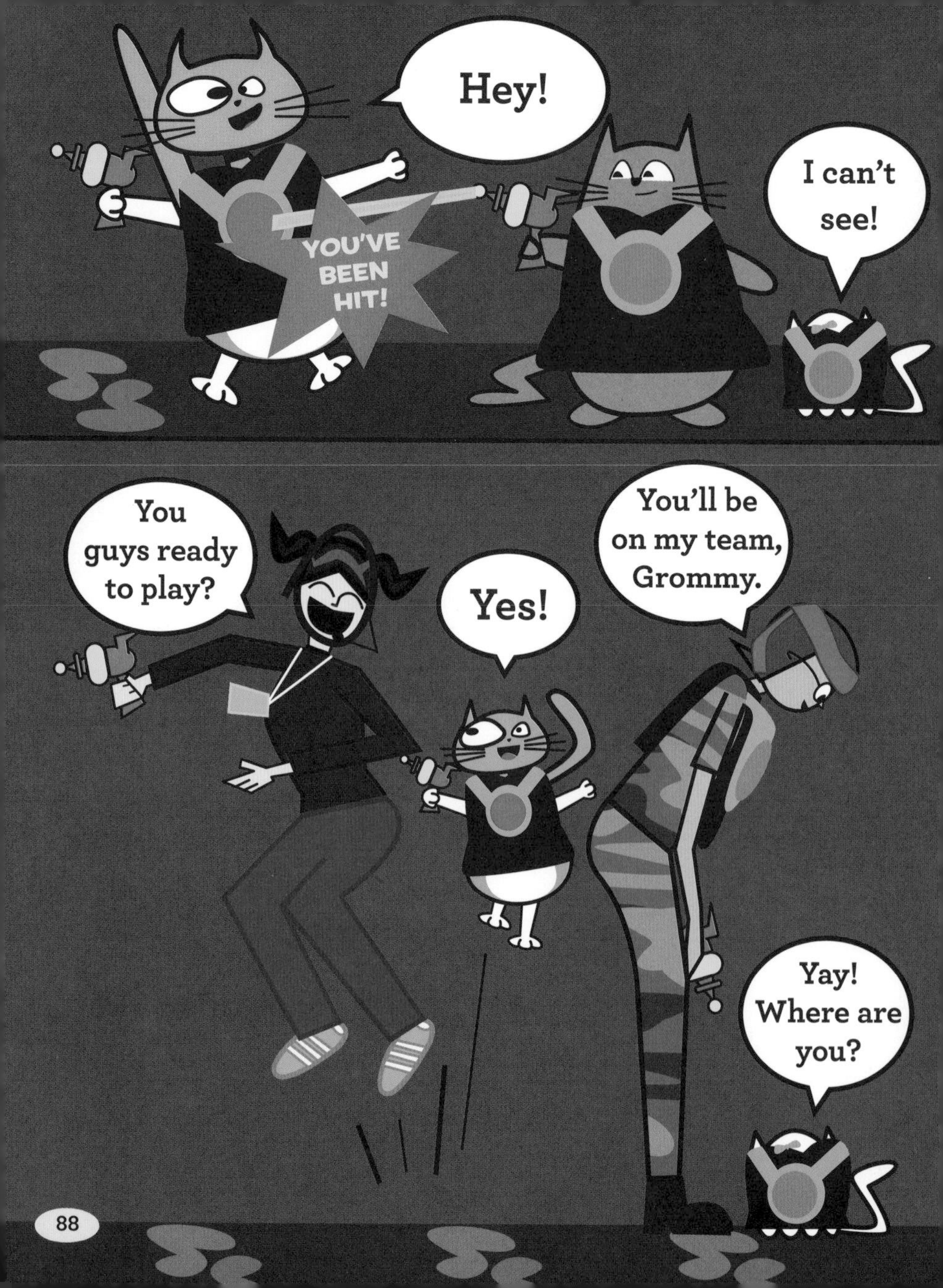
Hey!
YOU'VE BEEN HIT!
I can't see!
You guys ready to play?
Yes!
You'll be on my team, Grommy.
Yay! Where are you?

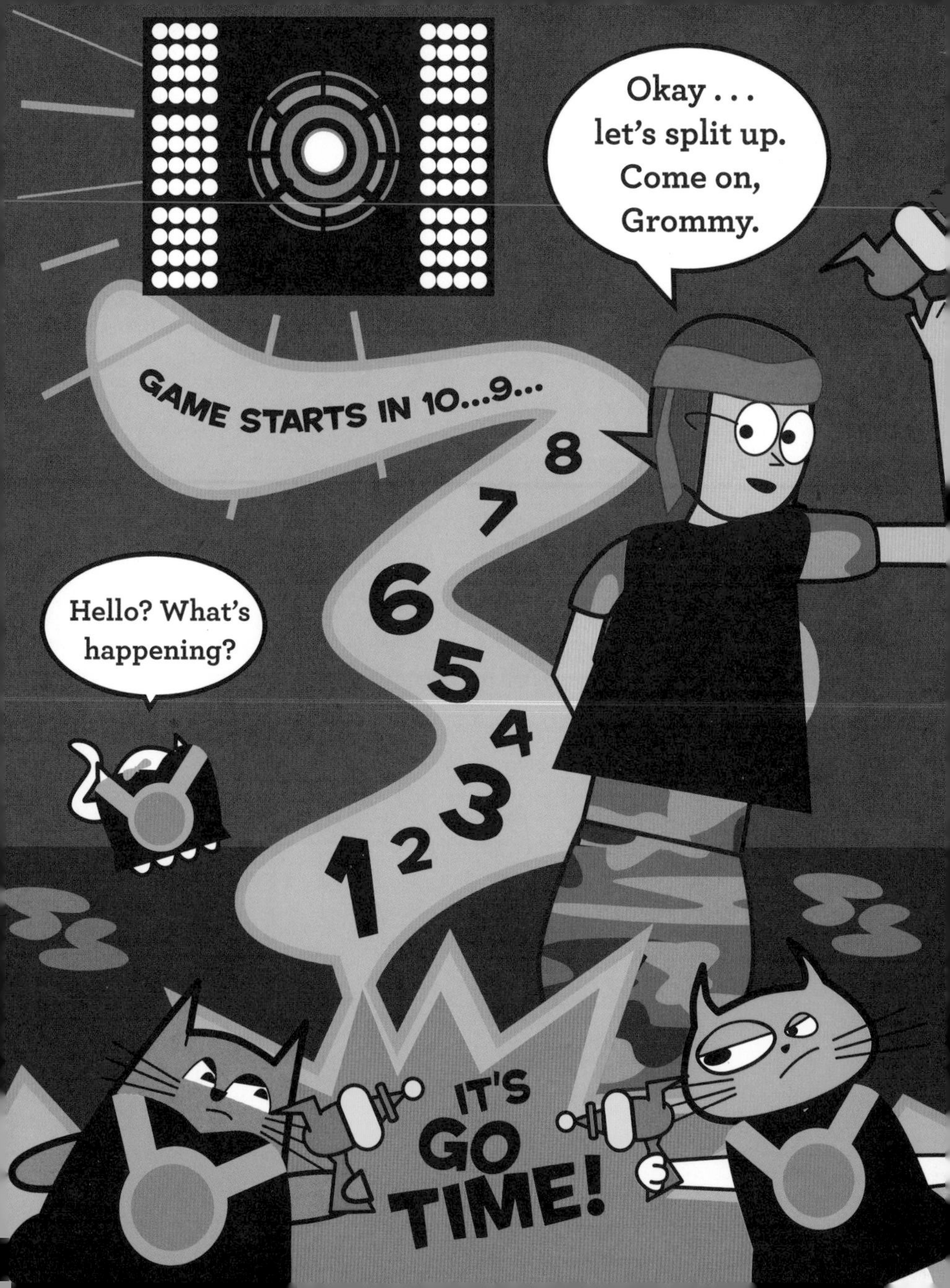
Okay . . . let's split up. Come on, Grommy.
GAME STARTS IN 10...9...
8
7
6
5
4
3
2
1
Hello? What's happening?
IT'S GO TIME!

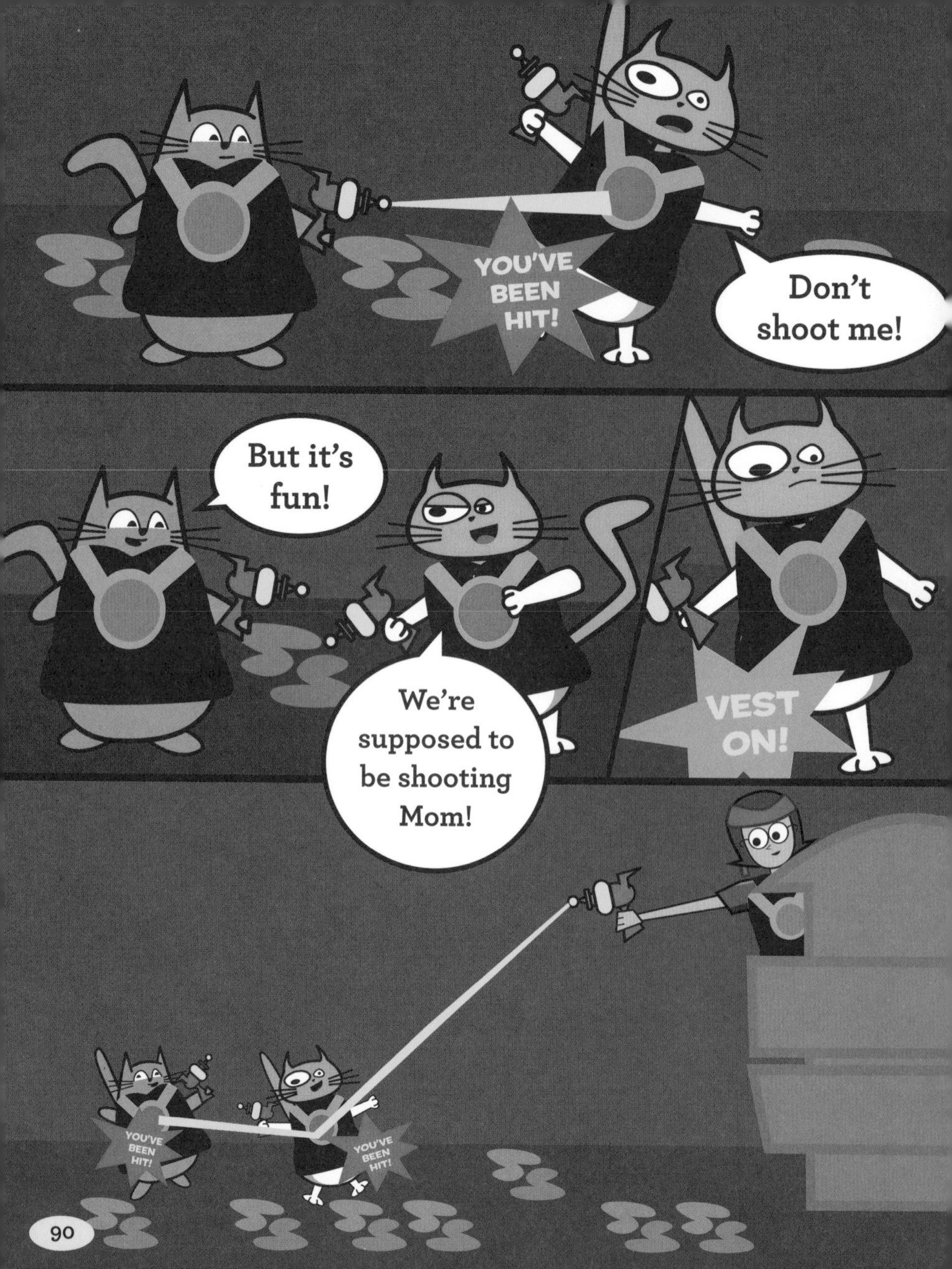
YOU'VE BEEN HIT!
Don't shoot me!
But it's fun!
We're supposed to be shooting Mom!
VEST ON!
YOU'VE BEEN HIT!
YOU'VE BEEN HIT!

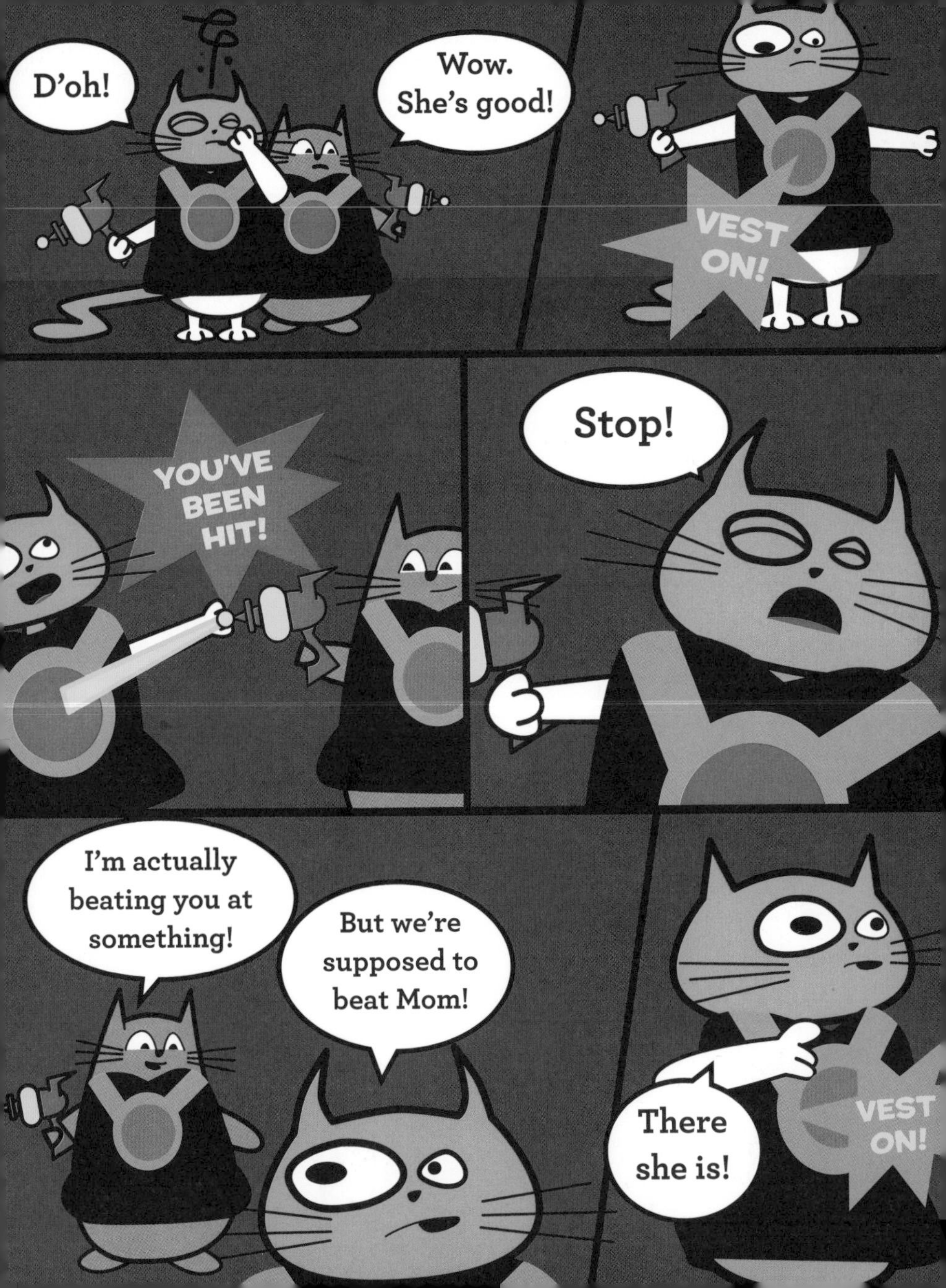
D'oh!
Wow. She's good!
VEST ON!
YOU'VE BEEN HIT!
Stop!
I'm actually beating you at something!
But we're supposed to beat Mom!
There she is!
VEST ON!

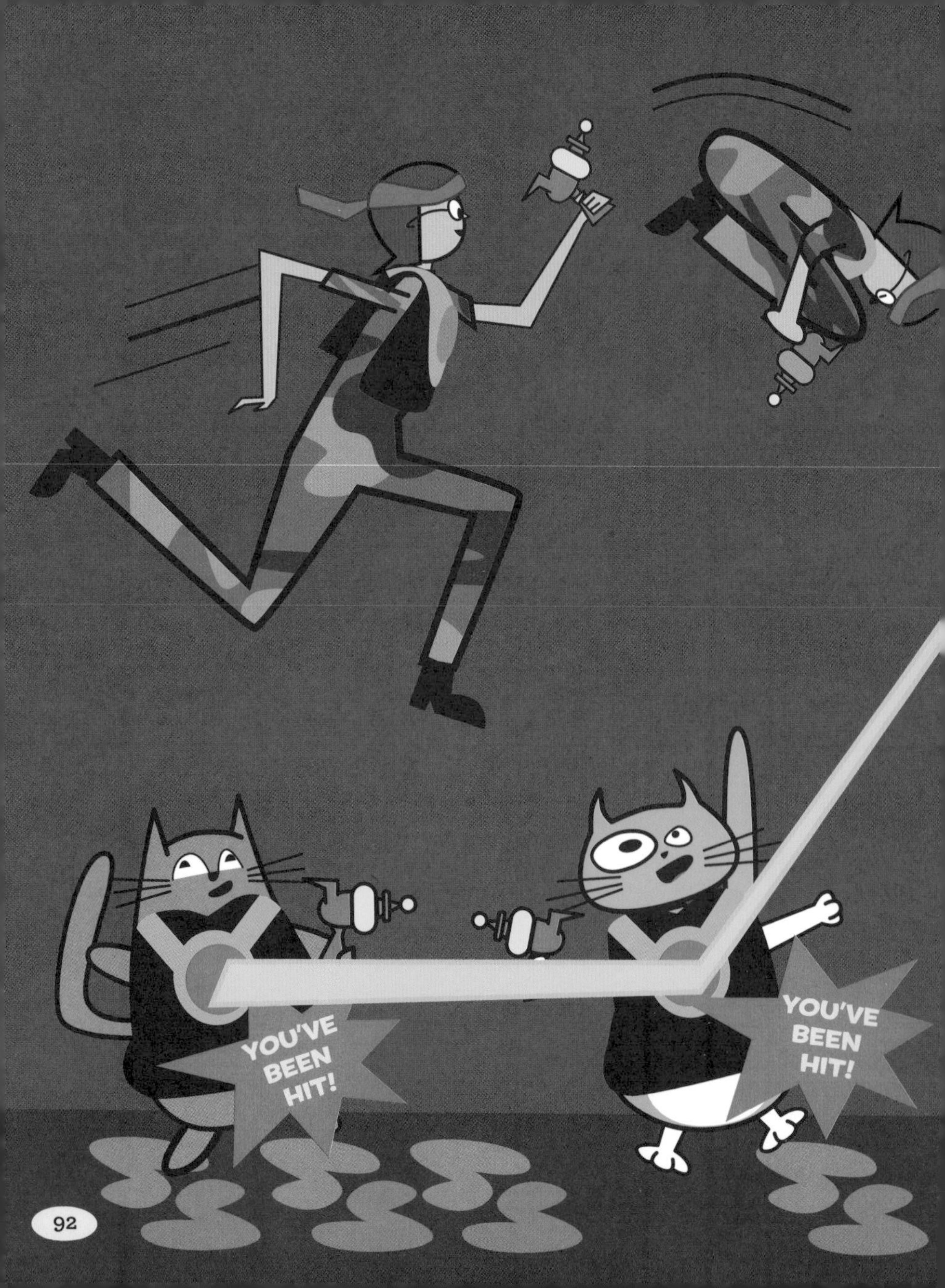
YOU'VE
BEEN
HIT!
YOU'VE
BEEN
HIT!

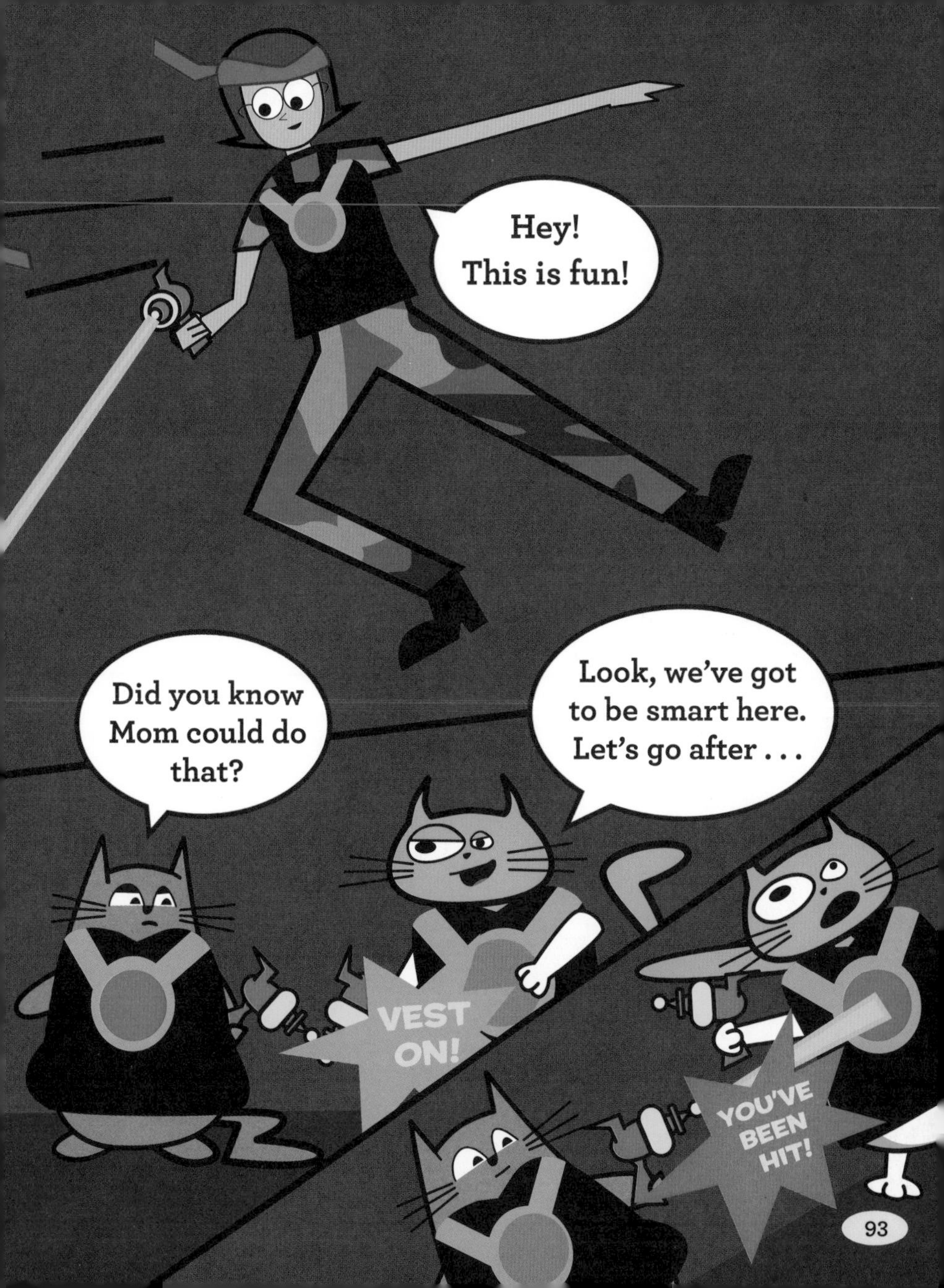
Hey!
This is fun!
Did you know Mom could do that?
Look, we've got to be smart here. Let's go after . . .
VEST ON!
YOU'VE BEEN HIT!

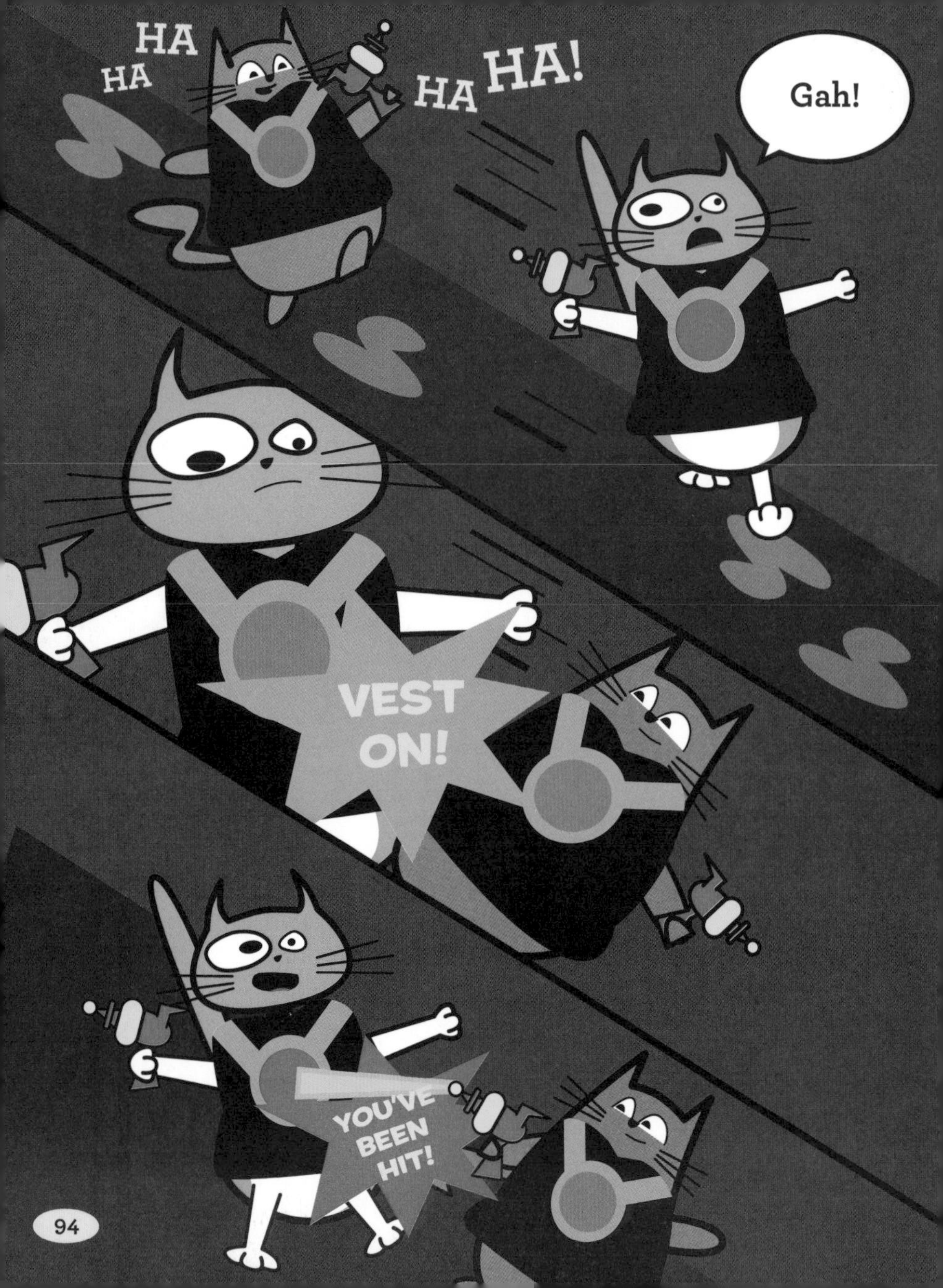
HA
HA
HA HA!
Gah!
VEST ON!
YOU'VE BEEN HIT!

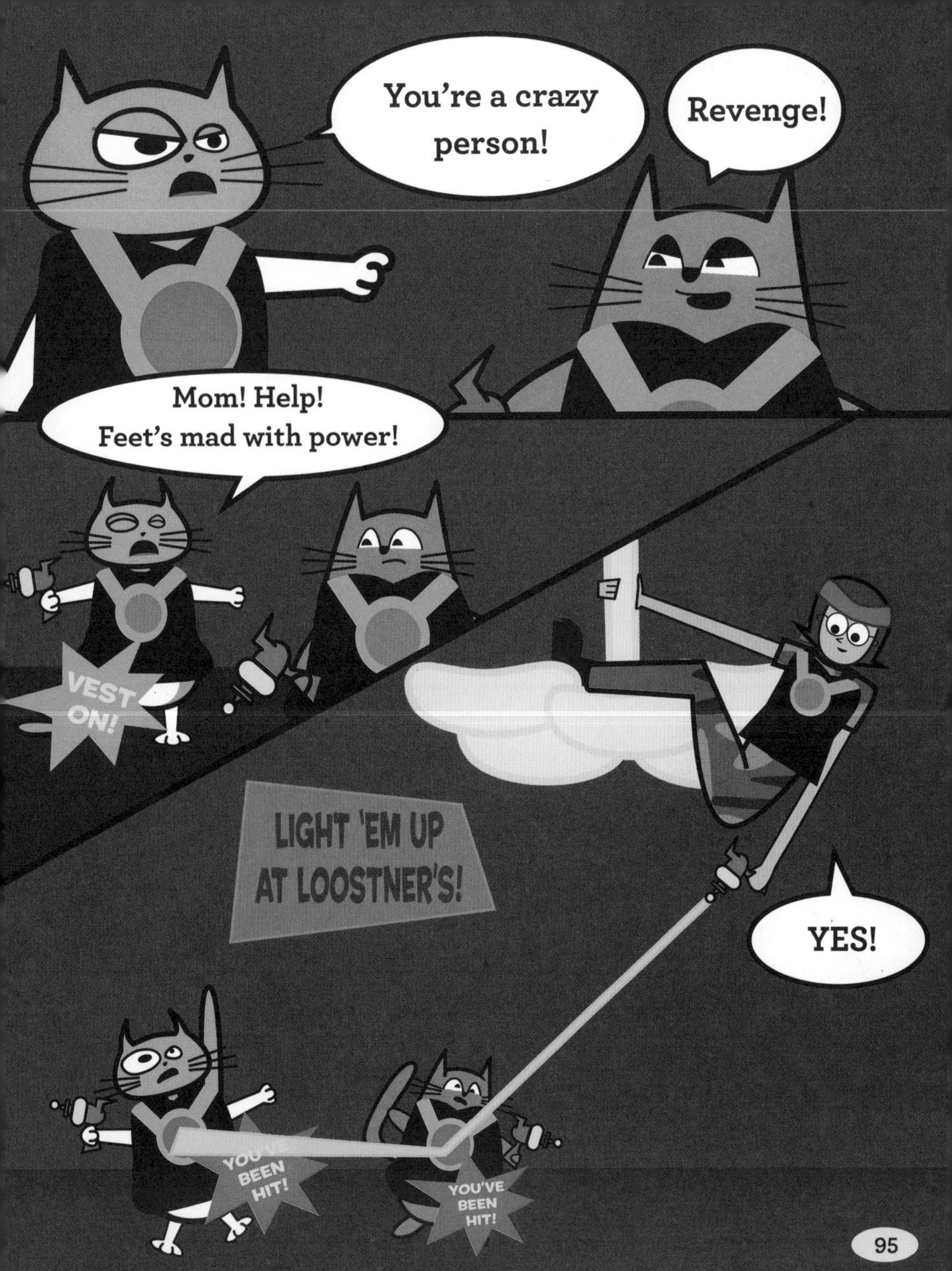
You're a crazy person!
Revenge!
Mom! Help! Feet's mad with power!
VEST ON!
LIGHT 'EM UP AT LOOSTNER'S!
YES!
YOU'VE BEEN HIT!
YOU'VE BEEN HIT!

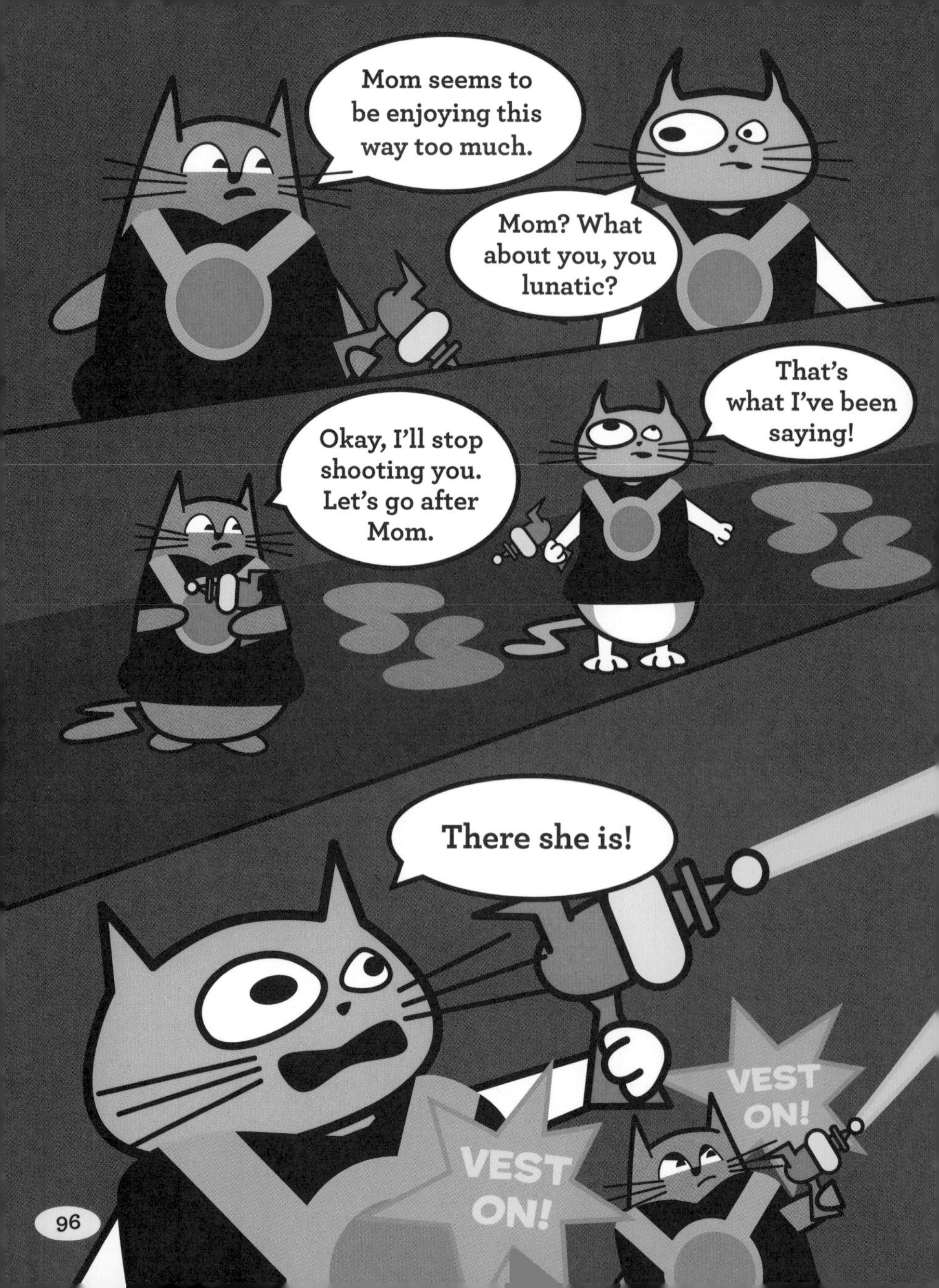
Mom seems to be enjoying this way too much.
Mom? What about you, you lunatic?
Okay, I'll stop shooting you. Let's go after Mom.
That's what I've been saying!
There she is!
VEST ON!
VEST ON!

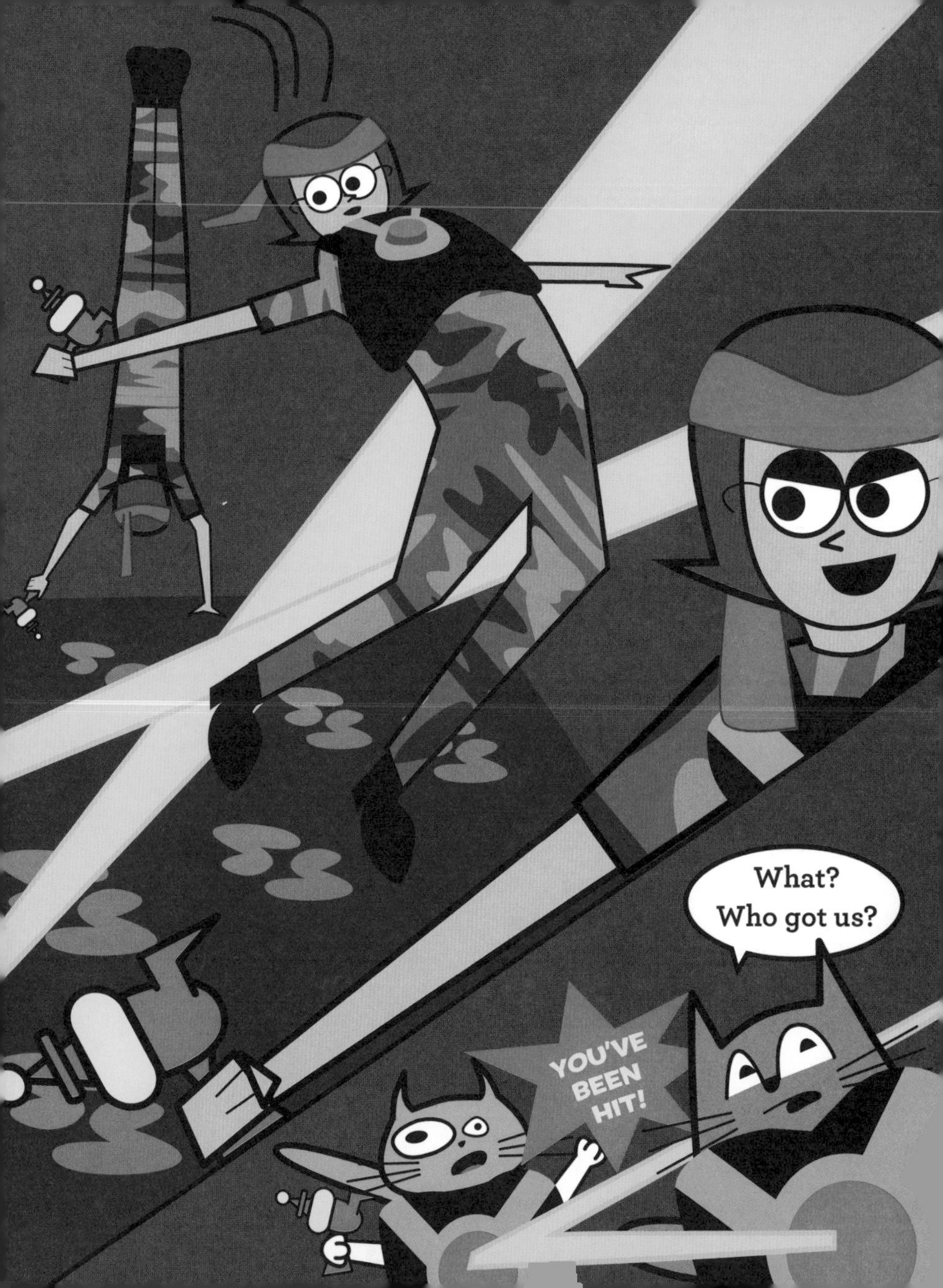
What?
Who got us?
YOU'VE BEEN HIT!

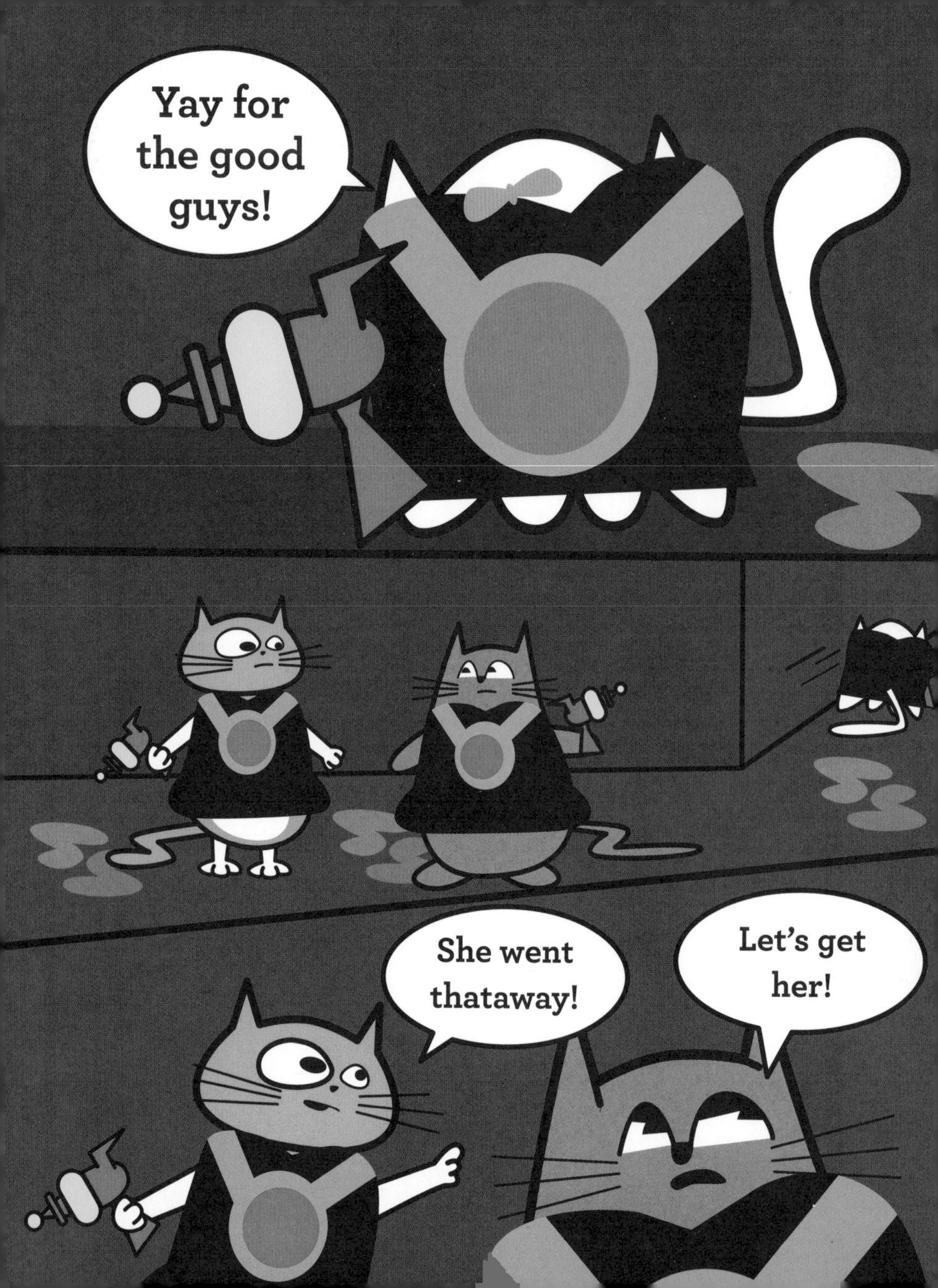
Yay for the good guys!
She went thataway!
Let's get her!

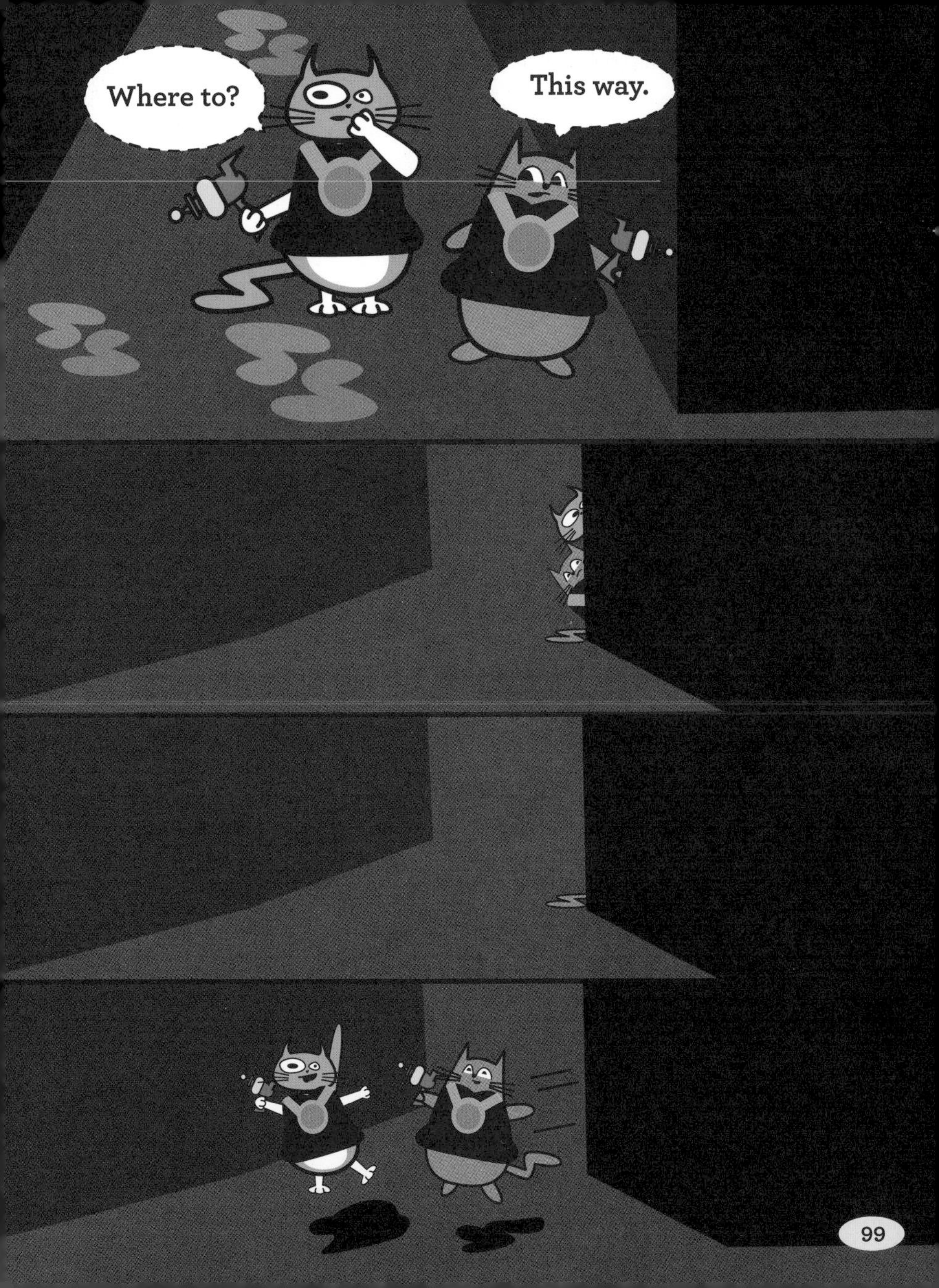
Where to?
This way.

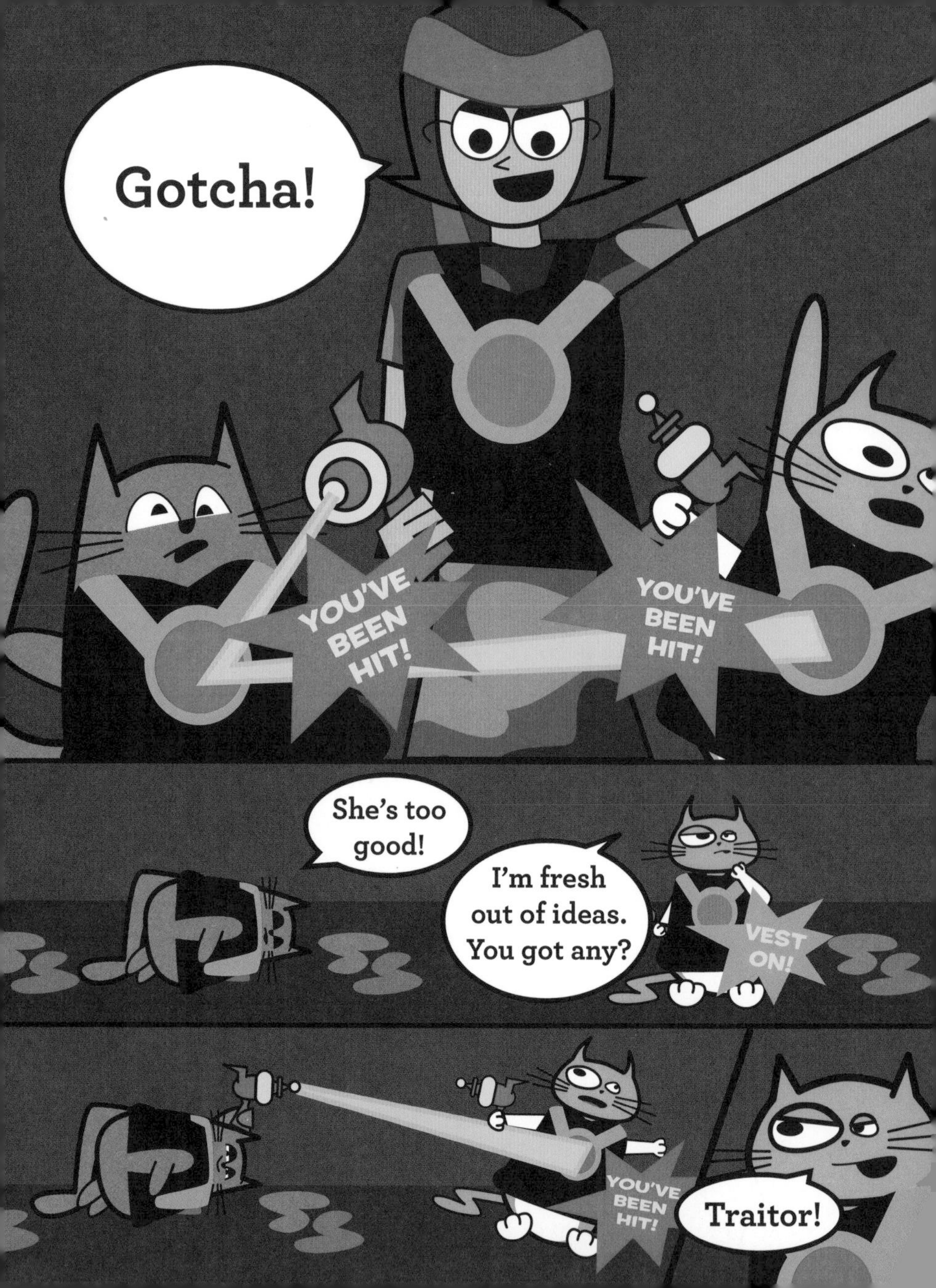
Gotcha!
YOU'VE BEEN HIT!
YOU'VE BEEN HIT!
She's too good!
I'm fresh out of ideas. You got any?
VEST ON!
YOU'VE BEEN HIT!
Traitor!

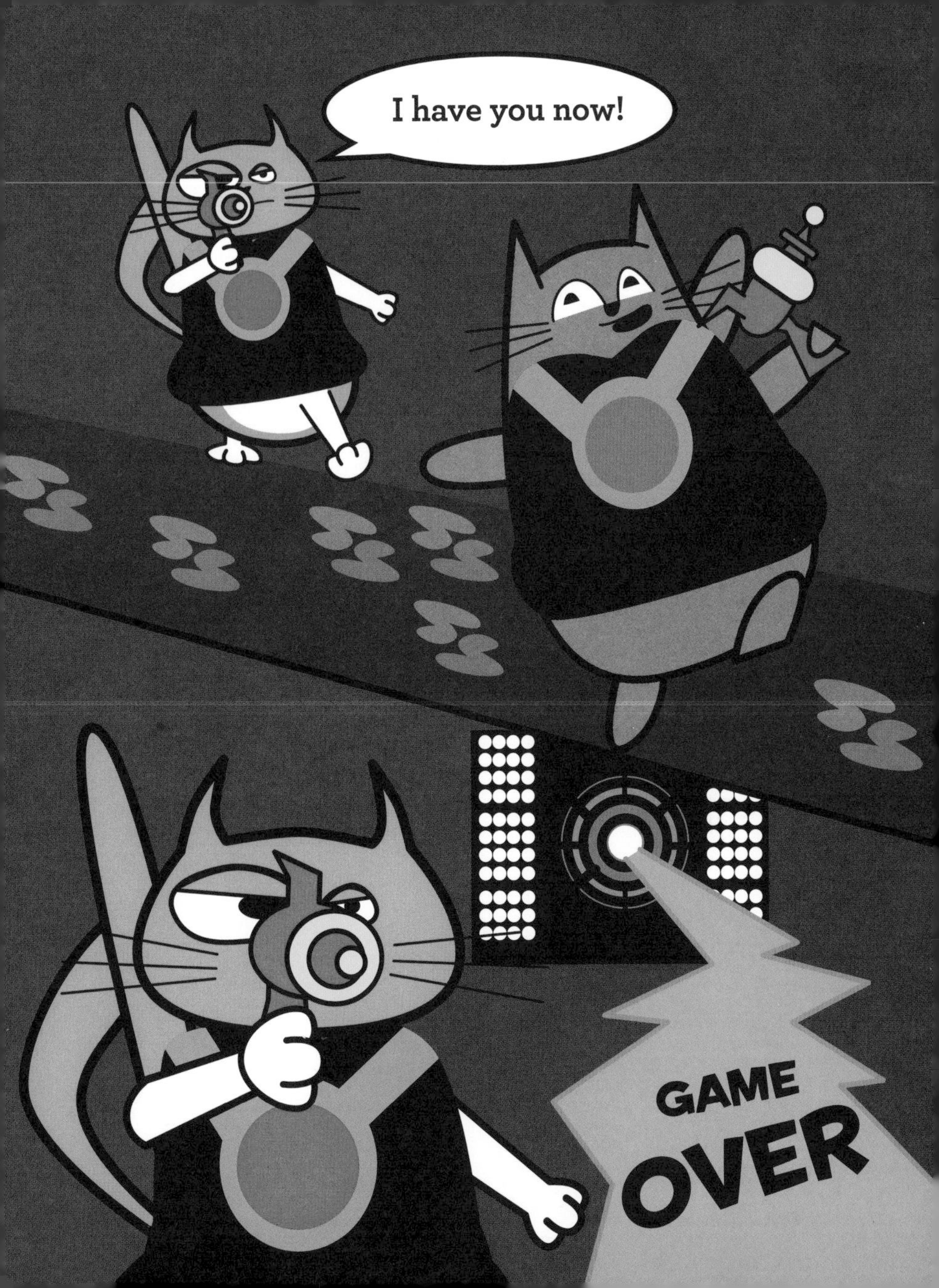
I have you now!
GAME
OVER

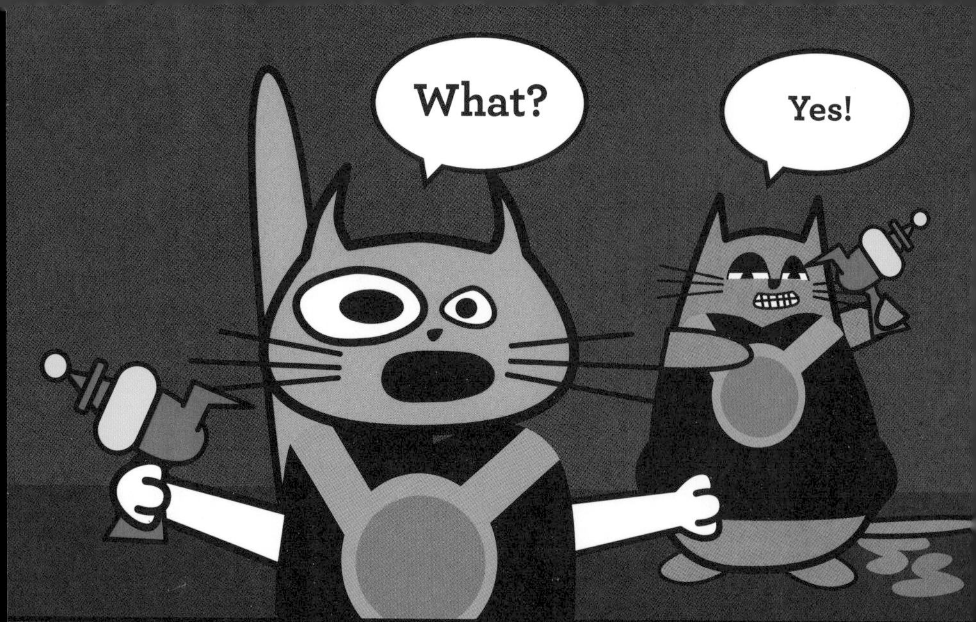
What?
Yes!

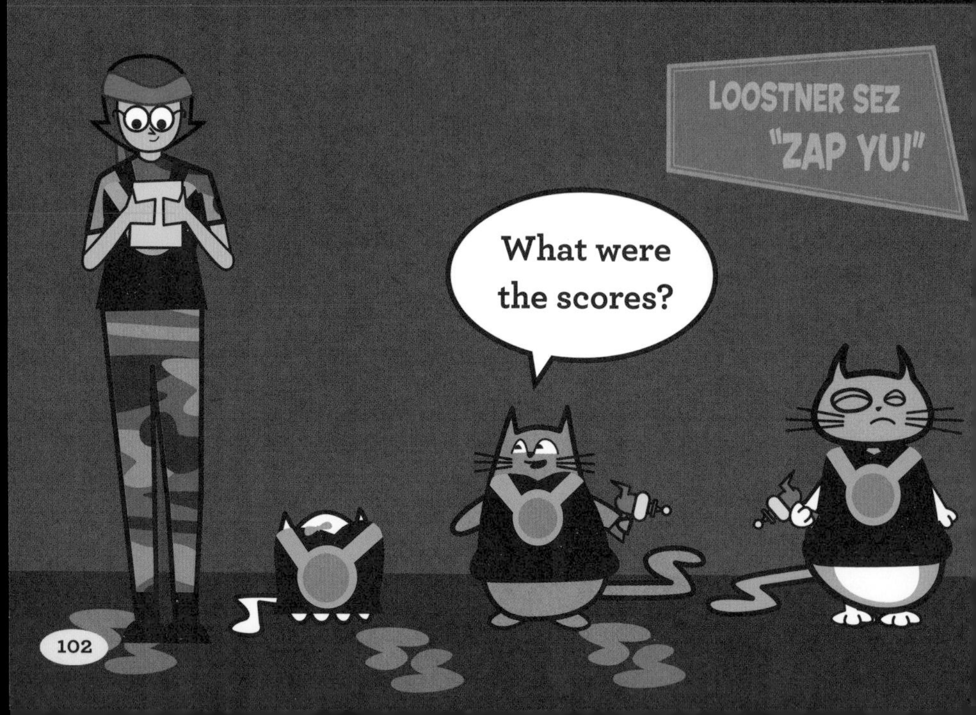
LOOSTNER SEZ "ZAP YU!"
What were the scores?

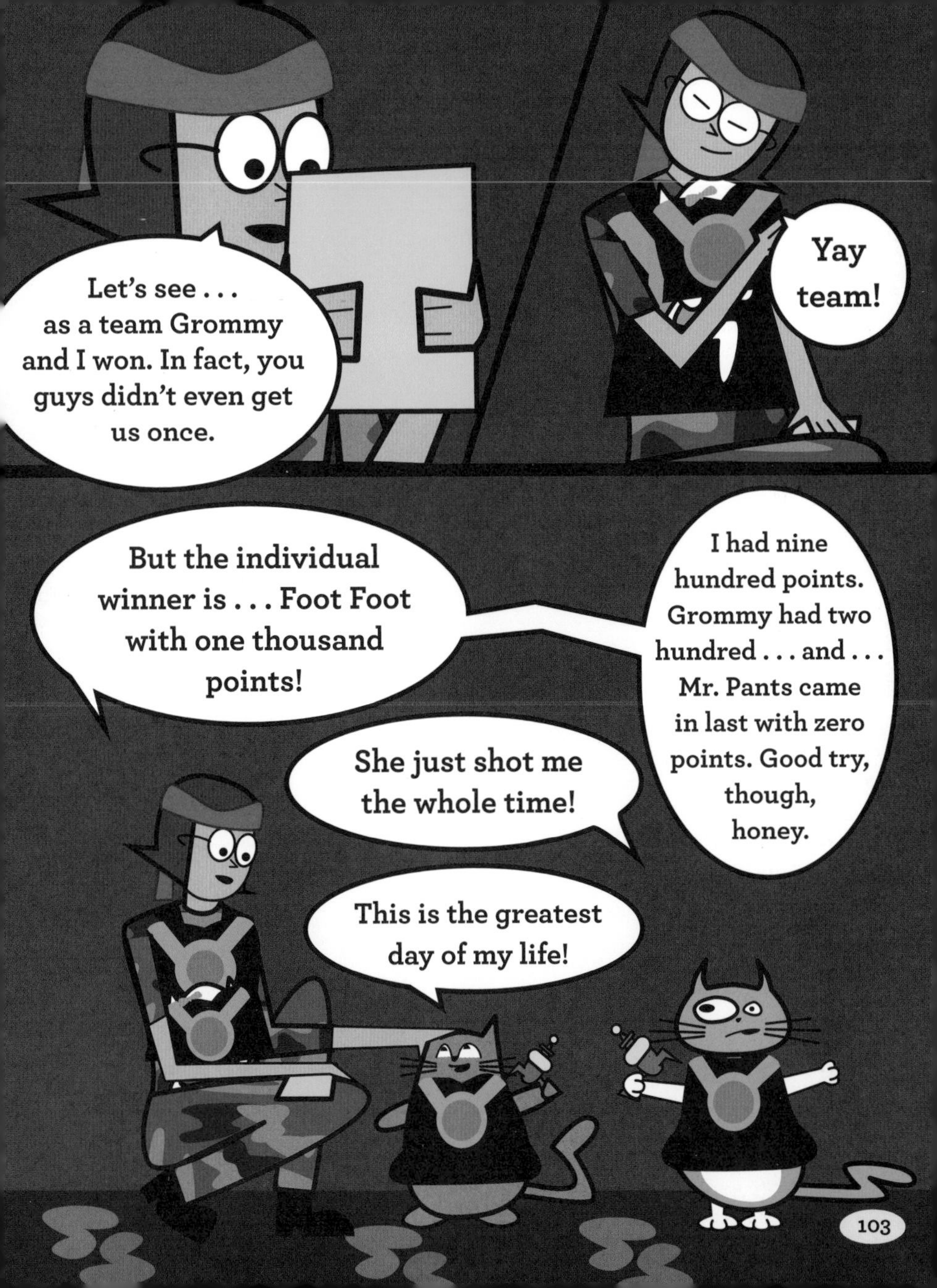
Let's see . . . as a team Grommy and I won. In fact, you guys didn't even get us once.
Yay team!
But the individual winner is . . . Foot Foot with one thousand points!
I had nine hundred points. Grommy had two hundred . . . and . . . Mr. Pants came in last with zero points. Good try, though, honey.
She just shot me the whole time!
This is the greatest day of my life!

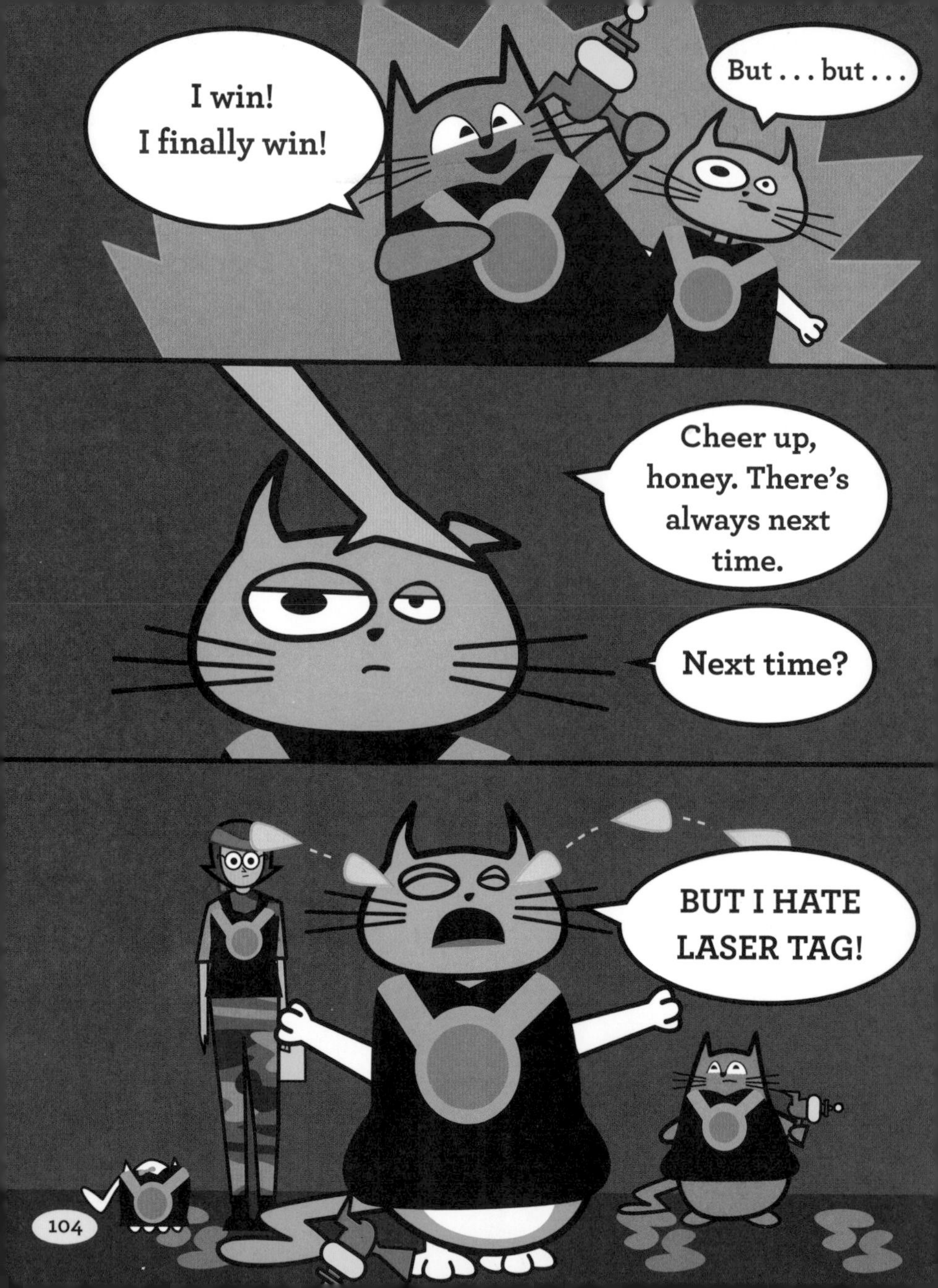
I win!
I finally win!
But . . . but . . .
Cheer up, honey. There's always next time.
Next time?
BUT I HATE LASER TAG!

Chapter Six: BATTLING BEDTIME STORIES

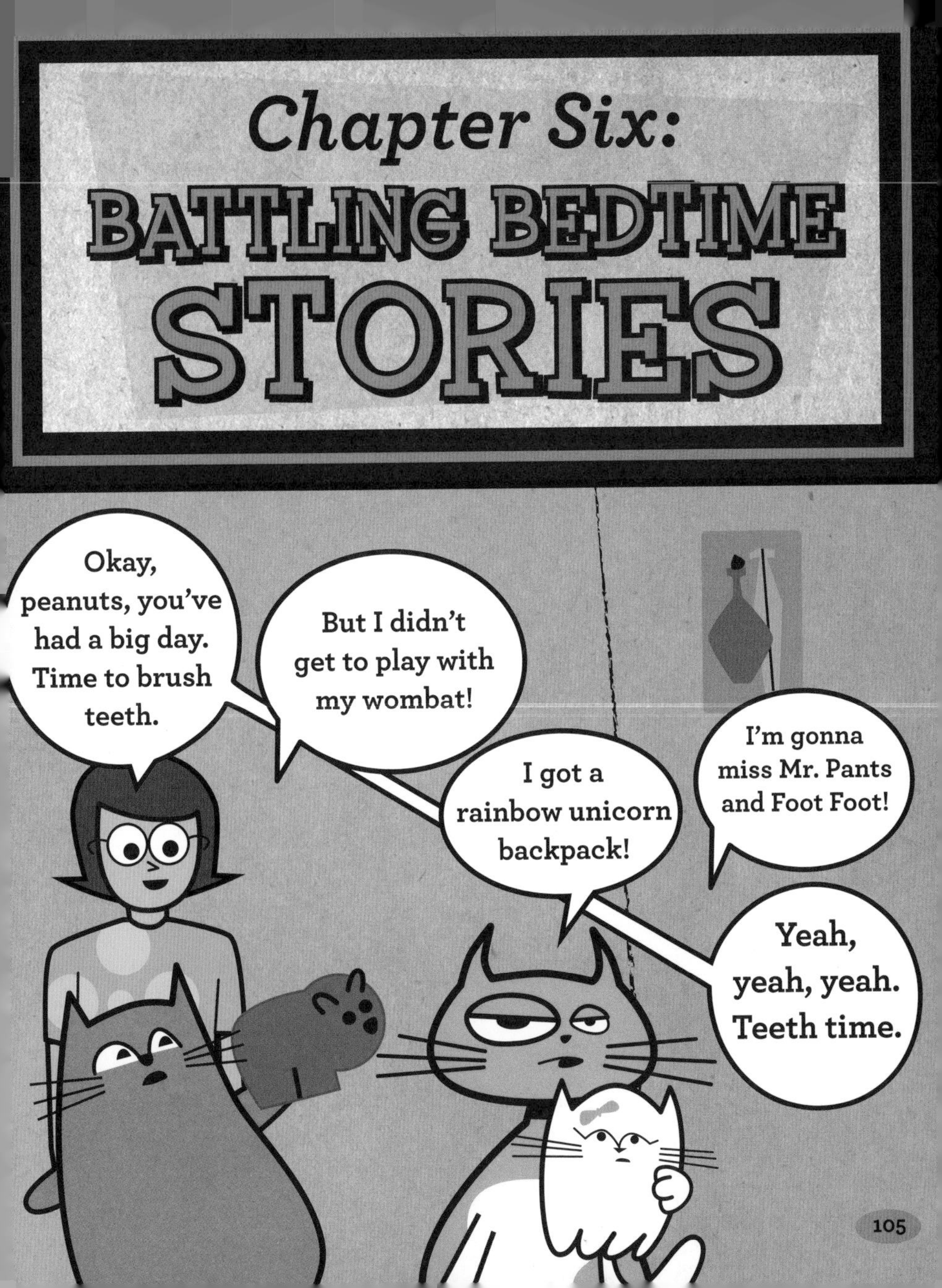
Okay, peanuts, you've had a big day. Time to brush teeth.
But I didn't get to play with my wombat!
I got a rainbow unicorn backpack!
I'm gonna miss Mr. Pants and Foot Foot!
Yeah, yeah, yeah. Teeth time.

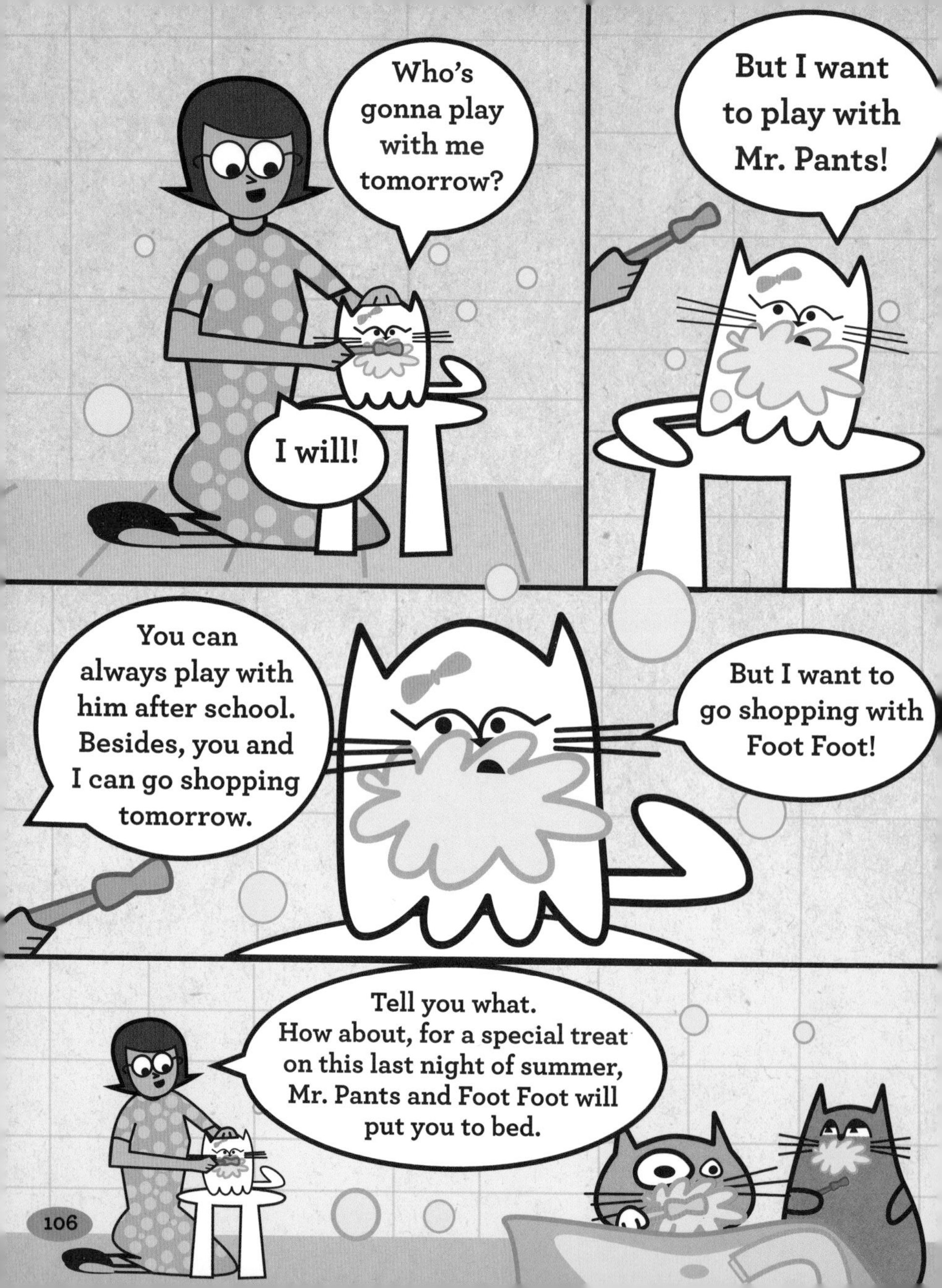
Who's gonna play with me tomorrow?
I will!
But I want to play with Mr. Pants!
You can always play with him after school. Besides, you and I can go shopping tomorrow.
But I want to go shopping with Foot Foot!
Tell you what. How about, for a special treat on this last night of summer, Mr. Pants and Foot Foot will put you to bed.

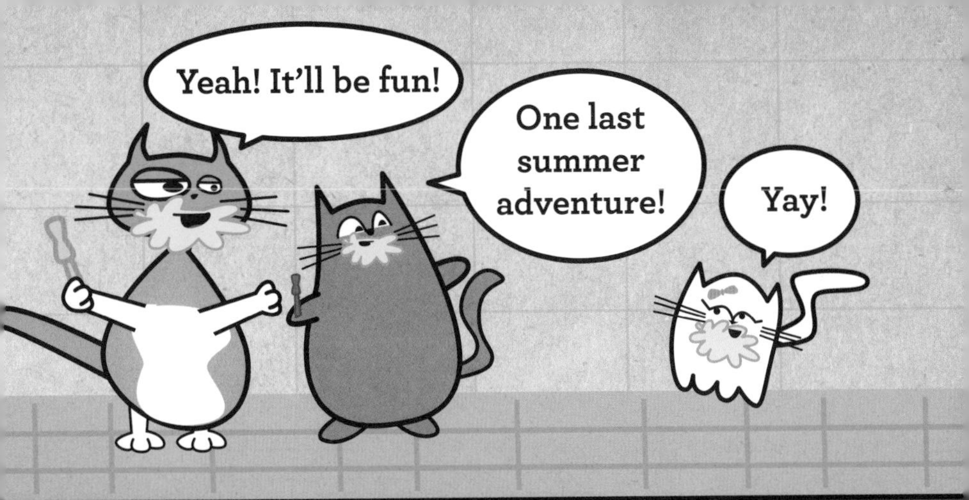
Yeah! It'll be fun!
One last summer adventure!
Yay!

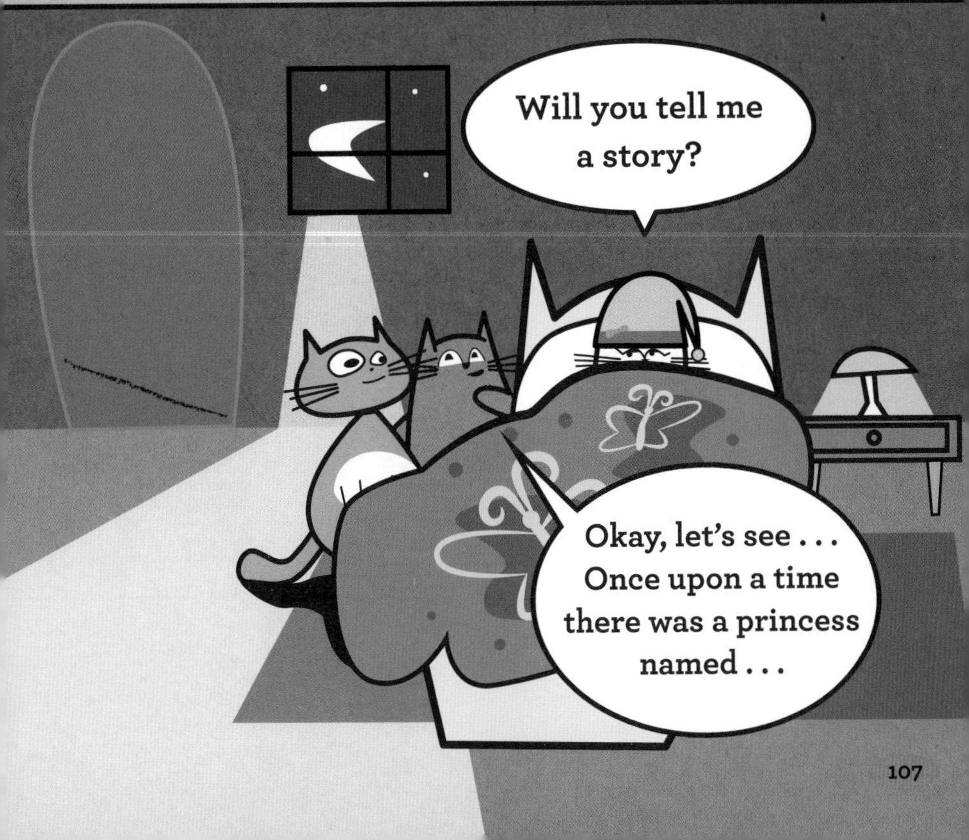
Will you tell me a story?
Okay, let's see . . . Once upon a time there was a princess named . . .

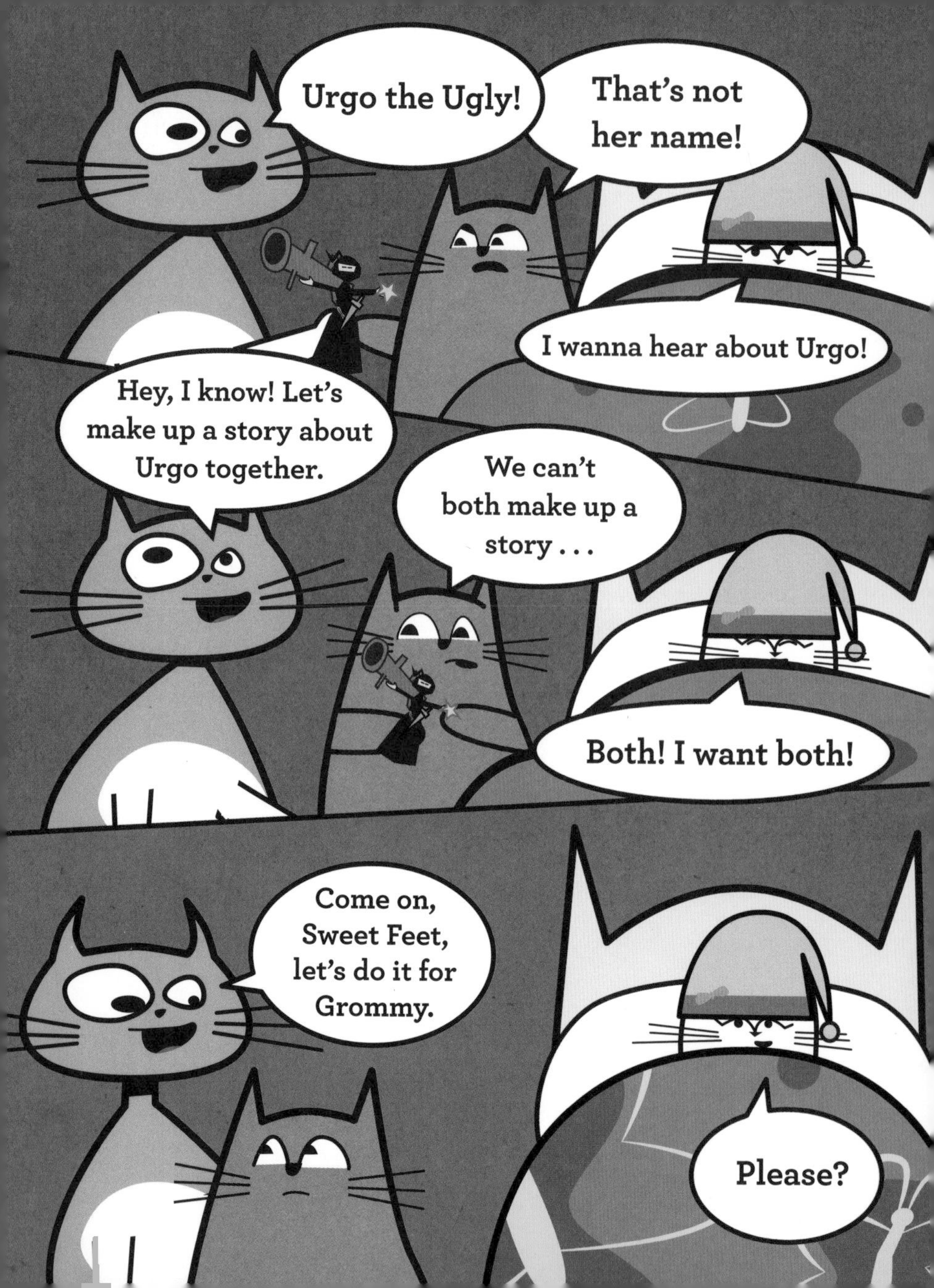
Urgo the Ugly!
That's not her name!
I wanna hear about Urgo!
Hey, I know! Let's make up a story about Urgo together.
We can't both make up a story . . .
Both! I want both!
Come on, Sweet Feet, let's do it for Grommy.
Please?

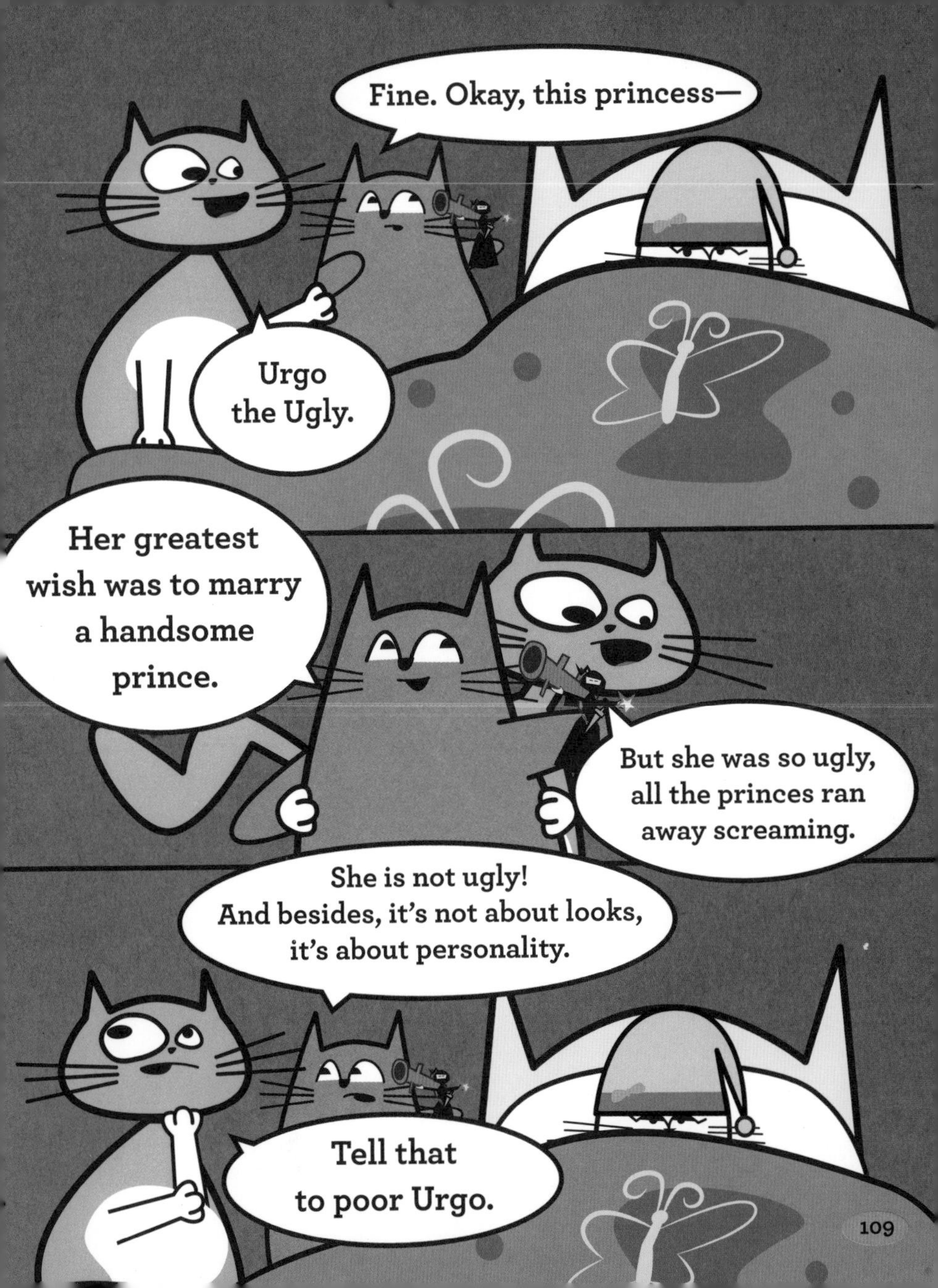
Fine. Okay, this princess—
Urgo the Ugly.
Her greatest wish was to marry a handsome prince.
But she was so ugly, all the princes ran away screaming.
She is not ugly! And besides, it's not about looks, it's about personality.
Tell that to poor Urgo.

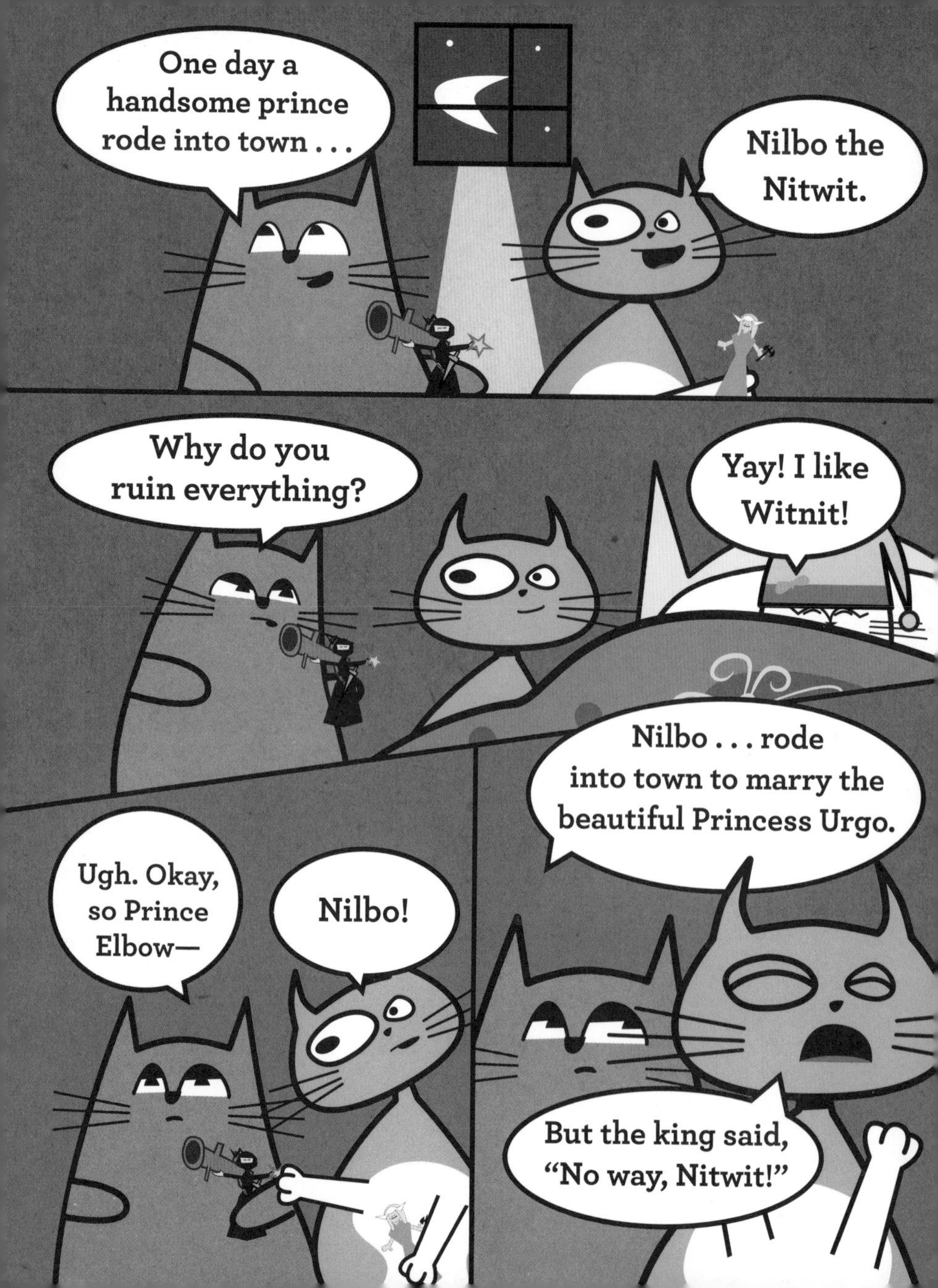
One day a handsome prince rode into town . . .
Nilbo the Nitwit.
Why do you ruin everything?
Yay! I like Witnit!
Ugh. Okay, so Prince Elbow—
Nilbo!
Nilbo . . . rode into town to marry the beautiful Princess Urgo.
But the king said, "No way, Nitwit!"

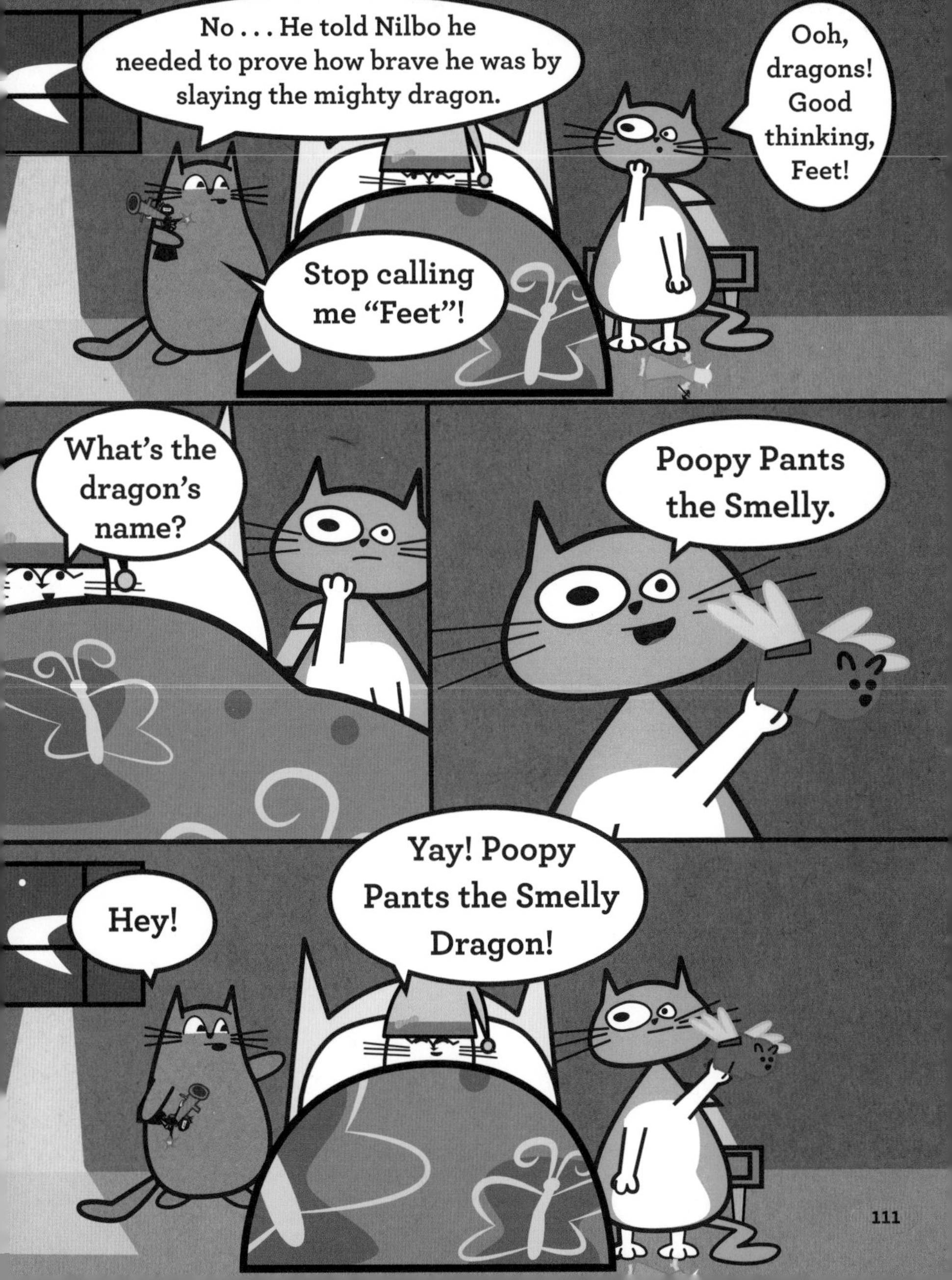
No . . . He told Nilbo he needed to prove how brave he was by slaying the mighty dragon.
Ooh, dragons! Good thinking, Feet!
Stop calling me "Feet"!
What's the dragon's name?
Poopy Pants the Smelly.
Hey!
Yay! Poopy Pants the Smelly Dragon!

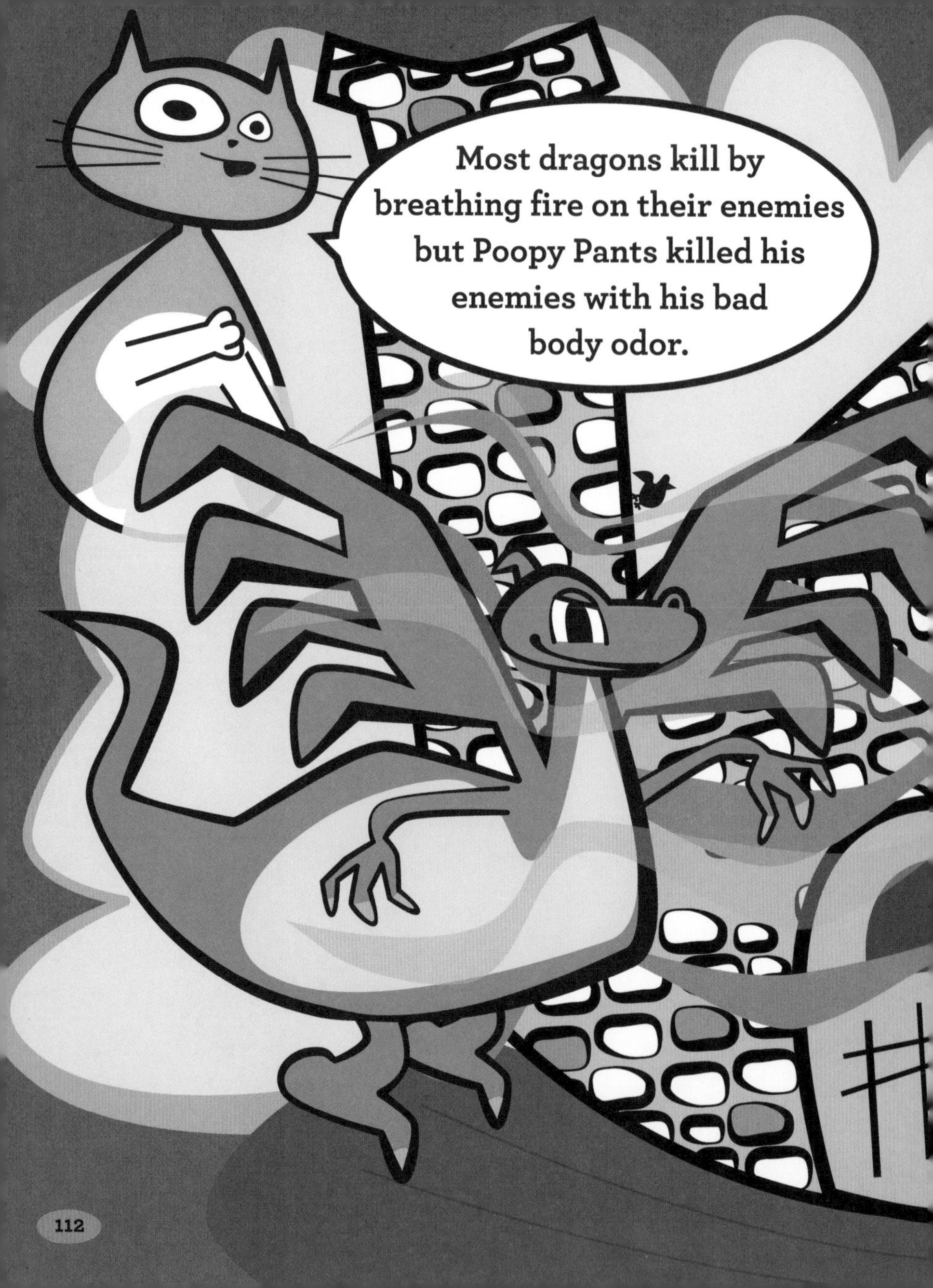
Most dragons kill by breathing fire on their enemies but Poopy Pants killed his enemies with his bad body odor.

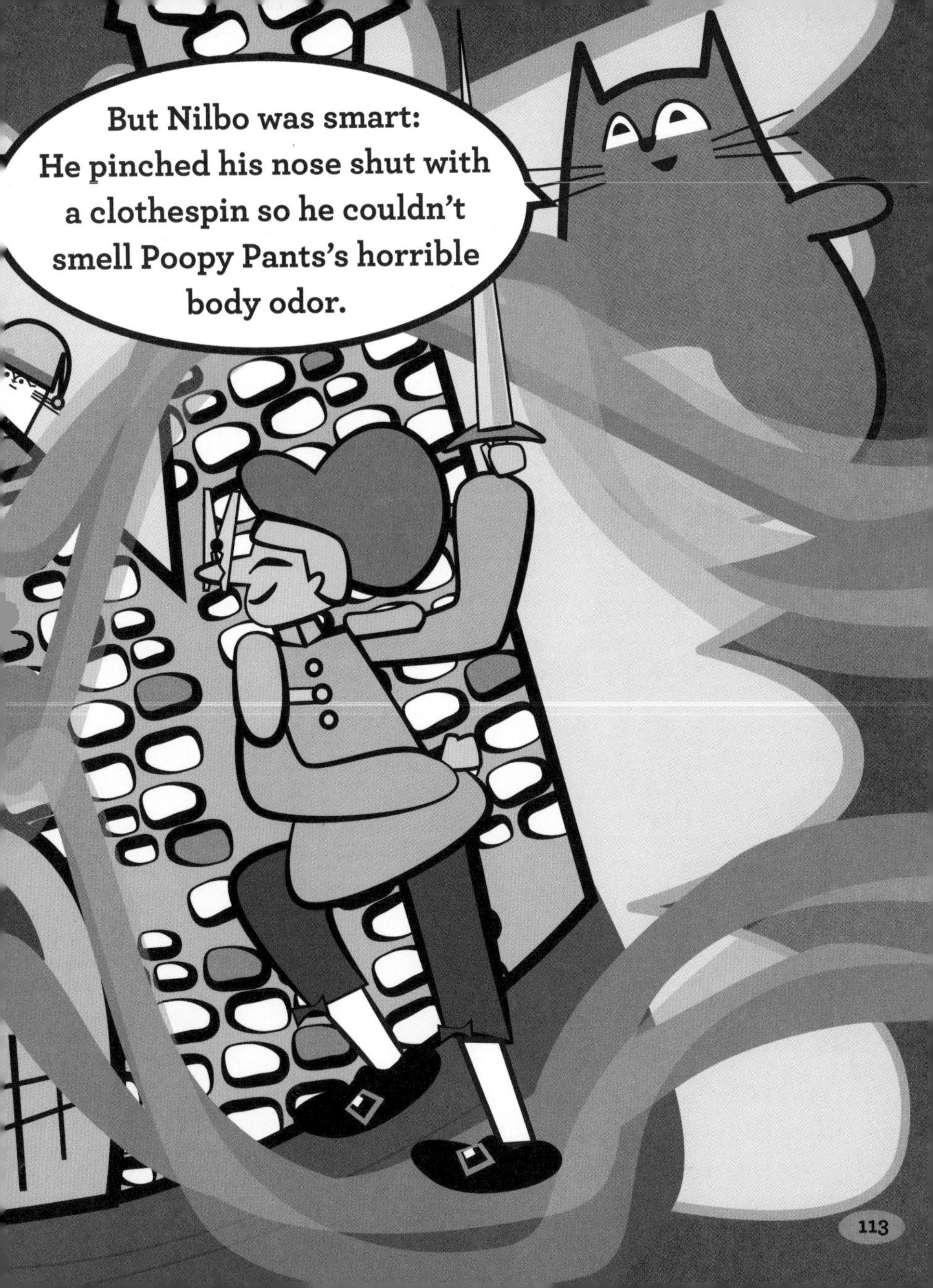
But Nilbo was smart:
He pinched his nose shut with a clothespin so he couldn't smell Poopy Pants's horrible body odor.

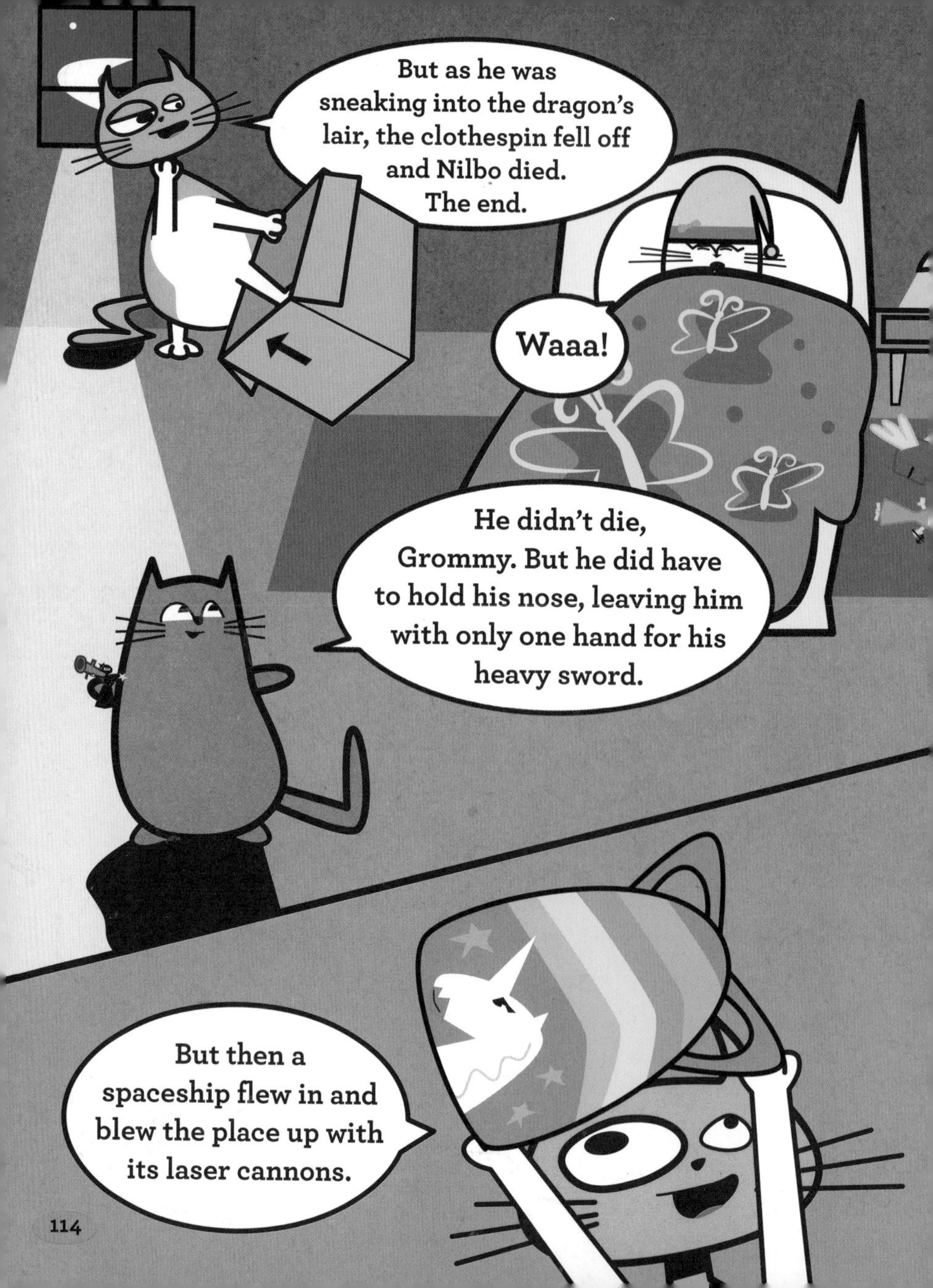
But as he was sneaking into the dragon's lair, the clothespin fell off and Nilbo died. The end.
Waaa!
He didn't die, Grommy. But he did have to hold his nose, leaving him with only one hand for his heavy sword.
But then a spaceship flew in and blew the place up with its laser cannons.

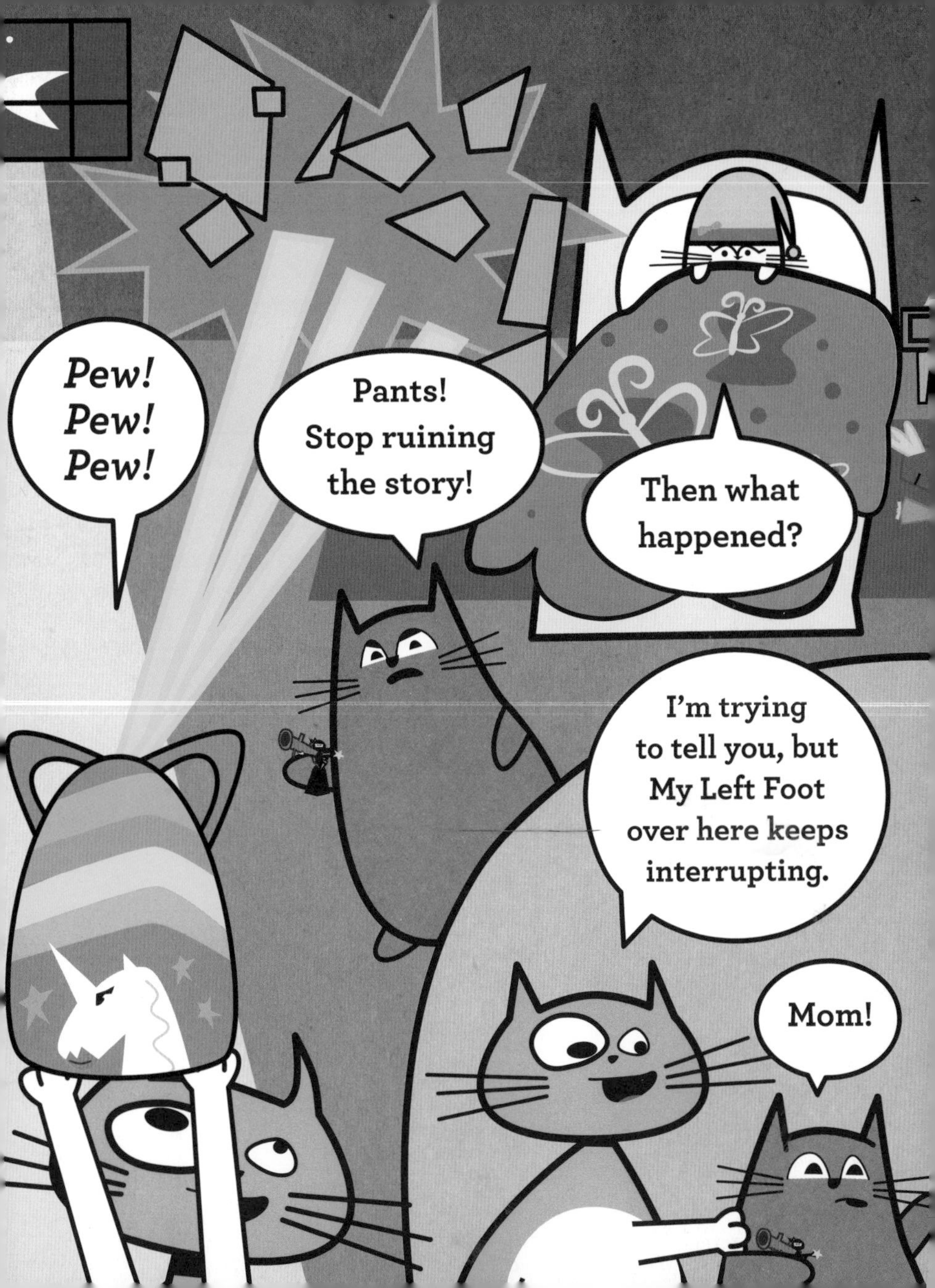

Pew! Pew! Pew!
Pants! Stop ruining the story!
Then what happened?
I'm trying to tell you, but My Left Foot over here keeps interrupting.
Mom!

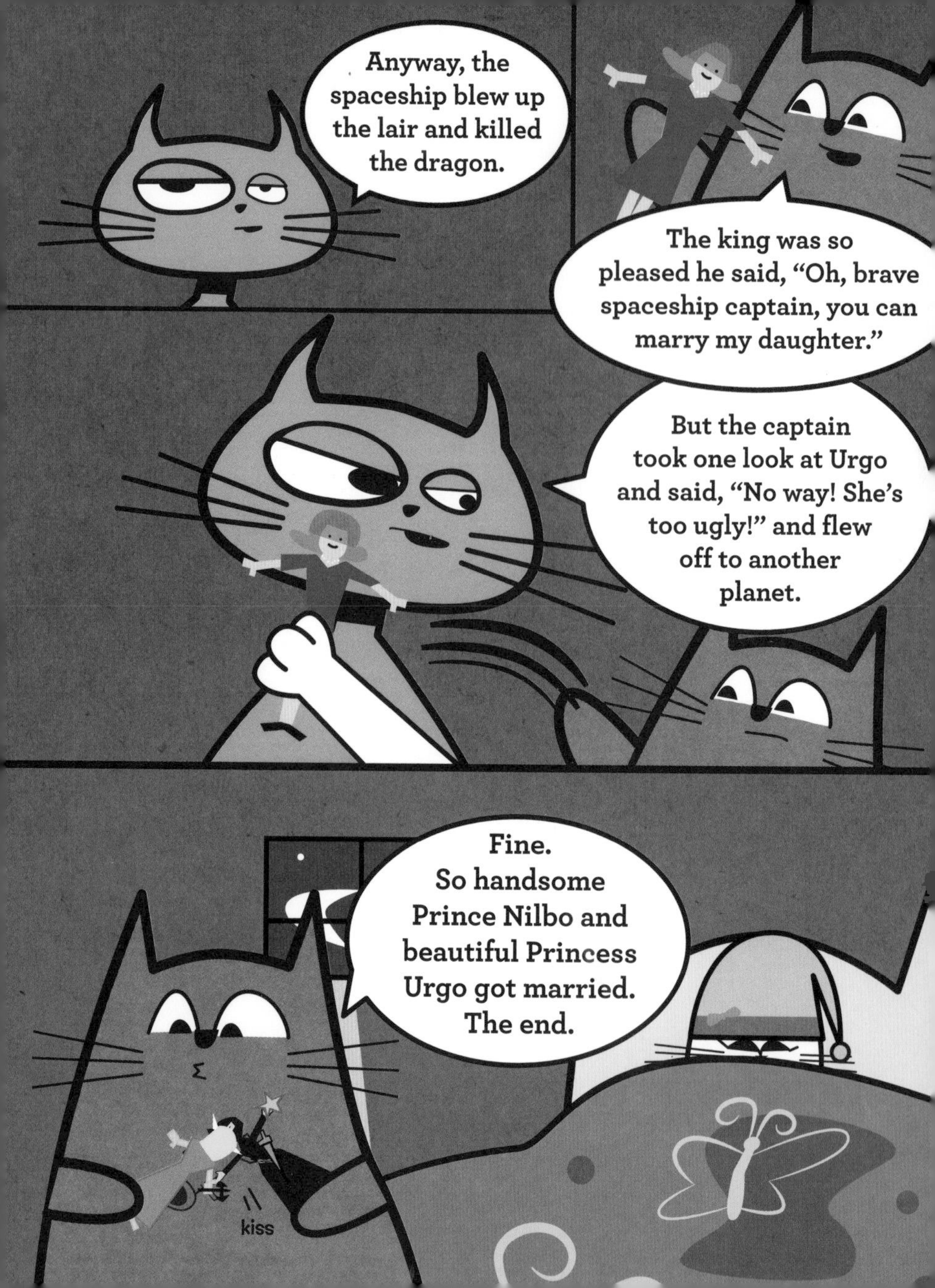
Anyway, the spaceship blew up the lair and killed the dragon.
The king was so pleased he said, “Oh, brave spaceship captain, you can marry my daughter.”
But the captain took one look at Urgo and said, “No way! She’s too ugly!” and flew off to another planet.
Fine. So handsome Prince Nilbo and beautiful Princess Urgo got married. The end.
kiss

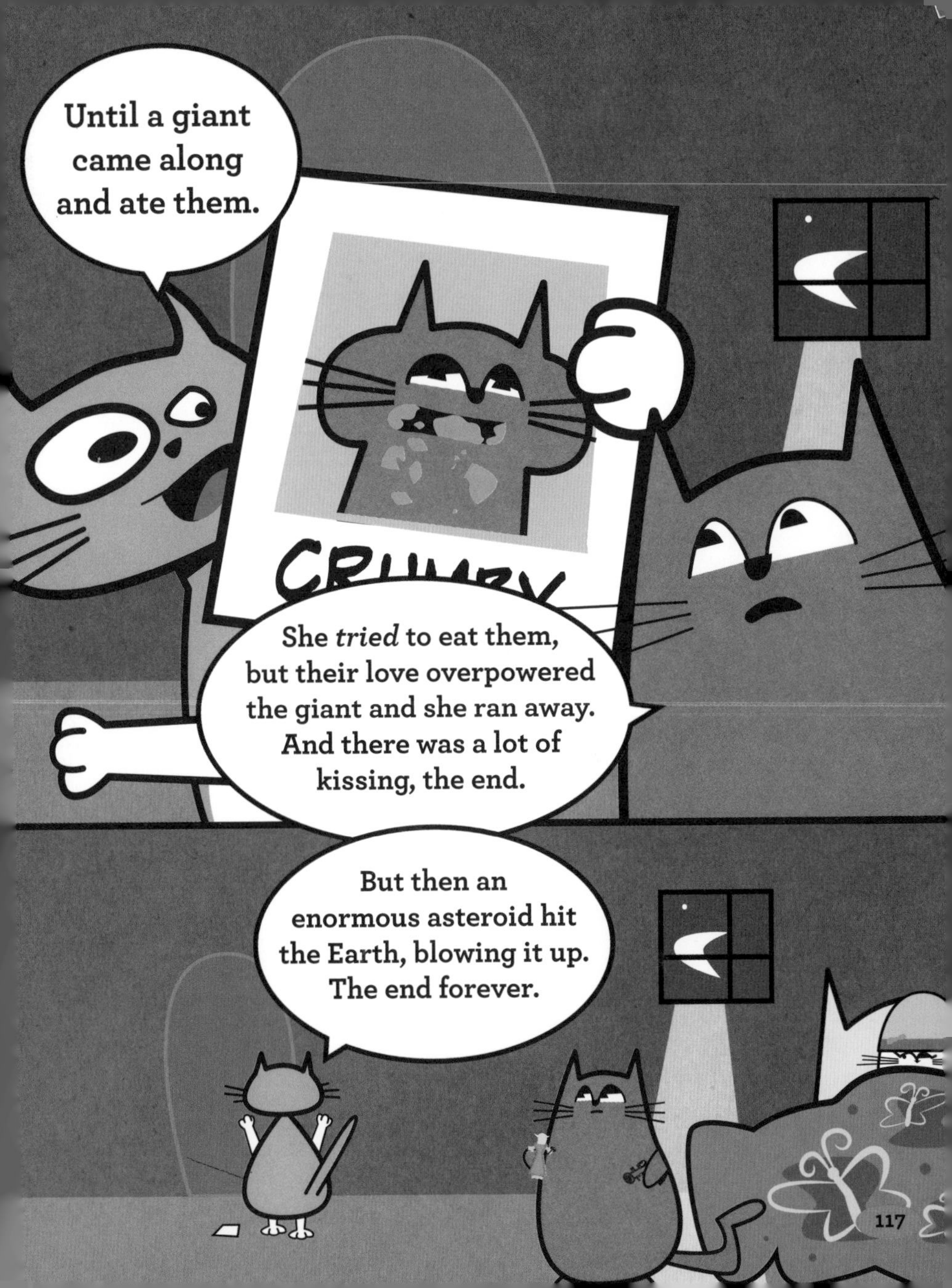
Until a giant came along and ate them.
She *tried* to eat them, but their love overpowered the giant and she ran away. And there was a lot of kissing, the end.
But then an enormous asteroid hit the Earth, blowing it up. The end forever.

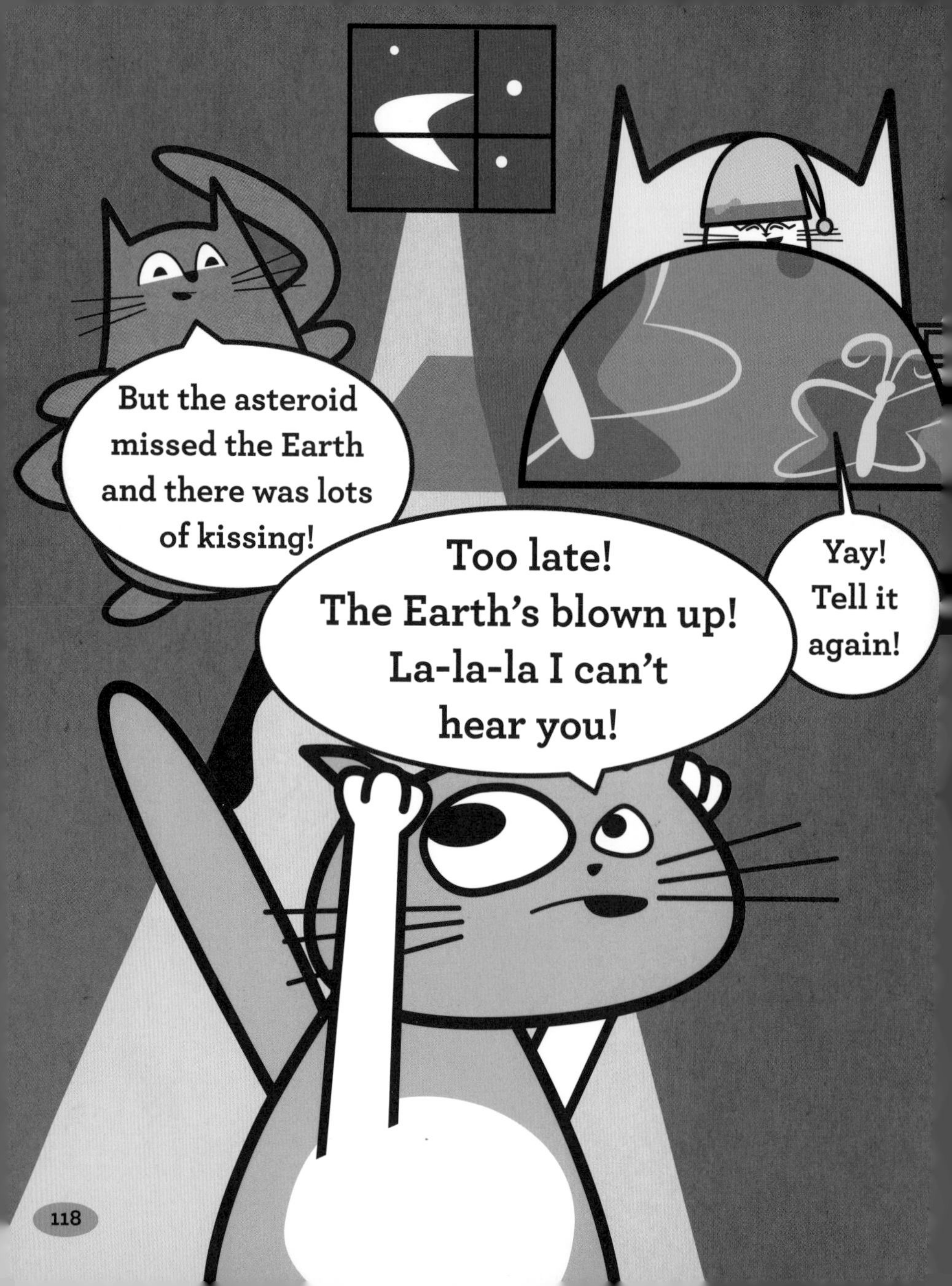
But the asteroid missed the Earth and there was lots of kissing!
Yay! Tell it again!
Too late! The Earth's blown up! La-la-la I can't hear you!

Chapter Seven:

WUB-BY! WUB-BY! WUB-BY!

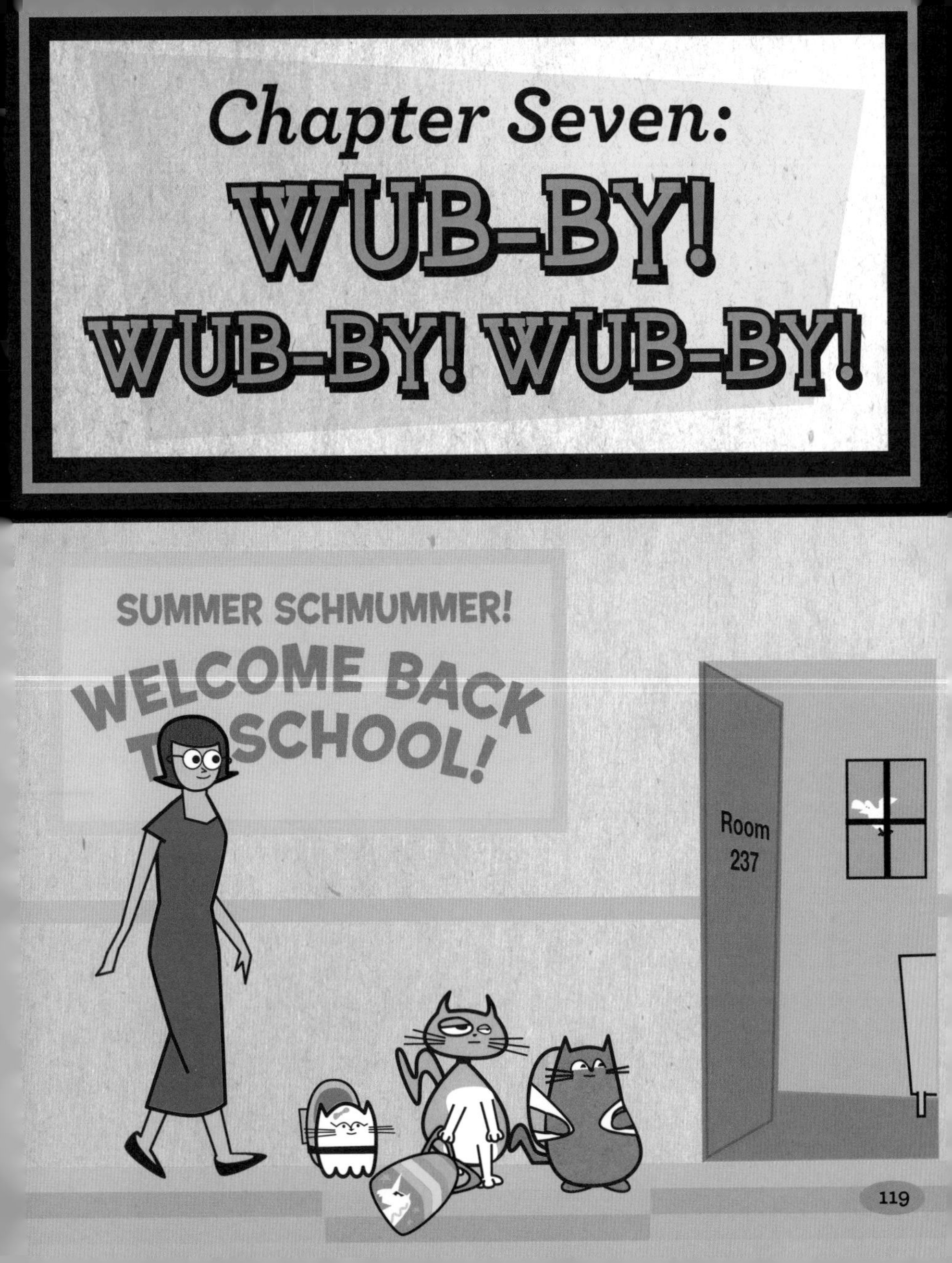

SUMMER SCHMUMMER!
WELCOME BACK
T SCHOOL!
Room 237

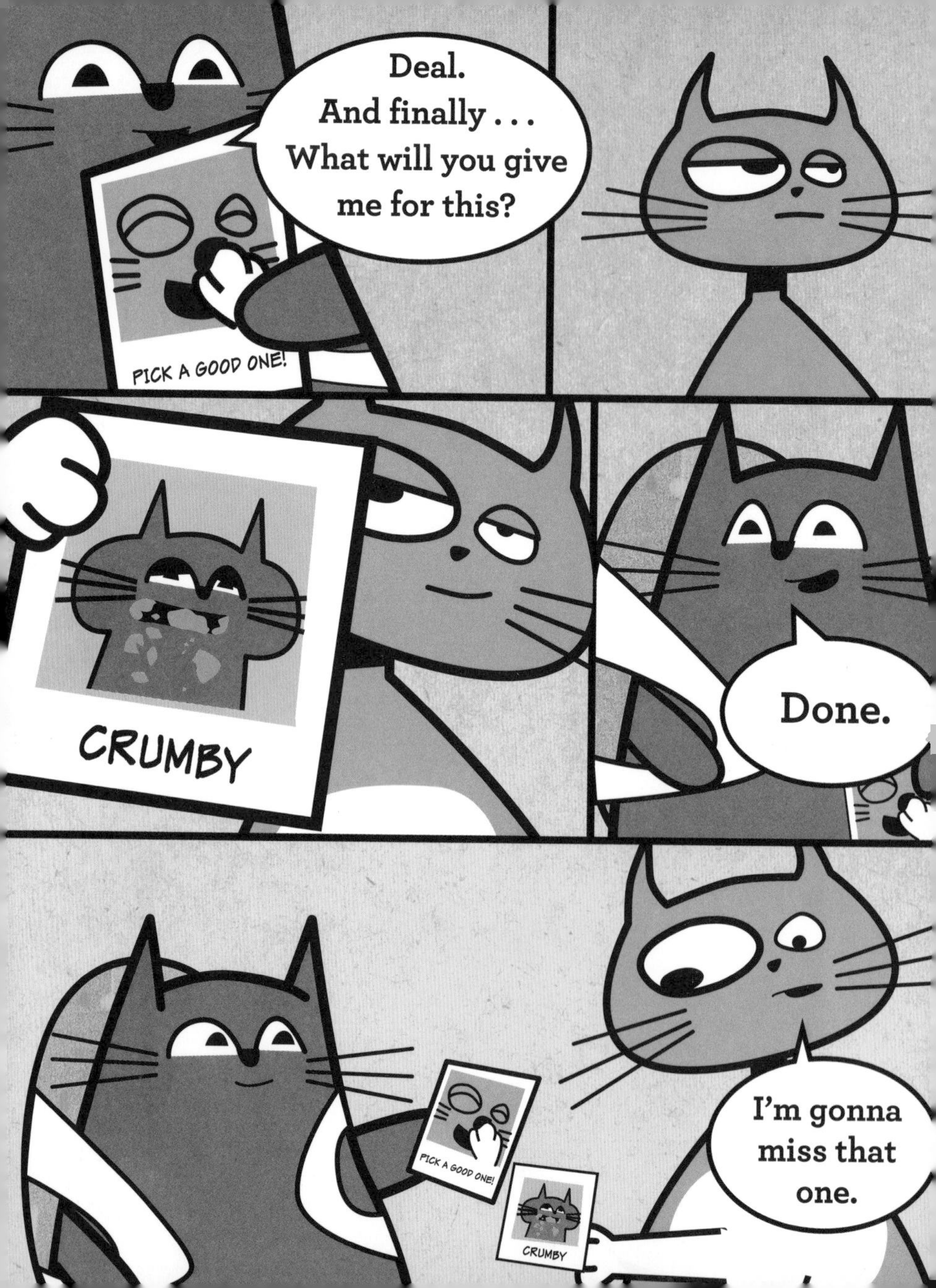
Deal.
And finally . . .
What will you give
me for this?
PICK A GOOD ONE!
CRUMBY
Done.
PICK A GOOD ONE!
CRUMBY
I'm gonna
miss that
one.

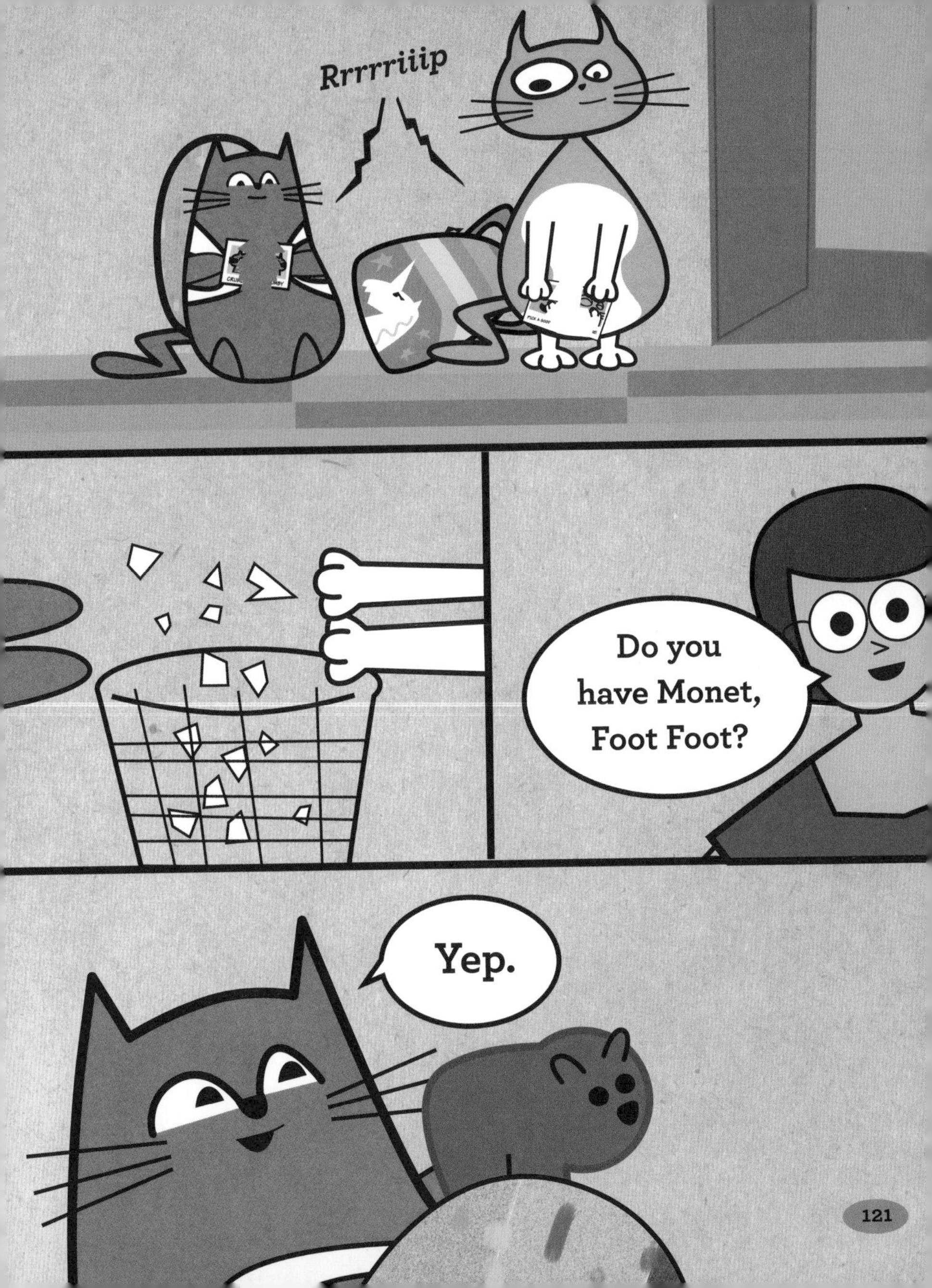
Rrrrriiip
Do you have Monet, Foot Foot?
Yep.

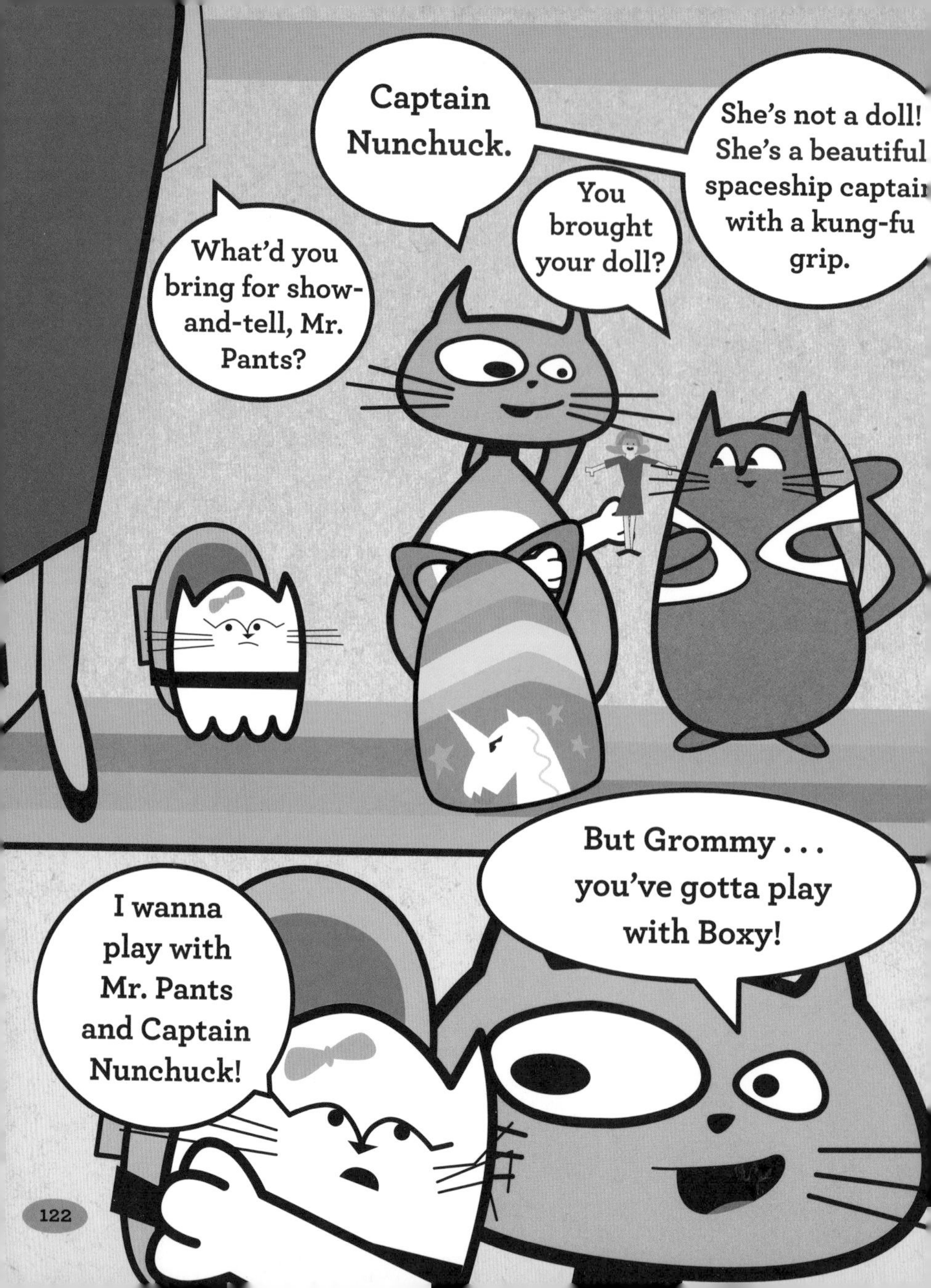
What'd you bring for show-and-tell, Mr. Pants?
Captain Nunchuck.
You brought your doll?
She's not a doll! She's a beautiful spaceship captain with a kung-fu grip.
I wanna play with Mr. Pants and Captain Nunchuck!
But Grommy . . . you've gotta play with Boxy!

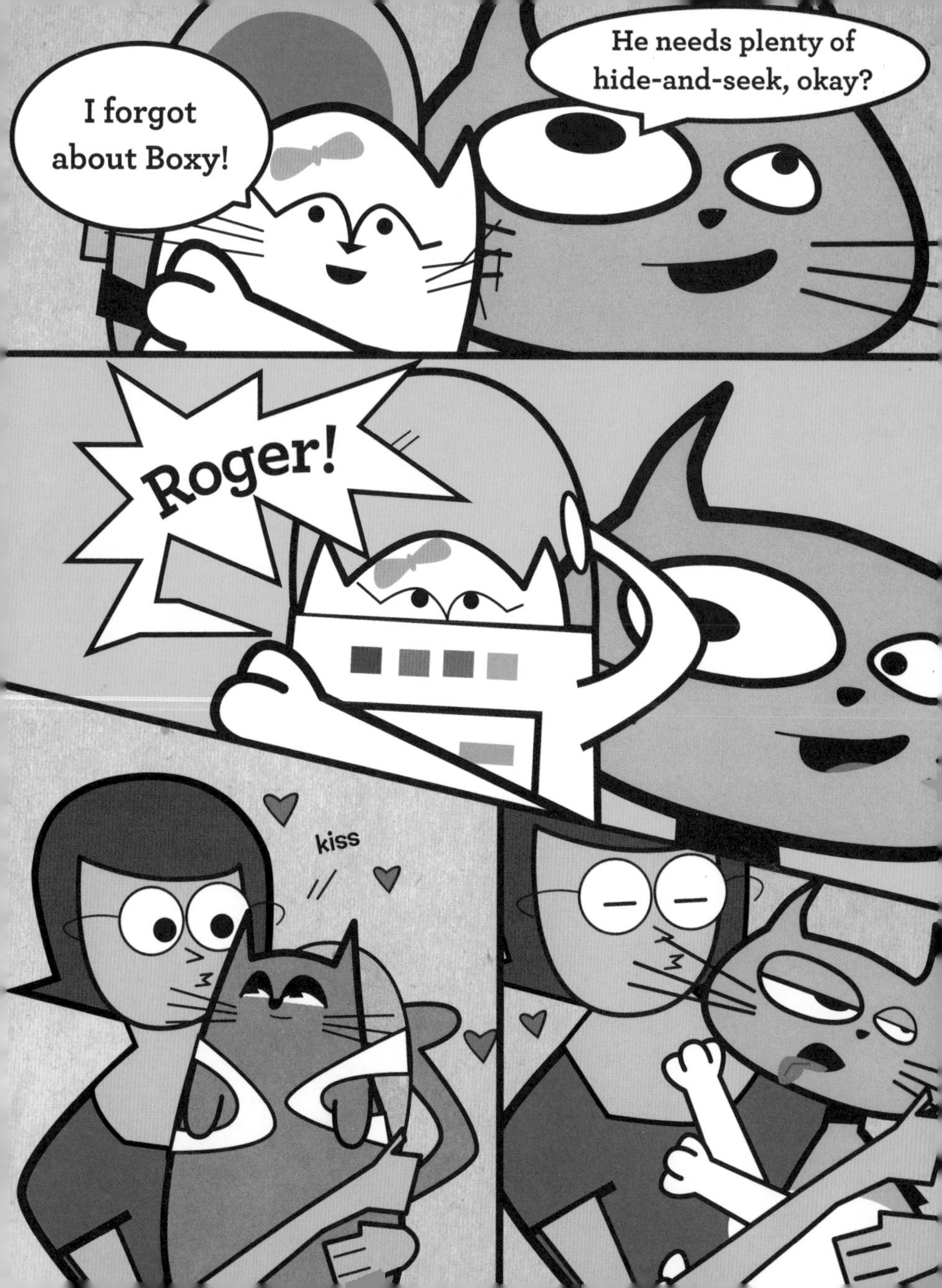
I forgot
about Boxy!
He needs plenty of
hide-and-seek, okay?
Roger!
kiss

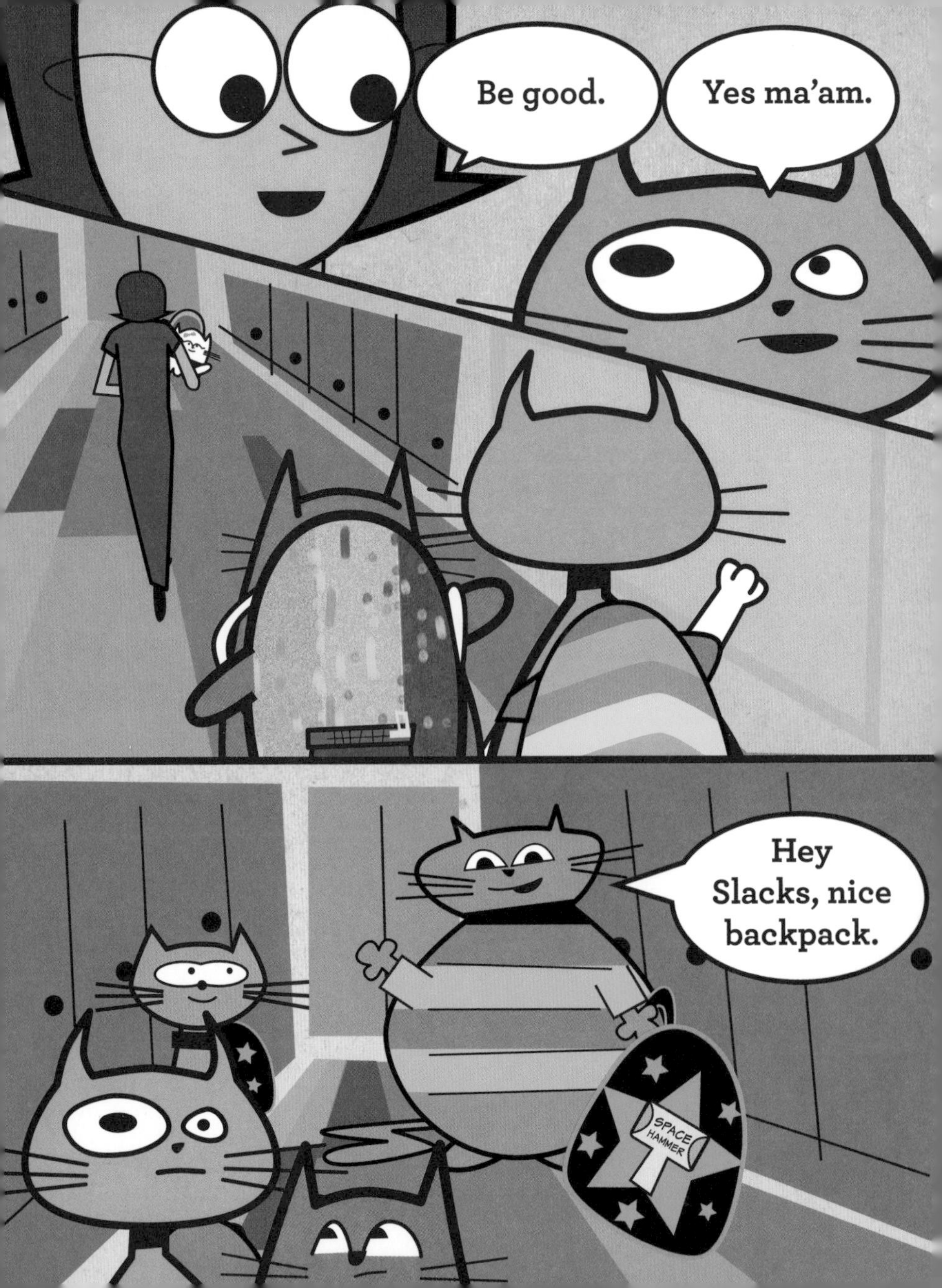
Be good.
Yes ma'am.
Hey Slacks, nice backpack.
SPACE HAMMER

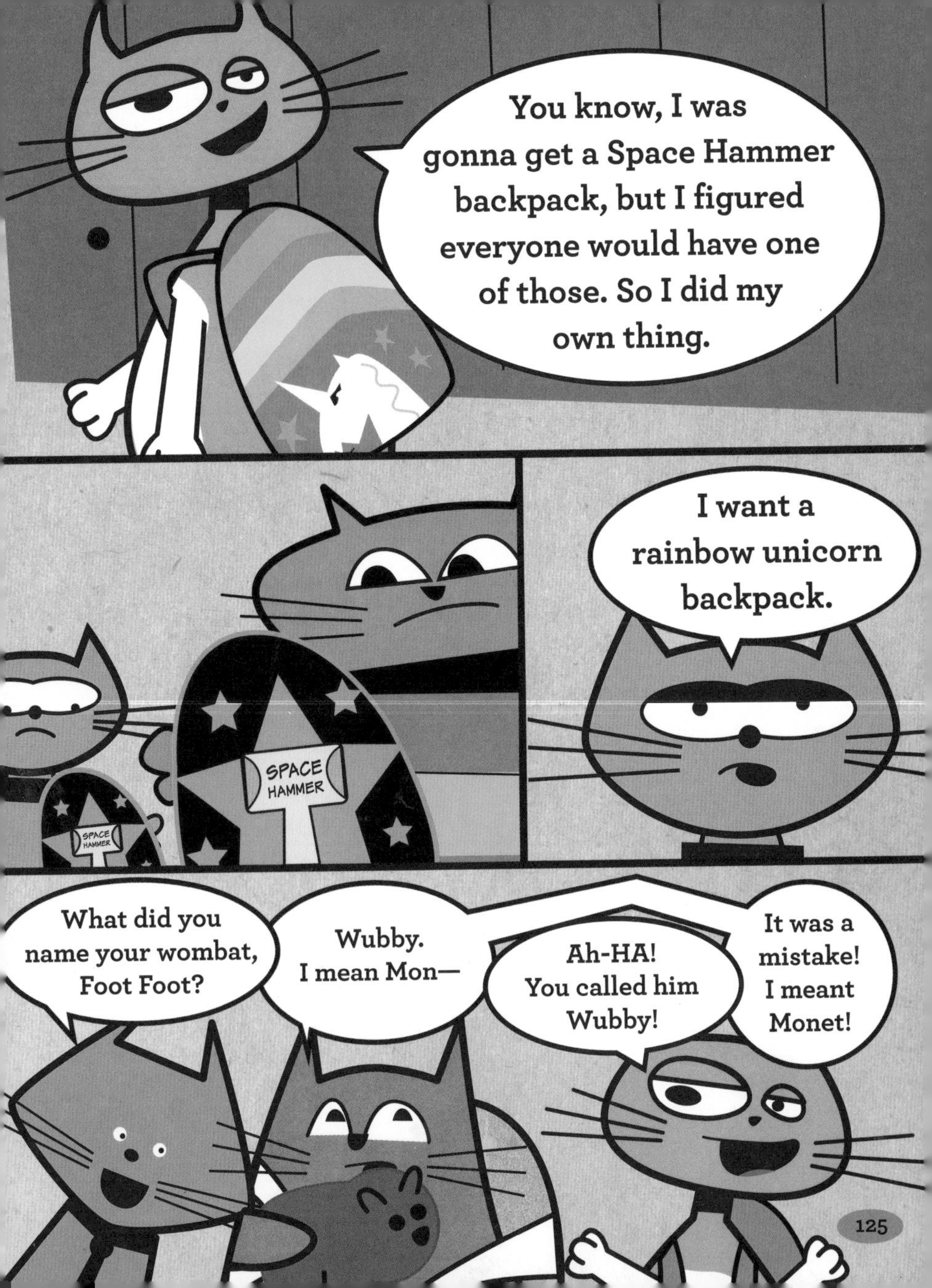
You know, I was gonna get a Space Hammer backpack, but I figured everyone would have one of those. So I did my own thing.
SPACE HAMMER
SPACE HAMMER
I want a rainbow unicorn backpack.
What did you name your wombat, Foot Foot?
Wubby. I mean Mon—
Ah-HA! You called him Wubby!
It was a mistake! I meant Monet!

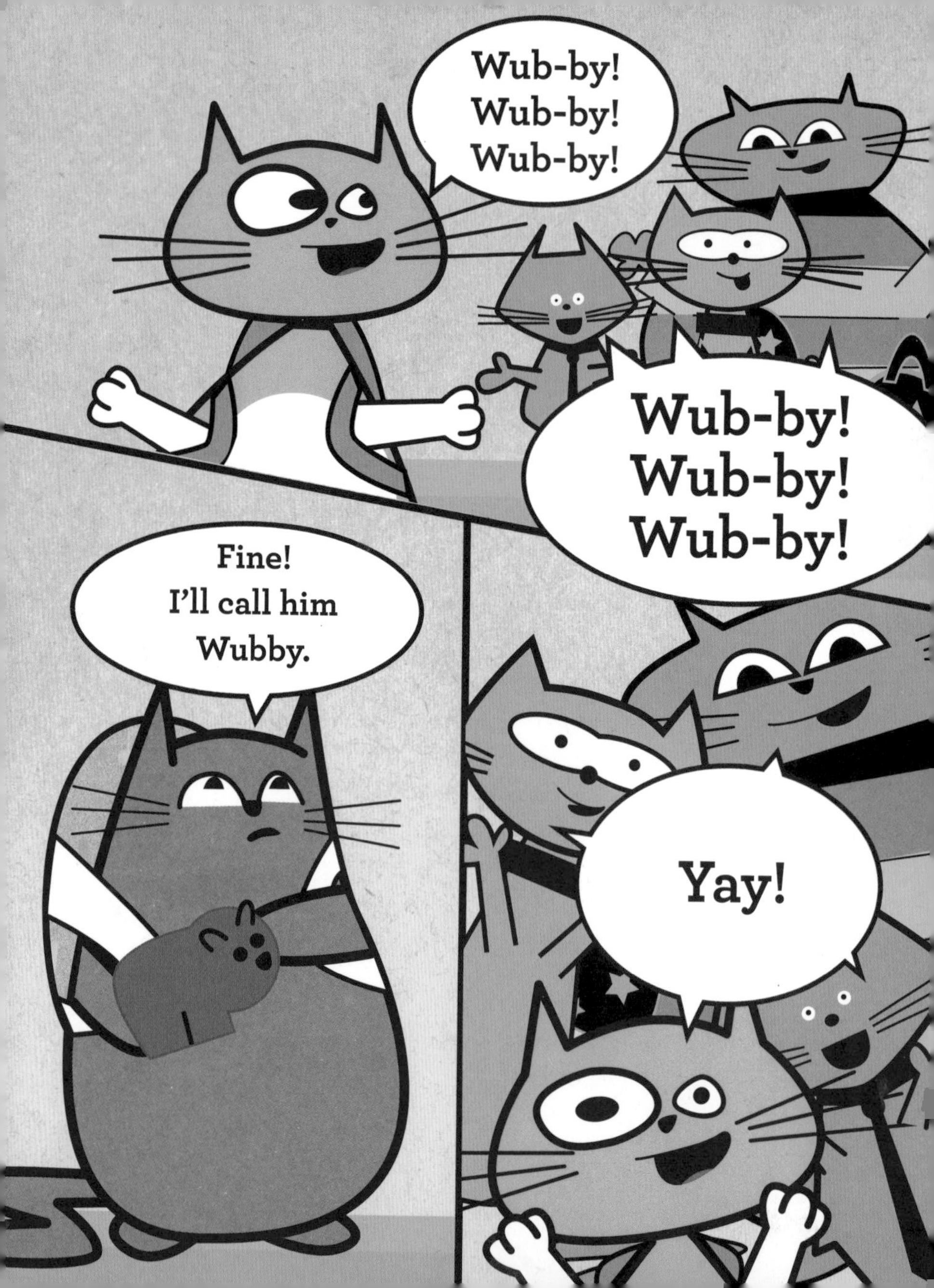
Wub-by! Wub-by! Wub-by!
Wub-by! Wub-by! Wub-by!
Fine! I'll call him Wubby.
Yay!

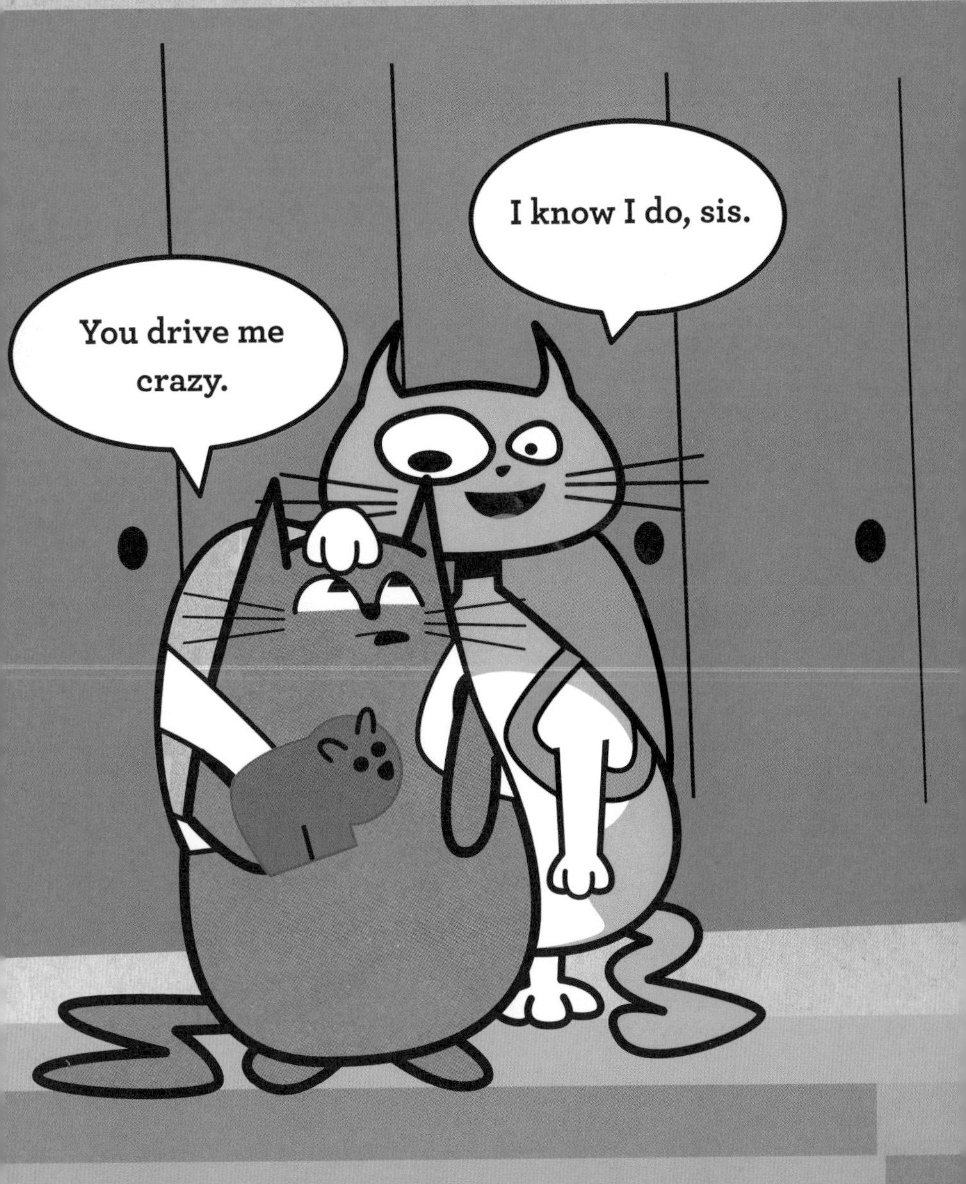
You drive me crazy.
I know I do, sis.

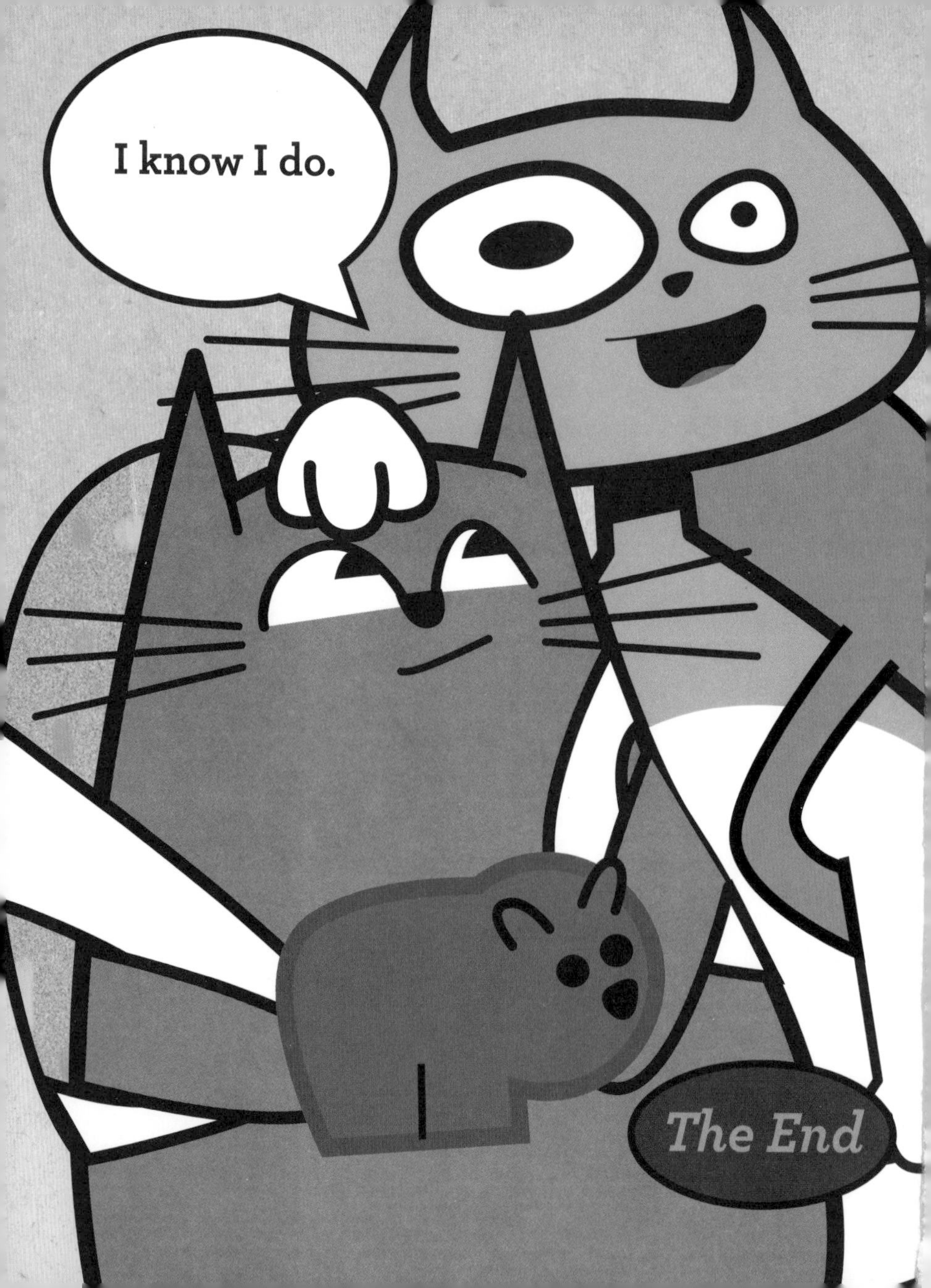
I know I do.
The End